I0598904

Loaded
for
Justice

Dark Sheriff Series

ROMEN GRAPHICS - San Antonio, Texas

Check out other books
by Roger Mendoza

Non-Fiction:
My Little Cowboy: My Reincarnation Story
Migrants: Exploring the Colors of my Family History
Jesus Mendoza: His Life through Letters

Fiction:
Purging Purgatory

Loaded
for
Justice

Dark Sheriff Series

ROGER MENDOZA

Published by Romen Graphics
www.RomenGraphics.com
Author Website: www.Roger-Mendoza.com

Cover Design by Roger Mendoza

ISBN-13: 978-1-938962-32-5 (Hardback)
ISBN-13: 978-1-938962-35-6 (Paperback)

Library of Congress Control Number: 2024910458

To my mother – Carmen.
She called me to this life and nurtured and cared for me.

TABLE OF CONTENTS

CHAPTER ONE

It's About That Time

Randall's heart was heavy, longing for the days he felt alive. He'd spent a decade away from the thrill of a stagecoach robbery. Back then, he had a loyal ally in Deputy CJ. Randall had reason to trust him. CJ had risked his career as a deputy, his family, and even his life for Randall. CJ had informed him whenever there was a stagecoach with cargo worth robbing. Randall and his gang — his brother Joseph, the sharpshooter Juan Cortez, and the strategy expert Sam Williams — had made a fortune from raiding the stagecoaches. They had worked well together for several years and often enlisted like-minded men in the robberies.

Now, at fifty, Randall was alone and bitter. He couldn't shake off the overwhelming sense of loneliness that engulfed him. Most everyone he trusted had either met their end or turned their back on him. Even his best friend, CJ, had left him behind without even a word.

Sam Williams, a ranch hand for the Pruitt family for decades, was the only one who stayed. Though his mind was not as sharp as it once was, his dedication to Randall and the land remained unyielding — or at least so it seemed to Randall. Sam was the same age as Randall but looked old and worn with his leathery, dried skin. The sun and the hard work had taken a merciless toll on his wire-thin frame.

"Ten years is long enough," Randall muttered. He drank the rest of his whiskey and slammed the glass on the table. He grabbed his rifle and started for the door. It was time to begin again with the stagecoach robbing. A corrupt new friend had told him that a coach carrying a wealthy bank customer was headed south from New York City. "There's a lot of money on that coach, and it's poorly protected," his informant said.

Randall went outside and shut the door behind him. Thomas, his nephew, was next to his horse while Frank, Sam's boy, was up on his, rocking forward and backward, chomping to go.

"Are you two ready to leave?" asked Randall.

Frank, at twenty years old, idolized Randall. Frank was clean-cut, well-dressed, and clean-shaven. He sat up tall. "Yes, sir!"

Thomas, also twenty, had long, oily, unkempt hair and could stand to have a proper bath now and again. He grunted as he climbed up on his horse. "No one's getting hurt, right?" asked Thomas.

Frank snorted.

Randall shook his head at Thomas. "You boys ride up ahead. I'll be there in a few minutes. Sam and I need to talk."

Frank smiled. "Sure thing." He threw a sideways glance at Thomas and then raced away.

Thomas snapped his reins and chased after Frank. "Hey, wait for me!"

Randall stared, glassy-eyed, as the two boys disappeared behind a cloud of dust. Pride swelled in his chest for Frank, his loyal protégé, following in his footsteps. Alternatively, his rebellious nephew Thomas seemed to revile him. Randall recalled a much younger Thomas, his face etched with innocent fear, clutching Randall's leg and sobbing, "Don't go. Uncle Randall, I love you." The echo of his soft voice, laced with a desperate plea, was a stark reminder of a bond severed by time and circumstance. Randall, his face wrinkled with disappointment, muttered, "He'd sooner see me dead than say he loved me." He kicked at the dirt and then went to Sam's place.

Randall pushed open the creaky door of the rundown shack.

"Frank?" yelled Sam from the room at the back. He was in bed recovering from a gunshot wound.

Randall closed the noisy door behind him. "It's me." The inside was neat and orderly. He walked to Sam's bedroom.

Sam sat up and grinned, his teeth stained yellow. "I thought you left already."

"The boys went ahead. Let's talk about yesterday."

Sam's face soured. "That Alexander Johnson shot me in the chest." His eyes darted away from Randall. "The doctor says I was lucky; the bullet went clear through me. I'll be back in the saddle in a few days."

Randall clenched his jaw and glared at Sam as he closed in on him. Randall rested his hand on his holstered gun. "Why did you shoot at Alexander after I told you not to?" He lowered his voice to a whisper. "He hadn't seen us. No one had."

Sam's eyes shot back to Randall. "I couldn't believe my eyes seein' him all grown up. He'll be trouble for us whenever he's on one of those stagecoaches."

A wave of disbelief washed over Randall. His jaw slackened, lips parting in a silent gasp as if he'd been struck speechless. "You know damn well I swore to his pa that I'd care for him, no matter what. None of us would be this well-off if it weren't for CJ."

Sam's gaze narrowed into slits, his nostrils flaring as his breath hitched in his throat. "CJ helped and clued us into which coaches to rob; that's true. But then, all of a sudden, he got sloppy, drinkin' all the time. That lawman was turnin' out to be a big problem for us. Eventually, he would have turn us all in."

Randall gripped his gun. "CJ would sooner die than betray us. You never liked him. You taunted and bullied him. That man didn't deserve being treated that way."

Sam's cheeks reddened with rage, and his forehead ridged with hate. "A good-for-nothing drunk, that's what he turned into. Always whining about him missing his dead wife and having to take care of that boy all on his own."

Randall narrowed his eyes and leaned in. "CJ thought the world of his son. I'm telling you again, leave Alexander alone."

Sam snarled at Randall and sat taller. "As soon as I'm on my feet, I'll hunt him down and kill that troublemaker, just like I did his—pa." Sam smiled. "His gun is hidden in the closet." He used his chin to point.

Randall, his face drained of color, cocked his head back in shock. "You told me that CJ up and left." His breathing slowed, his heart pounding. "After he disappeared, I went searching for him."

The edge of Sam's lips curled upward, and his eyes lit up bright with fire. "The coward was walking away from me when I shot him." Sam scoffed and leaned forward with a cold, defiant look. "Always following you around like a puppy dog, looking at you funny. It wasn't natural. I did you a favor. That stinkin' body is buried behind the barn."

A wave of nausea hit Randall hard.

Sam moved to stand and then winced as bright red blood oozed, staining his white shirt. He examined his wound. "Shoot. I'm bleeding again."

The loud click of a cocked gun broke the silence. Sam gasped. Randall had his weapon pointed at him.

Randall spat on the floor. "He was my one true friend." Randall holstered his weapon and then headed to the door.

Sam's eyes, crazed with rage, shouted, "Wasn't I your friend? You up and left me here. You took most of our bounty and bought that huge ranch down south. And worse yet, you took my son and Joseph's boy and left me alone to care for this place. And then you moved back here after ten years — wanting to rob stagecoaches again."

"The boys and I came up and visited now and then."

Sam scoffed. "With my cut of the money we made back then, I should have lived rich all this time — you with your fancy boots and expensive clothes."

"I gave you plenty."

Sam's jaw clenched tight, and his eyes narrowed to icy slits. He hissed, the words barely escaping through his gritted teeth, "I know your damn secret. I know all about it. CJ told me everything."

Betrayal flashed across Randall's face, momentarily erasing the rage. Randall's face crumpled as if he'd been physically struck. "No! You're lying."

Fury contorted Sam's face, his chest heaving as he lunged at Randall.

Randall, a lightning draw, sent a bullet into the oozing wound on Sam's chest.

Sam fell back into his bed, his eyes wide with shock. He looked at his chest and then back at Randall. "I knew you'd be the one to kill me."

Randall stood emotionless and silent as the life fled from Sam's body. Almost a minute passed, and the bright red stain still ate away at the once-white shirt. Randall shook his head.

Randall went to the closet, which was neat and orderly. He spotted an old, tattered wooden box hiding at the back of the top shelf and pulled it down. Sam needed a ladder to reach that high, he thought. The smell of linseed oil and stain escaped when he opened the box. A cleaned and oiled six-shooter was inside, wrapped in an oiled rag. The handle was smooth and faintly engraved with CJ's initials. No doubt, Sam had tried to erase the last of CJ from the gun.

It was the late 1850s in New York City. In his early twenties, Alexander Johnson, a tall, well-dressed bank manager, walked into his office carrying a stack of ledgers and loose papers. Alexander plopped them down on his large, ornate desk that was too fancy for his liking. Wallace Holt, the bank owner, told him, "All of our customers, especially the wealthy ones, regard the bank's appearance as an indicator of wealth and stability. We must maintain this image!"

Alexander took his two six-shooters out of the side drawer. Six bullets were nestled safely in the first one's chambers. He holstered the gun and picked up the other one. He'd cleaned it the night before and hadn't loaded it—he always cleaned his guns after firing them. A bullet from that weapon had found its mark in an outlaw's chest. He, along with another two or three masked men, got away.

He put six shiny bullets into the gun's chambers. He glanced at the papers on his desk as he holstered the second gun. The journals seemed to be beckoning to him to address a severe error in the account of a wealthy customer. He checked the time and shook his head. He'd promised Wallace he'd ride on the next stagecoach headed out of town instead of his regular one. Alexander figured he had enough time to examine the records again to exonerate his good name. He plopped down onto his chair. The barrels of his weapons dug hard into the side of his legs. He pulled both guns, put them on the desk, and returned to the ledgers.

He worked for several minutes. Then, he took a blank piece of paper from his center drawer, scribbled some numbers in a column, and drew a line under the last one. He added them and wrote the answer beneath the line. He compared it to another number in the ledger belonging to Mr. Swanson's account. He returned his pen to its holder and then smiled.

Sharp, rapid knocks startled Alexander. A short, stout Wallace

Holt stood behind the wood-framed glass of Alexander's door.

"Come in," yelled Alexander as his self-congratulatory smile disappeared.

Wallace opened the door, huffing—almost hyperventilating—and rushed to Alexander's desk. "Why aren't you on the stagecoach with Mr. and Mrs. Swanson?"

Alexander grinned. "There's still fifteen minutes before the coach leaves."

Wallace gasped. "Mr. Swanson is not a patient man. He withdrew another $1,000 in cash, and he's taking it to the college his daughter attends."

"That coach isn't going to leave without me."

Wallace shook his head. "He's outraged because I won't fire you."

Alexander shrugged. "He's a damn fool."

"Mr. Swanson said he plans to withdraw the rest of his money if we don't fix this. Let me assign his account to someone else."

"No. I can do both jobs," said Alexander, although it had been two days since Mr. Swanson had discovered the discrepancy in his account. Another more skilled accountant who didn't have to split his time between protecting stagecoaches and balancing books would likely not have made a mistake.

Alexander pointed to the ledger where he had solved the mystery of the accounting error.

Wallace raised a brow. "I need you riding with them to ensure they get to the next station. The men at *Sanctuary Station* will guard the coach the rest of the way."

Alexander scoffed. "I'd rather go on the coach headed to Boston at 10:00 a.m. That's the one I'm usually on."

Wallace shook his head. "I have someone else on that one. You're the best stagecoach protector we've got."

Alexander's face tightened. "Let me show you something first."

Wallace exhaled hard and glanced at his timepiece.

Alexander moved the books over so that Wallace could see them better. "Here's the cause of the supposed discrepancy in Mr. Swanson's account."

Holt's eyes tensed with dread. He braced himself for the bad news and leaned in toward the ledgers. Loud, forceful knocks interrupted his suspense. He gasped.

Alexander gritted his teeth and shouted at the deputy behind the door's glass, "Come in."

The deputy burst into the office and yelled, "The stagecoach with Mr. Swanson left."

Wallace, his heart racing, looked at his pocket watch. "The driver was supposed to wait for Alexander. That coach wasn't due to leave for another fifteen minutes, at least."

The deputy cleared his throat. "Mr. Swanson came out of the coach, created a huge spectacle, and said Alexander could go to hell."

Alexander chuckled. "The damn fool is going to get himself killed. Do me a favor and get my horse ready." Alexander turned to Wallace and said, "It'll serve Mr. Swanson right if the stagecoach robbers rob him blind."

"Alexander! He's our wealthiest customer. It'd be a tragedy if anything happened to his mon—" Wallace blinked several times and shuddered, "...if anything happened to him."

Alexander snickered.

"Mr. Swanson and his money will be fine. Those outlaws wouldn't be dumb enough to stop a coach between here and *Sanctuary Station* two days in a row."

Wallace gasped.

The deputy shook his head. "I'll wait outside."

Alexander went back to the books.

The deputy slammed the door when he left.

Wallace winced. "How bad is it? Did you account for the $20,000 shortage?"

"A simple missed decimal point, that's all it was. There is no shortage. I've added proper ledger entries to bring Mr. Swanson's account into balance. He'll be satisfied once he examines these ledgers."

Wallace sighed. "Mr. Swanson wants another manager assigned and said that this is the third time he's discovered an error." Wallace chuckled. "Swanson's daughter is the one who found all three of the accounting errors."

Alexander shook his head. "But this time, the mistake was

minor." He stood and put his guns in their holsters. "We sure do cater to Mr. Swanson's independent nature."

"When he returns, we can clear this whole thing up," said Wallace, his face returning to its pallid color. "Perhaps I could explain it to him in a more diplomatic manner—"

Alexander retrieved his rifle from the cabinet by the door. "When I catch up with him, I'll tell him we resolved the issue."

Wallace blinked several times. "The bank can't lose him as a customer."

Alexander grinned. "Don't worry, I'll be gentle." Alexander patted Wallace on the shoulder and left.

Wallace half-smiled as he picked up the ledger and examined the journal entries. He gazed out the window. Alexander was putting his rifle in its leather holder hanging from the saddle. The deputy was a few feet away, bobbing his head as he waited on his horse. Wallace was curious about the deputy's nervous habit, but not enough to ask the deputy about it.

CHAPTER TWO

Stagecoach Robbery

The robbers were escalating their attacks on the stagecoaches. Banks, desperate to safeguard their money, resorted to concealed strongboxes hidden within the stagecoach or beneath the driver's seat. Yet, even these measures felt inadequate. Each journey became a dangerous gamble, relying on a heavily armed trio: a rifle-wielding rider inside, a vigilant lookout perched atop the coach, and the driver himself, ever watchful with his weapon under his bench. Most of the time, the passengers were safe if they gave up the bank's money.

The driver sat on the stagecoach, waiting to leave New York. Inside were his two passengers, Mr. and Mrs. Swanson.

As he waited, Mr. Swanson yelled fiercely at the deputy inside. He only caught part of the conversation because he was "resting" his eyes.

"I'll follow behind on my horse instead of inside, and Alexander can catch up with us later," said the deputy to Mr. Swanson.

Soon after, the deputy tapped the driver's shoulder.

The driver jumped and gasped for air as he awoke.

"Mr. Swanson wants you to go. He said to give you this," said the deputy. "I'll follow you on my horse until Alexander shows up."

The deputy handed the driver twenty-five dollars. The driver smiled as he took the money. Confident in the short one-hour trip to their first stop, the driver felt safe. It was a beautiful, clear day, and he was confident he could manage any difficulty. Traversing these roads was routine, and he had never encountered a situation he couldn't handle. Of course, he couldn't remember the last time he'd traveled without an armed companion sitting next to him. No matter, he thought, Mr. Swanson was handy with his six-shooter if they got into trouble. And with the deputy riding behind, it should be okay.

The driver shook the reins to go. The coach began its trip out of New York through the wilderness to its first stop at *Sanctuary Station*.

The driver whistled a song and imagined what he could buy with his newfound fortune. He had always appreciated Mr. Swanson, who had helped pay for a modest house for him and his wife.

Inside, the wealthy couple sat on the rear bench and swayed to and fro as the stagecoach went. The ride was relatively smooth.

Mrs. Swanson said, "I brought my mother's necklace and a few other jewelry pieces for Martha. We have to encourage her to wear the dresses I'm bringing for her."

"So that's what's in that heavy trunk up top — Lots of dresses."

She chuckled as she rolled her eyes. "There are a few things for Gertrude, too."

"If Martha dressed more like a lady, she might attract a potential suitor."

Mr. Swanson smiled. "Most women, if not all, are happy to marry and have children. Just look at how joyful you are."

Mrs. Swanson winced. "I know we agreed to allow Martha to attend the college, but I'm worried about her."

"She's fine. Our daughter knows how to care for herself and must have had a good reason for punching that boy. I'm sure it's not as bad as it seems."

Her body shuddered as if she'd tipped her toe in ice-cold water. "Oh dear, that is never how a proper young lady should behave."

He patted his wife's hand. "The telegram I received from the school indicated that they would permit our daughter to attend a second year."

"Your generous donation likely influenced their decision in her favor."

Mr. Swanson's brows rose as he tilted his head with an amused smile. "My money can be quite persuasive."

"I'm beginning to regret that you and Martha 'persuaded' me to allow her to go to college. She needs to settle down, marry, and raise a family. Only then will she know what being a woman is."

He rolled his eyes. "We can't deny her this opportunity to go there and learn in a disciplined manner. After she finishes, she can live her life as she pleases."

Mrs. Swanson guffawed.

The corner of his lips curled upward as he glanced sideways at his wife and said, "I hope she gave that boy a good wallop!"

She laughed and sat up taller. "She's exactly like you."

"When we first met, you were energetically independent."

She inhaled and let it out in a huff. "Why can't she funnel that energy in a more positive, lady-like way? Just as I did."

"Agreed." He looked at his watch, returned it to his pocket, and said, "We should arrive at *Sanctuary Station* in twenty minutes."

She tried getting comfortable in her seat, and the pillow she had placed on the hard bench didn't help much. "I'm so glad Martha is staying with my dear Gertrude."

"Those two are inseparable."

Mrs. Swanson smiled. "Yes. Gertrude has always treated Martha as if she were her daughter. Martha adores her."

"We're fortunate that Gertrude came into our lives."

"When Joe brought her home to meet us all those years ago, I didn't know what to make of her. She was very loud—and talkative." Mrs. Swanson sighed as a tear fell to her cheek.

"I'm sorry that your brother...."

She squeezed his hand as a cloud of remembered pain overcame her. She took a slow, deep breath and put her head on his shoulder, trying to forget about her brother's tragic death.

Not far behind them, three men on horseback rode furiously along a dusty road. Randall Pruitt led the way, followed by his nephew, Thomas Pruitt, and Thomas's long-time friend, Frank Williams.

Randall, more than twice his nephew's age, was a tall, gruff man. He was a meticulous planner who liked robbing stagecoaches. Those coaches almost always carried lots of money, especially those leaving the big banks of New York and heading to the smaller town banks that littered the well-traveled roads. "You catch 'em in those parts where they have to slow down," he had told Thomas and Frank. Randall didn't like robbing banks. There

11

were too many lawmen in and around the building. Robbing a stagecoach was fun and exhilarating. He'd tried often to get his nephew, Thomas, to share his enthusiasm for robbing stagecoaches. Thomas was too much like his father in that respect. Thomas, with his scrappy appearance, was a bit quiet and too reserved.

Frank, on the other hand, was like Randall. Frank was outspoken, neat, and well-dressed. Randall was proud of Frank. Randall liked that Frank never questioned him and was always eager to follow his orders.

That day, Frank was distracted because his father had been wounded during a botched stagecoach robbery the day before. He and his father had a long, disturbing conversation early that morning. Frank consoled his father as best he could. Frank was bothered that his father had also mentioned disparaging things about Randall. Frank didn't pay much attention to them since most of it was none of his business. He never liked gossip.

Randall roared, "Those bastards are early. Hurry up! They're getting away." Randall was angry that he was short a man. If only Sam were here, he thought. "Doggone it!"

Randall spurred his horse onward, the animal leaping into a faster gallop with a startled snort.

Alexander jumped on his horse outside the bank and smirked at the deputy.

Alexander winked at him. "Sorry about that."

"That's okay. You were being an ass as usual." The deputy laughed and took off.

Within minutes, Alexander caught up to him, and both rode side-by-side.

After twenty minutes, Alexander said, "Are you sure they didn't leave earlier? We should have seen them raising dust already."

The deputy shrugged. "Come on. We're going too slow. Let's see who can get to Swanson's stagecoach first."

Alexander and the deputy raced past each other as swirling plumes of dust followed behind them.

* * *

Far ahead, the stagecoach carrying the Swanson couple thundered down the road. Its wheels, occasionally, leaped high above the ground. The driver caught a glimpse of three robbers bearing down on them. The driver, a mask of terror replacing his usual stoicism, flayed the reins, his voice ragged, "Faster!" Every lash echoed his rising panic, urging the horses to a speed well beyond their limit.

The animals pounded hooves in frantic unison down the trail headed toward what was aptly called *Sanctuary Station*. The driver knew he couldn't outrun the outlaws, yet every muscle screamed to push the horses harder. If he could get close enough, he might be able to get help. He glanced to the side, angry that he was alone on that perch. His knuckles were strained as he snapped the reins harder. The horses shrieked, but getting there was his only hope.

The couple inside clutched tightly to each other as they jostled about.

"We'll be fine, my love. You'll see!" Mr. Swanson reassured her as he took his gun from his bag.

"Dear God, please protect us," she prayed.

Closing in on the stagecoach, Randall saw the trail of dust loom over the path where it went. Further away was the smoke coming from a lone house — *Sanctuary Station*. The coach would soon be out of reach unless they could slow it down.

Frank pulled his six-shooter and fired several shots at the coach.

"Come on! We got 'em," Randall shouted and then pointed at Frank. "Get up on that ridge and shoot that damn driver."

Frank raced ahead and rode up the hill. It was full of trees and shrubs, which gave a shooter like him good cover. He jumped from his horse, grabbed his rifle, and ran to the edge. He narrowed his eyes, aimed at his target, and fired.

"Yeah!" Frank shouted when he hit his target. "Damn! I'm good!" He rushed to his horse.

The driver gasped as the molten metal pierced his arm, and he almost lost control as the coach violently shook. The coach veered left, nearly smashing against a large outcrop. A heavy trunk slid from behind him and struck his head. He felt dizzy as he instinctively pulled back on the reins, using his might to command the horses to slow down.

The horses' muscles shuddered as the coach's immense weight smashed into them. Panicked whinnies erupted as the horses skidded chaotically, and the coach bore down on them. A cacophony of scraping hooves echoed as the coach slowed to a crawl. The stagecoach finally stopped when one of its wheels collided with a rock jutting from the ground. The horses stood trembling, choking, and gasping for air. The driver slumped over motionless.

Inside, Mr. Swanson helped his wife into a compartment below the front seat, usually reserved for the strongbox. It was barely big enough to hold her. She peered up at him with tears and fear in her eyes. He gestured for her to keep silent. She pulled herself tight as he closed the cover over her. He grabbed his pistol and crawled out the small window opposite the door.

Randall and Thomas jumped from their horses and ran to the cockeyed stagecoach.

Randall walked cautiously to the door. "Come on out." He slowed as he drew closer, his weapon drawn.

There was no answer.

Randall narrowed his eyes. "Come on out. You ain't got a chance. We won't shoot. No one has to get hurt."

Both Randall and Thomas pointed their guns at the door. Randall signaled to Thomas to open it.

Thomas cocked his head back, a simmering anger replacing his surprise, and then turned back to the coach. Trepidation laced Thomas's movements as he inched toward the door, his grip tightening around his six-shooter. His weapon trembled, betraying a flicker of doubt. With a sharp exhale, he reached for the latch and flung the door open.

Inside was empty. Relief flickered across Thomas's face as he holstered his gun. A humorless scoff escaped his lips as he met Randall's gaze. "There's no one in there. No wonder they were able to go so fast."

Randall blinked, curiosity etched in his brows. He stepped past Thomas and poked his head inside. "What the hell? They had to have gotten in at the hotel."

Thomas snickered. "Maybe they got out earlier. Jumped, maybe?"

Randall offered no response and shook his head at the absurdity of the suggestion. As he turned, a jolt shot through him. Frank was charging toward them, his gun drawn, aiming at the coach, yelling something at him.

Thomas looked inside again and heard a click. His mouth fell open when the glint of metal caught his eye. A gun was pointed at him from the window opposite him.

Outside, as Frank approached, he saw Mr. Swanson pointing a weapon into the cabin.

A booming shot rang out. Thomas fell back to the ground.

A woman screamed.

Frank jumped from his horse, smoke oozing from his gun's barrel, and ran to Thomas. "Thomas, are you okay?"

Thomas stood up and felt his chest for a bullet hole.

Randall sprinted to the other side of the coach. On the ground was a wounded Mr. Swanson groaning in pain, reaching for his pistol.

Randall kicked the gun away as Frank and Thomas walked up.

A gold money clip was hanging out of Mr. Swanson's pocket.

Frank bent over and snatched it from him. "You won't be needin' this anymore. Serves you right for trying to shoot my friend. What's wrong with you?"

Mr. Swanson moaned and glared at Randall. "Randall! Back to your old ways."

Randall smirked and then nodded at Thomas. "He just withdrew money from the bank. Make sure you get every last cent. It's probably in the strongbox inside the coach under the front seat."

Thomas went to the stagecoach.

Frank walked up next to Mr. Swanson. "What do we do with him?"

Randall pointed his gun at Mr. Swanson's face and grinned.

Mr. Swanson's eyes widened in horror as Randall pulled the

trigger and fired.

Blood splattered on Frank's dusty boots.

Frank jumped back. "Doggone it, Randall! These dang boots were new." Frank kicked at the ground, trying to get the dirt to soak up the blood splatters.

The ground was too hard to let go of anything more than a small cloud of dust.

"Damnit!" said Frank, wiping his boots on Mr. Swanson's pant legs.

Mr. Swanson's watch was hanging half out of his pocket. Randall leaned over and picked it up. He pulled on the chain and tried to dislodge the end of it from the man's coat. But it broke anyway. Randall grimaced and examined the watch. The watches he'd seen before were all metal, mainly gold or silver. This one had a painted picture of a young, beautiful woman on the front. He winked at the dead man as he put the fancy watch in his pocket.

Thomas came running from the other side of the coach, pulling Mrs. Swanson by the arm. His eyes widened with fright when he saw Mr. Swanson on the ground.

Mrs. Swanson screamed when she saw her husband, rushed to him, and knelt next to his side.

Thomas glared at Randall. "You swore we weren't gonna kill anyone."

Randall chuckled. "No, I didn't. Besides, Son, he was trying to shoot ya."

Thomas narrowed his eyes at Randall.

Randall stepped toward Mrs. Swanson. "Who do we have here?"

She wailed in horror at Randall and shouted, "You're a monster!"

Thomas's eyes widened, and he jumped away from Mrs. Swanson. Thomas remembered his mother yelling the same thing at Randall the day she died.

Randall glared at the woman and then drew his gun.

She started to stand. "I'm not afraid of you. You killed my dear friend, Rose."

Randall almost choked as if punched in the gut. He glanced at

Thomas.

Thomas, his lips tight, stared accusingly at Randall.

Randall's eyes narrowed to deadly slits and darted toward Mrs. Swanson. "You don't know what you're saying."

She wailed even louder, "You miscreant, good-for-nothing murdering monster."

A guttural growl rumbled from Randall's chest. "Shut it!"

"I'm—"

Randall pulled the trigger.

Mrs. Swanson fell silent next to her husband.

Thomas gasped and approached the dead couple. "That woman was talking about my mother. Wasn't she?"

Randall walked up menacingly close to Thomas. Thomas cowered.

The red faded from Randall's face, "That woman was crazy. All that screeching. You know as well as I do your pa killed your ma."

Thomas stepped back as if trying to avoid something more lethal than a bullet. His gaze fell to Mrs. Swanson, and she seemed peaceful. The gruesome scene reminded him of the day he'd seen his mother's lifeless body lying on the floor. His mother had been wearing a similar, fancy dress as the dead woman. It made sense that his mother would have been friends with Mrs. Swanson. Thomas gritted his teeth, and his narrowed eyes darted to Randall.

Randall was staring at him. "Son, she ain't worth your pity." He shook his head and strolled away.

A silent battle raged within Thomas between thoughts of revenge and his intertwined thoughts of Mrs. Swanson's and his mother's deaths. He took a deep breath and exhaled slowly to calm himself. His gaze fell on Mrs. Swanson. She was clutching something. It took some effort to pry it from her clenched hand. It was a photograph. He wiped the blood from it with his fingers and saw the image of a young, beautiful woman. He looked closer, and his eyes widened in shock. When he turned it over, his mouth fell open.

"My dearest Martha" was written on the back.

Randall walked up to him. "Whatcha got there?"

Thomas snuck it into his pocket. "Nothing."

Randall's eyes darted to Thomas's pocket and then back to his face. "Go help Frank get the money out of the strongbox. It's up top. And hurry it up so we can get back home and check on his pa." Randall winked at him and then started for his horse.

Thomas's face soured, and he went to the front of the coach.

Frank was leaning over the driver.

Thomas stood on the ground, looking up at Frank. "Is he alive?"

Frank glanced sideways at Thomas, pulled out his six-shooter, and pointed it at the driver's face. "The man might be breathing. I can't tell."

Thomas climbed up next to Frank and pushed Frank's weapon away. "Leave him be. You aren't a cold-blooded killer."

Frank chuckled and holstered his gun. "You're right. Let's get this done so I can get back to Pa."

Thomas and Frank dislodged the strongbox and threw it to the ground, and it fell open.

Frank laughed. "It ain't locked."

They jumped down. Frank gathered the money and stuffed it into a pouch. Thomas noticed the glint of what seemed like precious stones. It was a necklace and other pieces of jewelry. He put them into his pockets.

Randall rode up on his horse. "Let's go! Riders are coming."

The stagecoach stood eerily motionless, crooked on the road, hiding its tragic, bloody scene from Alexander's and the deputy's approach.

With their guns drawn, the deputy and Alexander approached cautiously, the deputy on the left and Alexander on the right.

Alexander crept slowly toward the coach's open door and jumped forward, his gun pointed inside. The inside was empty except for the luggage thrown about.

The deputy moved along the coach's left side and stopped when he saw the bodies. "We're too late," the deputy rasped, his voice tight with disappointment. He shuffled toward the couple, his weapon disappearing into its holster.

Scrambling up top, Alexander stood next to the slumped-over driver.

The deputy rubbed his neck, his face pained with disgust, as he paced back and forth beside the bodies. "They're dead."

The deputy looked up at Alexander, shaking his head in disbelief. His voice creaked as he yelled, "If we'd arrived just a few minutes earlier, they'd still be alive."

Alexander sat where he should have been earlier, meant to protect the passengers. The scene that unfolded below was brutally clear. Mr. Swanson lay sprawled on his back, and Mrs. Swanson crumpled beside him. Crimson stained their clothes, while the hard-packed earth had become slick mud from the blood spilled mere moments ago. Guilt gnawed at him. "This is all my fault," he choked out, the words lost in the wind.

A sudden moan jolted him from his self-flagellation. The driver, eyes fluttering open, clutched his right arm, dark with dried blood.

"You're alive," Alexander breathed, a flicker of relief warming the icy grip of dread in his chest.

CHAPTER THREE

From Past to Present

Randall raced home, followed closely by Frank. Thomas trailed far behind the other two. Frank almost crashed into Randall when he suddenly slowed and turned onto a narrow, winding trail. This path was one Randall used long ago to 'escape' from any pursuer. Anyone following them would be met with an uninviting labyrinth, most trails leading to treacherous dead ends.

Randall yelled, "Thomas, ride up here with us. You don't want to get lost in here."

Thomas wrinkled his face. "I'm good."

The trio pressed on for thirty minutes, navigating a dark maze of gnarled trees and unforgiving terrain. Emerging from the dense canopy, they skirted the edge of Randall's land. On one side, the forest they'd just traversed loomed like a brooding giant, its secrets hidden in the shadows. On the other, a stark contrast: a flat wasteland choked by tall weeds and scraggly shrubs where, long ago, vegetables once flourished. Back then, the air smelled green with life. His mother had toiled in the fields with her two boys. His father, who worked as a deputy, was tainted with corruption.

Randall took a sharp right turn into a narrow path just beyond the weedy land. His house came into view. He rode up to the hitching post.

Randall tied his horse. He excitedly pulled the saddle bag, loaded with cash, and rushed to the door. About to go inside, he glanced back. He took a deep breath and exhaled through his words, "Frank, after you're done, go see if your pa is well enough to come on over. We got some celebratin' to do."

"Yes, sir," said Frank, grinning.

Frank was tying his horse when Thomas stopped next to him.

Thomas bristled as he got down. He took an apple from the pouch hanging from his saddle, where he kept snacks. He cut two slices and gave one to his horse—she whinnied with delight.

Frank waited for Thomas to toss him the other one for his horse, like he usually did. Instead, Thomas gave the second piece to his horse.

Frank's face wrinkled as he narrowed his eyes and said, "Show some respect for your uncle. We made a lot of money today. And it wasn't easy for him."

Thomas shook his head, "Randall murdered that couple in the stagecoach just like he killed my ma."

"Randall didn't kill your ma," said Frank.

Thomas scoffed.

Their conversation carried through the open window.

Inside, Randall grunted. "Damnit! I told that boy what happened," he muttered. He took a glass and the whiskey from the cupboard, poured himself a drink, and sat at the kitchen table. Now and again, a smooth glass of spirits was well deserved, especially after the thrill of a successful robbery. Today's chase was exciting. He was skilled at robbing stagecoaches. And after a ten-year hiatus, he was back at it. He took a sip. A cursed memory, one that he had relived many times, snapped at him as he slammed his empty glass down. He gazed into nothingness as the memory accosted him.

Ten years before, he and his brother sat across from each other, drinking at the same table.

A grinning Randall poured a little whiskey into a glass and slid it over to Joseph. "What were you and Juan talking about all hush-hush? Are you two planning on robbing a stagecoach without me?"

Joseph glanced at the glass and shook his head. He licked his lips and stared disdainfully at Randall.

Randall smiled. "Have a drink." It bothered him that his brother was keeping something important from him.

Joseph took a sip. He hardly remembered the last time he'd tasted anything this smooth. The whiskey comforted him like an old friend who was always there for him, at least until the next day when he'd have to go looking for more. He drank the rest down.

Randall filled both glasses.

"Rose won't like me drinking," said Joseph as he eyed the

glass, mesmerized by the reflection of the late morning sunlight swimming on its surface.

Joseph sat, his eyes fixed on the glass. He took a drink and wrinkled his face. He closed his eyes for a few seconds, his head swaying slightly. "I don't trust you. I've told you a million times to keep your hands off my Rose."

"Rose? Nothing is going on. I want nothing to do with that toad of a wife you got. She ain't family." Randall shook his head. "You imagine things when you drink."

Joseph glared at Randall and leaned in. "She's my wife, and that makes her family. I can see why she wants to move on out of here. She doesn't like it here. Mostly because she doesn't like you."

Randall winced, the vein growing thick on his throat. He shifted uncomfortably in his chair. "You're moving? We got a good thing going here. You could help—"

"I'm not interested in robbing stagecoaches. I want to be a lawman out West who protects innocent people from the likes of you." Joseph drank the rest of the whiskey and shoved his empty glass closer to Randall.

Randall snickered and filled Joseph's glass halfway. "Like Pa? Bad is in our blood, brother. There's nothing you can do about that. He was as crooked as you are."

"That's not true." Joseph drank the whiskey in one shot, put the empty glass down, and stood. "I'm nothing like our pa. I have respect for the law."

Randall scoffed.

Joseph half-smiled. "Juan is organizing wagons to get us to California. We're leaving tomorrow. Rose is at his house, delivering the last of our provisions for the trip."

Randall flinched and glared at Joseph. "What the hell! Juan is going, too? You can't leave. Pa left this house to both of us and wanted us to stay here." Randall took another drink.

Joseph guffawed.

Randall almost choked. "You're my family, and I need you with me."

Joseph spun around to Randall, held up his arm, about to say something, and then lost his balance.

Randall jumped from his chair and reached for Joseph, but missed. Joseph crashed head-first to the floor.

"Damnit, Joseph!"

Joseph pushed himself up and was already kneeling when his eyes flashed open. Reaching to cover his mouth, he jumped up and bolted out the front door.

Randall rushed after him. Joseph was leaning over the railing, vomiting. Joseph wiped his mouth and staggered to the bench, avoiding Randall's gaze. The world was spinning out of control. He plopped down on the bench and closed his eyes. The chaos faded as he fell into an unnatural slumber.

Randall relaxed when he saw his brother's breathing return to normal. Randall went inside and returned with a pillow and put it under Joseph's head. It'd been a long time since Joseph had touched whiskey.

Earlier, Randall had heard Rose and Joseph whispering to each other. Rose had shushed Joseph after he mentioned something about Juan. The whiskey was the only way to discover what secret Joseph was hiding.

Randall was about to enter the house when Rose and young Thomas arrived. Thomas rushed around and helped his mother down. Rose's eyes darted from Randall to Joseph. Joseph was asleep on the porch. The smell of whiskey accosted her as she stepped toward the house. Dread filled her heart as she heard Joseph's incoherent mumblings. Joseph hadn't touched any whiskey since she'd threatened to leave him so many years before. Rose glanced at Thomas and forced a smile.

She went to the back of the wagon and pulled out a box of things she'd bought to prepare a cake for Thomas's birthday. She and Joseph hadn't told Thomas of their plans to move. She placed the container on the porch and turned back to Thomas.

"Thomas, take the wagon to the barn and see that one of the ranch hands takes care of the horse." Rose always referred to Frank and his father, Sam, as ranch hands instead of calling them by their names.

Thomas's eyes darted to Randall, who stood stone-faced and towering over Rose.

She smiled stiffly at Thomas, "Get going."

Thomas nodded slowly and suspiciously, unhooked the horse

from the wagon, and then led the horse away.

She waited until Thomas disappeared into the barn and then turned to Randall. He grinned and narrowed his eyes.

She rushed to Joseph, shaking him. He didn't respond. She glared at Randall, "What the hell is wrong with you, getting him drunk? This is your doing."

"He's sleeping it off. He's not that drunk. He puked most of it up," he said with a chuckle.

"You know very well that he doesn't drink anymore. Why did you do this to him? You must hate your brother even more than I realized."

Randall cocked his head back, his face pained with surprise. "Before you came along, Joseph never kept anything from me. My brother trusted me." He took a step toward her. "You turned him against me by talking him into leaving here. You've made a mistake gettin' between us like that! You're trying to take him away."

Rose stepped back, shock painted on her face. Joseph wasn't supposed to tell Randall about their plans to move away. Her breathing went heavy. She leaned toward Randall. "You're no good for Joseph. He's a good man, and you want to corrupt him. I won't let you do that."

Randall burst into laughter. "You won't last. My brother doesn't love you. Sooner or later, he'll leave you for someone who cares for him. I know my brother better than you."

He went inside and slammed the door behind him.

Rose's eyes filled with rage. She kicked the door open and ran in after him.

"My husband loves me. You're just jealous. No respectable woman would ever love you. If your mother knew that you scour the whorehouses for love, she'd certainly be disappointed in you."

"The women there are more respectable than you." Randall stepped toward her, his eyes icy cold. "Didn't your mother work there?"

That comment choked the breath out of her. She had confided in Joseph long before that her mother had worked in a brothel for many years.

"You're a cruel monster," she shouted as she slapped Randall.

He shoved Rose hard to the floor. She wailed in pain and howled when he pulled her up by her arm.

He glared at her. "You—"

Randall recognized the click of the hammer of a six-shooter cocked and ready to fire. Joseph stood in the doorway, his hand trembling as he pointed a gun at him. A loud blast from Joseph's gun filled the room as a bullet grazed Randall's left arm. Randall, his jaws clenched, glared at Joseph. Embers of fury smoldered in Randall's bloodshot eyes.

"Let her go, Randall! Or else the next bullet will go through your cold heart," Joseph roared. He pointed the gun at Randall's chest.

Rose's eyes went wide with shock, and her jaw dropped. "Joseph! Put the gun down," yelled Rose. "Everything's going to be fine."

Randall released Rose's arm. His mouth held an insidious grin as he tilted his head down and locked eyes with Joseph.

Joseph relaxed his shooting hand.

And then, in one sweeping movement, Randall grabbed Rose and shoved her hard into Joseph's gun.

Rose screamed.

Joseph's gun went off, and Rose fell to the ground.

A hint of a smile crossed Randall's lips.

Joseph gasped, dropped his gun, and pulled Rose into his arms. "Rose!"

Rose whispered, "This is Randall's fault. Take Thomas away from here before it's too late."

She took one last breath.

Joseph roared as he grabbed the gun and jumped at Randall.

Randall wrestled the gun away from Joseph and stepped back, pointing the gun at his brother.

Randall shook his head as he thought of a way to spin this so that all blame fell onto Joseph. "What the hell, you drunken fool? Why did you kill her?" Randall glanced at his sleeve, which was quickly soaking up blood from the bullet that grazed him. His voice began to quiver as he said, "You shot me, you bastard. Damnit, I'm your brother. I wanted you to stay here and help me out. But it won't be good to have a killer like you hanging around here. You've always been a bit slow, but now you're plain stupid!" He knew Joseph bristled whenever someone called him stupid. "You were going to kill me, weren't you?"

Joseph backed away slowly without saying a word.

Randall's eyes filled with rage as Joseph stepped back. Randall cocked the gun, ready to shoot.

"I want you to leave, take your horse, and go. I don't care where you go, but I'll kill your boy if I ever see you again. You got that?"

Joseph stood defiant. "You love my son. You aren't going to hurt him. I'm taking him with me."

Randall growled at Joseph, "Thomas is a mama's boy, and by killing his mother, you've destroyed his life. Ain't telling what this is gonna do to him. Thomas needs someone strong to teach him how to be a man. You, for sure, ain't got what it takes to—"

"What's going on?" yelled Thomas from outside.

Thomas burst through the front door. His nose twitched from the acrid smell of spent gunpowder. His eyes, filled with horror, darted from Joseph to Randall to the gun in Randall's hand. And then Thomas's gaze fell onto the heart-wrenching sight on the floor, and his breath caught in his throat.

His mother was lying lifeless on the floor. The blood was seeping slowly away from her.

Joseph, his eyes moist with guilt, reached for Thomas. "It was an accident."

Randall shook his head. "Your pa just killed your ma. That's what happened."

Barely enough air to speak, Thomas rushed to his mother, kneeling at her side.

"Ma!" He picked up her hand and held in his tears as best he could.

Randall turned to Joseph. "Once I alert the sheriff about what you've done here, he's going to hunt you down and string you up." He used the gun barrel to point the way to the back door. "Your boy needs a father, not a drunken fool who killed his mother."

Joseph's face contorted in shock, and he whispered to his son, "I'm sorry."

Randall bared his teeth like a mad dog. "Yeah. You are. Now

get going."

Joseph reached for Thomas. "Let's go, son."

Randall stepped over Rose's body and pushed Joseph. "You're not taking him anywhere." He turned to Thomas. "Did you know they were leaving for California tomorrow?"

Thomas sucked in a sharp breath, his hands flying to his temples. He rubbed them in tight circles, trying to quell the rising panic.

Joseph gasped. "Your mother and I were going to tell you. We wanted to surprise you."

Randall shook his head. "I wonder what else they were keeping from you."

Thomas's shoulders drooped as his hands dropped to his side in surrender, and he walked next to Randall.

Randall's lips curled upward slightly. "It's time to go, Joseph."

Joseph shuffled out the door. Randall, his gun poking his brother's back, followed behind.

Once outside, Joseph pivoted and lunged at Randall.

Randall quickly shoved him to the ground. "You're slow. Maybe it's the whiskey. Now off you go, little brother!"

Joseph got on his horse and glanced at the door where Thomas stood. Thomas winced and then turned away and disappeared into the house.

Randall laughed. "You ain't wanted here."

Joseph snapped at the reins and left.

Randall went back inside and found Thomas crying over his mother's body.

"Thomas, let's go get some air." Randall pointed to the door with the gun that had shot Rose.

Thomas, his lip quivering, ran out of the house and kept on running until he got to Frank's house.

Frank jumped down from the porch. "What's wrong?"

"He killed my mother."

Frank gasped. "Randall? No!" He glanced down and then locked eyes with Thomas. "This morning, Randall told me he wanted Rose dead. He said she was turning your pa against him. I thought he was joking."

Thomas's mouth fell open. "What?"

Frank pulled away from Thomas as Randall rode up.

Randall strained to smile, the tension evident in the tightness of his jaw. "Thomas, you should stay here tonight."

A shiver went up Thomas's spine at the feigned smile. He gripped the porch railing, knuckles white. He inhaled deeply, the air catching rough in his throat. He exhaled loudly. Things were about to get complicated between him and Randall. Thomas's eyes narrowed like slits as he watched Randall's smile disappear. Thomas turned and marched up the stairs.

Randall's eyes were narrowly fixed on Thomas as he continued into the house. Randall jumped when Thomas slammed the door behind him.

"Frank, come over here."

Frank rushed over.

"Where's your pa?"

"He's still out in the fields."

"Tell your pa that I'll come by later. Watch Thomas while I get the sheriff. And keep him here. Joseph killed Rose."

In the present, Randall poured himself more whiskey and glanced out the window. Thomas and Frank were out of earshot and headed to the barn.

Once inside, Frank asked, "Why are you mad at me?"

"I'm not mad at you."

"Well then, what's wrong? You've hardly said a word since we robbed that stagecoach. And just now, you didn't even give my horse a piece of apple like you usually do."

"Sorry." Thomas took a deep breath. "I've been thinking. That woman said that Randall killed my ma."

"That woman didn't know what she was saying. When I asked Randall what happened, he told me how Joseph shot your ma."

Thomas exhaled loudly. "Remember that day my mother died when I snuck out of your house?"

"Yes. You wouldn't talk to me for a long time after that. That's the day that I lied to Randall for you. I'd never kept the truth from him before that day. That's when I went looking for you 'cause I knew you were upset."

"I know." Thomas half-smiled at his friend. "Anyhow, I heard

28

them arguing that day. I was in the barn putting the horse up. Ma screamed 'Monster!' just like that woman on that stagecoach today. I dropped everything and ran to the house. Then, Ma yelled at my pa to put the gun down."

Frank straightened up. "See! Your pa did shoot your ma. He had the gun."

Thomas's voice rose a notch, his words laced with urgency and simmering frustration. "Later that night, I went to look for my pa. When I got near that little shed, he called out to me with a tune he would whistle now and then." Thomas whistled a bit of it.

"Oh yeah. I remember," said Frank.

Thomas nodded as the memories overwhelmed him.

Ten years before, Thomas peeked out the window and saw Frank and Randall talking. Randall had told Frank, "Joseph just killed Rose." Thomas gritted his teeth and then snuck out the back door. Having decided to chase after his father, he bolted to the barn to get his horse. A familiar, whistled tune caught his attention as he walked past the shed.

Thomas turned toward the melodic sound. The full moon's light partially lit a silhouette of a man standing at its entrance. Thomas squinted at the apparition.

"Thomas," yelled Joseph.

Joseph ran to Thomas and hugged him. "Son, I'm sorry. I'm so sorry."

"Pa, what happened? Why did you shoot Ma?"

Joseph led Thomas to the shed. "It was an accident — a terrible accident. Randall was hurting your mother. He shoved her. I was drinking, and the gun went off."

"Why don't you come back? Tell that to the sheriff. It'll be fine."

"I can't." Joseph hesitated. Randall had threatened to kill Thomas if he returned. A wave of nausea hit him. "Randall will kill…."

The moonlight caught Thomas's face as he turned away to wipe his tears.

Joseph gasped at the sight of Thomas's eyes. They were filled with a deep, raw pain that tugged at Joseph's heart. "Everything is going to be okay, son." He walked over to a corner of the shed and removed some boards from the floor. He pulled a wooden box from the dark hiding place and held it where the light was better. "Your ma made me promise I'd take you from here."

Thomas scrunched his face, confused. "To California?"

Joseph nodded. "Your ma and I arranged to travel by wagon train. We wanted to surprise you with this for your birthday, and we thought you'd be excited about it. Juan organized the trip."

"Mr. Cortez?" asked Thomas. Thomas didn't know him all that well. It'd been about two years since he'd last seen him. Before that, Mr. Cortez used to come by the house almost daily.

"Yes. We're going to meet at his place tomorrow."

Thomas's shoulders dropped. "But I don't want to go. I like it here."

"Son, there's no life for us here. Staying here will lead to a life of stagecoach robberies and who knows what. Your mother and I wanted so much more for you. We'll have a great life there. Did you know there's gold pouring from the ground in California?"

Joseph withdrew two pouches from the wooden box. "This will be enough for us to make the trip and set us up once we get there. You need to go back for now, and don't tell Randall you saw me."

Thomas stepped back. His world was crumbling too fast for him to know what to do. "Yeah, but...."

Joseph didn't notice the doubt creeping into his son. "I'll be waiting for you at that mine just west of here in the morning. Let's say 9:00 a.m. That'll give you ample time to do your chores and leave unnoticed. Can you do that?"

"Yes."

"We'll ride to Juan's place and head out to California. He's expecting us."

Off in the distance, they heard Frank calling out to Thomas.

Joseph jumped. "You better get back."

Thomas nodded. He thought about his mother and started to feel more comfortable about the idea of leaving. "I'll see you at 9:00 a.m."

Thomas returned to the house and found Frank sitting on the front steps.

Frank smiled at Thomas. "Randall came by while you were gone, and I told him you were asleep, even though I knew you weren't."

"I couldn't sleep, so I went for a walk."

"Did you find your pa?"

A wave of surprise crashed over Thomas. Had Frank followed him, he thought.

Frank half-smiled. "If I were you, I would have done that."

Thomas took a deep breath. "My father is leaving town and wants me to go with him. We'll meet at 9:00 a.m. at the mine where we used to hang out. Why don't you come with us?"

"Leave Pa? No way!" Frank's voice cracked with desperation, and his eyes glistened with disbelief.

"Your pa can come with us. It'll be great," said Thomas.

"No." Frank stammered, his face etched with worry, "He can't.... He won't." He ran a hand through his hair, the gesture betraying his agitation. "Look, maybe... maybe I could visit you one day. But, I can't just...."

The following morning, Thomas finished his chores early. After he cleaned up, he collected some of his things and left. It was 9:00 a.m. sharp when he arrived at the mine. There was no sign of his pa. Several crows were cawing from their trees above. Thomas had always been fascinated with crows.

"They're intelligent and cunning," His pa had told him. "Don't let 'em look at your face. They'll remember you and attack you if you do them wrong,"

"They're just birds," Thomas scoffed, dismissing the memory with a shake of his head.

Loud chatter came from up ahead. He ran in that direction and stopped dead in his tracks. Frank was on his horse, and Randall stood a few feet away. Randall was holding a small leather pouch like the one he'd seen his father with the night before.

Randall walked up to Thomas and tossed him the pouch. "Your pa left without you. He asked me to give this to you. He said something about it being for your future."

Thomas opened it and found it contained bits of gold, some paper money, and some jewels. He narrowed his eyes at Randall.

"You ran him off, didn't you?"

Randall's face held a sly smile. His eyebrows bumped up.

Thomas's eyes darted to Frank. "Why?"

Frank looked away.

Randall chuckled. "Son, I don't see why you would want to go with your pa, especially since he killed your ma. He's probably on his way to California by now. I guess you're stuck with me. I'll take care of you. Family takes care of family."

Randall got up on his horse. "It's best you put that pouch somewhere safe. You never know when you might need it." He started to leave and then abruptly turned back. "Oh, and I wouldn't hide it in the shed. I'd find someplace else. That's where your pa and I hid stuff from your grandpa."

Thomas stood alone, holding the leather pouch as Randall and Frank rode away.

Back in the present, Frank and Thomas walked out of the barn. Thomas said, "I miss my pa."

"I know." Frank smiled and patted Thomas's shoulder. "I'll go get my pa," he said as he rushed away.

Thomas went to the kitchen to prepare supper.

Randall had a good fire burning in the stove and had seared several pieces of meat. Thomas avoided Randall's gaze as he poured the cut vegetables and seared meat into the deep stove pot. A mouth-watering aroma filled the air.

Minutes crawled by, heavy with unspoken tension. Thomas, a statue of silent fury, stirred the stew — enough for four.

Frank shuffled in.

Thomas glanced at him and stopped stirring the pot. Frank stood wide-eyed, his breathing shallow, in the doorway. His face was pallid.

Randall didn't look up and said, "Hope you're hungry." Randall reached into the cupboard, pulled out three plates and three bowls, and set them on the table.

Thomas, his voice filled with unease, rushed over to Frank. "Where's your pa?"

Randall turned to Frank, stone-faced.

"My pa is dead," said Frank.

CHAPTER FOUR

Expulsion

Long, raven hair, nearly black, framed Martha Swanson's face, cascading a few inches past her shoulders. Flecks of gold danced within her warm, hazel eyes. Independent and fiercely self-reliant, Martha was more than ambitious; she was audacious. At seventeen, she'd charted her course: college, a respectable career, perhaps travel, culminating in marriage—bold aspirations for a young woman carving her unique path in a time of limitations. Unafraid of dissenting whispers, she remained committed to her goal. While she loved her parents dearly, their approval wasn't her compass. Her father, a successful businessman, cautioned against the difficulty of her chosen path. Her mother firmly believed a woman's place was in the home, caring for her husband and children. Yet, they nurtured her love for learning, filling their library with books that became her silent mentors. In them, she envisioned a life exceeding even her father's achievements, a future she was determined to claim. One day, she sprung a surprise on her father. It challenged their dynamic and set her destiny in motion.

"Father, I've read many of the books in your collection. I especially enjoy adventure books that take me to the farthest outskirts of my imagination. Someday, maybe I'll go see those places myself."

Martha walked over to the shelf beside the fireplace, pulled down two books, and said, "These two books seemed odd to me."

"Odd? In what way?"

She flipped through their pages. "They depict women as tools for the men to use as they please."

He cocked his head back, revealing an unflattering second chin. "Tools? That's a bit harsh, don't you think?"

She looked at her father, astonished. How could he not agree with her about this, she thought. "The men in these books comment on the human condition and claim to have all the answers. And most of the time, they are nonsensical. A woman's perspective should have been included to balance the extreme views. Almost all the pages have spelling and grammatical errors."

Martha held the two books so her father could see them.

Mr. Swanson guffawed. His face relaxed, his cheek bright red. "Oh! Those books. They're rubbish! Your uncle, Joe, rest his soul, gave me those two books years ago. He raved about them and insisted I read them. He told me that if more people read them, they would help solve serious social issues plaguing society." He shook his head. "He had some very extreme views and obnoxious ideas."

Mrs. Swanson walked in. "He most certainly did! I found them last week while cleaning here. They'd fallen behind a shelf."

Mrs. Swanson took the books from Martha and began paging through one of them, shaking her head.

Mr. Swanson nodded and winked at Martha. "I was going to give them back to Gertrude." He raised his brows. "Perhaps she might want them as a memento."

Mrs. Swanson shook her head. "These blasted books would only stir memories of my brother's most uncharitable views on the fairer sex. There is nothing but rubbish in these books." She tossed the two books into the fireplace. The fire flared from the dry fuel of propaganda. "May his soul rest in peace."

Martha almost choked as she inhaled.

Mrs. Swanson hugged Martha. "I've always admired your voracious appetite for reading. Your father and I have always made it a point to add books to this library to feed your thirst for knowledge. We've avoided the many books that use falsehoods to paint the changing times negatively."

Mr. Swanson nodded, his brows raised.

Martha cleared her throat. "Thank you both. I appreciate it, and I do love reading. But it's not enough." Martha's gaze floated from her mother to her father and then back to her mother. "I want to go to college."

Mrs. Swanson gasped. "What? We have every sort of book imaginable. There's no reason for you to go to college."

Martha kissed her mother's cheek. "Mother, you know better than anyone why I must go there. These books leave me thirsty for much more."

Mrs. Swanson half smiled and left without another word.

A part of Mr. Swanson understood the truth of Martha's words, yet a flicker of indecision remained in his eyes.

Martha's voice cracked with desperation. "Father, please talk to her. You know I have to do this. Tell her I promise to consider marriage after I complete my schooling."

Mr. Swanson looked into Martha's eyes pensively. "Be patient while your mother and I discuss it."

Martha smiled. This meant her father had decided in her favor when he said this. She could hardly contain her glee and nodded. "Yes, Father. I'll be patient. But so you know, the Fall session begins in August, and Gertrude lives a few blocks from the school."

Soon after, Martha's father enrolled her in college.

The college was reluctant to accept 17-year-old Martha because only men (and one or two women unofficially) were allowed to take classes there. They demanded an 'accommodation' fee even to consider Martha's admission. After Mr. Swanson donated twice the fee amount, the college made a narrow exception to its admission policy, allowing Martha and only her to attend. Mr. Swanson agreed to give them a similar amount for each additional term she was permitted to attend.

Mr. Swanson knew this was a bribe, plain and simple.

Martha began her first year of studies on Monday, August 16, 1858. She lived with Gertrude, not far from the college. She enjoyed her independence. Attending college was the most exciting thing she had ever undertaken. Of course, as a woman, Martha was required to take typing and other skills needed in an office. The school counselor had advised her to take classes in the arts lest the more challenging courses might overtax her. Much to his dismay, she ignored his advice and took courses like bookkeeping, accounting, mathematics, and philosophy. She wasn't the only woman attending that college. As far as she knew, she was the only woman "allowed" to take classes designated for men. Her father's generous donations ensured she could take those classes, no matter how controversial it was for a woman.

In her first term, she worked hard to learn her lessons. Many of the instructors resented her in their classrooms and graded her harshly. Amongst themselves, they complained about her taking a seat away from a young man who would better utilize his education than she could. Even so, she demanded fair treatment. By the end of her first term, she had gained their respect and was consistently faring better than the other students. Her academic prowess inspired awe in some students, while her quiet demeanor earned her the trust of others.

In January, she began her second term in college and found more support as she advanced to the next level of classes. Most of the instructors no longer resented her. Instead, they encouraged her by challenging her with more complex problems and rooting for her success. Unlike the previous term, nearly all her classmates supported her. She thought they might have become accustomed to her or felt less threatened by her. Her second term ended in April.

May brought the third term, culminating in July, with mastery of accounting and bookkeeping. While economics proved more difficult, Martha tackled it with unwavering determination.

August ushered in Martha's second year; initially, things were sailing smoothly. But the calm wouldn't last. A month into the term, an incident outside the school turned her world upside down. Two instructors witnessed her in an altercation with a passerby, claiming they saw her knock the individual to the ground before he scrambled away, triggering a chase by several students. Thankfully, the instructors intervened, diffusing the tense situation. However, the repercussions were severe. The school contacted Gertrude, and an urgent telegram summoned Martha's parents for a crucial meeting. The air crackled with unspoken questions and a rising tide of worry.

Soon after, Martha's parents had wired her and Gertrude that they were coming.

On the day Mr. and Mrs. Swanson were due to arrive, Martha and Gertrude sat on a park bench holding umbrellas. Some ducks swam in the pond before them, and others rested under the nearby shade trees. The clear, blue sky provided no shelter from the sun, high in its zenith. A gentle breeze felt heavy, doing little to cool the two women dressed in attire Martha's mother would approve of.

Gertrude patted Martha's hand. "Are you okay?"

Martha half-smiled. "Do you think Mother and Father are upset with me?"

"Your parents are coming to settle the school's ruffled feathers. The school has threatened to expel you."

"They won't expel me. They like the money my father gives them too much," Martha grinned. "Besides, the man who snuck up on me and surprised me deserved what he got. I didn't know who he was. And then he had the nerve to say I didn't belong there. Well, I showed him!"

Gertrude chuckled. "Maybe next time you could just walk away or something."

"But Gertrude. All of my dreams are coming true. Nobody's going to take a single dream away from me."

Gertrude took a deep breath and snorted a little as she exhaled. Her face warmed as she took Martha's hand. "Child, I'm very proud of you. Your parents are, too. Your father will do whatever he can to keep you in school."

Martha nodded. "Mother is disappointed in me. She wants me to settle down, get married, and become a good servant to a husband."

"Servant?"

Martha shrugged uncomfortably. Her mother had told her Gertrude's mother was an enslaved person in the South. It wasn't easy to tell by looking at Gertrude. She inherited her father's fair skin and his light, emerald-green eyes.

Gertrude patted Martha's arm. "Your mother admires your strength, even if it scares her some. She wishes she had the courage to live the life you dare to dream."

"Really?"

"Yes. She doesn't understand why you would choose a needlessly difficult life. However, she and your father have made peace with your decision and hope you'll marry after you graduate."

Martha chuckled warmly. "That's part of my plan, too. But only after I've worked for a year or two and maybe traveled." Martha took Gertrude's hand. "Did your dreams come true?"

Gertrude's face softened as the edge of her lips curled up.

"They did — in a round-about sort of way."

Martha looked puzzled. "Round-about?"

"Well," Gertrude said as a flood of memories surfaced. "My father told me I was born in 1809 and was a rambunctious, wildly independent little girl. I loved playing in the field behind the house, picking flowers, and watching the birds."

"Where was your mother?"

"I never knew her. My father told me she went down South and never came back. That's where she was from. She worked on a huge plantation there." Gertrude took a shallow breath. "Anyhow, my father had difficulty keeping food on the table for us. There were quite a few times I went to bed hungry. When I was about ten, my father dropped me off at the orphanage."

"Oh, that's sad."

"It wasn't so bad. However, I did miss my father a lot. I was never hungry and loved assisting the staff with the other children. And I did have chores." Gertrude reached into her bag, withdrew a fan, and used it to cool her flushed face. "Yes, sirree, I had chores. It was hard work, and I loved every minute of it. When my eighteenth birthday drew near, the orphanage elders offered me a job. I jumped at the chance and officially became their housekeeper, mostly cleaning and helping with the children."

Martha gasped. "Wait. You were in the orphanage for eight years, and no one had wanted to adopt you?"

Gertrude smiled. "No way did I want to be adopted. Whenever prospective parents showed even an inkling of interest in me, I knew exactly what to say and do to dissuade them."

"Why? Didn't you want to be happy?"

"I was happy. I hoped my father would return to find me if I stayed there." Gertrude sighed. "He never did."

"I'm sorry. Have you seen him since?"

"Nope. I never saw him again. But as I said, I was happy. I was. That's where I met your uncle."

"Really? You've never told me about you and Uncle Joe. Mother cries when I ask her about him. How did you meet him?" Martha sat upright and leaned in toward Gertrude with an expectant smile that could melt any heart.

"Well, one day, I was working in the front yard while the young ones tended to their chores in the garden. He came up the walk and asked to speak with the headmistress. He complained about the children being too noisy. He was beautiful, handsome, and smart. I loved him from the moment I saw him." Gertrude smiled. "Well, maybe not the first moment. At first, he was a little condescending toward me. Perhaps, at the time, he had little experience with women. I set him straight rather quickly."

"I read a couple of the books he had loaned to Father. They held some—extreme views." Martha stifled a chuckle. "Mother burned them in the fireplace."

Gertrude turned to Martha, her face caught in a question, and then a broad grin filled her face. "Oh, yes! Your mother told me, and we both laughed about it."

"Mother told me you were perfect for her little brother and brought him out of his shell."

"Joe was introverted in an extroverted sort of way."

"I know what you mean. They're sensitive and hide it in a flagrant, extroverted manner as if it were a weakness." Martha rolled her eyes. "Many of the boys at school are like that."

"Have any of those 'boys' caught your eye?"

"Gertrude, I'm not interested in them like that."

"Are they respectful of you?"

"At first, they weren't. Now, they kid around a bit, but they're all respectful. I respect them, too. They're good-natured. Although sometimes you must dig a little to reach that part of them."

Gertrude chuckled. "What about the boy you punched?"

Martha rolled her eyes. "Like I told you, he snuck up on me. He was tall with ragged, unkempt, long hair. The only thing not disgusting about him was his piercing blue eyes." She scrunched her nose and continued, "His clothes were worn and smelled of sweat. I had never seen him before that day. That man had no right to be familiar with me."

Gertrude narrowed her eyes with concern. "In what way?"

"Oh, I don't know. He was older and rude — and most definitely not a student. I told him to go away. When he surprised me by grabbing my arm, I punched him in the face. A couple of my classmates intervened, roughed him up, and then he ran away. When the principal discovered I was at the center of the conflict, he told me he was disappointed in me."

"The school should have taken steps to protect you and not have suspended you," Gertrude said, her voice firm.

Martha bobbed her head rapidly in agreement. "It's going to work out. Let's get back to your story. You were getting to the good part."

Gertrude smiled and took a deep breath.

"After three years of courtship, Joe proposed. By then, he had become confident and optimistic and developed a healthy attitude toward women. He would have burned those books himself that he'd loaned to your father."

Martha laughed. "When did you both get married?"

"It was a beautiful spring day on our wedding day. I wore a gorgeous, billowy, lacy dress. Everything was perfect. Earlier that day, his friends invited him to go for a ride. Joe took his prized horse. As they neared the house, the horse got spooked and threw him. He must have hit his head. His friends took him inside, but he insisted he was okay."

Martha moved closer to Gertrude and nodded affectionately.

Gertrude half-smiled. "Already in my wedding dress, I rushed to him. He whispered, 'Isn't it bad luck for the groom to see his bride on their wedding day?' I fought back my tears. We were married an hour later, and he fell when we left the church. I knelt at his side and held his hand. His eyes were locked with mine, his face etched with regret."

Gertrude wiped away her tears. "Then he told me he loved me. Joe, I said, I will always love you and only you. A few seconds later, his life left him."

Martha hugged Gertrude tightly. "Gertrude, I'm so sorry. I had no idea."

"Child, I'm fine. I feel him with me always. I'm never alone. After that, I moved in with your parents, and five years later, I helped the doctor deliver you. Both you and your parents brought me so much joy. I was incredibly grateful, and I still am. I was thrilled when your parents asked me to move here. You know that we're living in your mother's and Joe's childhood home, and this is the park where the wedding reception was to take place."

"Oh my! It's beautiful here."

"Yes. In those days, they owned a hundred acres of land where the house sat. Even this park was part of their property. Your mother donated most of it to the city and kept only the house."

When Gertrude stood, the ducks near the water's edge jumped into the water, swam away frantically, and quacked.

Gertrude laughed. "I'm getting hungry. Let's go. After lunch, I want to freshen up your parents' bedroom before they arrive."

Martha took Gertrude's hand. "I can hardly wait. Thank you for sharing that part of your life with me. I love you very much."

Gertrude said, "I love you, too."

Martha and Gertrude walked hand in hand, each with their umbrella providing shade.

As they approached the house, a teenage boy was waiting on the front porch.

Dread shook Gertrude's voice. "Young man, what are you doing here?"

"My supervisor instructed me to personally deliver this telegram to you. I'm sorry."

Gertrude half-smiled and looked over at Martha.

"Martha, please get the table ready for lunch. I'll be there in a moment."

Martha hesitated and then went inside.

The courier awkwardly handed Gertrude the telegram.

She reached into her pocket and gave him a coin. He almost smiled and then left.

The telegram read: "MR MRS SWANSON KILLED IN STAGECOACH ACCIDENT — COME HOME — WALLACE HOLT."

CHAPTER FIVE
All Cleaned Up

The Thursday morning following the funeral, Martha was in the study reading one of her favorite books, *The Adventures of Daniel Boone*. She sat in a thick, overstuffed leather chair opposite the desk where her father read the newspaper each afternoon. She loved sitting in that chair because she could see the beautiful oak tree through the window behind the desk. A hint of a smile crossed her lips when the sound of clacking heels grew louder from the hallway. Gertrude always wore soft-soled shoes or was barefoot at home unless she was going out. Martha glanced up from her book when the sound stopped.

Gertrude peered in from the doorway.

"Why don't you come shopping with me? I heard they got a shipment of lovely new fabrics at the general store," said Gertrude.

Martha sat taller, stretching her arms and legs. "I'd rather stay here and read if you don't mind. I'm happy here, reading my father's books."

Gertrude rushed over and tickled Martha's side.

Martha held her lips tight as she suppressed the urge to giggle.

Gertrude gazed up at the many shelves overflowing with books and said, "Your father always knew when you borrowed a book."

Martha smiled proudly. "When I pulled this book from the shelf earlier, my first thought was to remember to replace it exactly where I found it. He was...meticulous about their placement." Her voice trailed off, a memory surfacing. "Years ago, I absentmindedly put it back wrong after finishing it. He lectured me about putting things in their rightful place."

"When I first met your mother, she was an avid reader." Gertrude glanced at the shelves. "Most of these books came from your mother's family when she married your father."

Martha tilted her head. "Really? The only book I'd ever seen her read was the Bible. Mother was always doing housework or other chores expected of a woman."

Gertrude raised her right brow. "Years ago, she decided to be a model mother to you and dedicate herself to your father. She spent her free time entertaining and socializing with the elites."

"Odd that she didn't tell me that."

"Your mother enjoyed so much happiness with the life she chose. Your father and you both brought her joy." Gertrude chuckled. "She told me that after you left home for college, she started reading the newer books to see what you found so alluring about them. She felt closer to you the more she read. Murder mysteries were her favorite. Last month, when we talked, she read something written by a man named Poe."

"Edgar Allen Poe? I read his short story *The Murders in the Rue Morgue*. I loved it!" A tear rolled down Martha's cheek.

Gertrude's lower lip trembled. "Dear, why don't you get some fresh air outside?"

Martha scrunched her nose. "I need a few more days." She walked over to a small bookcase next to the doorway and shuffled through the stacks of newspapers and magazines. She pulled out the magazine issue with the story. She rushed back to her seat and paged through it. "I know it's in this issue." She held it up for Gertrude to see.

Gertrude nodded and smiled. "I'll be back in a couple of hours."

Martha leaned back, trying to get more comfortable, and said, "Have a good time." She flicked the pages one after the other and gasped when she found the story by Edgar Allan Poe.

As Gertrude turned to leave, a glint of dark metal caught her eye. A six-shooter was lying on the desk. Gertrude walked over and picked it up.

"Child, why is your father's six-shooter sitting here?"

Martha walked over and picked up the weapon. "It needed a cleaning. I guess my father fired it before he...."

Martha opened the side drawer, and several bullets rolled around the bottom. She arranged them in a small stack and placed the gun beside them. She sighed and smiled at Gertrude. She shuffled to her chair and fumbled to find her place in the magazine.

Her face pained with worry, Gertrude said, "Are you alright, Martha? I can go shopping tomorrow."

"Yes. Don't worry about me, I'm fine." Martha returned to the magazine, and then her eyes darted to Gertrude. "Oh, can you buy some bullets? I think it's time I sharpened up my shooting skills. You never know what life might throw our way."

"Sure."

Martha grinned. "You should practice, too."

Gertrude shook her head. "No thanks. I don't like shooting those little guns. I prefer my shotgun. Hard to miss with one of those." She smiled and patted Martha's shoulder as she walked past her.

Martha smiled and watched as Gertrude left out the front door. Martha's gaze lingered there as tears blurred her vision. She stared at the front door for almost a minute as she thought about her parents, especially her mother. She rubbed her eyes and went back to the magazine. She was surprised her mother kept her book-reading a secret from her. She loved her mother but felt closer to her father because of their love of books.

Two knocks at the front door, one loud and one soft, jolted her back from her abyss of sadness. She stared at the front door. Sometimes, that door shuddered from an occasional gust of wind. She glanced out the window. The leaves from the big oak tree in the front yard swayed gently in the wind. Her sadness abated when she remembered how much her father loved that tree. She took a deep breath and went back to reading.

A few seconds later, several more knocks came forcefully from the door.

Martha snapped out of her reading, annoyed. With her magazine in hand, she rushed to the front door. She put the magazine on the entryway table, open to where she left off. She flung open the door. A tall, handsome, well-dressed man stood carrying a huge bouquet in one hand and a small box in the other. She fixated on the flowers.

He shifted from foot to foot, avoiding eye contact. "My condolences for your loss."

He practiced that line as he rode from the hotel. He cleaned himself up and dressed in the suit Frank had given him. Shame

44

and guilt clawed at him, preventing him from meeting her gaze. He offered her the flowers. He thought his picture of her didn't do her justice.

She took the flowers and smiled. "Oh my! These are beautiful ... and big."

"I— I got carried away."

"I don't mind them." She leaned in slightly. "You knew my parents?"

"No." Thomas's eyes shot down to the ground, haunted by the sound of her mother's scream. His face grew flushed. "I was at the college. That's where I met you."

She scrunched her forehead. He looked familiar, but she couldn't place him for sure. "I didn't have any friends there. Were you a student?"

He shook his head. "I'm not that kind of fellow. I had a beard and long hair. I didn't take too good of myself, my appearance." He raised his head and locked eyes with her.

She stepped back and brought her hand to her mouth. She recognized those distinctive blue eyes. Her face went blank as her eyes darted across the man's face. She remembered his long, stringy hair and unwieldy beard. Back then, his clothes held a pungent odor that clung to him like a second skin. The man before her had short, slicked-down, light brown hair, a tasteful mustache on a clean-shaved face, and a well-tailored suit. His piercing blue eyes accented his chiseled jawline. She cleared her throat as she tried to speak. He smelled sweet to her. The dramatic transformation from the unpolished, disgusting man she met at college to the man standing before her was extraordinary.

She stared at him as she tried to remember why she had punched him before.

He cleared his throat.

Embarrassed, her eyes darted to the flowers. She smelled them, and slowly, her gaze floated back to him. "Thank you for the flowers. I'm sorry, I don't remember your name."

"It's Thomas."

Thomas handed her the small box he was holding. "These are for you."

Martha opened the aromatic box and smiled as she realized the sweet smell came from the chocolate candies.

Thomas smiled. "I sure hope you like chocolate. I wasn't sure if you preferred hard candies instead."

"Chocolate is my weakness, my absolute favorite. I appreciate your thoughtfulness." She closed the box and put it down next to the flowers. She wondered why their first encounter at the college went so wrong. Even worse, she was embarrassed that she punched him in the face and that her classmates roughed him up. Now, he seemed the perfect gentleman. As she gazed at him, silence settled between them.

Thomas blinked nervously. "Are you okay?"

Martha nodded. "I'm fine." She rubbed her right hand, remembering the pain from punching him. "It's just that you look so different. I'm sorry for how my classmates treated you. I didn't realize then that they would pursue you and—"

"Think nothing of it. I'm sure I deserved it."

Martha smiled awkwardly.

"I got something else for you. I didn't know if it was appropriate to give them to you directly or take them to the sheriff's office."

Martha's smile faded, replaced by a flicker of worry.

He withdrew a pouch from his side pocket and handed it to her.

She took the pouch and opened it cautiously. Inside, she found a bracelet, a necklace, and a distinctive gold chain. One end of the chain had a clasp with a small fob hanging. She read the initials on the dangling gold fob — "C.S." The end of the chain had a bent link that was supposed to be attached to a buttonhole. She imagined the thief yanking her father's watch. She gasped.

"I'm sorry. I thought you'd be happy to have those things back."

Tears welled in Martha's eyes. "How?"

He extended a handkerchief, crisp and white. "Forgive me."

She hesitated. Finally, she reached out and took it. The familiar aroma of cologne sparked a warmth that soothed and complicated her emotions. It reminded her of her father. "Thank you," she whispered, the words barely audible.

"My friend and I passed this stagecoach on the side of the

road all by itself."

"The bank's responsible for returning anything recovered from the stagecoach. I wonder how they could have missed these."

"Those things weren't in the stagecoach. Perhaps they'd been thrown from it."

Martha nodded as she pressed the gold chain tightly to her chest. Her jaw fell open when she examined the necklace from the pouch. It belonged to her grandmother, and Martha's mother promised to give it to her when she married.

Thomas pulled the picture from his pocket and handed it to Martha.

"This photograph was with the other things. That's how I knew they belonged to you."

A wave of emotion overwhelmed Martha. Tears welled up in her eyes, spilling over like a dam bursting. Her lower lip trembled uncontrollably. She gave that picture to her mother the day she left for college.

Thomas leaned forward and patted Martha on her arm.

She pulled her arm back and wiped her tears away with the handkerchief.

"My aunt will be back soon. Perhaps we could wait here and talk on the porch until she arrives," she said as she pointed to the bench.

Thomas stepped back.

"Sorry, but I have to get back home. We're getting ready to head out of town in a couple of days," he said, clearing his throat.

Martha smiled.

He turned to leave and unexpectedly spun back, startling Martha.

"It seems to me you need some cheering up. We could go dancing if you want."

Martha shook her head. "Dancing? I hate dancing."

"You do?" Every woman he ever knew loved dancing, even his mother.

Martha shuddered at the thought. "I don't think so. My parents just died. I—"

"I just thought...."

She stared at him, not knowing what to say.

Hope drained from his face. "Sorry."

"Thank you so much for these things," she said and went inside, closing the door behind her.

From behind the door, she heard him utter, "Damn it! I'm so stupid. What was I thinking?"

A pang of guilt shot through her. She hurt his feelings. She peeked out the window.

Thomas was halfway to his horse.

She opened the door and yelled, "Thomas!"

Thomas and his horse jumped, surprised.

Martha's voice rose slightly. "Could you stop by tomorrow afternoon? We could go for a stroll in the park and talk."

Thomas's face lit up bright with a huge smile. "Sure thing." He climbed up on his horse.

Martha smiled and stood at the door.

As he rode away, Thomas clicked to his horse and yelled, "Yahoo!"

Later that day, she told Gertrude about Thomas's visit.

"He was tall and handsome and had the most beautiful eyes." Martha showed Gertrude the pouch Thomas gave her. "He gave me these things that belonged to my parents. At first, it made me sad to see them. But then, I was grateful to have them."

Gertrude gasped. "Your mother loved this necklace." Her fingers traced the string of pearls, snagging on rough, dark specks. She frowned. Using her fingernail, she rubbed away the black, crusty speck on one of the pearls. Odd, she thought. It didn't occur to her that it was dried blood. She shook her head. "How in God's name did the bank miss these things?"

"He said they weren't in the stagecoach. Maybe those robbers dropped them as they fled."

"I suppose that's possible. In any case, the bank didn't properly search the area. I wonder what else they missed. We should check with Wallace in the morning."

Martha nodded. "We can ask him about my father's account, too."

Gertrude examined the other items briefly, smiled at Martha, and handed them back to her.

Martha smiled, her eyes moistened with tears, as she safely stowed each precious item into the pouch.

Martha brought the pouch close to her heart. "I told Thomas to call on me tomorrow and take me for a stroll in the park."

Gertrude cocked her head, pleased. "That would be wonderful. It's about time you stop lollygagging around here."

Martha rolled her eyes. "He asked me if I wanted to go dancing."

"Dancing? That would be wonderful for you."

Martha grimaced. "You know how I hate prancing around like that. It's embarrassing," she said as she turned and glided smoothly across to the kitchen, waving her arms in a swan-like movement.

Gertrude chuckled. "Didn't you just say you didn't like dancing?"

"I suppose I could be persuaded to dance if the right fellow came along."

Gertrude smiled at the happy Martha, who was starting to shine through the oppressive grief holding her niece captive.

Martha grinned, her eyes sparkling with life. "I'm tingling all over with happiness. I can hardly wait for tomorrow."

CHAPTER SIX

Help Wanted

Alexander twiddled a pencil the following morning while examining Swanson's journal at his desk. His gun sat before him on top of a stack of papers to the right.

Wallace hurried into Alexander's office. "The driver woke up, and he's talking up a storm."

Alexander dropped his pencil, holstered his gun, and handed the journal to Wallace. "This is ready for you to review."

Wallace, whose face was riddled with worry, followed Alexander out the door. "We gotta get that money and catch those lawbreakers."

Alexander stopped at the door. "After I talk to the driver, I'm going to grab a few men and ride out to the spot where the Swanson's coach was robbed and clear out the brush and some of the trees where those robbers were likely hiding."

Wallace nodded, "That's a good idea. The sheriff has people ready to help."

"That's good. I'll chat with him about that after I'm done with the driver." Alexander winked at Wallace and then left.

Wallace shook his head and went to his office to examine the journal more closely.

Minutes later, a carriage pulled up to the bank. Martha and Gertrude stepped down and marched to the entrance. Martha smiled when she noticed a "Help Wanted" sign hanging conspicuously on the front door. She opened the door for Gertrude and followed her inside.

Wallace Holt sat at his desk examining Swanson's journal. His eyes were fixed on the last line of the page that held the balance. "What to do? What to do?"

A series of soft knocks came from the door. An audible gasp escaped his mouth when he saw Gertrude standing in the doorway. He cleared his throat and stashed the journal in his top drawer.

"Come in," he said and smiled broadly.

Gertrude walked in.

Mr. Holt stood quickly. His smile faded when Martha entered. In all the years he'd known Mr. Swanson, he'd met Martha a handful of times. The last time he'd seen her was when Mr. Swanson arranged for a payment to the college for Martha's second year. She sat quietly, waiting while they discussed the details of the unusual donation.

"Mr. Holt, I don't know if you remember me, but I'm Martha Swanson, and you know Aunt Gertrude."

"Of course I do, Miss Swanson. Please accept my deepest condolences." He turned to Gertrude, smiling, and nodded.

Gertrude half-smiled. She had known Wallace for years.

He pointed to the ornate, plush leather chairs facing the desk. "Please sit." They were a bit large for the office. "Would you like something to drink?"

"No ... thank you," said Martha.

Gertrude shook her head.

The two women sat.

Martha sank into the fancy, overstuffed chair that lacked the welcoming embrace of the worn leather armchair in her father's library. A pang of longing shot through her as she settled in.

"Your father was a good friend. He...." Wallace paused and stood uncomfortably. He quickly sat down. "Mr. Swanson was one of our largest account holders, and I cared deeply for him."

Gertrude grimaced. "Mr. Swanson was concerned about a discrepancy in his account balance."

Wallace gasped. "My manager examined the books personally and fixed some minor irregularities in the records. There is no discrepancy."

Gertrude nodded. "Minor irregularities? In the telegram Mr. Swanson sent me, he described it as serious."

Wallace cracked a small, guilty smile at Gertrude.

"It certainly appeared that way at first. But let me assure you, it was a trivial accounting error, a rather unattractive one, I'll admit. Mr. Swanson was correct, and your money, all of it, is completely safe here. My accountant has assured me of that."

Gertrude winced.

Martha's mouth went crooked. "We'll see. May I see the records?"

"What?!" he blurted out, his surprise mirroring the disbelief in his wide eyes. "I can't…"

Gertrude's lips stretched into a smile that danced between amusement and 'did you just say that?' incredulity. "Wallace, Martha has been studying bookkeeping for a year now. She's a bookkeeping expert, perhaps even more so than your accountant. Need I remind you that she was the one who found the accounting errors in Mr. Swanson's account?"

Wallace cleared his throat. He retrieved the journal from his desk and handed it to Martha.

Martha said, "Thank you." She quickly opened it and leafed through its pages.

Wallace watched as she ran her fingers down one side of the page and mouthed some words. She was quiet for almost a full minute, then shook her head and softly grunted.

She glanced up at Wallace and noticed a photograph hanging on the wall behind him. She returned the journal to him.

Martha went to the picture and said, "The account appears in balance. Your bookkeeper made several simple mistakes that resulted in the $20,000 error. It's a common mistake that beginners make. Certainly, he's not your best."

"This will never happen again." Wallace turned, curious about what Martha was looking at.

Martha turned to Wallace. "At least your accountant was transparent in making the entries that brought the account back into balance."

A perplexed wrinkle formed between Wallace's eyes as he blinked rapidly. "Transparent? What does that mean?"

Martha chuckled, "He documented his corrections and did not hide the mistake."

Wallace relaxed. "Yes, of course. He's beyond reproach and would never conceal something this important."

Martha pointed to the man standing in the middle of the photograph. "This man came to my house yesterday."

Wallace squinted at the picture. "You must be mistaken. That man is Joseph. I'm on the left, and the other man is Juan. That was taken almost twenty years ago. I put on a lot of weight since then."

Martha squinted at the image to examine the detail. She motioned for Gertrude to see.

Gertrude rushed over. She cocked her head back, surprised, and pointed to the man in the middle. "He doesn't have a mustache."

Wallace sat at his desk. "They moved with their wives to California about ten years ago. My brother in Sacramento wrote me that Joseph is a sheriff and lives with his wife in a nearby town."

They examined the picture for a little longer and returned to their seats.

Martha leaned in. "Thomas brought me some of my parents' jewelry and told me they were near the stagecoach."

Wallace raised his brows. "During a robbery, things get very chaotic. I suppose it's possible. Items are strewn about at the site, and a passerby could come upon a crashed stagecoach. It's not a pretty sight."

Gertrude narrowed her eyes at Wallace and grimaced.

Wallace cleared his throat. "I'm sorry. I didn't mean to be insensitive. The bank's practice is to return belongings found to their owners. Frankly, I'm surprised that we missed valuables there. The strongbox was empty."

Gertrude took a deep breath and let it out all at once.

Wallace sat up quickly. "Don't worry. The bank will replace the stolen money, and I'll send some men to scour the site again."

A gentle calm settled over Martha. "Could you notify me if they find something more?"

Wallace leaned back, relieved that their meeting had ended well. "Of course."

Gertrude stood and reached over to Martha. "We'd better get going."

He rushed around the desk to them. "If there's anything I can do for you, don't hesitate to ask."

Martha furrowed her brow. "There's a 'Help Wanted' sign outside."

Wallace nodded excitedly. "The banking business has been

bustling these days. It's hard to keep up."

Martha dreamed of working at the bank after completing school. "I would like to work here."

Wallace's voice cracked and then grew higher in pitch. "What? You don't need a job. You have all the money you could ever want in your account."

Martha chuckled. "Yes. That's right, more than I know what to do with."

Gertrude locked eyes with Wallace and winked at him. "I'd suggest you give her the position. With her college experience, I'm sure she's better at adding numbers than your accountant."

Wallace nodded slowly.

Martha, her chin extended. "When can I start?"

Unblinking, Gertrude fixed Wallace with a stare that seemed to pierce his soul.

Wallace returned to his desk, shuffled through the things in the top drawer, and then pulled out a piece of paper. He scribbled something on it. He figured she would take her money to another bank if he refused her. "I suppose you'll need a week or two to prepare."

Martha smiled. "I'll be here at 7:00 a.m. sharp Monday morning."

Wallace tilted his head. "That's barely enough time to inform all the staff and set up a space for you to work." He wrote something more on the paper. "Your desk will be ready. The workday begins at 8:00 a.m. here."

"Don't worry. It's just until the next school year begins."

Gertrude raised her brows, surprised at Martha.

"Please fill this out and give it to my assistant outside my office. We'll expect you at 8:00 a.m. on Monday." He handed her the paper.

Martha took it. "Thank you, Mr. Holt. You won't be disappointed."

She lowered her voice and said, "I don't want anyone here to know who I am. I'd like to have a separate account to deposit my wages."

"That won't be a problem. I'll take care of it myself."

Martha nodded, strutted to the door like an elegant swan, and opened it wide. She turned back to Gertrude.

"Gertrude, would you mind if we stopped at the dress shop?"

"Of course not."

Gertrude followed Martha out the door. Gertrude turned and winked at Wallace.

Wallace's legs went wobbly as he rushed back to his desk.

Outside, Gertrude and then Martha stepped up onto the carriage.

Martha pointed to a small shop down the road. "That's the dress shop where I want to go."

Gertrude shook the reins, and the horses obliged.

Neither Martha nor Gertrude had seen Thomas sitting on the hotel porch across from the bank.

Later, Martha and Gertrude were on their way home. Several boxes were stacked neatly in the cart behind them.

Martha sat holding the reins and turned to Gertrude, "Mr. Holt seems like a nice man."

"He was worried you'd withdraw all of your money."

"Where would I put it?"

Gertrude laughed. "I've known Wallace for many years. He's an honest man but a bit obsessed with wealth."

Martha's eyes lit up with curiosity. "Is he married?"

Gertrude rolled her eyes. "Yes, he is."

Later that afternoon, Martha was alone in the backyard with her father's gun and the two boxes of bullets Gertrude had bought. She lined up six cans on a log and then rushed back ten yards to the bench that held her gun and the ammunition. She aimed and shot each target dead center, one after the other. She liked how some flew in the air, twirling around as they fell to the ground. She set the cans back up, reloaded, stepped further back than before, and shot them all dead.

At the front of the house, Thomas got down from his horse. He pulled some flowers from his side saddle and started for the porch. He heard shot after shot coming from behind the house. It reminded him of when he and Frank would practice shooting.

Thomas walked briskly to the backyard. Martha stood assuredly, aiming at a line of cans. He smiled as each flew up into the air after being shot. He was astonished at her deadly accuracy.

"Martha," he yelled to her.

Martha turned around and smiled when she saw him.

"You came," she yelled, waving him to come over. She turned back to the cans and shot three, one after the other.

He sauntered over to her as she loaded her gun. "That's excellent shooting."

Martha shot the fourth can and missed. She gritted her teeth, winked at him, and returned to her targets. She quickly shot the fifth and sixth cans dead. "I got a job at the bank."

"Congratulations!"

Martha reloaded again. "We told the bank owner about you."

Thomas's smile faded. "What did you tell him?"

She aimed at the can she had missed and dispatched it effortlessly.

"Not much, except that you were very kind to have returned my parents' things to me."

When he arrived, she hadn't noticed the flowers, but now he was holding them toward her. She put her gun down and then rushed over and took the bouquet.

She brought them to her nose and closed her eyes. "They're lovely." She let out a small sigh and glanced at Thomas. "They need water."

Martha started toward the house and spun back at Thomas. "Do me a favor and grab my gun."

He collected the bullets and the gun and caught up to her.

She smiled at him. "Thanks. I'd rather chat with you instead of shooting cans."

When they reached the house, Martha approached his horse and patted its face. "You're so beautiful," she said.

The horse cocked her head up and whinnied. Her ears were pinned back, her body tense with suspicion.

Thomas clicked at his horse and walked between her and Martha.

He rubbed his horse's face. "She's a bit temperamental sometimes."

Martha nodded and went to the porch. "She doesn't know me yet."

Thomas followed Martha. "Where'd you learn to shoot like that?"

Martha grinned. "My ma taught me."

Thomas blinked in surprise. "Really?"

"Nah. I'm just fooling. My pa taught me. He always hit his targets. This is the gun my father had with him on the stagecoach. A bullet was missing when the bank returned it, so I'm hoping...." Martha shivered as she brushed away her thoughts of the robbery.

Thomas glanced away as he remembered Mr. Swanson pointing that gun at him.

Martha took a deep breath and exhaled through her nose. "My pa and I used to shoot cans together."

Would she ever shoot him, he thought. "You ever shoot anyone?"

"Nope, but as soon as I find those scoundrels that killed my parents, I'll kill them. They won't have a chance against me."

Thomas blinked, nervous that she would want to shoot him.

"How about you?"

Thomas shook his head quickly. "No."

"Hmm." She pointed to the porch bench and said, "Sit here. I'll be right back. These flowers are begging for water."

Thomas felt his anxiety lifting as he sat on the bench. Martha's optimism was soothing to him.

Gertrude walked out. "My goodness, those flowers are lovely."

Thomas jumped to his feet.

"They sure are." Martha smiled. "This is Thomas, and he brought me this gorgeous bunch."

Thomas lowered his head slightly. "Pleased to meet you."

Gertrude stepped back when she saw Thomas holding a gun.

Thomas gasped and turned to Martha. "Don't forget your gun."

Martha took the gun and put it in her pocket. "Thank you. We'll be right back with some refreshments."

Thomas sat and realized that he still had the box of bullets in his hand. He smiled and placed them on the bench.

Ten minutes later, Gertrude and Martha walked out with two glasses of lemonade.

Gertrude half-smiled and nodded at him. "I'll leave you two.

You don't need an old lady making you feel uncomfortable."

She patted Martha's shoulder, started for the door, and said, "I'll be inside if you want me."

"Thank you, Gertrude."

Gertrude glanced back at Thomas for an instant and then went inside.

Martha smiled at Thomas. "She got worried when she saw you with my gun."

"I can understand why," said Thomas, pointing to the box. "There's your bullets."

"Thanks. So, are you a good dancer?" Martha asked.

Thomas tilted his head as a smile crept onto his face. "I haven't had any complaints."

"We can go dancing when you return from your trip."

Thomas wrinkled his face. "I thought you didn't like dancing."

She smiled as she reached for his hand. "Maybe that's because I haven't had a good partner. My ma loved to dance."

Thomas gasped. His horse neighed. He remembered dragging Mrs. Swanson over to her dead husband. He glanced at the door. Gertrude stood watching him from the front door.

Martha turned cockeyed at Thomas. "What's wrong?"

"Nothing. My ma loved dancing, too. I still miss her."

Martha sighed. "I miss my ma, too."

His chest tightened.

Gertrude stepped out onto the porch. "Thomas, are you related to Joseph? He and his friend, Juan, left for California about ten years ago."

Thomas went pale.

Gertrude noticed as she continued. "He used to live somewhere around here. Now, he's a sheriff in California and lives there with his wife."

Thomas's jaw dropped, his eyes wide with surprise. "That sounds like my pa. He's the sheriff there? And he has a wife? How do you know?"

Martha leaned in. "Wallace, the bank owner, told us."

"I haven't seen him since he left with Juan. My pa killed my ma before he left."

Martha choked out a loud gasp.

Gertrude cocked her head in surprise.

A flicker of sadness danced in Thomas's eyes.

Martha's heart felt heavy. "Are you okay?"

"I'm fine. I have a long ride ahead of me. I'll call on you when I get back into town if that's okay." He forced a smile at Martha.

"Of course."

Still donning a semblance of a smile, he kissed her hand, nodded to Gertrude, and went to his horse.

His horse neighed as Thomas rubbed the side of her head. The horse pointed his ears curiously at Martha. He climbed up, gazed affectionately at Martha for a second, and then rode away.

Martha and Gertrude stood on the porch as he disappeared down the road.

Gertrude narrowed her eyes at the mystery. "That young man was mighty surprised, certainly shocked, hearing about his father being a sheriff and that he had a wife."

Martha shook her head. "I hope he's okay."

"You can never tell much about people these days," said Gertrude as she hugged Martha.

Thirty minutes south of the town, Randall was on his porch cleaning his gun as Alexander rode up. Randall holstered his weapon and rushed down the stairs to greet him.

A smile cracked across Randall's face. "Well, if it ain't my all-time favorite. How'd you know I was here?"

"I saw you riding out of town earlier today. I would have ridden after you if I'd been near my horse."

Alexander's horse whinnied as he came to a stop next to Randall. "How long has it been?"

Randall chuckled. "It's been ten years since you told me you never wanted to see me again."

"I'm sorry about that. After my pa disappeared, you went a little crazy. It was hard being around you. You kept insisting that my pa was still alive somewhere."

Alexander got down from his horse and didn't notice Randall wince at the mention of Alexander's pa.

Alexander and Randall shook hands.

"It's good to see you. It's been way too long," said Randall. "I should have listened to you back then. There's no way your pa would have left without telling me goodbye."

Alexander shrugged. "I shouldn't have treated you that way. You were a good friend to my pa. But, honestly, you were always the pa that I wished I had."

Randall smiled. It was a genuine smile and not his usual sinister one.

"I promised your pa I'd look out for you even though I knew you could care for yourself."

"Didn't you buy a big cattle ranch about sixty miles south of New York?"

Randall nodded. "My partner and I bought that plot of land a while back. It made us a good chunk of money, but business slowed down. He wants to buy me out. So I decided to fix this place here in case I move back."

Alexander cleared his throat. "As long as I'm here, I was hoping you could help me with something."

Randall smiled. "Sure. What is it?"

"There was a big stagecoach robbery about eleven days ago."

"Shoot, no! Who'd be dumb enough to rob stagecoaches these days? Those coaches have plenty of firepower to thwart off any assault; ten or so years ago, it would have been easier."

"You wouldn't know who could have done that, do you?" Alexander's voice held a hint of accusation.

Randall shrugged, feigning indifference. "Heck no."

"I'm desperate to find those robbers. I'm at a loss to figure out why they would have shot the passengers."

Randall's blood was simmering to a boil, threatening to expose him. He kept control. "What? They killed them! That's not good. In my day, thieves took the money without shedding innocent blood."

"Yeah."

"Do you want to ride with me? I was about to inspect the fences on the property's south side," Randall said, trying to change the subject.

"I enjoyed it when you and I rode around your property. I liked our talks. But I have to get back."

Randall reached out to shake hands. Alexander grabbed

Randall's hand and then pulled him into a tight hug. Randall felt disarmed and froze for an instant. He gasped, and then the tension eased away as he exhaled. Randall patted Alexander's back.

Alexander climbed up on his horse.

"Don't be a stranger. Okay?" asked Randall.

"Yup," said Alexander. "It was terrific to see you— Pa."

Randall's heart almost stopped beating. He stood motionless as Alexander left, and the sound of his galloping horse faded into the distance. He was close to shedding a tear. Lost in thought, a tap on his shoulder startled him. He turned quickly, pulled his gun, and pointed it at the deputy.

The deputy raised his hands and backed up. "Whoa. I thought you heard me."

Randall grimaced, an expression he felt comfortable with. "Don't sneak up on me like that again."

"Sorry."

Randall holstered his gun. "Now, what the hell are you doing showing up here at my place?"

"You said no one would get killed when I told you about Swanson's stagecoach. If Alexander finds out I was involved, the sheriff will hang me next to you on those gallows."

"As long as you keep your mouth shut, no one's gonna find out. Is that clear?"

"Absolutely."

"Wait here while I get your money, your cut."

"Yes, sir," said the deputy.

CHAPTER SEVEN

Nowhere to Hide

Early Saturday morning, the smell of burnt wood tainted the cool, still air. Thomas, Frank, and Randall rode up to the base of the hill, where, almost two weeks before, Frank had shot at the driver of the Swansons' coach from the top. The horses sloshed through small puddles of water on the road left by the recent rains.

Randall cursed under his breath. "What in the...."

He didn't wait for a reply, leaping off his horse with an agility that belied his weathered exterior. With practiced ease, he secured the reins to a nearby tree stump, eyes scanning the scene.

Frank dismounted more slowly, his hand instinctively reaching for the holstered gun at his hip. "It's so different than before."

Thomas mirrored Frank's apprehension. "It looks like someone cleared out the brush and trees and took a torch to the rest," he muttered, his gaze lingering on the scorched remains.

Randall, however, was visibly shaken. "You two stay put," he said. "The stagecoach is due any minute."

Frank, ever the loyal follower, nodded. "Yes, sir."

Randall ran to the crest of the hill. His eyes scanned the barren landscape in disbelief. Gone was the thicket of trees that once offered the perfect cover for two or three robbers. Now, the naked ridge stretched before him, offering no shelter, no concealment.

"Dangit!"

That vantage point gave him an unobstructed view of the road coming from New York. But that same open vista made him a glaringly visible target. Even crouching low and crawling to the edge wouldn't guarantee his safety. Firing a rifle with any accuracy from that precarious position was downright suicidal.

He was lost in thought as his plans to rob stagecoaches unraveled. Someone had deliberately destroyed his perfect hiding spot. If they knew about this place, what else did they know? Did they know about him?

As he stood in the desolate landscape, he was distracted by a conversation drifting from below. He heard bits and pieces of Frank and Thomas chatting. He clenched his jaws when his name was mentioned. He shook his head and started down the hill.

Frank and Thomas continued talking next to their horses.

A perplexed wrinkle formed between Frank's eyes. "I'm surprised you wanted to come with us today, especially now that you're all clean and nice-looking."

Thomas chuckled.

"What were you doing in town yesterday? Randall thinks you've met someone."

Thomas's eyes lit up. "What if I did?"

"I was beginning to wonder about you."

"You're such an ass sometimes." Thomas glanced behind him at the trail where Randall had gone. "Yeah, I did meet a girl."

"Nah. Really?"

Thomas nodded. "She's incredible. I talked to her before, but she didn't like me much then. I don't blame her. I used to look crappy."

"You did." Frank pinched his nose. "And you smelled almost as bad as a skunk."

Thomas grimaced and shoved Frank's arm. "I called on her. I could tell she liked me. At first, I wasn't sure, but we saw each other again yesterday, and I'm positive now."

"Hey, I'm glad for you. My Sunday clothes look sharp on you, and of course, they look better on me."

Thomas's face soured. "There's one thing, though."

"What?" Frank tilted his head, his smile fading.

"She's the daughter of that old couple Randall killed from that stagecoach we robbed."

Frank's jaw dropped, his eyes filled with shock. "No!"

"That old lady was clutching a picture of her. That's how I knew who she was."

Frank's eyes narrowed with concern. "Shoot."

"Yesterday, when I saw her, she said the law was looking for us?"

"What? They know who we are?"

"No! Of course not. They don't have a clue."

Frank rubbed his neck as he shook his head. "This is way too risky."

"The bank owner says my pa's living in California, and he has a new wife."

"Nah. That can't be true. I thought your pa was dead."

"Randall lied about killing my ma. He probably lied about my pa, too."

A twig snapped loudly. Both jumped. Randall stood behind them, red-faced.

"With all the trees and vegetation cleared away, sound travels." Randall's eyes turned to icy slits. "I don't know how many times I gotta tell you, your pa killed your ma."

Thomas glared at Randall. "Why did you tell me my pa was dead?"

Randall winced.

"He's dead to me. Should be to you, too, after what he did."

Thomas spat back, "He's living in California and has a wife."

Randall was silent, his face growing a darker crimson, his eyes narrowly focused on Thomas.

Thomas stepped toward Randall. "I'm going to find my pa."

"You ain't going nowhere. Your pa don't want to have anything to do with you."

Thomas pulled back, stunned. His eyes darted from Frank to Randall. "I don't believe you," he said.

Randall smiled. "I get a letter from a friend out there occasionally, and he's told me plenty."

Thomas was speechless. He shook his head and stormed away to his horse.

Randall's face contorted with rage. "Where are you going? We've got a stagecoach to rob. It'll be here any minute."

Thomas kept walking.

Randall's eyes narrowed to slits, his pupils sharp as daggers. "Don't turn your back on me, son."

Frank's gaze darted nervously between Randall and Thomas. Taking a deep breath, he rushed toward Thomas's side.

Thomas cast a sideways glance at Frank. "Don't! You can stay with him. I'm done with his lies. I'm going to find my pa. Randall's something much worse than a monster."

Fire exploded in Randall's eyes. "I could have killed your pa instead of letting him go, but I didn't. I don't kill family."

Thomas, his heart racing, glanced back. "My ma was family, and you killed her!"

Randall flinched. Irrational rage consumed him.

Frank stepped back as his loyalty tugged at him from both sides.

Thomas grunted as he reached up to hoist himself onto his saddle.

Molten fire erupted from the barrel of Randall's gun, slamming into Thomas's leg with a sickening thud.

The world seemed to slow down for a nightmarish instant. Thomas crumpled to the ground, a scream erupting from his throat. "What the hell is wrong with you?!" he roared, his voice laced with betrayal and agony.

Randall, his face contorted in a mask of rage, the gun still smoking in his hand. "You ain't leaving me now, you hear!" he bellowed, his voice hoarse with fury and desperation.

Frank scrambled toward Thomas, his mind reeling. "You're bleeding bad!" he yelled, his voice cracking with fear he'd never felt before. Randall's face, twisted with a rage he'd never witnessed, burned into his memory.

Frank moved quickly to stop the bleeding, wrapping a leather strap around Thomas's leg and wrapping the wound, dirt and all.

His eyes darted from Thomas's leg to Randall. "He needs a doctor," he stammered, his voice thick with terror and confusion.

The sight of Randall, his face a mask of fury, sent a shiver down his spine.

The sound of a fast-approaching stagecoach echoed from behind the hill.

Randall aimed his gun squarely at Frank's chest. "You keep him quiet."

Frank managed only a silent, sharp nod. This was the first time Randall had threatened him this way.

Randall holstered his gun and grabbed his rifle from his saddle with a hand that trembled slightly. Randall, a surge of adrenaline coursing through him, bolted up the hill. His heart hammered in his chest, a frantic drumbeat against his ribs. Reaching the ridge, he dropped to the ground, his breath ragged. He inched forward, his gaze on the approaching stagecoach.

A tall man with a rifle sat beside the driver, and a barrel was pointed out of the cabin window.

Randall shook his head. "Damnit." As the coach approached, he recognized Alexander by the driver. Alexander was holding a rifle pointed squarely at him. A booming shot rang from the stagecoach. A cloud of debris flew up inches from his head. Randall peeked out. Alexander aimed for a second shot. Randall crawled backward where Alexander's bullets wouldn't matter. Two more gunshots came from the coach. Randall muttered, "What the hell is he doing on that stagecoach?"

Randall waited a few minutes for the coach to pass. He kicked at the dirt and marched down to his horse.

An unsettled stillness hung in the air. Thomas sat motionless on his saddle, his eyes half closed, holding firm to his reins. Mounted on his horse, Frank held tight on the reins as if readying himself for a sudden escape.

Randall glared at Frank. "How'd he hear about his pa?"

A spark of defiance flickered in Frank's eyes as he met Randall's gaze for a fleeting moment. Then, he looked down, his voice soft, "I— I don't know."

Randall narrowed his eyes. "Get that ingrate home. And keep him at your place, or else I might accidentally kill him."

Randall shook his head as the sound of the stagecoach faded into the distance.

"He needs a doctor," said Frank, his voice tenuous.

Without saying a word, Randall untied his horse from the tree stump and climbed up on his horse.

Frank sat dumbfounded as Randall rode away.

Thomas grunted and then spoke gibberish.

"I'm gonna take care of you. Just hang on. I'll get you to a doctor," said Frank, his voice shaking with uncertainty.

A strangled gasp escaped Thomas's lips. His breathing was labored. "Can't...It hurts..." he rasped. Then, silence.

"You're going to be fine. Just hold on. Don't let go."

Thomas closed his eyes and choked out, "Okay."

Thomas's leg was dripping blood even though Frank had tightened the leather strap around it.

Frank clicked to Thomas's horse. The horse looked at Frank and whinnied in confusion.

"Come on, girl. We gotta get Thomas to the doctor." Frank rode out front. Finally, Thomas's horse began to follow.

CHAPTER EIGHT

Absent Thomas

Thirty minutes later, the doctor's office came into view. Frank clicked for the horses to go faster. Thomas grunted when his horse stopped abruptly in front of the office. Frank jumped from his horse and ran up the porch.

Next to the door, behind the window, was a sign that read, "Dr. Martin." He tried the door, but it was locked. Underneath was a smaller sign: "Back at noon."

He knocked repeatedly and waited a few seconds. Nothing. He pounded on the door.

There was a commotion from inside. The door opened. The doctor stood there, pointing at the sign. "What the hell is going on here? Can't you read? I'm eating my lunch."

Frank pointed to Thomas, still up on his horse. "My friend is hurt. He got shot. I tied something around his leg, but the bleeding won't stop. You gotta help him."

The doctor's brow furrowed as he approached Thomas.

Thomas was slumped forward on his horse, his hand hanging to each side.

The doctor winced after seeing the bloody leg and said, "You sure he isn't dead already? That's a lot of blood."

The doctor grabbed Thomas's arm. "Help me get him down."

Frank and the doctor struggled to drag Thomas inside onto a small bed in the front room.

The doctor exhaled sharply, the weight of the situation settling on his shoulder. "I'll do what I can. He's pale as a ghost and still losing blood."

Frank pulled his pistol. "I—"

The doctor was used to dealing with sick and dying people. "Don't get yourself in a tizzy; You wait on the porch while I patch him up. I'm not going to put up with your nonsense. He'll live. I don't know about his leg, though."

Thomas groaned and mumbled something.

Frank narrowed his eyes at the doctor. "Call me if he—"

Thomas moaned loudly, grabbed at his leg, and screeched in pain. "He tried to kill me. The bastard shot me."

The doctor stood shocked.

Frank handed the doctor a crisp $20 bill. "It was an accident."

The doctor grimaced and took the money, and then gave Thomas a dose of ether.

Thomas relaxed. His breathing slowed, and his eyes shut.

"If you please," said the doctor, pointing to the door. "He won't be waking up anytime soon. You can wait out front."

Frank trudged outside to the porch, his boots thudding heavily on the weathered wood. Collapsing onto the creaking bench, he squeezed his eyes shut, the day's events replaying in his mind. Randall's rage-filled face, the echoing gunshot, and Thomas's crumpling form – the scene refused to fade. Why, it gnawed at him, would Randall shoot Thomas? It didn't make sense. Randall, the man who'd always been his unwavering rock, the one he'd followed with blind faith – was he capable of such calculated cruelty to his own blood?

A seed of doubt, long dormant, sprouted within Frank. Had Randall lied to Thomas about his pa's death? All these years, Thomas had barely spoken of his pa. Now, the silence seemed deafening. Was there a connection, a dark secret that fueled Randall's fury?

Thirty minutes later, the doctor stepped out to the porch.

Frank was staring at nothing in particular, lost in thought. His eyes were moist with guilt.

The doctor hesitated for an instant before speaking. He cleared his throat.

Frank wiped his nose and looked up at the doctor.

"He's still sleeping. I might have given him a bit too much of that ether. I dug out one bullet. That's all I found in there."

Frank's voice was tight but beginning to relax. "There was just one." Relief was painted on Frank's face.

The doctor smiled. "He's going to be okay. His leg wasn't as bad as I thought. He was lucky. He won't be able to walk on it for a while. You can see him now if you like."

Frank's eyes grew bright with excitement as he rushed past the doctor. The doctor followed him to the examination room.

Thomas mumbled, his eyes fluttering beneath their lids. "Martha."

Frank stood next to Thomas and started to rest his hand on his arm. Instantly, he pulled his hand away as if he'd touched a hot stove. "I gotta get him home."

"He's in no shape to be moved. He can stay the night, but only until tomorrow."

Frank nodded. "I'll stay with him." His stomach growled.

The doctor's eyes darted to Frank. "I'll get you something to eat."

"Thanks." Frank took another twenty-dollar bill from his pocket.

A flicker of suspicion danced in the doctor's eyes. "You've given me enough," the doctor said, checking the patient's bandages before leaving.

Frank stood next to Thomas.

Across from him was a full-length mirror with his reflection. Thomas's left hand was partially showing on one side of it. Frank's eyes widened as he realized the image the mirror had captured stared back at him in shame. He had not been loyal to his friend. He turned to his right, and just beyond the bed was the cupboard's glass door ajar. A faint image of Thomas was there. Many dark bottles with torn paper stuck to the front of each were lined up behind the glass door.

The mirror caught a fleeting glimpse of him as his eyes darted to the other side of the room. A coat rack stood between the mirror and the closet door. On the floor, a bloody trail led from the office door to the bed where Thomas was.

Frank put Thomas's left hand back on the bed.

The doctor rushed in and tapped Frank's shoulder. Frank pulled his gun and pointed it at the doctor.

The doctor narrowed his eyes and let out a huff. "You gonna shoot me now…after mending your friend?" asked the doctor. He walked past Frank and examined Thomas's bandages. "I fixed you some meat and potatoes. I got coffee, too."

Frank holstered his gun. "Sorry. I'm a little jumpy."

"He's not bleeding anymore. I gave him an injection.

Otherwise, he'll be in a world of pain when he wakes up. Come get something to eat. Your stomach's been howling like a pack of hungry wolves since you arrived."

Frank held his lips tight as he patted Thomas's shoulder.

"He'll be fine. We can leave the door open, and you can hear if your friend needs you. But, I think he's out for the night." Frank followed the doctor to the kitchen.

Frank ate while the doctor poured himself some coffee.

"I've got some food here for him, too, if he does wake up."

Frank nodded and kept on eating. All that he'd had that day was a cup of coffee.

"You got far to go to get home?"

"Yeah. It's a ways away. At least an hour at a normal pace, probably longer in his condition."

The doctor sipped his coffee and said, "He's likely to start bleeding out again if he moves too much, even with those splints."

"Can't we stay here another day?"

"My wife and son are visiting my cousin. They'll be back tomorrow afternoon."

Frank thought for a second. "I'll rent a room at the hotel."

"That's a grand idea. I'm there every morning right after breakfast. I have a little space in there." The doctor's eyes lit up. "I have a wheelchair in the closet. It'll be easy to wheel him there. Make sure you get a room on the first floor."

A hint of a smile broke through Frank's worried face. "Thanks for patching him up. I'm gonna go sit with my friend."

"Glad I could help. There's a cot folded up in the closet. You can set it next to him."

Early the following day, Frank took the horses to the stables behind the hotel and rented a room. When he returned to the doctor's office. The doctor was examining Thomas.

Thomas lit up bright when Frank walked in. "Frank, you're here."

The doctor grinned proudly. "Frank stayed right here with you all night. You've got a good friend. He saved your life."

Frank nodded. "How are you feeling?"

"The doctor here gave me a shot. I feel great!"

Thomas sat up. He closed his eyes as a wave of nausea accosted him.

The doctor shook his head. "You've got to take it easy. You lost quite a bit of blood. It'll take a few days to get back to normal."

Thomas opened his eyes. "I'm okay." He took a deep breath and exhaled slowly. "The room started to spin on me."

Frank chuckled. "We're gonna stay in the hotel. I got a room for us, and everything is all set. We'll be there for a day or two and head home if you're doing well."

Thomas narrowed his eyes, and the corner of his lips curled downward. "What about my uncle?"

"Don't worry about him."

Thomas grimaced.

The doctor examined Thomas's leg. "You're a lucky man. The bullet nicked your bone. You'll be okay; just don't stand on it. You could break it if you're not careful. It won't take long to heal, maybe two or three weeks. I'll give you an injection for the pain each day you're in the hotel. After that, if you can't handle the pain, I have pills that'll help. Just don't take one unless you need it."

Thomas blinked. "I can handle pain."

Frank chuckled.

"But just in case, give me the pills."

The doctor nodded. "That shot I gave you is potent."

Frank said with a playful grin, "How about we move you while you're still smiling and pain-free?"

Thomas let out a weak chuckle.

The doctor brought the wheelchair next to the bed.

"Shoot, I can walk," said Thomas as he hung his legs over the side.

The doctor yelled, "No!"

Thomas fell back onto the bed; his eyes rolled back unnaturally and closed. Bright red blood oozed from the bandaged leg.

Frank's jaw dropped, his eyes white with shock.

"He's not thinking straight, not enough blood pumping to his head yet," said the doctor.

The doctor attended to Thomas's leg and wrapped it with fresh bandages.

Five minutes later, Thomas opened his eyes. The doctor and Frank were staring at him.

Frank's face was pale and etched with worry. "Don't do that again."

The doctor stifled a chuckle. "Let's sit him in the wheelchair. We have to go slow. Once he's in the chair, you can wheel him over...even if he passes out again."

Thomas rolled his eyes and let out a huff. "I'm fine. I just moved a little too fast."

Frank and the doctor helped Thomas into the wheelchair.

Frank patted Thomas's shoulder. "You okay?"

Thomas closed his eyes as his head bobbed up and down slowly. "Yup. And nothing is spinning." He opened his eyes, fixated on the doctor.

The doctor pulled out a large, dark bottle from the cupboard. After reading the label, he poured out seven pills. He put them in another bottle and handed it to Thomas, "If you can handle the pain, you shouldn't need these. It would be best to use them sparingly— or not at all. Is that clear?"

"Yes, Doctor," said Thomas as he grimaced. "I understand."

Frank tilted his head, surprised that Thomas seemed suddenly alert.

The doctor started to push the wheelchair. There was a knock at the door.

Frank pulled his gun. The doctor shook his head at Frank as he rushed to the door.

"Nervous?" Thomas grinned at Frank and noticed the pain pills in the open cupboard.

Frank peeked around the corner to see who the doctor was talking to. "It's just a woman asking the doctor to come by and see her sick boy." He kept his gaze on the interchange until the woman turned to leave. When Frank turned back, Thomas was grinning at him.

"What's wrong?"

The pitch of Thomas's voice rose. "Nothing. Shouldn't we be

going?"

The doctor rushed back in. "I have to go. Are you two okay?" He grabbed his bag.

"Yes. We'll see you tomorrow morning." Frank pushed the wheelchair and followed the doctor to the porch.

Thomas laughed. "Wheee! Faster."

The doctor chuckled. "Remember. Keep off that leg."

"Of course," Thomas said.

The doctor glanced at Frank and smiled. He locked eyes with Thomas. "You're fortunate you have a good friend. You owe him your life."

A huge grin warmed Thomas's face. "He's my best friend."

Two hours later, Thomas slept peacefully in the hotel bed while Frank sat in the guest chair, waiting for Thomas to wake up.

Thomas awoke disoriented. It took him a minute to realize where he was. Frank was asleep in the armchair in the far corner. Thomas was propped up with several pillows under his back and head. A cool breeze was blowing in from the window.

Determined to see outside, he gritted his teeth and began a slow, agonizing ascent. Nausea swirled in his head, but his gaze remained fixed on the window. He could see the bank's entrance across the road. Perhaps he could get a glimpse of Martha, he thought. She had told him she got a job at the bank. No one was going into or out of the building. He took a deep breath and let it out quickly. A dull ache pulsed in his leg, and he saw the room transform into a dizzying blur. He leaned back and closed his eyes. A few minutes later, everything returned to normal except his throbbing leg.

When he opened his eyes, Frank was smiling at him.

Frank stretched his arms and yawned. "How do you feel?"

There was a knock at the door. Frank jumped from his chair, gun drawn, and rushed to the door.

"It's Dr. Martin," came from the hallway outside the door.

Frank holstered his gun and let the doctor in. Dr. Martin rushed in with his bag and went to Thomas's bedside.

"How are you doing?" Dr. Martin asked. "It looks like your color is starting to come back."

"My leg is killing me."

The doctor shuffled through his bag.

Before Thomas could say more, Dr. Martin had a syringe ready. He held Thomas's arm and injected the potion into it.

Thomas looked pleased at the doctor.

The doctor stowed the spent syringe and examined Thomas's leg. He looked at Frank. "He's healing well. As long as you secure his leg, you can move him tomorrow. You can use my cart if you need it. It shouldn't be hard to lay him down on the back of the cart. Your horse should be able to pull it easy."

Frank nodded.

"I have to go. I've got half a dozen patients waiting for me." The doctor picked up his bag and nodded at Frank.

Dr. Martin narrowed his eyes at Thomas and said, "And for god's sake, don't put any pressure on that leg. Once you get home, stay in bed for two or three weeks to give your leg time to heal. I'll stop by in the morning with another injection for you."

Thomas grinned. "Thanks for the shot."

Frank felt better that his friend was mending well. "Thanks, Doctor. Tomorrow, I'll come by for the cart." Frank nodded as the doctor left. He looked at Thomas, who was still grinning ear to ear.

Thomas raised his brows, his head bobbing slowly. "Whatever that doctor gave me is making me feel real good. It's not like drinking."

Frank walked up and handed Thomas a glass of water. "Drink up. I'll get you something to eat if you're hungry."

Thomas drank it all down.

"I'm starving." Thomas pointed to the window. "Why aren't there any people at the bank?"

Frank chuckled. "It's Sunday. It's not open today. Why? You want to rob it?"

Thomas chuckled.

"We'll head home tomorrow. You can have my pa's room. I promise I'll take care of you." Frank, relieved that the worst was behind, said, "You'll have to stay in bed until you're healed. You hear me?"

Thomas nodded and glanced at the window.

"I'll be back with some food," said Frank as he left.

"Frank!" yelled Thomas.

Frank rushed back in, alarmed. "What's wrong?"

"Nothing." Thomas smiled. "I just wanted to thank you. You're a good friend."

Thomas's words hit Frank like a warm wave, washing away the tension coiled in his stomach. He met Thomas's gaze, his smile trembling with relief. "Don't even think about it." His voice was thick with emotion. He lingered for a moment, taking in the gratitude on Thomas's face, before stepping away, unable to meet his eyes any longer.

CHAPTER NINE

Martha's Job

Promptly at 7:45 a.m. Monday, Martha and Gertrude rode up to the bank in their carriage.

Martha handed the reins to Gertrude and hopped down. "I don't know why I'm nervous and excited about my first day here."

"You'll do fine. This reminds me of your first day at the university."

"I was a mess. It's one thing to fight for what I want, but a whole different matter to walk in and expect others to treat me like I belong there."

Gertrude nodded. "Once they get to know you, they'll love you. Most people appreciate talent and skill."

"When I saw the 'Wanted' sign outside the bank, I knew the job was meant for me. It was one of my dreams. I knew I had to ask for it." Martha glanced at the front door. The sign was gone. "I knew I would be good at it."

"I like how you act on opportunities."

Martha shuffled to the door and waved goodbye to Gertrude. She motioned for Martha to go inside. Martha smiled and went in.

A woman about Gertrude's age walked up to her. "Martha!"

"Pleased to see you again," said Martha.

"Mr. Holt asked me to show you to your workplace and assign you work."

"Thank you."

The woman offered a warm nod. "This way," she said, leading Martha to a cluster of identical, oak-stained desks. Her desk was closest to the three enclosed offices of the owner and the two managers.

Martha smiled as she sat at her desk. It had a dozen journals stacked on top.

The woman stood beside her and said, "The workday starts at 8:00 a.m. Please don't be late. Starting at noon, you may have 45 minutes for lunch, but considering that you are a woman, perhaps one hour now and then would be okay. You may leave at 4:00, but most employees stay until 4:30."

Martha was amazed that this woman had so plainly utilized the biases imposed on women to create the office rules for her. I need only thirty minutes to eat, she thought. But then she thought an occasional picnic with Gertrude might last longer. And working until 4:30 was fine. It was enough time for her to rush home and help Gertrude prepare supper. She admired this woman's no-nonsense, direct manner.

"Any questions?"

"No." Martha smiled and brought the stack of accounts close.

"Those journals contain the accounts of the other bookkeepers. You are to scrutinize each one and make any appropriate corrections."

She whispered to Martha, "I'm sure you'll find a lot of errors."

Martha stifled a grin.

"One more thing. I would appreciate it very much if you cleaned up the writing," said the woman, loud enough for all to hear.

The other workers chuckled.

Martha glanced at the others. She wondered if they thought of her as a maid there to clean up after them.

The woman turned to leave and then doubled back.

"I almost forgot. I'm Mrs. Holt, and if you have any trouble here, let me know. I can take care of that for you. My husband has told me all about you. I'm only here in the mornings."

"Thank you. It's a pleasure to meet you. I'm sure everything will be perfect."

"Wonderful," said Mrs. Holt, and then she walked away.

Martha sat smiling as she put the first journal in front of her. Her mouth fell open at the scribbles that filled the pages.

It was half past four when Gertrude marched up to Martha's desk. Martha, oblivious, remained hunched over the second journal, scribbling numbers.

"Martha," Gertrude said.

Martha continued to write.

Gertrude roared, "Martha!"

A startled yelp escaped Martha's lips as she fumbled to catch her falling pencil. Her cheeks flushed crimson as she looked up at Gertrude. "I lost track of time completely!"

"I've been waiting outside for thirty minutes."

Martha checked the time on the wall clock beside Mr. Holt's office. The other bookkeepers were long gone.

Martha was stunned. "I only sat down a minute ago."

"It's time to go." Gertrude picked up Martha's bag. It was heavier than she expected. She looked inside. "You didn't eat that lunch I prepared for you, did you?"

"I ate a cracker, I think," said Martha.

"Let's go home and have dinner."

"I have so much to tell you." Martha stacked the two finished journals on the right and the other ten on the left. Then, she followed Gertrude out of the bank to the carriage.

Soon after, Gertrude and Martha sat at the kitchen table. Gertrude served the food.

Martha said, "The work is wonderful, although when I walked in, it was obvious that the men were suspicious of me. While not impolite, their eyes flitted toward me subtly, almost imperceptibly, making me feel like I didn't belong."

"I'm sure they'll get used to you."

"Mrs. Holt works there. I can tell that she is a delightful person. When she greeted me, she had a dozen journals on my desk, ready to review. I examined them before writing anything; they were a mess. After correcting the many errors, I made them legible."

Gertrude chuckled. "Slow down and eat something. It sounds like your first work day went well."

"It went very well...."

They continued to chat about working at the bank, with Martha doing most of the talking.

Gertrude was happy that Martha hadn't said a word about Thomas. She had a gnawing feeling that Martha was better off without him.

When Gertrude and Martha had supper after the second day of work, Martha mentioned Thomas.

"As I finished the last journal today, I lost myself in thought.

Why hasn't Thomas called on me? I know I just met him, but his smiles and lingering glances…felt like affection. Was I mistaken about him?"

"Focus on your work and let the rest work itself out."

Gertrude hoped that Martha's job at the bank would serve as a distraction from Thomas.

On Saturday morning, after her first week of work, Martha told Gertrude, "I miss Thomas. Am I in love or just infatuated?"

Gertrude cocked her head back in surprise. "He's probably gone out West to find his father."

Martha grimaced. "I'll give him a few more days. If there's no sign of him, I'll move on."

By Friday, the end of the second work week, Martha was sad that Thomas had not called on her and annoyed with the simple work the bookkeepers gave her.

She copied entries from one journal to another. "You write much nicer than I do," each would tell her. She corrected their mistakes as she went. All but one of her coworkers didn't like it when she reported their mistake.

When she first started, she somewhat enjoyed it. But now, it seemed that the others were taking advantage of her. They seemed to rush through their work and made many errors, expecting her to make corrections.

On the Monday morning of her third week at work, Mr. Holt walked to Martha's desk. He cocked his head back, surprised that Martha hadn't acknowledged him. Martha was leaning over a journal, mumbling numbers. "Twenty-two, Twenty-three, and Twenty-four."

"That's it," she said as she drew an underscore on the bottom of the page. She plopped her pencil down and smiled. She leaned back and gasped in shock. Her desk shook when she pushed her chair back to stand. "Mr. Holt! I'm so sorry. I didn't see you there."

He gave a curt nod. "Stop by my office after lunch, would you? I should be back around 1:30."

A sliver of apprehension replaced the usual warmth in her eyes. "Yes. Of course," she stammered, her voice barely above a whisper.

"Thanks, Martha. See you then." He rushed away.

In the sudden silence, Martha's hand drifted to her chest, where a dull ache had settled. Her gaze darted toward the door where Mr. Holt joined Mrs. Holt, and they left, hand-in-hand.

With a sigh, Martha collected her bag and hurried away.

Five minutes later, she reached the park, where she and Gertrude planned to have lunch.

Gertrude spread a bright red tablecloth on the wooden table and pulled the bread from the basket. "You're a bit early. I'm almost done setting everything up."

"I'm going to be fired."

Gertrude froze. "What? Why?"

"I was told to report to Mr. Holt's office today at 1:30 p.m. It's very unusual."

Gertrude served Martha a plate of food and prepared one for herself. "Maybe he just wants to talk? He wouldn't dare fire you."

Martha shrugged and then took a bite of the chicken. "This is delicious."

Gertrude nodded. "I cooked it just the way you like it."

Martha smiled. She picked up another small chunk of chicken with her fork and held it near her mouth. "That job is almost mindless. I'm bored to death."

Gertrude's gaze drifted from Martha's face to the bobbing piece of chicken on Martha's fork. "That's something you should tell him. Perhaps there's something more you could do with those journals."

"Hmmm. I thought I was making a difference at first. But now I'm not so sure."

"Things will feel better after you've eaten."

Martha glanced back at the bank and then smiled. "I guess it won't be the end of the world."

Gertrude worried the meat on Martha's fork had cooled. "Eat up. That way, you'll return to the office with a full stomach. It'll be easier for you to talk with Mr. Holt."

Gertrude relaxed when Martha finally ate the chicken piece.

Martha finished the rest of her lunch. "Why don't you tell me about the latest town gossip? That always cheers me up."

Gertrude's eyes lit up bright. She loved talking about her friend, Agnes. "Well, you know, Agnes. Well, her two sons...."

They chatted for almost an hour.

Martha stood and started to pack up the picnic basket. "I have to go. I'd hate to be late for the meeting with Mr. Holt."

With a gleeful glint in her eye, Gertrude said, "I'll take care of this. You run along and go get fired, okay?"

Martha stifled a laugh, her eyes moist with tears. "Okay."

Martha walked into the bank.

She gasped. Mr. Holt had already returned. She hurried to his office and knocked.

"Come in, Martha. Please close the door behind you."

Martha, her heart beating hard, closed the door, marched over, and sat in the chair facing Mr. Holt.

"I've heard good things about your performance."

"I like working here."

"That's what I wanted to talk to you about."

A heavy sigh escaped her lips. "Most of my assignments are too simple. Perhaps if I were given something more challenging...."

"I see."

"I do want a challenge. Maybe you could assign me a larger account. My father's account?"

"Oh, no. I couldn't do that. That would be inappropriate. I trust you to work on any of the other accounts."

Martha scowled.

Wallace stood, his face filled with apology. "That's not—I mean—I do trust you."

Martha slumped back in her chair. "Are you firing me?"

Wallace cocked his head back, his face riddled with confusion. "Of course not. It would be foolish of me to fire you. What gave you that idea?"

"Most of what I do here is menial. I don't feel useful here."

Wallace shook his head. "One of the managers suggested to me this morning that I give you something more substantial."

"Really?"

"Martha, I must admit that I had my doubts when you asked for this job. All those little corrections you make while transcribing those books have saved the bank a lot of money. Those pennies do add up."

Martha smiled.

Wallace sat down and closed a folder that was on his desk.

Martha straightened up. She wasn't sure if he would start his following sentence with 'but' or something more palatable.

He stood up and handed her the folder.

"These are your accounts. They're smaller than your father's, and every penny you save your clients matters to them."

Martha took it and jumped up from her chair. She ran around and hugged Mr. Holt.

He was surprised by Martha's hug. He glanced at the door to ensure no one had seen them.

"Thank you, Mr. Holt. You won't be disappointed. I'll be glad to help the others transcribe their entries." Martha smiled. "Their writing is quite sloppy."

Wallace laughed. "Congratulations."

Martha's heart raced as she hurried to the door and flung it open.

Alexander Johnson, who was about to knock, jumped, surprised.

"Hello, Mr. Johnson," said Martha, her eyes alive and vibrant. She flew past him, holding her collection of valuable clients close to her.

A faint smile crept onto his face.

"Come in, Alexander."

Martha rushed to her desk and opened the folder. She sat on the edge of her chair and wrote down the account numbers of the three accounts before her. She went to the back room, withdrew the journals for the accounts, and returned to her desk. She spent the next several days scrutinizing those accounts. By the end of the week, each penny was accounted for. She asked one of her counterparts to check her work for her, and of course, the books were in good order.

CHAPTER TEN

Moving On

Martha loved working at the bank, especially now that she had her accounts. She found it much more enjoyable than studying for hours back at the college. It occurred to her that she might delay her return to college for a little longer. Martha grew more comfortable with her coworkers. Her exuberant and infectious personality helped. She made people feel valued and appreciated, fostering a solid camaraderie among her colleagues.

Martha arrived at 7:50 a.m. She spent the first two hours assisting her fellow workers with their journals and then worked on her accounts. After a short lunch break, she continued working until 4:30 p.m. Sometimes, she had tea and biscuits in the afternoon with another worker, but only if they discussed work matters. Now and then, she left early to tend to some personal issues, but she always made up the time the following day. On those days, she would come in earlier or leave later. She found it curious that Mr. Alexander Johnson, one of the managers, would often be absent. She knew when he was there because his office was directly across from her desk.

Near the end of the workday of her third week, Wallace walked from his office to Martha's desk carrying a large envelope. He motioned for the other employees to come. The two managers joined in. Wallace stood smiling at Martha as everyone gathered.

Once the commotion settled, Wallace said, "Martha, we all are very proud of you."

Martha sat uncomfortably. "What's going on?"

Several workers smiled with delight.

Wallace continued. "I would like to express my gratitude for your superb work here and honor you with this small token of appreciation."

Wallace handed her the envelope. "You've saved the bank more than just a few pennies."

Martha blushed as she nodded. She opened the envelope and

read it out loud: "Employee of the Month: Martha S."

Everyone cheered and clapped.

Martha smiled, her eyes moist with tears. "Thank you."

Wallace offered his hand to shake Martha's.

Martha grinned and shook Wallace's hand. "Thank you." She looked nervously at her desk. "Well, I guess I'd better get back to work and improve my performance for next month."

Laughter filled the air.

Wallace waved his hands. "Yes. Everyone, back to work."

Alexander lingered a bit longer, leaned over, and said, "Congratulations."

Martha pointed to the award. "I appreciate this very much."

Alexander's lips formed a wrinkled smile, and he almost bowed before he walked away.

Martha blushed at his awkward exit. Something in his recent glances made her skin tingle. At first, she thought nothing would come of it. But, for the last few days, those odd glances from him seemed to happen more frequently. It didn't bother her; instead, she appreciated his respectful attention. She admired his work ethic. He arrived on time each day and was hard at work at his desk when she left, except on the days he was out protecting stagecoaches.

Martha finished tidying her work area, and her gaze drifted to the window, drawn by something outside. A man was in the square across the way. She leaned closer and squinted at the man. It was Thomas. The bank sign partially obstructed her view. She smiled with excitement. Even though she had ten more minutes of work, she grabbed her bag and moved briskly to the exit. Alexander stood as she ran past his office.

"Martha," he said a little too softly for her to hear. He went after her, the scent of her perfume lingering in the air, only to catch the loud thud of the closing door.

Alexander was curious as to why she ran out the door. He looked at the clock and narrowed his brows. "That's odd. Ten minutes early." He went to the window. Martha was running toward the alley next to the hotel. He grabbed his coat and went after her.

When Alexander stepped outside, Martha disappeared around

the corner of the hotel. Alexander stood watching with concern at her erratic behavior.

Martha bolted across the road toward the hotel, her eyes scanning for Thomas. She shook her head, disappointed. She thought he returned to make good on his date. She heard a noise come from behind her and looked back at the hotel, expecting to see Thomas standing there, calling to her. It wasn't him. A mix of disappointment and resolve set in as she trudged back to the bank, her stride firm despite a lingering sigh. Perhaps it was for the better, she thought. It was time for her to move on.

Alexander went inside the bank, but something felt wrong. He doubled back and walked out the door. Martha was there looking backward and barreling toward him.

Alexander choked out, "Excuse me!"

He tried stepping out of the way, but it was too late.

Martha barreled straight into him. "I didn't see you there." She pushed back and righted herself, and then realized that it was Alexander. His scent was of a cologne similar to her father's. It was sweet, aromatic, and clean. Even as she pulled away, his fragrance stayed with her.

Alexander's face froze. "I followed you. I thought—"

Martha's embarrassment morphed into annoyance. "What? You followed me. That's very inappropriate."

Alexander gasped. "Forgive me. Yes, I did. I thought something was wrong. When I called out to you to ask you something, you didn't answer. You seemed distressed. I was alarmed for you."

Martha was breathing hard. She took a deep breath and quickly calmed herself. Alexander's face seemed tight, and his eyes filled with worry. She'd hurt him, and she regretted it. "I'm sorry."

Alexander tilted his head down. "I'm the one who should apologize."

Martha's heart raced. "What did you want to ask me?"

"If you would do me the honor of accompanying me to the church picnic this Sunday, it would be a wonderful opportunity to learn more about each other." He took a breath. "I was hoping to catch you after you completed your work. It would be inappropriate to discuss personal matters before then."

Martha wanted to smile. He presented a calm demeanor with just the right amount of sophistication. She liked how he answered directly about the picnic and then meandered afterward.

A cool breeze swept past her. Her hair, usually kept tight to her head, came loose and tickled her cheek. Her heart was melting away, but she decided to stand her ground lest she appear weak. "Why would I want to go with you? You know nothing about me, nor I about you."

Martha was both annoyed and intrigued. When Mr. Holt introduced her to Alexander, his courteous and considerate nature impressed her. At that time, she felt a flicker of a spark from him, but brushed it away because she thought about her obligation to wait for Thomas.

Alexander smiled. "That is precisely why I invited you to the picnic. It's the perfect place for us to become acquainted amid our 'God-fearing' neighbors."

A spark of excitement ignited bright within her. "And why would we need to learn more about each other? What about the other workers, Mr. Johnson? What would they say?"

"They would wish you well, Martha. And please call me Alexander."

Most everyone called him Alexander, except for Martha. She maintained a strictly formal manner around him. Alexander was not very patient; however, as one of the bank's managers, he often dealt with demanding customers. He somehow managed to subdue his shortcomings. But Martha was not a delicate woman. Alexander truly admired a robust and determined woman such as Martha.

"Alexander—" Martha began, a flicker of uncertainty crossing her features.

"Or Alex," he interjected with a wink.

Heat crept up Martha's neck. "Mr. Johnson—I mean, Alexander! Perhaps we should maintain a professional distance for now."

Alexander raised an eyebrow, a playful glint in his eyes. "Distance? But the picnic is supposed to be about getting to know each other, wouldn't you say?"

Martha blinked, her eyes studying his. She remained silent.

A trace of a smile still loomed on his lips. "Alexander will do just fine," he said.

A reluctant smile tugged at the corners of Martha's lips. "Perhaps," she conceded, a hint of amusement replacing her initial fluster.

"You may call me Martha. Now, what time did you say the picnic starts?" Martha asked.

Alexander's face warmed, his eyes filled with hope. "It starts at about 10:00 a.m. May I call on you at 10:30?"

Martha whisked away a fleeting thought of Thomas.

"No, you may not. I would prefer that you call on me at 11:00 sharp. My sister and I will be ready by then." She glanced away when she realized she had referred to Gertrude as her sister. No matter, she thought. Gertrude would be their chaperone, just like a big sister.

Alexander tilted his head, confused. "Your sister?" Wallace told him that Martha had an aunt and no other relatives. Perhaps he misunderstood Wallace. "Yes, of course. I'll pick you up promptly at 11:00. Good day, Martha. I look forward to seeing you and your sister on Sunday."

"Good day to you, Mr. Johnson." She walked away with a pronounced lightness about her step, gliding away like a beautiful swan.

"Mr. Johnson?" he muttered to himself. "It's Alexander."

Alexander smiled as she disappeared down the road, and he strolled back to the office.

When Thomas arrived at the hotel twenty minutes before, he saw a woman selling flowers next door. He wanted to surprise Martha with a bouquet after her workday ended. He left to get the flowers and gave her some coin for the best bunch. By the time he returned, Martha and Alexander were by the bank, talking passionately with each other. Portions of their conversation wafted over to him. It infuriated him how Alexander imposed his charm on Martha. She responded to Alexander's advances with a look of feigned embarrassment. Thomas found the whole affair disgusting. He shook his head, tossed the aromatic bunch to the ground, and limped away defeated.

As he climbed onto the wagon, the seeds of betrayal and hatred were planted deep in his heart— betrayal by Martha and hatred for Alexander. Both would fester in his heart.

Thomas sat rigid in the wagon, his body trembling with rage. He swallowed a pill to dull the searing pain in his leg, yet his mind churned with confusion. Alexander—the man who had shot Frank's father.

Thomas swallowed another pill, his mind lingering on whether to confront Alexander.

A current of excitement crackled within Martha as she hurried home, her steps fueled by the need to tell Gertrude the fantastic news.

Gertrude looked up from the stove as Martha walked into the kitchen. "The food is almost ready. How was your day?"

"Something odd happened. I was about to leave work and thought I saw Thomas. But when I went outside, he wasn't there. I could have sworn it was him."

"Child, that young man is long gone."

Martha set the table. "At first, it disappointed me. Then, someone at the bank surprised me. And he invited me to a picnic."

Gertrude grinned ear to ear. "A picnic?"

Martha nodded excitedly. "Yes. He's the most wonderful man I have ever met." Words flew out of Martha's mouth with hardly a breath of air between each one.

"For a few days now, he's been stealing glances at me." Martha inhaled and continued. "Well, today I tripped and fell into his arms."

Gertrude cocked her head in surprise. "What?"

"Oh, it was so embarrassing. I was going back into the bank and crashed into him. He was quite the gentleman. But I didn't punch him. That would have been terrible if I'd done that. It wouldn't have been proper to punch my employer. Although it might have been funny." Martha giggled.

Gertrude didn't laugh. Instead, a warm smile spread across her face as she watched Martha, enthralled by her infectious excitement.

Gertrude served two plates of food.

"Gertrude, are you listening to me?"

Gertrude's face warmed.

"Yes, Martha." Gertrude grinned. "I wish your mother could see you now. She would be so happy for you."

Martha nodded. "I hope so."

Both sat and continued to chat as they extended their napkins.

Gertrude smiled. "This young man sounds like a real gentleman. I already like him. Now tell me more."

"He IS a gentleman. I'm sure that you've seen him. He's the manager there."

Gertrude's smile softened. "Which manager?"

"Mr. Alexander Johnson."

Gertrude winced. "Oh yes. I've heard of him. Let's talk some more after dinner before the food gets cold." Mr. Swanson often complained to her about Alexander's inadequate bookkeeping skills. "I'm happy you found someone special."

CHAPTER ELEVEN

Alexander

A smile lingered on Alexander's face after Martha disappeared down the street, his heart still buzzing that she had accepted his invitation. He checked his watch, a touch reluctantly, before returning to the bank, the memory of their conversation warming him from the inside out.

Alexander walked past the front counter, where customer transactions occurred, through the door to the employee area. A modest grouping of desks was in the open space, bookended by three offices. The first one belonged to Wallace, the second was his, and the third to the other manager. Each of them had a glass panel inset in a wooden door through which they could see all the workers. The doors contained their names and job titles stenciled in black letters. Alexander's door held **Mr. Alexander Johnson, Bank Manager.**

He entered his office and sat at his desk, an oversized oak specimen whose top was covered with carefully placed stacks of journals, receipts, invoices, and other essential papers.

Alexander picked up the statement he had been working on earlier before rushing to intercept Martha. Something caught his eye through the glass of his door. Martha's desk was cluttered with papers and a still-open journal, and her chair was pulled away. A modest-looking shawl hung over the back of Martha's chair. The scene triggered a memory. When he was a child, his mother always kept a shawl draped over the armrest of her favorite rocker. Martha reminded him of his mother in a delicate sort of way. He admired Martha as a bright and independent woman who brought warmth into his heart. Memories of his mother began to play out in his mind. Alexander chuckled, puzzled as to why the memories had surfaced. Perhaps it was Martha who sparked life into the recollections of his mother.

Alexander loved how his mother would fuss over him. The last time he remembered being happy was when his mother and he picnicked together in the nearby park while his father was working. Alexander was eleven, awaiting his twelfth birthday.

"I want to be a lawman just like Pa," he told his mother.

"You are so much like your father," she replied. "But remember to stay on the right side of the law."

Less than two months later, he understood why his mother said that.

Alexander snapped out of his distractions when Wallace knocked and opened the door. "Have you made any progress on the Swanson robbery?"

Alexander put his pencil down. "We scoured the site again and couldn't find anything else near that coach. The stagecoach driver thinks he heard two, maybe three men."

Wallace shook his head, standing in the doorway. "We've got to get those criminals."

Alexander nodded. "We'll catch them and get that money back, too."

"You're skilled at protecting those stagecoaches. If you focused on them instead of inside the bank, it—"

"Ever since you gave me this job, I've worked hard here. I like working on these journals: adding numbers, balancing accounts, and more. You know that."

Wallace half-smiled. "No one around is as good as you at caring for those stagecoaches."

Alexander grimaced and gathered the paperwork on his desk into a neat stack. "Except when I was hell-bent on finding a damn accounting error instead of protecting Swanson's coach."

"Are you ready for tomorrow's 9 a.m. stagecoach?" Wallace turned to the door. Martha's desk stood on the other side of the glass door.

"Absolutely."

"Fantastic!" Wallace reached for the door.

"Wallace, on another matter, what do you know about Martha?"

Wallace froze and found Alexander's eyes peering innocently at him. "She's an excellent worker."

"I asked her to the picnic."

Wallace tensed up, pulled his timepiece from his pocket, and looked at its face.

Alexander tilted his head, confused. Wallace seemed anxious.

Wallace forced a smile. "Are you sure that's a good idea? I mean, she's going back to the university soon."

Alexander forged ahead. "She's quite the remarkable woman."

Wallace glanced at his watch again and returned it to his pocket. "I don't think you should," he said.

Alexander cocked his head to one side. "Why?"

Wallace withdrew his pocket watch again and gasped when he popped it open. A picture of his wife staring emotionless at him was on the inside, opposite the clock face.

"Shoot! My wife will have my hide if I'm late for dinner. I've got to go." Wallace snapped his watch shut. "Please understand that Martha has been through a lot."

Wallace hesitated for an instant and scuttled away.

Alexander stood, wondering why Wallace had acted out of character. He cleaned up the top of his desk. The sun had not yet settled down for the night, and he was anxious to get home.

Outside, a man limped toward Alexander as he walked to his horse.

"Sir," snarled the man as if challenging Alexander to a duel.

The impeccably dressed man was wearing a hat that cast a dark shadow over part of his face.

Alexander nodded to the stranger.

The man walked with a pronounced limp and with determination. He brushed hard against Alexander's arm and then marched away, saying nothing.

Alexander bristled at the man's rude manner. Alexander was tempted to follow him and confront him about his crude behavior.

The man hesitated near the edge of the building as if about to turn back, but instead disappeared around the corner. As Alexander walked to his horse, the man's rudeness bothered him, triggering more profound thoughts.

As Alexander rode home, memories of his past relentlessly assailed him.

The memory of his aunt's visit ten years before, just after his father had gone missing, was particularly persistent. She arrived with a wagon full of furniture, crates, and trunks, and the horses seemed distressed at pulling the load.

"Your mother, rest her soul, asked me to keep these things for you. You should have them now that your father is gone," she said calmly.

Alexander and the driver managed to bring the cargo into the house.

"Alexandria asked me to provide you with the rest of your inheritance."

"Inheritance?"

"She expected you to be older when you received it. She wanted to ensure you continue your education in primary school and then attend college like your grandfather." His aunt handed him a case. "And then honor his legacy by working for the bank. If you do well in your studies, Mr. Holt, the owner, has assured me that he will hire you."

The case contained bank notes, several gold coins, and a letter folded inside an envelope. As Alexander opened the envelope, he noticed a delicate fragrance that reminded him of his mother. He unfolded the letter and read.

"My dearest son, I love you with all my heart. I wanted to ensure you wouldn't have to worry about your future. I'm sure that my sister has told you as much...."

Alexander's mouth quivered as he finished the last page and put the folded letter away.

His aunt leaned forward and hugged him. "She would always tell me how proud she was of you."

Alexander smiled. "I miss her."

After graduating from *The Academy of Accountants*, Alexander watched his aunt, who had been his guardian for six years, embark on a new chapter. Seeing him reach adulthood at eighteen, she felt her obligation fulfilled and free to pursue her happiness. She accepted a wedding proposal from a Southern gentleman who had been courting her and, on her wedding day, declared with conviction, "I'll never come back here. The anti-southern sentiment here is distasteful." Shortly after, she left with her husband for Louisiana.

The memory of the day his aunt gave him the letter faded as

he wiped an errant tear from his cheek. A warm feeling gently caressed him. The letter was safely stowed in the desk in his study.

Alexander lived in a modest house on five acres of land. An eight-foot-long hitching post greeted him as he arrived. An overgrown garden with tall weeds and brush lay off to the left. Further still, a barn with the same dark-colored, weathered wood as the house stood behind a windmill. Both the house and the barn could have used some paint.

Alexander walked up the steps to an expansive porch that stretched the entire width of the house. He remembered when his father moved the stairs from the center of the porch to the side where the hitching post was. When his mother discovered what he'd done, she told him, "The house appears lopsided. The stairs should be across from the front door."

A loud growl from his stomach interrupted Alexander's memory. He went into the kitchen. When he opened the icebox, he wrinkled his nose from the smell of stale, sitting water. A small clump of ice, barely the size of his fist, was on the bottom. He took a bowl of beans out and smelled them. He smiled, grabbed a spoon, and headed out to the porch.

Alexander sat on the creaky swing chair on the side, away from the hitching post. His gaze remained fixed on the worn stairs as he ate his beans. When he turned twelve, three months after his mother died unexpectedly, he found his father slumped in a drunken despair, sitting on the top step.

His father slurred, "Now that your ma is gone, I promise I'll be the father you deserve."

"You're a dirty lawman," young Alexander shouted. "You're nothing but a stain on Ma's memories. It's your fault she's dead."

His father's face became still, his mouth hanging open in surprise. Frantic blinks flickered across his eyes. He staggered away in silence without a word. That was the last day Alexander had seen his father.

In the present, Alexander jumped when an enormous, dark crow flew onto the porch and stared at him. Alexander smiled, grateful that the creature saved him from the abyss of unpleasant reminiscences.

"Hello," said Alexander. He tossed a bean to the crow.

The crow blinked several times, picked up the bean, and flew away.

Newly energized, he brushed his horse and then spent the next couple of hours doing odds and ends, less than his place needed. Now and then, the thought of Martha made him smile.

CHAPTER TWELVE

It's a Date

Gertrude sat on the porch swing, enjoying the cool morning breeze.

Martha walked out smiling.

Gertrude snapped out of her solitude. "My, don't you look pretty?"

"I figured I should dress nicely since we're going to a picnic full of old women who spend hours making themselves look beautiful."

A playful grin stretched across Gertrude's face. "I'm one of those old ladies. I'm as old as the hills."

"I'm not talking about you. You're a natural beauty, inside and out."

"Thank you, dear. There'll be plenty of young people there."

Martha sat. "I shouldn't be going out. It's not right."

"Why not?"

"I told Thomas I'd go out with him when he returned. It's like I'm cheating on him."

"Martha, listen to me. That Thomas of yours isn't cut from the same cloth as you. Something seems off about him."

"I thought you liked him," said Martha. "You were happy about me going dancing with him. You know how I feel about prancing on the dance floor like a fool."

"I got distracted because I was excited for you to get out and have fun."

Martha sighed. "I wonder why he didn't come back. Maybe something important kept him from coming."

"Even if he got stuck somewhere, he would have gotten word to you. It's not that hard to write a letter or send a telegram. He could have told someone."

"I suppose you're right."

Gertrude took a deep breath and then exhaled slowly. "You

should move on."

Martha shook her head and let out a huff. "Letting things go without a good reason doesn't make sense."

Gertrude hugged Martha. "I love you, darling."

Martha narrowed her eyes playfully at Gertrude. After a brief hesitation, Martha said, "You win. Let's go on this 'date' and get it over with. It'll do me some good to get out and stop my moping around the house."

Gertrude laughed. "Okay. No more nagging from me. I won't say another word about it."

A faint rumbling of horses echoed from the distance. Martha jumped up. A dark stagecoach with long plumes of dust trailing behind was coming their way.

Gertrude squinted at the fast-approaching conveyance. "My God, is that man bringing a stagecoach to pick us up? What in the heck? It's 10:50 a.m."

Gertrude rushed inside.

Martha smiled. She straightened out her dress and looked at her reflection in the window to ensure her hair was carefully placed. She calmed herself and walked to the edge of the porch, just above the stairs.

A beautiful, shiny, black stagecoach drawn by majestic horses thundered past the grand fountain and screeched to a halt before the porch. Despite its grand appearance, the coach was smaller than the lumbering behemoths typically used for transporting passengers and money between cities.

Alexander, who sat next to the driver, jumped down. "Wallace loaned us his private coach."

A mischievous glint danced in Martha's eyes. "I've been waiting for ten minutes."

Confused, he opened his pocket watch. "It's not even eleven yet. I'm not late."

"I thought you'd arrive earlier."

Alexander chuckled. "Where's your sister?"

"My sister?" Her forehead scrunched, her eyes narrowed, and after a few seconds, she blushed. When she was younger, she told her mother that she wished she had an older sister who would look out for her. Her mother said, "Whenever you need a protector, think of Gertrude as your big sister. She loves and will care for you as much as I do."

Martha's heart warmed at the memory of her mother.

Alexander's eyes clouded with confusion at Martha.

"Oh! Aunt Gertrude is like a sister to me."

Alexander nodded.

The front door creaked open, and a thin, slim woman was hunched over, walking backward out the door.

He raised an eyebrow at Gertrude's peculiar exit. "Is she okay?" he asked, dumbfounded. "It looks like she's having... trouble," he said.

Gertrude turned to Alexander. "Come here and help me move this crate out of the house!"

Alexander rushed to the door and dragged the wooden box onto the porch.

"Just set it on the edge, next to the stairs. Agnes's sons will pick it up later today." Gertrude nodded affectionately at Martha.

Martha held her lips tight as she tried to smile. Even so, her lower lip trembled. The box contained most of her father's clothes and other things they didn't want. Much to Gertrude's dismay, Martha kept several trousers she hoped to alter to her liking. Gertrude insisted they keep her mother's dresses since Gertrude could alter them to fit Martha.

"Much appreciated, Mr. Johnson," Gertrude said.

Alexander's head cocked back, surprised. "You know me?"

Gertrude chuckled. Mr. Swanson had mentioned him many times, mainly in an unflattering light. "I've seen you once or twice, but I've never met you. I'm Gertrude, and you're Alexander Johnson; now, let's go!"

Gertrude smiled and rushed to the coach. With a wink, she acknowledged the horses before turning a mischievous gaze toward the driver. "Mighty beautiful steeds, you got there."

He tipped his hat at her. "Thanks, Ma'am. They are."

Gertrude walked to the coach entrance and waited for Alexander.

His jaw fell open as his gaze fell on Martha. "She's your aunt?"

Martha stepped down from the porch and nodded.

He stood puzzled as the color washed from his face. His eyes darted from the enormous house to Gertrude and then settled on Martha. "Is Mr. Charles Swanson your father?"

Martha's smile disappeared as uncertainty crept in. "Yes."

He gasped. "I didn't know. Wallace always dealt directly with...."

Gertrude shook her head and rolled her eyes. "Well, now you know. Now, let's go. I'm sure Agnes is already wondering where I am. She and her husband like to arrive early, and I have plenty to tell her."

Alexander rushed to the door. Confusion swirled in his eyes, and the edge of his lips attempted to curl upward. He offered his hand to Gertrude. She took it and entered the coach.

Alexander was distracted when Martha walked up.

She cleared her throat and extended her hand.

Alexander gasped and quickly took her hand. She placed her hand in his and stepped into the coach.

The driver was grinning, unabashedly reveling in Alexander's clumsiness. "Where to?"

Alexander shook his head as he smiled through gritted teeth at him. "The park. And please go easy."

"Sure thing."

Alexander knew almost all the drivers, but this one was the closest to one he would call his friend. He crouched awkwardly and climbed inside.

Martha and Gertrude sat together on the rear bench, and their conversation abruptly stopped when Alexander entered. He hoped to sit with Martha. A disappointed smile was on his face as he sat opposite them. He couldn't help but admire how Gertrude, like a loyal lioness, held Martha's hand, keeping her safe.

With a silent chuckle, he tapped on the ceiling for the driver to go.

Martha's gaze held a spark of curiosity as she met Alexander's eyes.

A hint of a smile played on his lips. Her eyes resembled Mr. Swanson's judgmental eyes peering back at him. How could he not have noticed before?

Gertrude settled onto the unforgiving bench, shifting and patting the worn leather beneath her in a futile attempt to find comfort. She turned to Alexander. "I like facing forward."

Alexander blinked, confused as if he didn't hear.

Gertrude leaned forward and shouted, "I like facing the front. That's why we sat in the rear seat.... I thought you were wondering why."

"Of course." He glanced at Martha. "Now I see where Martha gets her direct, no-nonsense nature. It's quite refreshing and impressive."

Alexander found it ironic that those same characteristics also belonged to Mr. Swanson. But with Mr. Swanson, those traits were grating and unpleasant. Wallace should have told him that Martha was Mr. Swanson's daughter, he thought.

As soon as the coach was underway, Gertrude talked about her friends, chickens, cooking, and other things. Periodically, Alexander and Martha exchanged quick, nervous glances at each other and then mechanically smiled and nodded at Gertrude. Both were a bit uneasy, him about her identity and Martha about how Alexander knew her father.

Alexander remembered when Wallace hired Martha. He had examined her application and had agreed with Wallace that her credentials were satisfactory. He may have known who she was had she put her last name on the paperwork. Instead, she had written 'Martha S' as her name. It was odd that a wealthy young woman would want employment at a bank as a bookkeeper. Even so, she was excellent at that job and very passionate about it. Perhaps she wanted anonymity to allow her to work without prejudice.

"That would make sense," he mumbled aloud.

Gertrude asked, "What would make sense?"

Alexander straightened up. "My apologies. I got distracted for an instant. Please continue. You were talking about your chickens?"

Martha chuckled.

"My chickens? That was minutes ago. I was talking about..."

Alexander's lips tightened into a semblance of a smile, and his eyes glazed over. Gertrude's voice faded away as he glanced at Martha. He felt a warm feeling in his heart as he focused on her. She exuded confidence and independence with an air of loving tenderness. He had an overwhelming sense that Martha was the only one for him.

Martha smiled at Alexander.

Alexander was charming, tall, attractive, and so much more. He was also confident, independent, and genuinely caring. It comforted her that Alexander knew her father. Her heart fluttered.

Gertrude stopped talking, her eyes darting from Martha to Alexander. "You two aren't listening to me at all!"

The coach came to a quick stop.

Alexander pulled the curtain back and looked outside. "We're here."

"Goodness. That was fast," Gertrude said.

Alexander exited first. Most courteously, Alexander held out his hand for Gertrude. She took his hand as she stepped down from the coach. Then, Martha stood gracefully at the threshold. Her beauty dumbfounded him, and the sun had captured her face with a ray of light. He immediately extended his hand, and Martha took a step, but the heel of her shoe got caught in the doorway. She lost her balance and fell into Alexander's arms.

Martha let out a soft scream that sounded like a sustained high note that varied slightly in pitch.

Alexander quickly righted her and stepped back, embarrassed. "I'm sorry. It was my fault. Please forgive me."

Martha, her face flushed red, looked at him, puzzled. His firm grip had saved her from falling to the ground. She pulled her stuck shoe from the doorway and chuckled. "It was the fault of these darn shoes. If they weren't so beautiful and expensive, I would have thrown them out long ago."

She held onto Alexander while she put her shoe on. "Thank you for saving me from a terrible embarrassment."

The three walked side-by-side, Gertrude on Alexander's left and Martha on his right. When they arrived, the picnic was in full swing. There were plenty of friendly people, and a band was playing in the gazebo.

Gertrude turned to walk away. "I'll check on you two lovebirds later."

Martha's heart pounded hard, her head shaking from side to side at Gertrude and mouthing the word, "No."

Gertrude winked at Martha and pointed to the group of her rowdy friends sitting at a table. "Agnes is sitting with those old ladies. I gotta go."

Martha chuckled as she glanced at the women and then back at Gertrude. "Have fun."

When Gertrude was halfway to the gaggle of women, she yelled her hellos at them.

"Well, it's just the two of us now," Alexander said, a little louder than a whisper.

Martha smiled. "Gertrude will keep a watchful eye on us. Let's walk."

Alexander took her arm and continued along a brick walkway through the park's center. "She sure can talk up a storm," he said.

"Yes, she does love talking. I'm so thankful that she's in my life. Gertrude has helped me through some difficult times." She glanced down as she pushed back a tinge of pain. The memory of her parents' death arose, but she forced herself back to the present.

Alexander nodded.

Martha looked from one side of the park to the other. "I enjoy picnics. They remind me of when I was a little girl. My parents would bring me to this very park."

Alexander smiled as he imagined Martha gleefully running through the park as a child. "It's a beautiful park."

Alexander's smile faded. He glanced at Martha and then at the ground. "I'm sorry about your parents."

Martha bit her lip, stopped walking, and faced Alexander. "Mr. Holt said you were looking into the robbers who killed my parents. Can you tell me about it?"

Alexander blinked. "Now?"

"Yes. Tell me everything."

"Well." He paused for a second. "I'm working with the law. There are two or three men involved in the robbery."

"Mr. Holt has said as much. Can you give me more details? Have you identified any of them?" Martha was determined to put a bullet in each of those scoundrels who killed her parents. She had been practicing shooting with her father's gun ever since she returned from college.

Alexander grimaced. "We will find them. Those outlaws are difficult to track because they choose remote locations, far from the city's safety."

Martha crossed her arms. "Whenever I ask Mr. Holt about it, he tends to be vague. He doesn't tell me much."

"He's very protective of you."

She relaxed and nodded. "Have you talked to the driver?"

"Yes. The driver doesn't know who shot him. He heard two young men talking. And one of them convinced the other not to kill him. He thinks there was an older man there, too."

"Maybe he can identify them by their voices."

Alexander shrugged. "Maybe."

A handsome couple passed by, holding hands, carefully balancing their plates with their free hands.

"Mmm. My mouth is watering," he said, hoping to change the subject.

"I'm starving." Martha pointed to the far side of the park toward several tents. "There's the food. I'll race you there."

Alexander stood confused while Martha raced away toward the food. "What?"

He chuckled and sprinted after her.

They reached the tents together, out of breath. After a minute to recover from their mad dash, they walked inside. There was an assortment of beverages, food, and desserts, and dozens of people were helping to serve the food. She meandered to the back of the tent, where people brought trays full of meats, vegetables, and freshly baked bread.

Martha peeked out the back. Several sizable smoky fire pits were heating various cast-iron pots filled with beans, potatoes, and other vegetables. A giant roasting pig was on one side of the pit, and cuts of beef were on the other. The air was filled with delicious flavors.

Alexander pulled the tent flap open next to her. His eyes grew wide. "It's a feast out there."

"Let's eat."

After loading their plates, they found a secluded table.

Martha's eyes flicked to Alexander's plate, which contained a mountain of beans dwarfed by a lone piece of meat and a modest slice of bread. Martha's plate overflowed with a chaotic variety of her favorites. With a shrug and a grin, she met his gaze.

Alexander grinned. "I couldn't decide what to eat— too many choices."

Martha poked at a rogue carrot and gobbled it up. "I took a little of everything."

Alexander put beans on his bread and took a bite. "These beans are delicious," he said, gobbling up the rest of the bean-laden bread. "Picnics are the best."

Martha took a drink of tea. "Aren't they? This one is a bit bigger than I'm used to. I prefer to bring a picnic basket with some of my favorite foods and an interesting book."

"You go alone?"

"Oh no. Gertrude and I go together. But, often, she finds one of her friends, and they chat endlessly. And I read my book."

"You are quite efficient with your time. I admire that about you."

Martha smiled and took another bite. "Are your parents living?"

"No. My mother passed a while back." A soft smile formed on his lips. "I'm named after her. Her name was Alexandria."

"That's a beautiful name."

"I was about twelve when she...died." He glanced away, his smile fading. "I miss her."

"I'm sorry." She gazed at him for a few seconds. He was gobbling down his food. "And your father?"

Alexander shifted in his seat and then slumped. "He was a lawman, Deputy Christopher Johnson. Everyone called him CJ." He shook his head. "He's long gone."

Alexander ate a spoonful of beans. "Beans are my favorite."

Martha reached over and touched his hand. He glanced at her hand and smiled.

Martha put her fork down. "I miss my parents. I'm sad they're gone but happy they're at peace."

"You're a strong woman who deserves to be happy for yourself, too."

Martha looked deep into his eyes, and a hint of a smile formed on her lips. "That's such a nice thing to say. I had no idea that you had a sensitive side. I thought that you were all about numbers and bullets."

Alexander chuckled. "I like that: 'numbers and bullets.'"

Martha nodded. "That pretty much describes me, too. Which one is your passion?"

"My passion is bookkeeping, which came from my mother," he said.

Martha smiled. "I like bookkeeping, although I'm not sure where I got that from. My mother refused to work on home expenses. She said that men should tend to those matters. I suppose that my father was okay at numbers. He would usually have me check his accounting records for him. On more than one occasion, I corrected discrepancies in his account. Mr. Holt is much better at owning the bank than working on balance sheets."

Alexander moved uncomfortably in his seat and blinked several times. He'd wondered how Mr. Swanson had quickly found his bookkeeping errors. Eventually, Mr. Holt told him.

"I manage that account."

Martha tilted her head, surprised. "You do?"

"Yes." Alexander thought she might disapprove of that and ask him more about why he managed it so poorly.

A hesitant nod betrayed her conflicting emotions. "What do you think you inherited from your father?"

"From my father, I suppose I got gun-slinging abilities."

Her eyes lit up bright. "That's my real passion— Shooting."

She picked up her fork and continued eating. "I've handled a gun ever since I was a young girl. And my bullets always reach their targets."

Alexander raised his eyebrows, surprised. "That's impressive."

"I've been practicing a lot lately. We should practice shooting together sometimes. I bet you that I could out-shoot you," she said.

Alexander was fascinated with Martha. At work, she was all about business, almost reserved. Now, she was more relaxed, vibrant, and excited. He believed that she was his equal in every way. She was the one that his heart had been searching for. He noticed her plate was empty.

Gertrude rushed up. The driver ran up behind her.

"Let's go. I forgot to put the chickens away. Those dang foxes will eat them." Gertrude stared expectantly at the driver.

The driver chuckled. He had seen Gertrude running to Alexander and Martha and was concerned that something was wrong. "I'll get the coach ready."

Gertrude turned back to Martha and Alexander. "Let's go."

They walked to the coach. Gertrude stepped into the coach before Alexander had a chance to assist her. She sat in the middle of the rear bench. Martha waited at the entrance and extended her right hand. Alexander graciously obliged her. She seated herself in the center of the seat closest to the driver and opposite Gertrude. Alexander entered and looked from left to right. Both women were sitting in the center of each of the two benches. If he were to sit next to Gertrude, would he be disrespectful to Martha? Did Martha want him to sit with her? Did Gertrude, acting as a chaperone, prefer that he not sit with Martha? Before he could choose, they laughed, and Martha moved to one side and made room for Alexander.

Gertrude yelled out the window, "Let's go."

The coach lurched forward.

On the way home. Gertrude talked about all the foods she sampled and the latest gossip she heard. Martha and Alexander were unable to utter a single word in the conversation. Alexander reached for Martha's hand as Gertrude described the ingredients used to make the apple pie in detail. Martha winced and then looked over at him. She felt a wave of comfort wash over her as he rested his hand on hers. That was the moment that Martha knew that her life was going to change profoundly.

Martha loved cultivating her garden of plans. She would carefully nurture her plans, rearrange them, and adjust them until they were right. Now, her garden of dreams was about to change drastically. Then, as if Gertrude could read Martha's mind, Gertrude said, "Child, only God knows what the future holds. Have faith in each other!"

CHAPTER THIRTEEN

Second Picnic

The following Sunday, Alexander, Martha, and Gertrude picnicked at the park. This time, they brought a picnic basket filled with food that Gertrude had prepared. After they ate, Gertrude went off to chat with Agnes. Martha and Alexander sat under the shade of a giant oak tree on a bench overlooking the water. They sat at ease with each other. After briefly exchanging pleasantries and comments about the weather, they settled into discussing each other's dreams and ambitions.

Martha said, "I love adventures — exploring the great unknown. One of my favorite books is Daniel Boone. I've lost count of the times I've read it."

"Mr. Holt has often suggested that I move to California and work at his brother's bank," said Alexander.

"Oh my. That sounds exciting. Why haven't you pursued that?" asked Martha.

"I don't know. I'm used to living here, I guess."

"It certainly would be thrilling to join you on that adventure."

"Really?" asked Alexander.

"I suppose so," she said.

"You're amazing," said Alexander. "I've never met anyone like you before."

"I have to admit, I'm surprised that you and I have so much in common. You are so focused at work, sitting at your desk."

Alexander grinned. "That's what I thought about you. I've seen people approach your desk and try to get your attention. You seem to shut out the world while you work on your accounts."

"We're like two peas in a pod," said Martha, laughing. "Except, I'm not on those stagecoaches shooting at outlaws." Martha blinked several times. A thought of her parents' stagecoach robbery suddenly nagged at her. "Mr. Holt mentioned that you're the best stagecoach protector he has. Too bad you weren't on that coach protecting my parents. Those outlaws wouldn't have had a chance."

Alexander gasped. "Martha, I need to tell you something."

Gertrude rushed up. "Hurry. Let's go. I got us tickets to a play, which starts in fifteen minutes. We gotta go right now."

Martha stood. "I'm not dressed for a play."

Gertrude exhaled sharply and dropped her shoulders. "You're fine. They usually perform in the theater up the road. They had a small fire there, and it's been closed for a few days. Today, they're set up in that tent over there. That play has been sold out for weeks, ever since it started. Martha, you know I've been dying to go."

Martha nodded at Alexander.

Panic overtook Alexander's face. "What about the driver? What is he to do?"

Gertrude grinned. "He already has his ticket and is saving our seats. It turns out he loves the theater. Let's go!"

The trio made their way to an enormous tent across from the playhouse. An usher handed them each a program that carried the particulars about the play. All the chairs were taken except for three in the front row. Gertrude sat next to the driver, and Martha and Alexander sat in the remaining two seats. The front of the leaflet held the play's name in large, bold letters: "A Husband to Order" by John M. Morton, Esquire. A grinning Martha pointed to the leaflet and held it up for Gertrude to see. Alexander saw it, too, and chuckled. The play's running time was below the title — one hour and twenty-six minutes.

Gertrude shrugged and winked at Martha. Martha shook her head and sat back in her seat as the announcer's voice boomed, "This is a story of Josephine, who must marry Pierre sight unseen so that her uncle, Barron de Beaupre, does not lose his fortune. Some might call this a love story between two people who initially seem undeserving of each other."

Gertrude whispered to Martha loud enough for Alexander to hear. "You're Josephine."

Martha rolled her eyes at Gertrude.

Alexander giggled.

Martha smiled and sat back in her chair as the play started.

Alexander opened his watch and noted the time. He thought

about Martha and her parents. Martha was right. If only he'd been on that coach like he was supposed to, they would likely have survived. As the play progressed, Martha glanced at him now and then, mostly when laughter filled the air. His guilt eventually dissipated as the humor and laughter got the better of him. Although a bit absurd in humor, the play was the perfect metaphor for their budding romance. Time flew by as the play concluded with a happy-ever-after ending.

Alexander examined his watch as the cast members took their final bows. He was pleased that it had lasted almost exactly as they had advertised.

Martha's face was bubbling with excitement. "That was fun."

Gertrude's head bobbed like a cork in a gentle current, her eyes twinkling with mischief. "I was sure you'd love it. It was trendy in London. I've only heard wonderful things about it, Josephine."

Martha's jaw dropped, a mixture of surprise and delight washing over her face. "Gertrude!" she exclaimed, her voice laced with laughter.

Gertrude grinned and nodded repeatedly.

The ride home was filled with giggles and laughter. After arriving at their house, Martha and Gertrude stood on the porch waving goodbye to Alexander.

"Let's go inside and relax. I have sewing to do," said Gertrude.

Soon after, Martha and Gertrude chatted in the living room.

Martha traced the intricate embroidery on her dress, her lips pursed in thought. "Gertrude," she began, "do you believe in destiny?"

Gertrude, mending a worn shawl, looked up amused. "Destiny, dear? Or wishful thinking?"

Martha sighed. "Perhaps both. Alexander is a wonderful man. He loves working at the bank, just like me."

"You must have had quite a conversation on your stroll with him today." Gertrude's smile widened. "There was a twinkle in your eyes when you and Alexander returned from your stroll."

"It was a lovely walk." Martha blushed. "He's going to be my husband someday."

Gertrude's smile softened. "Already? Marriage is a serious matter. Are you sure about Alexander?"

"He's kind and intelligent and shares my passion for numbers and order. Remember how I always dreamed of exploring the world? He talks of working at another bank in California someday. Imagine that! Together, we could..."

Gertrude placed a hand on Martha's. "But what of your dreams, dear? Independence, education, seeing the world on your terms?"

Martha hesitated, a flicker of doubt clouding her eyes. "Recently, things have changed. Working at the bank, meeting Alexander, and seeing how Mr. and Mrs. Holt work together, I see how fulfilling it can be to build something with someone you love. He respects my opinions, encourages my ideas, and..." She paused, looking down, "he reminds me of my father. Strong, capable, driven."

"Ah, so that's it." Gertrude chuckled. "You're just like your father, and you see a reflection of yourself in Alexander."

Martha met her gaze, a new resolve settling in her eyes. "Yes, and I like what I see. I'm done waiting for someone who might never come. Thomas, handsome as he is, seems lost. Alexander, however, chases his dreams with every fiber of his being, just like I chase mine."

A thoughtful silence fell between them. Finally, Gertrude spoke, her voice warm. "Alexander does seem like an honorable man. And let's be honest, he shares your love for ledgers and meticulous accounts."

"And shooting!" Martha laughed, the tension breaking.

Gertrude smiled, a glint of approval in her eyes. "I won't tell you what to do, dear. But remember, happiness has many paths."

After dropping Martha and Gertrude home, he went to the bank. Wallace was usually there each Sunday, catching up on his work because it was quiet and no one else was there.

When Alexander got there, the bank was eerily silent. He went to his desk and began writing a letter to Martha. Alexander tapped his quill against the smooth paper, the rhythm barely registering compared to the replaying scenes of his afternoon with Martha. His heart ached with a newfound longing for her laughter, the way her eyes lit up as they discussed the future, her hand brushing his. He needed to talk to Wallace, not about ledgers or loans, but about something infinitely more important — Martha.

Alexander smiled as he finished the note. He checked the clock. Wallace should have arrived already.

Wallace entered the bank a few minutes later and stopped at Alexander's door.

"Alexander, I'm surprised you're here on a Sunday evening now that you're picnicking with our star employee."

"Have you got some time to talk?"

Wallace nodded. "Come on over. We haven't had a heartfelt chat in a while."

Alexander followed Wallace to his office. Wallace sat behind a towering stack of papers and moved the stack over.

"I know that Martha is the daughter of Mr. and Mrs. Swanson," said Alexander.

Wallace gasped. He leaned forward and locked eyes with Alexander. "Martha seems to be doing well after losing her parents," Wallace said.

"She's doing remarkably well," Alexander said.

Wallace inhaled deeply and let it out all at once. He nodded in surrender. "Mrs. Holt scolded me for not telling you about Martha. She thinks you and Martha are a perfect match. I apologize for keeping it from you."

"That's okay. Mrs. Holt is right." He hesitated. "I want to marry Martha."

Wallace raised an eyebrow, a smile tugging at his lips. His wife was right, as usual. "You and Martha may be well suited to each other, but marriage is no light matter. It takes time to develop a relationship— Months. You've barely met her."

"She's intelligent and kind and shares my passion for order and building something meaningful. Remember our talks about your brother's bank in California? She and I could work there together!"

Wallace nodded, his smile fading into a thoughtful frown. "Has Martha expressed similar desires? Or might she be sacrificing her aspirations for yours? Her father told me about her peculiar aspirations, like going to college, working, and exploring the world. I didn't think she could do it, but she completed a year of college. And she's working here."

Alexander sat back, his face filling with doubt. He hadn't considered her dreams. Was her enthusiasm for working at the California bank genuine, or was it simply her supporting his? An unsettling doubt prickled him.

"I... I don't know," he admitted, shame tinging his voice. "We haven't spoken of her dreams, only the ones we could build together."

Wallace said, "Mrs. Holt, the poet in my family, would say, 'True love flourishes with shared and individual journeys.' Before proposing, make sure you consider her needs."

Alexander stared at a small nick on the edge of the desk's wood, the carefree certainty he felt before replaced by a newfound determination. He needed to talk to Martha about their future together and her aspirations and dreams. Then, he could take the next step with genuine love and respect, building a future on shared ambitions and a foundation of understanding and individual fulfillment.

"Thank you for the chat. I'll discuss it with Martha at the next picnic. I'll leave you to your paperwork."

Wallace smiled and then nodded as Alexander left. "I wish you the best of luck."

Alexander left the bank and walked to his horse.

"Alexander," yelled Randall from across the road.

Alexander turned and smiled when he saw Randall rushing toward him.

Randall extended his hand.

Alexander shook it heartily and said, "I was just thinking about you."

"Why were you thinking about me?" asked Randall, his tension rising.

Alexander glanced down, embarrassed. "It's about something personal. It's about a woman."

Randall, his tension easing, slapped Alexander's shoulder. "You've met someone? Congratulations."

"Thanks. I hope you don't mind me springing this on you right now. I remember when I was a kid, you always knew what to say to make me feel better, no matter how big...or little my problem was."

"I enjoyed our talks, and I miss them."

"Me too."

Randall chuckled. "Last month, when we talked, I asked you to ride with me to catch up. How about we have a drink and catch up?"

Alexander nodded. "That sounds great."

They walked to the saloon and sat in the corner, away from the noisy patrons.

"So what's bothering you?"

"I met an incredible woman recently, and she's all I think of. I don't know if I'm moving too quickly. I'm in love with her and want to marry her."

Randall winced as a painful memory poked at him. "Whatever you do, don't let her get away. You'll regret it the rest of your life." Randall took a sip of his whiskey. "Look, these days, people take their time. They have a long courtship, and then, if nothing goes wrong, they get married. That's a bunch of nonsense. Don't wait."

Alexander nodded and took a drink of his lemonade.

Randall leaned in. "I've been meaning to ask you. What do you do for the bank? I thought you did bookkeeping."

Alexander lit up bright, like a son bragging to his father. "Yes. I'm a manager, and I do bookkeeping for them. But lately, Mr. Holt has me riding those stagecoaches and protecting them. I'm good at that, but I'd rather be working the books."

Randall grimaced. "That's dangerous work."

CHAPTER FOURTEEN

Heartbroken Thomas

Frank's house was small, with two bedrooms, a large kitchen to fit an iron cook stove, and a table that could easily seat six. Just beyond the kitchen, next to the front door, was another spacious room initially designed for entertaining guests or relaxing. Instead, the room had two chairs, two saddles in various states of disrepair, and tools better suited to a shed or a barn. Frank sat, intently working on one saddle, stitching down the leather that had come loose. The other was perched precariously on the chair opposite him.

"Damnit!" yelled Frank as he tried to push a needle through the thick, dried leather.

Thomas, his hair disheveled, limped out of his bedroom. "What's all the racket?"

"It's about time you get up," said Frank as he continued to wage war against the saddle.

Thomas grimaced and spotted a pitcher of tea on the kitchen windowsill. Frank always made it fresh every morning and let the breeze cool it. "You should take those into town. They know to get the leather wet to get a needle through it." He poured himself some brew.

Frank narrowed his eyes at Thomas. "I know how to fix a damn saddle. My pa taught me how, and he knew how to fix 'em better than anyone." He got a sopping wet cloth from the basin and returned to work.

Thomas tried putting his weight on his injured side and winced. He limped out of the kitchen, sipping his tea. "Your pa did that kind of stuff in the barn. There's not enough room in here for all this junk. You should—"

"This one's almost fixed." Frank pushed a needle through the hole of the now-wet leather. "It was Pa's."

Thomas examined the worn-out saddle. It was in a bad state. "It's lookin' good."

Thomas went onto the porch and grunted in pain as he sat on the bench. His leg wound had healed, but he was left with a nasty soreness that came and went. Frank walked out as Thomas swallowed a pill.

Frank, his forehead creased with concern, glared at Thomas. "You're still using those pills? Didn't you only have enough for a week?"

"When we were at the doctor's office, I helped myself to a few more."

Frank sat across from Thomas. "They make you a little crazy," he said.

Thomas stretched out his leg. "My leg's all healed. Those pills rid me of that darn pain."

"You're depending on those pills too much. The doctor said to take 'em for just a few days. You ain't supposed to keep taking them."

Thomas chuckled. "After just one pill, I was able to drive the wagon to town last week."

"And when you got back, you were in a world of pain, yelling and screaming about killing Alexander. You would have healed sooner if you had stayed in bed longer."

Thomas rolled his eyes.

"There's no telling what trouble that scoundrel has stirred up. Movin' in on my girl."

"Your girl?" asked Frank.

Thomas narrowed his eyes, looked toward Randall's house, and then back to Frank. "Alexander's the one that shot your pa. Randall told me so."

"Don't make this about Randall."

Thomas smirked and drank the rest of his tea. "High time I head into town. Been itching to stretch these legs in the saddle."

Frank's face contorted in astonishment. "Randall said to stay put. Remember?"

Thomas let out a humorless chuckle. "Randall? That poor excuse for an uncle put a bullet in me. I'm not listenin' to him anymore." A spark of defiance ignited in his eyes. "I'm gonna—"

Frank bolted upright, his chair scraping back with a screech. "We can't afford to be seen! Lay low, that's the plan."

Thomas's gaze turned steely. "Plan? I'm gonna go see my girl."

Frank's jaw clenched tight. "What?"

Thomas grinned. "I had a nice little date with Martha the day before Randall shot me. She liked the flowers I brought her. She even told me she wanted to go dancing with me."

"Doggone it, Thomas!"

"Last week, I took the cart to see her and got flowers and everything. But then I saw Alexander flirting with her and asking her out. And she said yes to him!"

Frank shook his head. "You gotta stay away from him. That man is lethal, and he's working with the law. Randall told me he's searching for us."

"Randall killed that couple, not us."

"All of us robbed that coach. They ain't just looking for Randall."

"Does Randall know about Martha?" asked Thomas.

Frank shook his head. "No. You gotta stay away from her. She's liable to turn us in."

"Nah, she won't."

"Are you crazy? She'll give us up in a heartbeat if she finds out who we are. Even more of a reason to steer clear of her."

Thomas chuckled. "She wouldn't do that. She's gonna be my wife someday."

Frank almost choked. "Thomas, I always watch your back, but you're talking crazy. It's those pills…. You have to stay away from her. And, for damn sure, stay away from Alexander. We don't want that son-of-a-bitch skulking around in our business."

Thomas stood. "I ain't stupid. You shouldn't be telling me what to do. You ain't my pa!"

"I know, I ain't your pa. I'd put a bullet in that murderer for killing your ma."

Thomas narrowed his eyes and lunged at Frank. Thomas swung at Frank and caught his jaw. "I've told you a million times. It's Randall's fault that my ma is dead."

Frank crashed into the wall. "What the hell?" Frank shoved Thomas hard. "You ain't right in the head."

Thomas tripped and fell from the porch. When he landed on his sore leg, he let out a howl. He glared at Frank as he struggled to stand, grunting when he put weight on his bad leg. He brushed the dirt from his clothes and limped away. Thomas cursed under his breath at Frank and climbed onto his horse.

Frank's eyes grew wide with concern. "I'm sorry."

"I'm in love with her," Thomas choked out, his eyes full of fire, his heart racing.

Thomas clicked to his horse.

The horse neighed in confusion. She hardly recognized the man she loved so much.

"Get going!" Thomas roared and dug his heels in. A sharp pain traveled up his right leg. "Damnit!" He leaned in and flogged the horse with his reins. The horse lurched forward with a jolt, screeching each time the sharp straps stung her.

Thomas felt the wind blowing into his face, beckoning him to temper his fury. His leg had gone numb as he rode furiously on the road leading to town. A fleeting thought of Martha accosted him. The feeling of calm usually followed when he thought about her, but not this time. Instead, thinking of Martha came with thoughts of Alexander. Adrenaline pulsed through him as he remembered Alexander and Martha chatting outside the bank.

Thomas slapped hard on the reins, his face red with rage, as he nurtured his hatred for Alexander. Thomas kicked hard with his legs. His horse was not used to this sort of abuse. The horse whinnied in anger and lunged forward into a gallop. The horse snorted with rage as they went faster and faster.

Thomas forced his horse cruelly to keep going. When Thomas arrived at the hotel, his horse grunted and gasped for air. Thomas got down from his horse and removed his bag from the saddle. A boy, his eyes narrowed and filled with disdain, stared at him from the porch. Thomas glared at him and tossed him a coin.

"Get my damn horse some water."

The horse had never experienced abuse like this before. She didn't recognize the monster Thomas had become.

Thomas took two pills from his little leather pouch and limped onto the porch. When he reached the door, he turned to see the boy whispering to the horse. The horse whinnied quietly back to the boy as if crying and whimpering about how Thomas had mistreated her. Thomas grunted, then popped the pills in his mouth and went inside.

Soon after, Thomas walked out of the hotel, looking somewhat presentable. His horse was tied to the post outside the hotel, brushed, and calmer than earlier. As Thomas took the leather straps from the post, the horse jumped up and tried to pull away. Thomas yanked hard on the straps. "Settle down, doggone it," yelled Thomas.

A man on the porch shouted at Thomas, "That ain't no way to treat a horse."

"Mind your own business, old man." Thomas drew his gun and aimed it squarely at the man.

When the man heard Thomas's voice, he blinked in surprise. He raised his hands and backed away, his eyes seeing what his ears already knew. "Okay! No need to tell me twice."

Thomas holstered his gun. When Thomas was about to climb up, the horse tried to back away. Thomas snapped the reins, and his horse submitted to her fear.

Thomas climbed on his horse and screamed, "Let's go." With a defiant shudder, the horse refused to budge. When Thomas whipped the horse and dug his heels hard into the horse's side, the bewildered horse lurched forward.

When he arrived at Martha's house, Thomas drew on the reins; the snort from his horse echoed in the stillness. Dismounting felt like wading through molasses. His gaze drifted from the house to the open window, with its gently swaying curtain beckoning him. The knot in his stomach tightened.

Reaching into his saddle pouch, he retrieved a flask that once belonged to his father. He'd found it in the things left behind. Just as when his father used it, the flask was filled with whiskey. Thomas detested the harsh taste, but Frank had assured him long before that the amber liquid steadied nerves. With a grimace, he tipped the flask back and gulped the fiery liquid down.

A wave of dizziness washed over him as the alcohol and the pills he'd swallowed earlier conspired to numb his senses. The world before him appeared to sway, blurring the boundaries of rationality. After stowing the empty flask away, he staggered to the house.

Thomas stepped onto the porch, about to knock on the door. Inside, Martha was humming a tune.

Thomas almost smiled, and then a wave of nausea hit him. It

lasted a few seconds. He shook his head and knocked on the door.

Martha yelled from inside, "Alexander, you're much too early for our picnic. Gertrude hasn't returned from the store. I'll be right there."

Thomas felt his blood boiling and stood taller as all rationality escaped him.

A smiling Martha opened the door. Her smile fled from her face as if she were face to face with a ghost. Thomas was glassy-eyed and had a stubble-filled face.

"Thomas," she said at the tall, unkempt figure on the porch. "I thought—"

He leaned in at her with his eyes crazed with madness. She gasped.

Thomas grabbed her, pulled her toward him, and kissed her.

Surprised, she turned her face away from him and kicked him hard. Memories of the day she first met Thomas at the university rushed back to her. Back then, he had violated her space. This time, he'd gone far beyond that. Thomas fell back, nearly losing his balance. Martha slammed the door shut.

With fire in his eyes, Thomas kicked open the door, and Martha fell to the floor.

She screamed and kicked hard at the door, hoping it would shut him out.

Thomas shoved his foot between the door and its jam, thwarting her feeble attempt to block him from entering.

"What's wrong with you?" she growled.

Grabbing at her arm, he pulled her up like a ragdoll. She scratched at his face, trying to stave off the attack.

He let her go and shoved her hard.

She fell backward and banged her head against the unforgiving floor. Martha was dazed.

He shook his head at her. "I loved you. You told me you'd wait for me. You lied to me. I should have known you'd betray me."

Thomas leaned over her, pinning her arms down.

"I waited for you. You left me here looking like a fool. I was wrong about you. I've moved on to a man with integrity. You're nothing but that scruffy, disgusting vagabond I encountered at the university. My friends were right to beat you," she said as she struggled to free herself.

Thomas leaned closer and stopped a few inches from her face.

Martha recoiled from the foul smell of whiskey mixed with hatred oozing from his mouth. His eyes were more black than blue.

He grinned. "You have your mother's eyes."

"My mother's eyes? What?" she screamed.

Her eyes widened in horror at the realization. Her terror changed to rage as fury ignited her eyes.

Martha jumped to her feet and kicked him hard.

He howled in pain.

She ran to the office to retrieve her father's six-shooter.

He caught up to her and slammed her small frame to the floor.

Her head hit the side of her father's desk as she fell. She was bewildered; her vision blurred as she stood on the brink of consciousness.

Thomas laughed. "Your university school friends aren't here to protect you, and neither is Alexander. You're mine now."

He strolled to the front door and slammed it shut, leaving him and Martha alone in the house.

She struggled to stand.

"You're a monster," Martha screamed.

Thomas's eyes grew wide, his mouth agape. Monster? It occurred to him he had become indistinguishable from Randall.

A hard click from a gun ready to shoot stopped him in his tracks. He turned and leaped back as Martha pulled the trigger, but it was too late.

Outside, the horse grunted a loud whinny when a frightened scream came from the house. It sounded familiar. She looked expectantly at the front door and shuddered at a lone gunshot followed by Thomas's loud grunt. The horse yanked hard at the ropes, holding her prisoner to the post. She gave up after a long silence came from the house. She stared intently at the front door, waiting. She uttered a soft neigh. Her body shuddered, not knowing what would happen next.

Thomas burst out of the front door. The horse jumped in fright and screamed in fear of Thomas.

Thomas tossed the gun he was holding into the bushes and staggered awkwardly down the stairs in a seemingly drunken swagger. Blood was oozing down the right side of his leg.

Thomas snarled at the thought that another pair of expensive pants had been destroyed. He shook his head and climbed up to his saddle. He glanced at the front window curtains, waving gently in the light breeze, and smirked. It was quiet inside. There was no more humming coming from the house.

Thomas clicked at his horse and rode away to his home. Adrenaline pumping through him ate away at his madness. The faster he rode, the quicker the pain spread from his bloody leg to the rest of him. His new wound was inches from the one that had just healed. Twenty minutes later, and just moments from home, his entire body convulsed in pain. He slumped forward in his seat. Dizzy and disoriented, he moaned as his horse continued on the path to his home. He thought he heard Frank's voice.

"Frank," he whispered.

No answer. Thomas slouched as he continued to Frank's house.

"I'm sorry," he muttered. "I didn't mean to…"

His horse neighed in response as she continued on the road home.

She turned onto the path that led to Frank's house.

The road was blurry. Thomas struggled to keep from falling from his horse. As he neared Frank's house, he squinted at a hazy silhouette of two people standing on the porch.

"Frank?" he asked as he tried to get down from his horse. He tumbled to the ground and passed out.

Frank ran to Thomas. Thomas's right leg and the horse's side were drenched in blood. "His damn leg is bleeding. Looks like he got shot again."

Randall was on the porch, shaking his head. "What has that fool done now?"

CHAPTER FIFTEEN

Broken Martha

Gertrude arrived at the house with her groceries. She took her purse, pulled a box from the back of the carriage, and started up the stairs.

Odd, she thought. The front door was ajar.

As she stepped onto the porch, her gaze fell to the floor. There was a trail of blood leading to the door.

She dropped the box and ran inside. Martha lay crumpled on the floor, not moving.

Gertrude rushed to her and shook her. "Wake up."

Martha's breathing was shallow.

Gertrude dashed to the kitchen and returned with a small vial. She opened it and waved it under Martha's nose.

Martha groaned.

An instant later, her eyes flashed open. She scrambled to sit. She trembled with rage as if she'd just woken from a nightmare.

Gertrude said, "Everything's okay now."

"He—" Martha's breathing grew labored as her rage consumed her.

Gertrude, her eyes filled with tears, spoke with a firm tenderness. "Breathe."

Martha, her face stiff, her teeth clenched tight, gazed into Gertrude's eyes.

Gertrude's lips curled up slightly. "You're safe now."

Martha reached for the calmness from Gertrude's tear-filled eyes.

Gertrude smiled.

Martha's rage transformed to anger, and her breathing fell into an even rhythm.

"The threat is gone."

"I'm going to kill him. He took my father's gun," Martha rasped.

"You can worry about that later."

Martha trembled. Her face was etched with hints of revenge.

"Come sit." Gertrude helped Martha to the chair. "Who attacked you?"

Martha narrowed her eyes. Her breathing was steady, but the trembling persisted. "It was Thomas. He was crazed with rage."

Gertrude cocked her head back in shock.

Martha leaned back, her breathing almost regular. "He was glassy-eyed. Something was wrong with him."

A minute later, Gertrude hovered over Martha with a spoonful of sugar and a glass of water.

Martha was shaking her head, a simmering rage returning.

"Martha, take this. It will help you."

She scrunched her face at the sweetness of the crystals and quickly drank the water. Seconds later, her body calmed.

Gertrude retrieved a damp cloth and a small bottle filled with a milky liquid from the kitchen. She handed them to Martha.

"I'm going to get the doctor. You have to clean yourself up. Use the whole bottle if you have to."

Martha held the bottle and cloth, confused.

Gertrude closed the windows and doors and ensured they were all secure. Then, she hurried out the back door, locked it, and sprinted to her horse.

Martha was still in the chair, the damp rag in her hand, looking off into the distance, when Gertrude walked in with the doctor.

Dr. Martin gasped when he saw Martha. She had bruises, and her clothes were torn.

Martha bristled at him as he examined her.

"You've got a terrible bruise on your temple. You must have had a severe blow to have caused that. Who did this to you?"

"No one," Martha grunted. "I'm fine. No cuts, just a few bruises."

Dr. Martin shook his head. "That doesn't make sense." He handed Gertrude a bottle of dark liquid.

Martha rolled her eyes.

"Have her take one spoonful of this tonic each day for the next seven days. It will help her."

Gertrude patted Martha's arm. "Yes, doctor."

He glanced at Martha, "I'll notify the sheriff."

Martha sat up tall. "No!"

The doctor cocked his head back as if a strong wind had blasted him.

Gertrude quickly led the doctor out to the porch. "Please be discreet. This sort of thing could destroy her reputation."

He grimaced. "But Gertrude—"

Gertrude glared at him. "I'll tell the bank she's bedridden and won't return to work until she recovers."

Alexander arrived a few minutes later than he had wanted for their picnic. He meant to bring flowers but had a lead on one of the stagecoach robbers. Earlier, the Swanson's stagecoach driver sat outside the hotel. He recognized the voice of one of the robbers. He didn't know his name but could certainly recognize him now. He got an honest, good look at him while the man pointed a gun at him.

He got down from his horse and noticed the serene trees surrounding Martha's house. They stood like sentries standing guard around her home. A gentle breeze rustled through the leaves, causing shimmering shadows on the ground as the sun pierced through tiny openings in the dense foliage.

He tapped on the door. The window next to the porch was closed. Usually, they left the front and back one open to allow a cross-breeze through the house. They would close those windows whenever they left the house.

He knocked a little louder and heard footsteps rushing to the door.

Gertrude opened the door, stepped out, and quickly closed the door behind her.

Alexander's tentative smile faded slowly.

"Is Martha ready for the picnic?" asked Alexander.

"I'm sorry. Martha can't see you today. She's indisposed because she's fallen ill."

Alexander's eyes widened with concern. "Is there anything that I can do?"

Gertrude sat in the chair on the porch and pointed to the one across from her.

"Please sit down. We need to talk."

Alexander's face went pale as he sat.

"What's wrong? Is Martha alright?" He glanced at the front door, hoping to see Martha standing there.

"She'll be okay. I promise. We need to discuss the stagecoach robbery."

Alexander nodded.

"What have you found out?" asked Gertrude.

Alexander cleared his throat. "It appears that three men were involved. The driver said he didn't see them but heard three distinct voices. One sounded older, and the other two were younger. He believes he encountered one of the younger ones."

Gertrude moved uncomfortably. "When?"

"This morning. I just finished talking to the driver. That's why I'm late."

She took a deep breath and let it out all at once. "One of those young ones attacked Martha today."

"What?"

"He's the same man who visited the house shortly after her parents died."

"Can you describe him?"

"Yes. He's about your size, with light brown hair and blue eyes. Martha said he smelled of whiskey and was limping. She said that she shot him in the leg, and then they struggled for the gun. Judging from all the blood in the entryway, I'd say she got him good."

She handed Alexander a piece of paper. "I wrote more of what she told me and what I remembered about him."

Alexander read the notes. "This is very detailed." The description of the man seemed familiar to him.

"Martha wants to kill him."

"I can understand why," he said.

Gertrude's brow jumped. "She's a proud and brave woman. She suffered through this ordeal, but she's not one to let this bring her down. She's angry, and that's great."

"Martha knows that I love her. Right?" He sat up taller and glanced at the door. "Please tell her that I want to see her."

"I'm sorry, but she needs to be alone for a little while. Could you tell Mr. Holt she won't be at work for a week or two?"

His face was etched with pain. "Yes, of course."

"Thank you."

Alexander, ever the problem solver, leaned in. "Perhaps an outing away from here would be helpful. I can pick you both up for a picnic next Sunday."

"I know you mean well, but Martha needs some time."

Alexander's smile soured. "That's a whole week away, plenty of time to recover. An outing will do her good. And besides, she's a fighter, and nothing will hold her back."

"You're right. Martha is a fighter. She'll need time to heal from this assault. I'll talk to her, and I'll let you know. I promise."

Alexander nodded, a hopeful smile aching to show. "She's an extraordinary woman."

"Yes. She certainly is."

Alexander stood, pulled a letter from his pocket, and handed it to Gertrude.

"Please give this to her. I was going to surprise her with it at the picnic. Tell her that I love her."

"I will," Gertrude said.

Alexander went to his horse, glanced back at the house, and hesitated briefly before leaving.

Gertrude took a deep breath and exhaled slowly. She went inside, closed the door, and smiled at Martha sitting beside the porch window.

"Did you hear?" Gertrude gave Martha the letter.

"Yes. I heard everything."

Martha tore open the envelope, her eyes sparkling with anticipation. As she read the short letter, a playful smile bloomed on her face. She glanced up at Gertrude.

"I love Alexander with all of my heart. I feel safe with him. Martha wiped her tears away and cleared her throat. "Maybe we should go on that picnic."

"Child, I can see that nothing will hold you back from your destiny. We'll see how you feel in a couple of days."

Martha held out her arms. "These bruises will take a few days to fade. I'm sure I can hide them."

CHAPTER SIXTEEN

Picnic Surprise

On the morning after the assault, Gertrude hurried to the house after feeding the chickens. As she set the eggs on the kitchen table, she heard a noise from the front door.

"You should be in bed, Martha," she yelled in the direction of the noise.

There was no answer. She marched to the front door and discovered an envelope on the floor next to it. She rushed to the window and saw a plume of dust settling on the ground on the trail leading away from the house to the main road. She half-smiled and looked at the envelope. On its face was written: "My dearest Martha, the light of my life." It was from Alexander.

Gertrude was worried. Martha needed time to recover. Gertrude held the envelope up to the light. Inside, she could see the outline of a folded paper filled with words she couldn't make out. Was it wise for Martha to become emotionally involved with Alexander while she was recovering? Martha was strong, but she had never experienced such a brutal attack before. Gertrude got lost in her thoughts and worries, and then she chuckled. Martha is a fighter, and it's apparent that she's in love with Alexander. This letter most certainly expresses Alexander's love and devotion for Martha. Gertrude let out a sigh. "What was I thinking? This is exactly what Martha needs in her recovery," she muttered. Grinning, she rushed to Martha's room.

Martha enthusiastically read part of the letter aloud to Gertrude.

"Gertrude, listen to this. 'I adore you and will always support you, for you are stronger than I could ever be....' Isn't he wonderful?"

"What else did he say?"

Martha chuckled. "I'm not reading you the rest. It's gushy. He wrote 'I love you' twenty-two times in total. I counted them twice. He even scribbled it around the edge of the paper like a frame surrounding his words."

Gertrude smiled. "You counted them?"

Martha laughed. "I'm a bookkeeper. I like to add numbers. What can I say?"

"Have you decided to go to the picnic?"

"Yes. We have to go." Martha held out her arms. "The bruises will be mostly gone by Sunday. I'll wear my hair down to hide the bruise on my temple. Powder will take care of the rest." A brief thought of Thomas stabbed at her, and then a hint of a smile formed on her lips as she narrowed her eyes ever so slightly. "Not even a lower-class thug like Thomas will dissuade me from pursuing happiness."

Gertrude blinked with concern at Martha.

Martha noticed. "Don't worry, Gertrude. You know about my little garden of dreams and ambitions. I cultivate it to nurture my plans for the future. Yesterday, it was ravaged. I thought it was destroyed. Instead, it's grown a little. I'm making room for Alexander's love and adding some space for justice."

"Oh dear," Gertrude said.

"I'm going to be fine. Now, let's get on with our day. I need to practice my shooting."

Gertrude patted Martha on the back, pleased that Martha was pushing forward. "You are so much like your mother. I'll tell Alexander we'll be ready for a nice picnic on Sunday. Yesterday, he was quite insistent about us going."

The following day, and each day until Sunday, a letter from Alexander arrived under the front door. Martha laughed and giggled as she read sections of them aloud to Gertrude. The house was once again filled with laughter, singing, and humming. Gertrude was happy that Alexander had been the brightness that guided Martha back to her mighty self.

When Sunday came, rain threatened to cancel the outing. Martha and Gertrude sat on the porch, relaxing.

Martha stood and walked to the edge of the porch. "The ground isn't even wet. If the showers return, we can eat in the gazebo." Martha turned back to Gertrude. "I've been looking forward to this day, and nothing will keep us from this picnic. I must see Alexander. I won't wait another day."

Gertrude smiled at Martha. "You're right. The weather will do." Gertrude's jaw dropped as something caught her eye. A giant plume of dust was coming toward them. "It's that little stagecoach again, and Alexander is early."

Martha squinted at the approaching coach. "Yes. That's him. He's up on top with the driver."

Gertrude leaped to her feet. "I'm not ready."

Martha burst out laughing. "Neither am I."

They almost collided with each other as they rushed inside.

Minutes later, Martha and Gertrude ran out of the house and landed on the porch. The coach was next to the stairs. Alexander smiled as he jumped down. He hesitated briefly, noticing generous amounts of white powder on their clothes. Gertrude's hair was held tight to her head, and Martha's hair was draped gracefully over her shoulders. The last time he'd seen Martha, it was wrapped tightly around her head.

"Good morning, ladies. Beautiful as always."

Gertrude glanced at Martha, wondering why Martha was uncharacteristically quiet. Gertrude's eyes grew wide. A white powder was splattered on Martha's neck and dress. She saw it on herself, and her eyes grew wide with shock. She tried to brush the powder away. She feigned a smile at Alexander. "You're early. How considerate of you."

Alexander nodded and smiled at Martha, "Did you get my letters?"

Gertrude tugged at Martha's arm and turned to Alexander. "Yes, she did. Would you excuse us for just one moment?"

Gertrude pulled a surprised Martha toward the door.

"Gertrude?"

Gertrude pointed at the powder. Martha gasped and scrambled into the house with Gertrude.

Outside, Alexander stood confused until their conversation carried through the open window. "Gertrude, I look foolish with all this powder!"

Alexander chuckled. He heard Gertrude and Martha continue to talk to each other in loud whispers until one of them shut the window. A few minutes later, a grinning Gertrude walked out carrying a picnic basket. Martha rushed out and then locked the door. She peeked over at the window and then caught up to Gertrude.

Gertrude winked at Alexander and handed him the basket. Then she yelled to the driver, "We got food for you, too."

The driver grinned and tipped his hat. "Thank ya' ma'am."

Gertrude shook her head. "Ma'am?" She stepped inside and seated herself. She waited several seconds and wondered why Martha had not yet entered. She peeked out and chuckled.

Alexander and Martha were in an awkward, speechless exchange. Martha avoided Alexander's gaze as he tried speaking to her. Alexander's mouth was open, about to say something.

Gertrude cleared her throat. "Let's go before the rain comes. We don't have all day. I told Agnes that we'd be there today."

Alexander smiled at Gertrude. "Agnes?"

Martha said, "Agnes Jenkins is Gertrude's best friend. She was close to my mother, too."

"Oh. I've seen Mrs. Jenkins and her husband at the bank." Alexander extended his hand to Martha. "She's a person with extreme opinions. Mr. Jenkins is as quiet as a mouse."

"Let's go!" said Gertrude.

Martha chuckled and then nodded at Alexander. Her anxiety melted away, and her face warmed with a broad smile. She took his hand and entered the coach. Alexander noticed a faded bruise on her arm and said nothing.

Alexander followed her inside, carrying the basket. He sat next to Martha and then signaled the driver to go.

"Finally!" said Gertrude, her face filled with mischievous glee.

Gertrude did all the talking as they went. Alexander and Martha held hands, affectionately squeezing each other's hands as they listened to Gertrude.

When they arrived, they set the food on a table near the gazebo, knowing they could move everything into the structure if the rain dared to visit.

Gertrude served the driver a plate of food.

His eyes lit up bright. "Thank you. I'd better get back to the coach."

Gertrude smiled and handed him some apple slices. "These are for your horses."

He winked at Gertrude and then sauntered back to the coach.

Gertrude giggled. She watched him walk away for a few seconds, admiring his physique. He was tall and slender and reminded her of her husband, John.

As they ate, they chatted about everyday things. Gertrude didn't want to discuss anything that might upset Martha, so the conversations were more subdued than usual. Never once did they mention the assault or Thomas. Their most discussed topic was the weather.

Mid-sentence, Gertrude gasped and then squinted up at the sky. "Is that a drop that I felt?"

Martha giggled. "It looks like it might clear up."

Gertrude looked sideways at Martha. She was used to having a picnic on a sunny day, and overcast days reminded her of gloom and doom.

Gertrude put on her sweater. "You're probably right." She rummaged through the wicker basket, her movements methodical. Reaching in, she retrieved a freshly baked apple pie and a stack of mismatched plates. She cut the pie in half with a practiced hand and then cut four wedges from one side. "That should do the trick," she announced with a hint of pride in her voice.

Martha carefully transferred a slice onto a plate and slid it toward Alexander. She served herself a slice and another for Gertrude. Martha looked at the fourth slice, puzzled.

Gertrude chuckled. "That's for the driver." She held up an empty plate. "Serve that one up." Gertrude took the pie to the driver and returned a few seconds later.

Alexander eagerly tucked into the dessert, his eyes widening with each bite. "Wow," he exclaimed between mouthfuls. "This is the best apple pie I've ever had. It's delicious."

Martha served Alexander a second serving of the dessert. "It's famous around here. Her friends often ask her to prepare one for their church socials. No one has been able to bake one that is nearly as good. She creates her works of art in the kitchen better than anyone."

Gertrude nodded. She was pleased that Martha was more relaxed. A wave of relief washed over her. Gertrude began chatting nonstop about the latest town gossip. Alexander and Martha seemed comfortable with each other as they listened attentively to Gertrude.

After twenty minutes, Alexander shot up to his feet, about to say something, and then sat down again. Martha glanced at Alexander and half-smiled.

Gertrude took off her sweater as the sun peeked through the clouds. "My goodness, the weather has made a beautiful transformation."

Martha nodded. Gertrude spoke faster as she jumped from subject to subject. Alexander leaned forward and raised his hand as he tried to talk, but Gertrude wouldn't yield. Alexander, in a most abrupt manner, cleared his throat.

Gertrude stopped talking, shook her head, and then turned to Alexander, grinning. "What's the matter? If you've got something to say, spit it out."

Alexander gasped. He hadn't intended to be rude to Gertrude. He pointed to the end of the park, where he saw an old lady sitting with some young children. "Isn't that Mrs. Jenkins over there? Weren't you looking to chat with her?"

Gertrude rolled her eyes and then laughed. "If you wanted to be alone with your lovebird, why didn't you just say so?" She winked at Martha and wandered off to gossip with Agnes.

Martha giggled.

Awe washed over Alexander, his gaze fixed on Martha. At that moment, she radiated a light that eclipsed everything else, a precious treasure beyond compare.

Martha turned to Alexander. She blinked, her face full of surprise when she saw him staring at her. A hint of a smile started on her lips.

"Gertrude is quite well aware of your intentions. From your letters, she knows how you feel about me."

Alexander gasped and then blinked repeatedly. "She read them?"

"No," she chuckled. "I recited only a few choice lines to her, saving the juicy parts for myself."

"That's good." He looked down. "I wanted to put something more in my last letter, but writing words on paper would never do." His face flushed red with embarrassment. His voice tightened as he tried to calm his nerves. "I had to speak to you about an important matter." Alexander moved uncomfortably from side to side.

"Has something gone awry?" she asked. All of a sudden, he seemed nervous and unsure of himself. Until now, everything was going so well. What could be wrong on such a beautiful day as this? Dread reared its ugly head. "Am I being let go from the bank?"

"No, of course not. Please, let's sit for a moment. I have to ask you something."

"Oh dear." Her stomach was tight as she shuffled to the bench and sat.

He sat next to her and reached for her hand. He was silent as he gazed into her large, brown eyes.

Doing his best not to lose his nerve, he asked, "I want to ask you a question. But first, I have to tell you something." He fidgeted in his seat. "I sometimes work with the Law to safeguard the bank's stagecoaches."

"Yes, I know. Mr. Holt told me that already."

Alexander nodded. "Yeah, but I enjoy bookkeeping at the bank much more."

"There have been one or two occasions where I've corrected your balance sheets. I suppose I could help you a bit in that regard."

He winced.

Alexander glanced downward and took a deep breath.

"I failed you twice. I should have been there for you—"

She looked crooked at him.

A tear trickled down her cheek, fearing that he wanted to discuss her parents' stagecoach robbery. "I want to focus on the future. I don't want to talk about the past right now."

She wiped the lone tear from her face and smiled. Her face brightened. "It's time to be happy. I love my parents and miss them dearly. They continue to live in my heart." Whenever she thought of them, she couldn't help thinking about getting justice, too. A chilling thought of killing Thomas fluttered away— but not too far.

Martha rubbed her arms as if trying to warm herself. "I'm anxious to return to work and go on more picnics on the weekends with you. There's so much more living to do."

A surge of courage grew within Alexander. "I wanted to talk to you about the future, too."

Calmness embraced her as she stared lovingly into Alexander's eyes and relaxed into a comfortable smile.

Alexander took Martha's hand, leaned in, and said, "Will you marry me?"

"What?" Martha's smile disappeared. "Marry?"

She cocked her head back in surprise. "I wasn't expecting this. I thought you and Mr. Holt had discussed a promotion for me at the bank. Or that you were thinking of giving me some of your accounts so you could have more time to protect the stagecoaches."

Alexander glanced down, almost defeated, and after a second, he smiled at Martha.

"You deserve a promotion, and I would be more than happy to transfer some of my accounts to you. I know you'd do much better with them than I would."

"Really?" Martha blinked several times. She hesitated as she realized that Alexander had just proposed. Her brows raised in surprise.

"I'm sorry, surprises overwhelm me right now. Everything's been changing so fast. You were my anchor when I was adrift, and your letters gave me the strength to stay true to myself." She locked eyes with Alexander and nodded. "Now, let's start over. I'm ready now. Ask your question."

Alexander giggled. He felt like the suitor, Pierre, in that play they'd seen: "A Husband to Order."

"Will you marry me?"

Martha's smile grew wide. This time, those four words exploded like fireworks in the sky. She thought about how proud her mother would be of her. What about college? What about her garden of plans? What about her future? All those questions came rushing at her. Her life kept turning in new directions. She knew that she'd found the love of her life. Gertrude told her on their first outing, "Only God knows what the future holds. Have faith." A flash of vulnerability she had never seen flickered across Alexander's deep brown eyes, stirring something tender within

Martha. "I want to say yes. But—"

"But what? I know what you went through with…" He didn't want to mention anything about the man who had attacked her. "I assure you the law will mete out justice to that scoundrel."

She tilted her head, confused. How much had Gertrude told him, she thought.

Alexander kissed her hand. "I want to marry you. We'll face the future together."

His heartfelt warmth washed over her. It was delicious. As she moved closer to Alexander, a tinge of doubt crept into her thoughts. She brushed away the disgusting images of Thomas as they tried to squelch her chance at happiness.

She hugged Alexander.

Gertrude cleared her throat, her face painted with worry. "What's going on here?"

Alexander and Martha jumped, surprised Gertrude was standing across from them.

Martha smiled through her tears at Gertrude. "Alexander has asked me to marry him."

Gertrude's face softened. "What was your answer?"

"I said… I said—"

A brilliant flash of lightning, followed by a booming thunderclap, blasted from above.

Martha almost glared at the sky, annoyed that Nature had dared to interrupt her moment of indecisiveness. A jolt of adrenaline pumped through her body, and her thoughts glistened with clarity. She locked eyes with Alexander and said, "Alexander, I love you. I would be honored to marry you."

Her past faded as she focused on the here and now. The fresh smell of the coming rain and the rumblings of the sky brought her a tingling sensation of hope. The present had crept up on her, allowing her to re-engage with her dreams.

Gertrude pointed to the sky. "Even the heavens applaud you."

Martha giggled with delight.

"We've got to go," Alexander said. "Looks like a thunderstorm is coming."

Alexander escorted the women to the coach. Gertrude stopped by the entrance, offered her hand, and waited for Alexander to open the door. Alexander gladly obliged. Gertrude seated herself in the middle of the rear bench. Martha entered next and sat on one side of the front seat. Alexander sat beside Martha. She reached for his hand and held it tight.

Gertrude quietly contemplated the bliss that Martha and Alexander had found. Gertrude had long dreamed about this day for Martha. Martha's mother and Gertrude had often discussed it. Years before, Gertrude had told Martha's mother that she would be delighted to help Martha with the wedding details. Ideas exploded with possibilities inside Gertrude's mind. "Where shall we have the grand event? Maybe we could have it at the house like your parents did."

Martha turned to Gertrude, and a flicker of something unspoken passed between them. A momentary glance at Alexander sent a thrill through her. It occurred to her that her 'happily-ever-after' had arrived.

But then, a dark thought, a fleeting image of Thomas, brushed against the edges of her joy. A shiver rippled down her spine, and she ruthlessly tossed the rubbish away.

As if sensing her momentary unease, Alexander gently squeezed her hand. Martha responded with a radiant grin, a surge of inspiration coursing through her veins. Unlike anything she'd ever known, she felt a surge of energy, a potent mix of newfound hope and a determination to leave the shadows behind.

Alexander leaned in. "Why not have the ceremony at the church across the road from the park?"

Gertrude's smile faded.

Martha quickly devised a solution to please everyone: "We can have the reception at the house. There, we would have the room to entertain all our friends."

Gertrude smiled, "That's an excellent idea! That's the perfect place for a grand celebration! Perhaps we could—"

"Gertrude, we'll have to make a few adjustments to Mother's wedding dress. It would be a bit too loose for me as it is."

Martha continued with the dress, shoes, flowers, and other ideas. Now and then, Gertrude would try unsuccessfully to get a word in, but Martha chattered away every detail of the plans. It became clear to Gertrude that Martha was intent on taking care of all of the details herself and that Gertrude would manage the reception. The one exception was the cake.

"The cake needs to be half chocolate and half yellow. Alexander's favorite is chocolate, and mine is yellow. And, Gertrude, I know that you like both."

Gertrude nodded, and before she could speak, Martha continued about the wedding ceremony.

Gertrude leaned back and smiled proudly.

Periodically, Martha would ask something, and either Gertrude or Alexander would nod in agreement, depending on who the question was directed to. Occasionally, Alexander said, "Yes, dear," or "I like that."

Alexander enjoyed Martha's enthusiasm. He was very excited about the wedding. He loved Martha and didn't care too much where or how they would marry. He wanted to be married to the woman that he loved with all of his might. She was the love of his life. He thought about the trauma she had experienced with that robber and was committed to helping her through it. Together, he thought they could get through anything.

CHAPTER SEVENTEEN

Peaceful Union

The sun shone brightly as Thomas and Frank sat on the porch of Frank's house. They prodded each other with jokes and riddles.

Randall rode up fast and furious and stopped next to the hitching post. He jumped down from his horse. He ran up the steps, two at a time, grabbed Thomas tight by his shirt collar, and shoved him against the wall.

Thomas gasped and let out a squeal.

Randall's face was bright red, the veins in his neck bulging. "I just got back from town, and Alexander told me that a man named Thomas attacked a woman. Not just any woman, but the daughter of that couple from the coach we robbed. Didn't I tell you to stay out of the city?"

Thomas, his eyes swimming in guilt, squirmed under Randall's grip.

Randall, with slits for eyes, growled at Frank. "Thomas here threatened the stagecoach driver." Randall's nostrils flared. "I thought you killed him."

Frank cowered and narrowed his eyes at Thomas.

Randall leaned into Thomas and tightened his grasp. "You're just like your pa!"

Thomas struggled to breathe as Randall's bloodshot eyes bore into him. Thomas couldn't avoid Randall's foul breath.

A hint of a smile cracked through the side of Randall's mouth. "Alexander plans to marry that woman you wronged."

With a grunt, he flung Thomas to the floor; a thud echoed when Thomas's head hit the wooden planks. Randall's gaze burned into the crumpled form lying at Frank's feet. Randall shook his head and then went inside, slamming the door hard. Thomas scrambled for the door, but Frank's hand closed around his arm, anchoring him in place.

Thomas's jaw clenched, his eyes spitting fire as they darted to Frank. With a surge of adrenaline, he wrenched his arm free and sank onto the chair, his head shaking. He glanced away toward the road. "Martha can't marry that good-for-nothing scoundrel."

Frank looked incredulously at Thomas. "Why would you attack her? I thought you liked her."

The fire faded from Thomas's eyes. "Things got hazy after she shot me. I think after we struggled for the gun, she wasn't moving anymore."

Frank grunted. "You're lucky she ain't dead. That's for sure." Frank shook his head and gritted his teeth. "It's those damn pills. I told you they make you crazy. Nothing would have happened if you stopped using them."

Thomas scoffed. "They get rid of the pain."

"They do a lot more than that!"

"That Alexander is a—"

A flicker of anger danced in Frank's eyes, and the corners of his mouth twitched in frustration. "You don't want to tangle with that man. Randall told us to keep away from him."

Thomas rolled his eyes. "Randall is afraid of him. You know that Alexander shot your pa. Right?"

"I know." Frank stood stone-faced, his eyes tainted with pain, his breathing shallow. "I have a reason to shoot Alexander dead. But—"

"You ain't gonna kill Alexander," shouted Randall as he walked out. He was holding a glass of whiskey. "We're moving back to my place in Middletown. We won't be coming back anytime soon. The driver he threatened recognized Thomas's voice. He's certain Thomas was one of the three robbers of Swanson's coach. Sooner or later, thanks to Thomas, they'll catch up to us."

Frank's heart skipped a beat, and then he glared accusingly at Thomas. "I thought we were okay. Doggone it, Thomas. I like it here."

Randall shook his head at Thomas. "We'll join up with my gang."

Thomas wrinkled his face like a sullen child. "I'm not leaving here."

Randall spat to the ground. "You ain't got a choice. There is no sense in giving up our freedom just because you were careless.

What the hell were you thinking?"

Thomas scoffed.

Frank stood between Thomas and Randall. Frank poked Thomas. "We have to do this."

Gertrude waved goodbye. Martha relaxed her face as several old women left in their buggies. She'd held a smile far too long. "I thought they'd never leave. Your friends went on and on about how I was so fortunate to have landed such a handsome man. Asking me so many questions about him."

Gertrude nodded. "Us old women still appreciate a fine-looking man."

Martha massaged her cheeks. "They were forward and unduly curious about my affairs."

"When you're as old as the hills, there's no time to be subdued or timid."

"I'm grateful that they offered to get the chairs and tables from the church for the reception."

"Yes. And don't forget that they are friends with the town's string quartet. And they assured me that they would perform at the reception. Now, let's figure out where we're going to put everything. How about the barn?"

A minute later, Martha opened the side door. A blast of warm, moist air rushed at them. Martha held her nose. "Oh! That smell. This will never do."

Gertrude quickly shut the door. "Yup. There's plenty of space in there, but not someplace people in fancy clothes would want to do any celebrating."

Martha laughed. "I think I know the perfect place. What about the clearing right behind the house? It's close to the kitchen."

They walked to the back of the house, which was flat, large, and shaded by two giant oak trees.

Martha pointed to the gazebo in the yard's far corner. "The band can perform in there." Off to the right of it stood a tall, covered structure with a weathered, wooden floor ideal for dancing. "I remember when Mother would have her dinner parties out here. This is where my mother would insist we have the reception if she were here."

"I'll get the neighborhood boys to clean it up a bit. Lord knows when it was last used."

"Yeah, that's because Mother lost interest in having gatherings outside. She preferred small, intimate gatherings inside."

Gertrude chuckled and then leaned in toward Martha. Gertrude did this when she was about to gossip. "It had something to do with those gossipy old ladies here earlier."

"Really?"

"Yes. Your mother didn't care much for a bunch of cackling women who shamelessly gossiped about the other guests at the party. Soon, her other friends stopped coming. They'd make up excuses and avoid her parties."

Martha's face shrank with concern. "That's not good."

"Your mother set them straight. They're still gossipy, but they're not mean-spirited anymore."

"That's a relief."

Gertrude said, "Let's get back to the planning." Gertrude surveyed the area.

Martha stared intently at Gertrude. She knew that within a moment, Gertrude would have everything accounted for.

"Okay, Gertrude. Let's have it."

Gertrude walked to the clearing outside the kitchen door. "This is where we can set up the tables to hold the food and the cake."

Martha nodded. "That makes sense. It would make bringing the feast from the kitchen easy."

Gertrude said, "With the band performing in the gazebo, the music will carry nicely to the guests. It won't be too loud for them to converse with each other."

Gertrude's eyes darted about as she sequentially tapped each finger in her left hand to her thumb. "We've got the band, the dancing, and the food. The guests' tables will be between the food and the band. Have I missed anything?"

"What about the decorations?"

"I've already taken care of that, the food, the cake, and your dress."

"Oh, Gertrude. You are the best."

* * *

On the wedding day, the backyard was transformed into a beautiful setting. There was a light, cool breeze, but not enough to disturb the tablecloths on the tables. The women who arranged to get the table and chairs from the church were preparing the food that would soon be moved from the kitchen to the area outside. The band set up their musical instruments in the gazebo. One of the performers took his violin to the church and waited to perform a song Martha had picked for her walk down the aisle.

In a modest room inside the church, Gertrude was helping Martha get ready. Martha was wearing her mother's beautiful, billowy, white wedding dress. After Gertrude took in the waistline, some fabric was left over. She managed to create several delicately stitched flowers from them. She added life to them by stitching small scraps of colorful fabric at their centers. Gertrude laced them beautifully onto the dress. Around her neck, she wore her grandmother's necklace.

Martha held a bouquet that Gertrude picked herself from the garden. Martha's hair was braided and carefully pinned atop her head. Wispy ringlets of hair softly caressed her temples and lay delicately in front of her ears. She exuded elegance with an air of nobility and the softness of femininity.

Gertrude smiled as her eyes fell on Martha. "You are the very definition of beauty."

"Thank you." A lone tear ran down Martha's cheek. "I miss my parents, and walking down the aisle today without my father will not be easy."

"You don't have to worry," Gertrude said, pointing to Martha's chest. "They are living right there in your heart."

Martha hugged Gertrude.

"Let's go," said Gertrude.

Martha stood up and almost lost her balance. She reached for Gertrude to steady herself. "Oh dear."

"You okay?"

Martha placed her hand on her stomach. "I've been feeling lightheaded the last few mornings. I think it's my nerves."

Gertrude narrowed her brows with concern, and then her eyes drifted to Martha's midsection. "I'll go get the doctor."

"No. I'm fine. Whatever it was has passed."

Gertrude's face grew thin. "Come sit for a moment."

"I don't want to be late for my wedding. I'm okay now. I'm sure it was my nerves."

"Okay," Gertrude said. She reached for Martha's hand.

Martha and Gertrude walked hand in hand to the back of the church. From there, they could see the pews, all filled with guests. Wallace, the bank owner, sat with several wealthy customers, including Charles and Victoria Adams, the owners of the account Martha managed. Dr. Martin and his family were next to Agnes in the front row. Agnes saved the empty chair to her right for Gertrude.

Martha winked at Alexander. He stood up front, swaying to and fro as he tapped his foot repeatedly. He was skilled at hiding his impatience, but not from her.

Thrilled and excited that he was about to marry the love of his life, Alexander caught a glimpse of Martha at the back of the church. Overwhelmed with nervous anticipation, he checked the time. "Right on time," he muttered. Calm descended over him as Martha smiled at him.

Martha brought the bouquet closer to her chest. "I'm ready."

Gertrude motioned to the musician and then took Martha's hand. The delicate music started. Martha and Gertrude began their slow march to the altar.

Martha focused on Alexander. He stood like an expectant schoolchild who was obediently awaiting his prize. Her gaze floated to the sea of smiling faces seated in the pews. Martha imagined her feet moving through molasses. She whispered to Gertrude, "We're moving way too slowly. Alexander's foot is tapping like crazy."

Gertrude's head bobbed up and down quickly, and the two doubled their pace.

Alexander smiled at his beautiful bride as she approached, slow at first and moving faster.

Alexander's brows went up as Martha stepped beside him and took her hand.

They faced the minister as the music faded to silence.

The minister smiled. "Let's begin."

Martha and Alexander nodded in unison.

The minister found his place in the book he was holding. "Alexander, do you love Martha?"

Alexander, his face flushed with love, smiled. "Yes, very much."

The minister asked, "Will you love and care for her, in sickness and health, forever and ever?"

Alexander said, "Yes, of course."

The minister turned to Martha. "Martha, do you love Alexander?"

"Yes, more than life itself."

The minister asked, "Will you love and care for him, in sickness and health, forever and ever?"

Martha's eyes got teary. "Oh yes. Yes!"

The minister stopped, distracted by loud sobbing coming from the pews. He stifled a chuckle. Martha turned toward the disturbance. Gertrude and Agnes were each wiping tears away.

Martha chuckled at them and felt the warmth of Gertrude's heart wash over her. She winked at Gertrude and turned back to Alexander.

The minister continued the ceremony. "Alexander, do you take Martha as your wife?"

"I do."

"Martha, do you take Alexander as your husband?"

"I do."

Alexander cleared his throat.

The minister turned to Alexander. "You wanted to say something more?"

"Yes. Just one thing." He blinked at Martha. "Together, we can face adversity with unity to keep our lovely family safe."

Martha nodded, her eyes moist with tears.

"I now pronounce you husband and wife, as God and these fine people bear witness. You may kiss your wife."

Martha stepped up and kissed Alexander.

The guests cheered and clapped.

Mr. and Mrs. Johnson faced the guests and walked from the church to the waiting carriage.

* * *

Everything was ready when the guests arrived at Martha's house for the reception. Over a hundred people were there, mainly wealthy bank customers. Everyone was anxiously awaiting the happy couple.

When Alexander and Martha arrived, there was a grand applause. All were quick to walk over and congratulate them. After fifteen minutes, Alexander noticed Martha seemed overwhelmed by the many well-wishers. Gertrude told him Martha hadn't eaten all day, and her excitement kept her awake the night before. Alexander raised his right hand to get the crowd's attention. Everyone went quiet. He was a little surprised that even the band stopped playing. He yelled, "Thank you, all. Now, let's eat!"

The guests wasted no time sitting at the tables while Gertrude and her friends served them generous portions of the tasty feast. There was chicken, vegetables, bread, and much more. Gertrude was proud that everyone was enjoying the food and having a good time.

Gertrude smiled as her gaze followed Alexander and Martha.

Alexander escorted Martha to the clearing near the band. The band played a delicate, whimsical tune as the night's last song. It was Martha's favorite. Alexander and Martha danced to that song in each other's arms.

Alexander gazed adoringly at his wife. As the music ebbed to its happy conclusion, Martha hugged Alexander.

Alexander whispered into Martha's ear, "I love you."

"I love you, too! Happiness belongs to us now."

Gertrude walked up behind them. "Indeed it does, you lovebirds. It's time for this grand celebration of joy to settle down for the night. The guests are leaving."

Alexander peered into Martha's eyes. "I love you."

"I now know what true happiness is."

Alexander kissed Martha's cheek. "Shall we?" Alexander extended his arm to Martha.

Martha walked briskly with Alexander toward the front of the house, resting her head on his shoulder as they went.

They stopped next to the stairs.

Martha said, "I'm so happy."

"Me too."

Gertrude rushed past them and opened the door. She held the door wide open and bowed toward the happy couple. Alexander chuckled and led Martha up the stairs to the door. He reached behind and picked her up.

Martha laughed with glee as Alexander carried her inside.

CHAPTER EIGHTEEN

A Little Change is Coming

Martha returned to work a week after getting married. At first, Martha was overwhelmed with the extra accounts from Alexander she'd been assigned. After organizing them and making minor corrections, they became less challenging.

Now, with less bookkeeping work, Alexander rode with the stagecoaches twice weekly. He expected the Friday payroll shipment to be the most difficult, but other than an occasional bandit or two attempting a robbery, they ran with little trouble.

Their day began at seven-thirty sharp with a shared journey to the bank in a dilapidated old wagon Alexander kept running. It was a slow ride filled with easy conversation. Occasionally, they would arrive late because of a broken wheel, axle, or countless other issues with that conveyance. Martha loved it because it used to belong to her father. Alexander maintained it as best he could, but after three months of tinkering to keep it working, he gave up.

"I think we need a new wagon," she said. "This isn't safe anymore."

Alexander jumped at the opportunity and bought Martha a new buggy. The following morning, he surprised her when he brought it to the front of the house.

When she walked out, she laughed. "Alexander! What have you done?"

"I never got you a wedding present.... Surprise!"

Martha rushed over and climbed in. "I like the low step-in height."

"It's the latest model." Alexander sat on the passenger side. "She's all yours."

Martha shook the reins and clicked to the horse. They lurched forward, and the horse launched into a graceful gallop. The ground blurred beneath them.

Alexander chuckled. "Whoa! We've got plenty of time to get to work."

The horse recognized Alexander's voice and slowed.

"This is marvelous! It takes off quite a bit faster than I'm used to."

Martha clicked sharply at the horse, and the horse responded with a quicker trot.

"You're a natural. I'm sure you'll grow to love this. This model is popular, and I got it for a good price."

The horse found its rhythm and settled on a smooth pace. Martha felt the sway become a familiar lullaby, and a smile bloomed across her face, chasing away any lingering tension in her arms.

Martha glanced sideways at Alexander and then back to the road. "I'd like to accompany you on your stagecoach assignments now and then," said Martha. "I think I'd be a natural for that."

Alexander's head cocked back. "Why would you want to do that? It's dangerous."

Martha tilted her head, "Dangerous? Please! I'm as good with my gun as you are."

"Yes, but—"

"Why should you have all the fun?" Martha grimaced. "Besides, you always ride with at least one other protector. I could be inside the coach if that would worry you less."

"Martha, I know you're an expert with your rifle—"

"And my six-shooter and my shotgun."

She pulled hard on the reins as they arrived at the bank.

Alexander scrunched his forehead. "I don't think it's a good idea. I'd rather you not. Maybe—"

Martha winced, clutching her midsection as a sharp pain coursed through her. She stifled a gasp, covering her mouth while squeezing her eyes shut against the agony.

Alexander's eyes filled with worry. "Are you alright?"

"I don't feel well."

Alexander took the reins from her, "We're going to Dr. Martin's."

Martha rested her head on Alexander's shoulder as Alexander snapped the reins. The horse bolted forward.

Minutes later, Dr. Martin examined Martha while Alexander

waited on the porch.

Inside, Martha sat still. "I'm fine now!"

The doctor moved his stethoscope from spot to spot and listened. "I'll decide that, Martha."

Martha grimaced. "Now and then, I get a bit lightheaded. But this morning, when it happened, I almost lost my breakfast."

The doctor half-smiled.

Martha furrowed her eyebrows at him.

"My dear, you are expecting."

"Expecting?"

Dr. Martin wrinkled his face. "A child."

After a second, Martha's face relaxed, a small smile formed on her lips, and a lone tear scurried down her cheek. Her dream of completing her education seemed to flutter away. Other dreams vanished, too: traveling the world, continuing to work, and other lesser aspirations.

The dream of bringing a new life into this world replaced them. Its addition disrupted her small garden of dreams she'd spent years cultivating and nurturing. Even so, having a child would be welcomed. The baby would bring joy to her and Alexander's lives, filling their hearts with hope and love. Before, she'd never paid much attention to bringing a new life into the world. She expected that to happen later.

But now, a new perspective suddenly snapped into focus. Her new garden presented itself in an expansive, different light that enriched her life in a way she hadn't anticipated. She realized, perhaps influenced by limiting views, that she created her garden of dreams in the smallest of spaces.

Her dreams hadn't fluttered away after all, as she thought. Instead, they settled nearby amongst other dreams she'd long forgotten. The ones closest to her held a higher priority than those further away. Having a child gave her a unique perspective, enabling her to see her full potential and navigate the vast expanse of her garden of dreams.

This revelation was beyond her wildest imaginings. For the first time, she was powerfully in control of her destiny. Perhaps realizing her greatest potential was what she desired, and it had come true profoundly.

Martha's face brightened with a huge grin, and she looked expectantly at Dr. Martin.

The doctor reached into his bag and pulled out a small bottle of liquid. "This tonic will calm your queasy stomach," he said.

"Thank you, Doctor." She jumped down from the examination table. "I'm very late for work today."

"I thought you left that job when you married." Dr. Martin shook his head. "You should get plenty of rest. Maybe you could go back to work after you've had your child, but I don't know where you would find the time. A woman's place is best at home, caring for her family."

A playful smile tugged at Martha's lips as she met the doctor's gaze. "Because you've given me ecstatically wonderful news, I will overlook any outdated notions you might have about women."

Dr. Martin wrinkled his nose, excused himself, and returned with Alexander.

"Your wife would like to share something important with you. I'll leave you two alone." Dr. Martin winked at Martha and walked away.

Alexander rushed to Martha's side. Martha was smiling, her eyes moist with tears.

"Are you alright, darling?" Alexander took her hand.

"Yes, dear. I'm fantastic. I'm afraid I can't go with you on our morning rides to work or on the stagecoaches to help you protect them. The doctor insists that I stay home for a while."

Alexander cocked his head in confusion.

Martha's eyes sparkled with excitement. "We are going to have a baby."

Alexander's face softened, and a broad smile followed.

The daily happenings in the Johnson household soon fell into a new routine. Gertrude still prepared the breakfast, and they all ate together at seven. Gertrude would ensure that Martha took her tonic each morning. Martha insisted that she take it after breakfast; otherwise, it would have tainted the taste of the delicious food. By seven thirty, Alexander rode off to the bank to work the books (including some of Martha's accounts) or, on Fridays, accompany the stagecoach. Mrs. Holt happily helped

Alexander with Martha's accounts. Although not as skilled as Martha, Mrs. Holt was proficient enough at bookkeeping to handle the job. She was the accountant for the bank itself.

At lunchtime, Martha had a hearty lunch. Most days, Alexander would have lunch with her and then rush back to the bank. After lunch, Martha enjoyed an afternoon nap. When she awoke, Gertrude had tea and biscuits ready for her.

After two weeks, Martha was better than ever. She was also bored.

As Martha, Alexander, and Gertrude sat for Sunday dinner, Martha announced, "Alexander, I've decided to return to work tomorrow."

Alexander gulped, finishing his last chew. A smile of surprise filled his face. "I was expecting as much. But are you certain that it's a good idea? I mean, you don't have to work. Mrs. Holt remarked on Friday that your excellent record-keeping makes it relatively easy to maintain your accounts."

Martha tilted her head down while eying Alexander. "The whole reason I was hired was to reduce her workload. And now, thanks to me, her workload has increased significantly."

"She does it happily," said Alexander.

Gertrude sat silent.

"Although hesitant, Dr. Martin suggested that working a few hours each day would not be too taxing on my constitution."

Gertrude giggled. "Constitution? He thinks women are frail, delicate things that can break easily."

Alexander chuckled. "It's not an uncommon view."

"I could work each morning until lunchtime, we could have lunch, and afterward, have my afternoon nap followed by tea and biscuits. It's perfect."

"What about Fridays?"

She rolled her eyes. "We could still ride in together. The only difference is that Gertrude would come at lunchtime and perhaps picnic with me in the park before going home."

"Okay," said Alexander. He went back to eating.

Martha turned to Gertrude, surprised. Martha and Gertrude looked at Alexander.

"Just like that? You're not going to challenge me and tell me it's a bad idea," Martha said.

Alexander grinned. "Of course, I'm worried about you, dear. But seeing you cooped up here, like a bird with clipped wings… hurts more than you know. Besides, the doctor spends the mornings at the hotel across from the bank. And I'll be there with you if you need me."

"Except Fridays when you're out on those stagecoaches."

Martha turned to Gertrude and said, "It's so nice being married to a person who thinks logically."

The corner of Alexander's lip curled up slightly. "I'll have the buggy out front waiting at 7:30 sharp."

Martha leaned forward, clasped her hands together, and cast a whimsical glance, her eyes dancing in glee at Alexander. "Could we leave at eight instead? I've grown fond of sleeping in."

Alexander laughed. "Of course."

The following morning, and each day for the next few months, Alexander and Martha rode into town on the buggy. Alexander drove while Martha sat beside him. Martha found that if she spent her time only on her accounts, she could easily keep up with her work. Unfortunately, this left her little time to help the others tidy up their accounts. Thanks to her prodding when she started working there, they tended to be more meticulous with their books.

Six months pregnant, Martha sat at her desk working on the last of her journals. Only Mr. and Mrs. Holt knew she was expecting. Martha hardly showed, especially since her dresses were looser than usual. Even so, the men she worked with didn't notice such things.

The rhythmic click-clack of her quill was the only sound that dared to break the office's quiet. She glanced at Alexander's empty office. He was away, protecting another stagecoach. Mr. and Mrs. Holt and the rest of the staff were at their desks, diligently hunched over their ledgers. Her stomach grumbled. One more hour until lunch, she thought.

Suddenly, a pair of thunderous booms echoed from beyond the office doors. A collective gasp rippled through the room. Martha's hand instinctively flew to her bag, the reassuring weight of her six-shooter calming a flicker of fear. With a frantic urgency, the other manager ushered Mrs. Holt and the bookkeepers into the back room where the customer journals were kept.

Mr. Holt, his face pale and drawn, rushed to Martha's desk, a trembling hand gripping a revolver. "The back room, Martha. You'll be safe in there."

"No." Her voice was laced with steel as she retrieved her weapon. Rushing to the door, she cracked it open, a sliver of the unfolding scene visible. A uniformed man, blood staining his shirt, lay crumpled on the floor. Two masked figures, barely out of their teens, brandished pistols, their bravado tinged with nervous energy. One customer crouched in the corner, his face twisted with fear, while a single teller behind the counter nodded his head.

Mr. Holt's voice, rough with panic, whispered, "Let the lawman handle this, Martha."

Spinning back, her gaze met his. "He's bleeding on the floor. There are only two of them, and they look scared. Besides," a steely glint flickered in her eyes, "I'm not letting them take one penny out of this bank."

Mr. Holt breathed hard. "This has never happened before."

A humorless smile played on her lips. "Don't worry. I know exactly what to do. But I could use your help." Her eyes flicked to his gun. "You know how to use that, don't you?"

Mr. Holt's scowl betrayed a mixture of fear and defiance. "Of course!"

"Good. Now, listen closely." Martha outlined her plan, her voice a low, urgent whisper. Mr. Holt, though visibly shaken, nodded curtly.

She grabbed her sweater and stuffed it under her dress to make her stomach area larger.

"Okay. Let's do this," she said.

With a bloodcurdling scream that sent shivers down spines, Martha flung open the door, Mr. Holt at her heels. The robbers, startled by the spectacle of a heavily pregnant woman in distress, faltered momentarily.

Seizing the opportunity, Martha launched into a performance worthy of the finest actress. Tears streamed down her face as she wailed about an imminent birth. In the blink of an eye, the facade shattered. Her hand shot up, her aim true as she fired at the more erratic of the gunmen.

A deafening silence descended. Mr. Holt, his gun trembling in his hand, had frozen. Taking charge, Martha whirled around, her gaze settling on the remaining outlaw. Another shot, swift and decisive, ended the standoff.

The first bank robbery Mr. Holt ever witnessed was over. He recovered his composure, securing the outlaws' weapons, his heart pounding. He looked at Martha, his eyes wide with awe. Her face, moments ago a mask of desperation, now held a quiet determination, the calm after the storm.

As Gertrude arrived at the bank, the sheriff and his deputy were escorting two injured young men out. She rushed inside. Dr. Martin was hovering over a man on the floor, bandaging his arm. Dread filled her heart as she went to Martha's desk in the back office. Martha was slumped over, her head in her arms, and still.

"Martha?" asked Gertrude.

Martha spun around with a massive grin and said, "You missed the greatest, most exciting thing ever."

Mr. Holt rushed over to Gertrude, his face bright red, his eyes glowing. "You should have seen Martha. She was incredible. Thanks to her, those bank robbers are going to jail."

Gertrude's jaw dropped as she grabbed at her chest, speechless.

That evening, Alexander and Martha sat having dinner. Gertrude was at Agnes's house telling her the latest gossip. This time, it was about Martha saving the bank from nasty robbers.

"You can't work at the bank anymore, Martha. It's too dangerous."

"It was exciting. Is that why you like working the stagecoaches?" Martha asked.

Alexander grinned. "Doesn't anything scare you?"

"Oh, I was scared, but that didn't stop me from calculating the best way to stop those criminals. They weren't much of a threat. It was probably their first time trying that; they were scared and inexperienced."

"You're not experienced either," said Alexander.

Martha cocked her head, surprised. She inhaled deeply and let it out. "This scared you. Didn't it?"

"I don't know what I would have done if you were hurt this morning. I love you too much even to fathom it."

"But I wasn't hurt. Let's start there."

Alexander rolled his eyes.

Martha smiled. "You can't live life worrying about what might happen if something were to go wrong."

Alexander blinked, confused.

"When you're on that stagecoach, holding your rifle, shotgun, or whatever. Are you thinking: 'What if I get shot?'"

"Nope. I'm thinking about shooting the lawbreaker before he has a chance to fire a shot at anyone."

"I think the same way you do. If it had been Mr. Holt, who had single-handedly foiled that bank robbery, you and he would have exchanged a tale of skill and adventure. He would have exaggerated parts of the story to make them more exciting. You would both laugh and likely share the story with others."

He chuckled. "Mr. Holt? Foil a bank robbery?"

Martha laughed. "You should have seen him. He froze the moment he came face to face with the robber."

"Martha, I love you," said Alexander in surrender.

"Worry about me if you must. But don't trap me in your worries like a caged bird."

"Okay. I'm sorry. You're right," said Alexander.

"I saw Dr. Martin at the bank today, and he recommended I take some time off to rest. I've already arranged to work one more week to organize my accounts and transfer them to Mrs. Holt. She'll keep them safe until I return in a few months."

Alexander's jaw dropped. He shook his head and laughed. "You're amazing!"

"You are, too!"

"Tell me every exciting detail about the bank robbery, and don't leave anything out," said Alexander.

As the weeks flew by, Martha's excitement grew, as did the need for loose-fitting clothing. Martha longed for the day when she would meet her newborn. Alexander often found Martha humming a tune early in the morning. Alexander lallygagged around the house to be with Martha instead of heading off to work. He preferred spending the mornings with her. He, too, was excited to welcome their new child. "Off you go," she would tell Alexander. "Gertrude and I have a lot to get done."

Martha and Gertrude decided on the room that would best serve as the nursery. They prepared the baby's room and gathered the items Martha wanted for the baby.

CHAPTER NINETEEN

Alex

One evening, several months later, Alexander and Martha sat on the porch swing, and Gertrude was in the doorway.

Gertrude stepped toward Martha. "There's a little chill in the air, Martha. Would you like a blanket?"

"No, thank you. I'm much too warm in all these clothes."

Gertrude walked up to Martha and felt her forehead. "You don't have a fever."

"I feel odd, but I'm sure it's nothing."

"It's something if you're feeling odd, Martha," said Gertrude.

Martha shut her eyes tight and then gasped. Her eyes shot open as nature announced the impending birth. "Alexander! The baby's coming!"

Alexander jumped and took Martha's hand.

Gertrude sat beside Martha. "It'll be okay. You have a little bit of time. There's no reason to get worried."

The color fled from Alexander's face. "Shall I get Dr. Martin?"

Gertrude looked at Alexander. "Yes, but first, I need you to help me get Martha inside where she can be comfortable."

Alexander nodded, took Martha's hand, and helped her up a little too quickly.

Martha moaned as she tried to stand.

Gertrude furrowed her eyebrows. "Alexander! Slow and easy. We got time."

"Yes, Ma'am." Alexander stood beside Martha, helpless. He couldn't bear to see his wife in pain.

Martha attempted a smile. "It's going to be alright, Alexander." She put her hand on her belly. "It must be a boy. He's kicking up a storm."

Uncertainty flickered in Alexander's eyes before he gave a series of quick nods. "Yes, a boy, yes." Martha was in distress, and he didn't know how to help her.

Gertrude smiled. She'd told Martha for weeks that she thought it was a boy. "Alexander, you can go get Dr. Martin now. Everything will be ready for when he comes. Okay?"

"Okay, Okay." Alexander took a breath. He grabbed his hat, nodded again to Martha, and then bolted out the door.

Martha, with tears in her eyes, moaned in pain. "The baby's coming. The doctor won't be here in time. I wanted Alexander here with me."

Gertrude's face was filled with a tense smile. "Don't worry, Martha. There's plenty of time. Everything is going to be just fine."

Twenty minutes stretched into an eternity before the door creaked open, and the doctor hurried in. Martha lay pale on the bed, her eyes wide with worry. Gertrude, a pillar of strength, held her hand, her voice a soothing murmur. "Breathe, Martha. Deep breaths."

Gertrude tossed the smelling salts aside and rushed over to receive the baby.

The doctor, his brow furrowed with concern. "What happened here?"

Gertrude's voice, usually calm, held a sharp edge. "She fainted, doctor. Once already."

The doctor cast Gertrude a curt glance. "I need space. Move aside."

Gertrude's jaw clenched. "No! You tend to her in case she faints again. The baby's coming." Her voice softened as she leaned closer to Martha. "We're almost there, dear. One big push when I say so, alright?"

Martha, eyes flitting between the doctor and Gertrude, managed a weak nod. The doctor set his bag down with a clatter.

Gertrude took a deep breath, her eyes locking with Martha's. "Okay, Martha. Push!"

A primal scream ripped from Martha's throat as she pushed with every ounce of her strength. A moment later, a relieved sigh escaped her lips, replaced by a whimper of pain.

Gertrude's face broke into a radiant smile as a tiny head crowned, followed by a slippery body. With practiced ease, she cradled the newborn in her arms, a precious bundle of life.

The doctor worked swiftly, severing the umbilical cord with a snip of the scissors. Relief flooded the room as he straightened, a smile gracing his lips. "All done," he announced, his voice warm. "Congratulations, you have a healthy baby boy, and quite a strong one. He's—"

Dr. Martin's breath stuck in his throat as Martha's eyes fluttered closed. He lunged for his bag and withdrew a brown vial, its contents glinting from the window light. His fingers fumbled with the cap before finally releasing a pungent aroma that filled the air. Waving the small bottle under Martha's nose, he said, "Wake up!"

A shallow and weak gasp escaped Martha's lips as her awareness flickered back to life. The world came into focus — blurry, then gradually sharpened. A searing pain, a white-hot poker jabbing at her, stole her breath. It radiated outwards, clawing up her spine and into her limbs. A strangled moan escaped her lips as the intensity ebbed, leaving behind a throbbing ache.

Martha forced herself to inhale, a shaky breath that filled her lungs with a burning sensation. As the wave of pain receded, awareness returned. Her gaze darted to Gertrude, and relief washed over her. The baby was safe. In Gertrude's strong arms, the tiny fingers and toes fanned out in a delicate exploration of the world.

A weak smile tugged at the corners of Martha's lips, a testament to the fierce love blooming amidst the exhaustion and lingering pain. The pure and potent joy was a balm, soothing the raw edges of her ordeal. In that moment, a mother's bond blossomed amidst the chaos and vulnerability.

Alexander rushed in.

Gertrude exclaimed, "It's a boy."

The baby cried through its first breaths.

"A boy!" said Martha. "It's a boy, Alexander." She extended her arms, crying tears of joy. The baby stopped crying and wobbled his little head when he heard his mother's voice — a sound he'd grown to love.

Gertrude brought the newborn to Martha. "Martha, his eyes are barely open, and you can see they're full of wonder."

Martha took her son in her arms. "My baby, I've been waiting for you. We all have."

She gazed at her son's face and then gasped. Her smile suddenly faded. Martha's eyes darted to Gertrude and then back to her baby.

"He's beautiful," said Alexander, not noticing Martha's reaction.

Gertrude exhaled as her shoulders slumped. She lent a supportive smile to Martha.

Martha, her breathing shallow, looked at Gertrude with concern and worry.

"Everything is going to work out fine. Your and Alexander's baby is lovely."

The baby started to cry softly and then broke into a loud wail.

Martha's heart melted. His cries awakened something deep within her.

"Now, my baby," Martha said. She hummed the same whimsical, soothing song she had sung each night for several months.

The cries softened as the familiar tune filled the room.

Alexander said, "His middle name should be Charles, in honor of your father."

Martha nodded and continued with the comforting melody as the baby's cries changed to soft, gurgling sounds.

Martha said, "Alexander Charles! We'll call him Alex for short." She puckered her lips and resumed the nurturing music.

Dr. Martin walked in. "Gertrude, would you take the baby? We need to wash him, and Martha needs to rest."

Martha smiled at little Alex and handed him to Gertrude.

Gertrude wrapped Alex in a fresh towel. "Today was quite a day for you. Welcome, little Alex."

After gathering his belongings into his worn bag, the doctor offered Martha a reassuring smile. With a final nod, he followed Gertrude out the door.

Martha watched as the doctor and Gertrude left the room with little Alex.

Alexander gently kissed Martha's hand.

Martha's gaze floated up reluctantly to Alexander. "I love you very much. I hope you will always love me and little Alex, no matter what."

Alexander tilted his head curiously. "Of course."

"Do you think we could move away from here someday?"

Alexander's face changed to one of concern. "To where?"

"Someplace far. Maybe out West. A place where—"

The doctor returned. "Alexander, may I have a word with you outside?"

Alexander leaned in toward Martha and whispered, "Someplace?"

Martha shrugged. "I don't know what I'm saying."

Alexander kissed her hand and followed the doctor to the hallway.

Gertrude walked back in with baby Alex. "He's all cleaned up."

"Gertrude, how is it possible that he looks like Thomas?"

Gertrude, her face pained, said, "It doesn't matter. This child belongs only to you and Alexander."

Martha closed her eyes. Her voice faded into slumber as she muttered, "I'm telling you it's impossible."

Gertrude, a pillar of strength, sat on the edge of the bed with Alex cradled in her arms. She watched as Martha's breathing fell into a soft, rhythmical pattern. She patted Martha's arm. "Don't worry. You'll feel better later."

Gertrude wiped an errant tear from her cheek, smiled at baby Alex, and gazed at his face.

The doctor spoke with Alexander outside on the porch. "I gave her a shot to help her sleep. She'll need to rest to recover her strength. Martha's body has suffered a great deal of trauma. I had to leave Gertrude with the birthing because Martha fainted. I revived her. Thankfully, I was quick."

Alexander furrowed his eyebrows.

The doctor said, "Martha is frail. This birth was too taxing for her."

Alexander thought that this was preposterous since Martha seemed fine.

"Ridiculous! Martha has a strong constitution."

Two weeks later, Martha was up on her feet. "I can't stay in bed any longer," she declared, a stubborn glint in her eyes. In no time, she returned to her usual routine, a whirlwind of activity fueled by love for her son, Little Alex.

Every gurgle and coo sent a thrill through her. She envisioned his future, whispering dreams of him following in their footsteps, a successful banker or accountant. Alexander, equally smitten, shared her pride. The sight of their son, ever the early riser, greeting the dawn with wide, curious eyes filled them with fierce love.

The first few months were a blur of sleepless nights punctuated by Alex's cries. But slowly, a rhythm emerged, nights became restful, and their days were filled with the quiet joy of parenthood.

With her head clear and well-rested, Martha yearned to return to work. She missed the ink smears on her hand and the whiff of the journal when she opened it. Seeing Mr. and Mrs. Holt working away at their desks had always made her hopeful. Although the bookkeepers mainly kept to themselves, she enjoyed collaborating with them. Most of all, she wished she could use her brain to add and subtract numbers, balance worksheets, work with ledgers, and so much more. She was on the back porch Saturday morning while Alex slept inside.

Alexander walked out and sat next to her.

"How are you doing, Martha?"

She inhaled and turned from the scenic backyard to Alexander. "I feel useless."

Alexander cocked his head back like Martha had said something in a foreign language.

"Aren't you happy?" he asked.

She smiled. "Of course I am. We have a beautiful son. I have a handsome husband and a loving aunt. I miss those accounts."

"Aha! I knew it. I'm surprised you've lasted this long without those ledgers."

Martha grimaced. "I've thought about it exhaustively and found no way I would want to be away from Alex."

"Even while he's sleeping?" he asked.

Martha rolled her eyes. "He has a nap in the morning and another in the afternoon."

"What do you do during his naps?"

Martha chuckled. "I usually sit out here and ponder. I'm good at that now."

"Well, it just so happens that Mr. Holt has asked if you would consider working for a few hours each day," said Alexander.

Martha gazed upward and shook her head. "I can't leave Alex. He's much too young. Perhaps when he's a little older."

With a mischievous smile and gleeful eyes, Alexander said, "Mr. Holt has proposed that I set up a desk in one of the spare rooms where you could toil over those ledgers. I wholeheartedly agreed, provided you would want to do that."

Martha jumped to her feet. Her face lit up bright. "That's a marvelous idea. I could spend at least four hours each day, sometimes more. I never deal with customers, so I have no reason to go to the bank. Except, how will I get the journals?"

"He said he would handle those details. He suggested a courier, or you could occasionally visit there, or I could transport the books. He's flexible. He wants your help desperately."

Martha sat and took Alexander's hands. "The room next to the baby's would be perfect. I could hear Alex immediately if he needed me."

"Gertrude said she'd happily take care of Alex while you worked. So you could be in a proper office," Alexander said. "I want to show you something."

Alexander led Martha upstairs. As they passed Alex's room, Martha peeked inside.

"Good, he's still sleeping," said Martha.

Alexander continued to the end of the hall and opened the door.

Martha rushed over, excited, and went inside.

In the large room, a desk stood stately at its center. A stack of journals, an inkwell, pens, and pencils sat on the desktop. A carved sign with her name, 'Martha S.,' was at the front. A guest chair stood next to the desk. Several bookcases lined the side wall, and the opposite wall held large windows.

Gertrude stood off to the side, waving her to the chair. "I got the sign from your desk at the bank."

Martha started to cry. "I don't know what to say."

Gertrude chuckled. "I think you need to get to work."

When Alex turned two years old, he seemed to have the energy to spare. He mastered the art of walking and exploited this newfound gift by traveling the far reaches of the house. He was never satisfied with sitting still. Alex wanted to explore the forbidden areas alone—like the kitchen, out on the porch, or better yet, the barn. He decided those places were his new frontier, ripe with exciting experiences.

Alexander was proud of his son's independence, but Martha worried Alex might wander into trouble. Alex had found himself confronted with the many perils that plagued their home, like when he saw his mother place a plate of cookies on the table. After she left the room, he set out on a mission to get a cookie.

Alex scooted his way toward the chair. He mostly crawled but also walked part of the way there, too. When he got to the chair, he peered over the edge at the inviting yellow cushion his mother had sewn. The tempting aroma of cookies wafted from high above.

He stood on his tiptoes, his little belly pressing uncomfortably against the seat cushion. Undeterred, Alex used his arms and legs to pull himself up and then sat. After a moment's rest, he knelt and, wobbly but determined, rose to his feet.

He peered over the tabletop and eyed the plate of cookies. Reaching over, he brought the plate closer to the edge and snagged not one but two cookies, one in each hand. With an air of accomplishment, he munched on the sugary treat in his right hand. When he finished the cookie, he licked his fingers clean.

He smiled at the cookie safely in his left hand. It was time to head to his toys and enjoy the second one there. Without letting go of his cookie, he tried several times to climb down from the chair. He ended up stomach down, one hand holding the cookie high, the other gripping the pillow tight, and his legs dangling an inch from the floor.

Alexander entered a few minutes later and stifled a chuckle. His son reminded him of a turtle on its back trying to right itself.

"Alex!" said Alexander, grinning. "Stop swinging your legs and let go."

Alex wailed, "Pa!" He swung his legs even more.

Martha rushed in. "Alex, my little cowboy, what are you doing?"

Alexander chuckled as he scooped Alex up. The remains of a broken cookie were in Alex's hands, and an outline of sugar and crumbs surrounded his mouth.

Martha said, "Oh my goodness!" She burst into laughter. She took a cloth and wiped the crumbs from little Alex's face. "Why didn't you ask for help?"

Little Alex said, "Got cookies. See." He held the broken cookie for her to see.

Alexander looked surprised at Martha. "He takes after you, Martha."

Martha nodded her head, laughing proudly.

At three years old, Alex was curious, a phenomenal problem solver, and determined when pursuing his goals. As he got older, he wanted to know why and how things worked.

Martha was happy that Alexander and her son were close. Alex often waited anxiously by the door for his father to come home, sometimes crying incessantly. Alexander would walk in and scoop Alex into his arms. Then, Alexander would ask Alex about the adventures that he and his mother had experienced that day. Alex would spare no detail in telling his tales.

Martha continued working for the bank in her private home office. Although now that Alex was three, she would often visit the bank to get a journal, return a journal, visit with Mr. or Mrs. Holt, or visit Alexander. Alex loved spending time with his father at the bank.

CHAPTER TWENTY

Juan Cortez

Wallace sat across from an impeccably dressed, mid-forties man in the late afternoon.

"It's been a while, maybe a dozen or more years?" Wallace asked. "I thought you were in California."

Juan nodded as he examined some papers. "My family and I decided to move back here."

Juan signed the documents and handed them to Wallace.

Wallace put them into a folder. "I thought things were booming out there."

"I earned a fortune there despite all the lawlessness. That gold doesn't attract only honest, hardworking folks like me. Damn robbers. They made it a challenge to hang on to my wealth." Juan chuckled. "I didn't mind it that much. They weren't that bright."

Wallace frowned and wrote 'Juan Cortez' on the top of the folder. "You don't have to worry about that. Your money is safe here."

Juan leaned back in his chair. "My wife hated living there. She demands that I find an upscale home on a large plot of land here."

"With an account like yours, you should be able to live anywhere you like. Where are you staying now?"

Juan's nose wrinkled as if he'd smelled something disgusting. "At the hotel across the way."

"I see."

Juan smiled when he noticed the photograph of the three men on the wall behind Wallace.

Wallace glanced at the picture. "I miss the old days when we'd go carousing about town, seeing what kind of trouble we could stir up."

Juan nodded. "That was a long time ago." He chuckled. "Our mutual friend, the sheriff, sends his regards."

"How's Joseph doing?"

"He's a well-respected man. After Rose passed away, he was a bit of a mess. His second wife keeps him on the straight and narrow."

"Wait, what?" Wallace stammered, his voice betraying his shock. "She died? The last time I talked to Rose, she made a big withdrawal and was excited about moving to California. What happened to her?" asked Wallace.

Juan moved uncomfortably and glanced away, and then back at Wallace.

"She got shot accidentally. Joseph and I left for California a day or two later. I thought you knew."

"Nope," said Wallace. "Douglas wrote me a while back and told me that Joseph and his wife lived in a town not too far from Sacramento. I guess I just assumed."

Juan shrugged.

"What about your house out West?"

"It's a spacious house that sits on a fair-sized plot of land. I bought it for an excellent price and fixed it up. It has a barn, a guest house, a huge garden area, and such."

"Oh yeah?" Wallace asked, a smile creeping onto his face. He glanced at the door as if Alexander were standing there.

"I loved that house. Your brother is taking care of it for me."

Wallace nodded. "Sounds like a grand place. You've left it in excellent hands."

"It's not doing me much good now that I'm here. I need to sell it."

Juan withdrew a small, thin book from his pocket. He opened it and pulled out an envelope.

"I almost forgot. I have a letter from Douglas. I put it in here to keep it flat." He handed the letter to Wallace.

Wallace smiled broadly as he took it and started to read it.

Juan was about to put the booklet away, but then hesitated.

"You can have this, too. I won't need it anymore." Juan placed it on the desk in front of Wallace.

Wallace glanced at the little book and then went back to the letter.

In the letter, his brother, Douglas, told him about the proliferation of stagecoach robbers and his desperate need for men to protect the stagecoach lines. Wallace chuckled when he read the part about how prosperous the banks of the West became.

Wallace put the letter down and smiled at Juan. He picked up the book, "A Journey to California Guidebook." He shuffled through the pages as his mouth widened into a smile.

"I know someone who might want to buy your house and sell you his mansion here."

A jolt of surprise shot through Juan. He leaned forward, his voice rising in pitch. "Wait, hold on, are you serious?"

Wallace let out a hearty chuckle, his eyes twinkling with amusement. "You may have to throw in some extras to sweeten the deal. Do you remember the Swansons' estate?"

Juan's eyes lit up. "Yes, of course. That house would exceed my wife's expectations. It would be ideal for my family. But—"

"It belongs to one of my bank managers. Actually, to his wife."

"Incredible!"

Wallace came around his desk and led Juan to Alexander's office. Wallace walked to the door, smiled broadly, and stepped inside. Juan followed close behind.

Alexander put his pencil down and looked up. He blinked as a vague look of familiarity crossed his face.

Wallace was grinning ear-to-ear. He glanced from Juan to Alexander. "I want to introduce you to my old friend, Juan Cortez. He arrived here from California a few days ago."

Alexander stood and shook Juan's hand, and then hesitated before letting go. "It's a pleasure to meet you. Although—"

Wallace rushed up to Alexander. "I have some wonderful news for you."

Alexander turned to Wallace. "I like wonderful news."

Wallace grinned as he handed Alexander the booklet, waiting for his reaction.

Alexander read the title aloud, "A Journey to California Guidebook."

Wallace hovered next to Alexander. "Juan gave me a letter from my brother. Douglas is doing quite well."

Alexander shuffled through the pages. "That's good to hear."

"I think you should move your family to California and work for my brother at his bank," exclaimed Wallace. "Juan is selling his house there and needs a house in New York. Juan and his family are staying at the hotel."

Alexander's jaw dropped.

Taking a step forward, Juan's face softened with reminiscence. "You were a young boy, maybe fourteen or fifteen, when I last saw you."

Alexander looked crooked at Juan and then smiled. "I thought I remembered you, Mr. Cortez," said Alexander. "You came to the house when I was a boy."

Juan nodded. "Please call me Juan." He sat in the chair across from Alexander.

Wallace rushed out the door, leaving Juan alone with Alexander. Alexander blinked, surprised.

Juan was annoyed that Wallace slinked away abruptly. He brushed the annoyance away and smiled at Alexander. "Wallace suggested that if you were to move to California, you might be interested in buying my ranch there."

"It's been a long time since I've thought about moving there, but—"

Juan leaned forward, his face glowing with excitement. "I own a beautiful ranch in Sacramento, California, with some animals, rich farmland, and a huge and comfortable house."

A sudden glint in Alexander's eyes betrayed a realization. A solution to a problem he didn't have presented itself. Before he and Martha married, they briefly discussed living in California, but that was his dream, not hers. They jointly decided against it. But then he remembered the day Martha asked him about moving somewhere far away. It was the day that Alex was born. She mentioned it a few times since, but not lately.

Juan tilted his head and leaned forward. "Alexander?"

Alexander blinked several times and then nodded. "Why would you leave that all behind?"

"Honestly, if it were just me, I would have stayed there for the rest of my life. It's the most beautiful country that I have ever seen. But all of my wife's family is here. And she has lots of relatives. My two sisters also live here."

"I see."

"Your father," Juan started, his voice carrying a hint of sadness, "Deputy Johnson. What happened to him? Wallace told me that after I went to California, he up and left and never returned."

Alexander shrugged. "He died fourteen years ago. No doubt he drank himself to death, or someone killed him."

Juan slumped slightly in his seat. "I'm sorry. I didn't know. Last time I saw him, he was drinking heavily."

Alexander paged through the booklet. "I was glad to be rid of him. We weren't that close." He glanced at Juan. "I thought it was a dangerous endeavor, going to California."

Juan raised his brows slightly. "It's not without its perils. It requires a bit of research and preparation."

"Is it safe for women and children to travel?"

Juan leaned back slightly and cleared his throat. "Yes, I have two young boys and an infant. There have been women who have given birth on the trips, too. My wife is one of them. As long as all are healthy, they'll be fine. I'm sure."

"How often have you made the trip?"

Juan smiled, proud of his accomplishment. "Twice. That booklet, 'A Guide to California,' contains useful information. It's a fast, quick read."

Alexander picked it up again and paged through it. His face softened, his cheeks rosy.

Juan straightened up in his seat. "It's an excellent little book. When we decided to move back here, my wife was going to have a baby."

"You traveled here in your wife's condition?"

"Yes. She gave birth to our daughter while on the trip."

Alexander's face flickered with surprise. "Amazing!" Alexander glanced at the booklet. "Do you miss California?"

"I do. I miss it very much."

"I see."

Alexander couldn't believe his ears—California? The distant dream that had quietly smoldered in the back of his mind now blazed to life, setting off a wildfire of excitement within him. "What can you tell me about the house?"

"I'm not looking to make a profit."

Juan picked up his satchel and placed a stack of papers on Alexander's desk.

Alexander's eyes widened as Juan spent the next half hour explaining the paperwork describing the house and the property in detail.

"The home is on fifteen acres with plenty of room to grow," said Juan.

"Is someone taking care of it now?"

"Yes. I hired a ranch hand to live there and care for the animals, the land, and the house. His name is Charlie. Wallace's brother, Douglas, is paying Charlie and looking after everything until I can sell it."

"He's talked about his brother before." Alexander chuckled. "Wallace has often told me that Douglas wants me to work for him out there."

"Douglas is a man of great integrity. The job and the house are perfect opportunities for you and your family. Would you be interested in the house?"

Alexander smiled broadly. "I would like to talk it over with my wife. She's mentioned, once or twice, about moving away. But I don't think she meant traveling across the country. Although before I left this morning, she was reading *The Adventures of Daniel Boone*. She's read that book more than any other in our library."

"The trip to California would be less perilous than Boone's and far more adventurous than just reading about it."

"Absolutely!" Alexander laughed. "Can we meet again tomorrow?"

Juan stood up. "Yes. I'll be back here at 10:00 a.m. Does that work for you?"

"It does." Alexander walked around and shook Juan's hand. "It was a pleasure speaking with you."

They both went outside, and Alexander watched as Juan rode away.

Alexander rushed back to his office and picked up the guidebook. He smiled broadly as he paged through it.

Alexander skimmed it, cover to cover. Each page sparked his imagination with a world of possibilities that hadn't existed an hour before. His heart raced with excitement at the thought of exploring new territories and the riches in the great unknown of the West.

"Martha would be so happy in our new home in California," Alexander muttered.

Alexander stayed well beyond the end of the workday and reread the booklet. "Martha will love this!"

He rushed home to share this fantastic adventure with his wife.

CHAPTER TWENTY-ONE
Real-Life Adventure

Martha was in the study, curled up with her well-worn favorite book. She checked the clock. She loved how the clock's pendulum swung back and forth like a carefree waltz. When she was younger, she imagined the pendulum's freedom as it traveled to and fro without worry. She snapped out of her distraction as rapid, soft footsteps approached from the hallway.

Martha smiled and sat up when Gertrude peeked in. "You're reading that again?" asked Gertrude. "It's about to start losing its pages."

"Daniel Boone's exploits are exciting." She planted her finger on the page where she left off. "Each time I read it, I feel like I'm there with him, trudging through the wild, undiscovered country."

Gertrude chuckled. "If I were there with him, he'd expect me to cook and clean."

"Sad but true." Martha's eyes darted to the door. "I wonder what's keeping Alexander."

"I don't know. I thought I heard someone ride up a few minutes ago. But it wasn't him. Sometimes, the wind carries the noise from the road."

Martha rolled her eyes. "He's bound to be working on one of those stubborn accounts of his. I love him so—"

The rumble of a galloping horse echoed into the house.

Gertrude jumped up. "That's got to be him, and he's riding fast. I bet he's excited about my stew. I'll be in the kitchen. It's almost ready."

Martha picked up the book, hoping to finish reading the last few pages before Alexander walked in. She calculated it would take Alexander ten minutes before he came in.

Less than a minute later, Alexander rushed into the study out of breath.

"Martha, you've got to read this. I'm sure you'll enjoy it. It's about going out West." Alexander caught his breath. He saw her holding her favorite book. "Much better than Daniel Boone."

She squinted at the small booklet Alexander held in his hand. Martha bookmarked her adventure. She would have finished it faster than ever with only four pages left.

Martha thrived on Alexander's infectious enthusiasm. She sometimes enjoyed living vicariously through his hopes and dreams.

"Is that what kept you late at work?"

"Yes. But I also chatted with an old friend of my father's, Juan Cortez. He had just arrived from California. The book is well written and describes what is needed for traveling there."

"California? We haven't talked about that since before we married."

"Things have changed much over the last four years. It's certainly safer now with all the people traveling there."

"I remember safety was my main concern."

"You've mentioned a time or two you wanted to move away from here."

"Yes, to a neighboring state, not across the country. Back then, I was motivated by fear. I desired to be out of reach of the harm from my past. I'm not afraid anymore."

"That's what I love about you. You're fearless."

"You're just trying to flatter me." She tilted her head. "Keep going."

"It would be quite an adventure to travel there. The guidebook says that many people have traveled to the West. We live in exciting times. We have a chance to be part of this great expansion. I think we can do this if we want to."

She set her Daniel Boone book aside, smiling at the coincidence between her old favorite adventure and Alexander's new one. She held out her hand to Alexander.

"Let me see that."

Alexander handed her the booklet. "I read it twice already."

"It's just a pamphlet."

She skimmed through it, slowly at first and then turning pages faster and faster. She sat up, a whirlwind of emotions swirling in her eyes, and cocked her head at Alexander. "Will Alex be safe? For that matter, will we be, too?"

"Juan said if we prepared adequately, we'd be safe. He and his wife traveled here with their children. This booklet says this is not a journey of endurance. It's one of exploration, adventure, and liberation."

"Liberation! Now, that alone would make it worthwhile."

"Martha, we have the means to do this. We could travel there with our neighbors, friends, and loyal bank patrons. Juan said it would be prudent to go with friends and family and outfit the wagons with enough provisions — food, medicine, tools, and spares."

A burning excitement crackled within Martha, its intensity growing with each passing moment. "I bet it wouldn't take much to convince others to join us."

"Juan has a ranch in California with an enormous house, a barn, farmland, and animals. He would like to give us that house in exchange for this house. He offered us extra money, covered wagons, oxen, supplies, and other odds and ends."

Martha's smile grew wide. "Does Wallace's brother still want to employ you?"

Alexander nodded. "Wallace assured me that Douglas would pay me double what I get here."

"Wow! Is there a job for me?"

"I'm certain we can work something out. Wallace says there's a lot of banking business with all the gold. Surely, they need bookkeepers."

"Where is Mr. Cortez and his family living?"

"They're staying in the hotel across from the bank. We don't have to decide this now. Juan said the earliest we could leave would be March or April. If we go too early, we could face harsh weather here. And if we go too late, we could face the same in California."

"How long will it take?"

"About four to six months."

"Hmm." Martha's eyes sparkled with adventure. "It would be a thrilling four to six months."

"The most thrilling ever." Alexander loved basking in Martha's passion.

Martha was deep in thought, planning all facets of their

journey to the West.

Alexander sat next to Martha. "In the morning, I'll tell Juan that he can stay in my old house until we decide whether or not we want to go to California. My house is not as nice as this one, but it would be more comfortable for them than the hotel."

Martha nodded. "That's a great idea."

Gertrude cleared her throat. "Dinner is ready."

The next day, Alexander met with Juan and Wallace over lunch. As they ate, they discussed the trip to California.

Wallace seemed more excited about the journey than Alexander. "I'm only thinking of what's best for you and your family," Wallace said. "I will miss you immensely."

"Thanks," said Alexander. "Juan, please tell us about your experiences in California."

Juan spent the next hour sharing his adventures there.

"Maybe someday I'll write a book about it," Juan said.

Alexander nodded. "I'm sure it would be exciting."

Juan put his napkin on his plate and pushed back his chair. "My wife is extremely displeased with the hotel. She says it's much too small for her."

Alexander's eyes shot open wide. "My old place would be a perfect temporary home for you and your family. If you're interested, we could go see it right now."

"That would be marvelous!" said Juan, standing. "Let's go."

Wallace bid them farewell, and Alexander and Juan left for the house.

When Juan saw the house, he said, "My wife will appreciate this much more than that hotel. When can we move in?"

"Tomorrow, if you like. The place is empty, but I need to clean it up. I've neglected it for a little too long."

"Don't bother. We'll take care of that."

Alexander returned to the bank and spent the afternoon on his accounts. When he arrived home, supper was on the table, and Gertrude and Martha were having a lively conversation about moving out West. Gertrude hurriedly served plates of food for everyone and sat with her plate.

Gertrude told Alexander, "Martha was just talking about the pros and cons of relocating to California."

Martha served Alex some carrots. "The oppression of this city is reason enough to leave."

Gertrude nodded. "We'll be giving up all the conveniences a big town affords, like shops, theaters, beautiful parks, and so much more."

Alexander shrugged. "I'm sure we can find those things out there, but without the hustle and bustle of New York."

Martha turned to Gertrude. "What do you think, Gertrude?"

"I don't want to interfere in these sorts of family matters. I will be fine with whatever you decide."

Alexander smiled. "I think it'll be exciting."

Martha sighed. "Growing up, life was slower. People back then took their time to enjoy each other's company. Nowadays, it seems that people only care about money and property."

Alexander said, "The pace will slow once we settle there. But, there's no doubt people there will continue prioritizing money and property above all else."

Chewing thoughtfully, little Alex observed the conversation, his eyes darting from person to person. He may not have understood every word, but the passion and enthusiasm in their voices painted a vivid picture of an exciting adventure. When there was a lull in the discussion, he looked up and said, "California!"

Martha chuckled and looked over at Alexander and then at their three-year-old son.

"Want California!" Alex repeated, his voice rising in pitch, and his eyes glowed with a mischievous gleam.

"Well then, Alex wants us to go to California." Martha smiled at Alex.

Alexander raised his hand. "Me too."

Martha raised her hand and turned to Gertrude. "Would you care to join us on our expedition to California?"

Gertrude raised both her hands. "I wouldn't miss it for the world. When do we leave?"

Alexander cocked his head back. "We should plan for the end of March."

"We'll be ready. This will be the most thrilling quest of our lifetime. I'll have to tell Agnes we've decided to go."

Martha grinned at Gertrude. "Agnes already knows?"

"I mentioned it to her this morning. There's very little that I don't tell Agnes. I wasn't there even ten minutes when she ran and told her two sons to prepare their families to move to California. They have three old wagons that they'll fix up. Her grandkids are excited about going, too."

"Yay," said little Alex. "I like playing with them."

Martha laughed. "That's wonderful."

Alexander looked puzzled. "Mr. Jenkins has trouble getting around. Is he thinking of driving?"

Gertrude perked up. "Agnes is looking for someone to help drive. Her sons and their families will be in the other two wagons."

Alexander's eyes lit up. "That's great news. Plenty of folks will want to join us on our trip."

Martha nodded. "Lots to plan and lots to do. This is going to be exciting!"

The days flew by as they planned every detail of their cross-country journey. Juan helped them with the oxen, the covered wagons, and the many supplies.

Only six weeks were left before their departure. A faint tremor of unease ran through Gertrude as she stood at the kitchen basin washing the last few breakfast dishes. The rhythmic clink of dishes competed with the disquiet in her chest. The window overlooking the backyard with its vibrant garden, usually a source of comfort, revealed a scene that mirrored her growing worry.

Martha sat frowning beside the still water of the pond. Oblivious to his mother's mood, Little Alex played a few feet away, his laughter a cheerful counterpoint to the storm brewing within Martha. But it was Martha who held Gertrude's attention. Martha's shoulders slumped, her gaze fixed on the water's surface as if lost in a labyrinth of worries. The world's weight seemed to press down on her, starkly contrasting with the carefree child beside her.

Gertrude wiped her hands on her apron. She took a deep

breath and strolled outside to Martha.

Martha forced a smile at Gertrude.

The disquiet Gertrude felt earlier only intensified.

Martha's gaze drifted back to the pond. She crumbled bits of biscuit and tossed them into the water. The bright gold and orange fish erupted in a flurry of activity. They splashed and darted, competing for the meager treats.

"I've always loved sitting in this spot," Martha murmured, the words tinged with a melancholic longing.

"It's beautiful here."

"I love the feeling of the sun on my face. And the cool breeze reminds me how sweet life is."

Gertrude relaxed a little. "Those fish appreciate you."

"I'll miss them." Martha tossed a few more crumbs into the pond. She looked over to Alex, playing with some small wooden toys, and then her gaze floated from the house to the gazebo and to the covered porch where she and Alexander danced on their wedding day. "I'll miss all of this."

"You can have all this and more in California."

A hint of a smile almost escaped Martha's lips. "I know."

Gertrude sat down next to Martha and kept an eye on Alex lest he hear something he shouldn't. "I can tell that something is bothering you. What is it?"

Martha looked crooked at Gertrude. "I'm fine."

"Before little Alex was born, you thought you could conquer the world and show everyone that a woman could do anything as well as any man. And you began to make your mark on the world. But afterward, you suddenly wanted to leave this town. And you've worn out the pages of that adventure book you read. And now your wish has come to fruition, and we're leaving this place."

"Things changed when I saw my son for the first time, that's true. I'm delighted that we're going on that account. But now…" Martha looked down and rested her hand on her belly. She wiped away her tears and smiled.

"I should have known. You're glowing as bright as a lantern."

"Oh, Gertrude, I'm both happy and worried all at the same time." Martha's eyes welled up with joy. "We're almost ready to leave. I thought Alexander might want to postpone the trip, so I visited with Dr. Martin this morning. He told me many women have traveled across the country while expecting a child. He said Juan's wife gave birth during their trip here." She wiped away her tears. "You'll be there for me, won't you?"

"Of course, you know I will. Why are you worried?"

Martha relaxed her shoulders and exhaled. "We'll be away from a doctor, the city, and the safety it affords. I'll be carrying a baby for the whole way."

"Perhaps you should discuss this with—"

Alex let out a loud chortle, "Pa!"

Alexander stood shocked, outside the house, holding a bouquet.

"Martha?" asked Alexander.

Martha jumped to her feet. She saw the flowers fall to the ground.

Alexander's face was riddled with confusion. "Why didn't you tell me this wondrous news?"

Martha sighed. "We can't postpone this trip. We're about ready to go."

Alexander collected the flowers and brushed off the dirt that threatened their beauty. He rushed to Martha and gave her the beautiful bundle of color and sweet aroma. "I'm delighted, my darling, that we're having another child." He leaned over and kissed her.

He winked at Gertrude, whose face was painted with a huge grin. "You'll help Martha along the way, won't you?"

"Of course." Gertrude went over and picked up Alex.

Alexander winked at his son and turned to Martha. "I'll place an advertisement in the paper to have a doctor accompany us."

A lone tear rolled down Martha's delicate cheek and stopped as a warm smile illuminated her face. "I'm so happy. When I spoke with Dr. Martin this morning, he said he'd been talking with Juan about our California adventure. The doctor gave me a list of things we needed. Maybe you could invite Dr. Martin to join us."

"I'll stop by his place tomorrow. He's been a doctor here for as long as I can remember. I can't imagine him leaving, but I'll ask."

"Where's the list?" asked Gertrude. "I have to go shopping anyway, so I might as well pick up whatever potions the doctor recommended."

Martha almost giggled. She liked Gertrude's adversarial but friendly relationship with the doctor.

"It's on the desk in the study. I wrote out several copies for the rest of the travelers."

Gertrude took Alex inside. Glancing back, Alexander and Martha were in a loving embrace.

The following day, Alexander enjoyed a hearty breakfast Martha made for him. "Have you seen Gertrude? She should come with me when I talk to the doctor."

"She took Alex to pick up the things the doctor suggested we bring: quinine, opium, whiskey, citric acid, and an assortment of tonics."

"I can't keep up with her.... I'll be back in time for lunch." Alexander kissed Martha.

Martha laughed. "No one can keep up with her."

Ten minutes later, Alexander reached Dr. Martin's house. When he arrived, he saw Mrs. Martin sitting on the porch and waved at her. She jumped up and ran into the house, yelling, "Alexander is here!"

Alexander was about to step up when Dr. Martin burst out of the front door, startling him. "Alexander! I was going to visit you at the bank. Your wife stopped by yesterday morning. She's such an inspiration."

"She is."

"I remember that she had a bit of trouble with your firstborn. I'd be happy to look after her while on the trip. I have some tonics that would be beneficial for her. Martha will be fine with the tonics, adequate rest, and minimal exertion."

"You're joining us?" asked Alexander, dumbfounded.

"Yes. Mr. Cortez said you were looking for families to go with you. I've already begun making the preparations. My wife and son are thrilled about it."

Alexander's face was riddled with surprise. "How old is he?"

"Eighteen."

Alexander nodded. "That's great. Traveling with your son will allow you time to care for patients."

"Absolutely! California has been a dream for my wife and me for years, and I've been researching it endlessly. You know I'm a man of science, so I believe in learning everything possible before attempting a monumental move like this. But after Martha's visit yesterday, she lit a fire under us. We decided it was finally time to make it happen. Thanks to her kind words, of course."

"I had no idea."

The doctor held the door open. "Please come inside. I want to show you some of my findings."

Alexander followed Dr. Martin into a room toward the back of the house. The doctor sat at his desk and motioned for Alexander to sit next to him. In front of him were piles of books, maps, and paper. He had never been in this room before. When he and Martha visited Dr. Martin, it was in the examination room near the front of the house.

"As you can see, I've researched traveling out West."

Alexander's eyes grew wide at the mountain of research. "I can see that."

"There are reports of cholera, dysentery, scurvy, snake bites, and other health concerns that travelers reported."

"Yes. Gertrude is in town shopping for those things from the list you gave Martha."

"Gertrude stopped by earlier this morning and asked me a few questions. Bless her heart."

Alexander chuckled.

"We discussed the care required for your wife."

"Gertrude gave me a list, too." The doctor showed Alexander the list.

Alexander picked up the paper and read from it. "Flour, bacon, and dried meats, fruits, and vegetables."

The doctor's eyes brightened. "Gertrude said she would give each of our wagon train travelers a copy of this list. I asked her to share mine as well."

Alexander said, "That's a good idea. Gertrude is bringing her specialties: wild plum and crabapple preserves. She's making a lot of it. They're my favorites."

Dr. Martin didn't take a breath between words. "Half of my

wagon will be full of provisions, and the rest with my books, papers, medicine, and instruments. I may have to leave some of it behind."

"Martha and I have chosen a small collection of our favorite books to take. We'll store the rest, hoping another wagon train might bring them. Or maybe we'll donate them to a library."

The doctor gazed at his shelves. "I wish I could take them all. I have many books, too."

Alexander looked at his pocket watch. It was eleven-thirty. "I have to go. There is so much yet to do. I'm so glad you and your family are traveling to California with us."

The doctor led Alexander to the porch where Mrs. Martin sat.

Dr. Martin said, "We're excited to be going. It's going to be quite an adventure."

"Yes, it will," Alexander said.

The doctor and his wife waved at him as he rode away.

He stopped by the bank for a short while and then went home.

Gertrude was setting the table for lunch when Alexander entered.

Alex ran into his father's open arms. "Pa!"

Martha rushed out of the kitchen. "What did the fine doctor have to say?"

"He and his wife are excited about moving to California with us."

Gertrude grinned. "He couldn't stop talking about it when I saw him."

Alexander kissed Martha. "They've wanted to go for the past few years," he said, looking at Martha curiously. "He mentioned that you convinced them to go."

Martha looked crooked.

"Maybe it was when he told me that you and I were courageous to follow our dream to California. I told him you can't let opportunities pass you by because they seem impossible or too difficult to attain. Letting them pass too often could lead to a regretful life."

CHAPTER TWENTY-TWO

Ready To Go

The early morning light poured into the barn when Alexander opened the doors. He rushed to the wagon, inspected it, and went to the left front wheel. He grabbed the top of the wheel and shook it hard. He tried all four wheels, and all were sound. His family would spend the next several months in this conveyance, and he had to be sure it would withstand the rigors of rough, unpredictable roads. Alexander climbed up to the driver's bench and peeked inside. It was fully loaded.

Juan strolled into the barn. "You've done an excellent job."

A surprised Alexander jumped from the coach and shook Juan Cortez's hand.

"It's great to see you! I think everybody is about ready to go, even Dr. Martin and his family," said Alexander.

Juan chuckled. "Dr. Martin's cousin is taking over his practice. My wife visited his office yesterday and is very impressed with him."

"Martha thinks he's as good a doctor as Dr. Martin."

Juan rolled his eyes. "My wife called him beautiful."

Alexander grinned. "He's young."

Juan glanced away. "On another matter, I'm trying to find an old friend. Wallace didn't know where he was."

"Who are you looking for?"

"Randall Pruitt. He used to have a place just outside of town."

A warm smile crossed Alexander's face. "When I was a kid, he always gave me gifts. He was always around. But after my pa left, Randall kept insisting he was alive. I couldn't handle it, so I asked him to stop coming by." Alexander's gaze dropped. "I regretted it later. He came back briefly about three years ago and said he had a huge ranch about sixty miles south of here. I haven't seen him since."

Juan smiled. "The deputy saw Randall in town yesterday. I'll ride to his old place and see if he's there."

Alexander's face lit up. "If you see him, tell him about us moving away."

"I'll be sure to tell him you sent your regards." Juan nodded. "I'd better let you finish up here. I'll check back with you, and perhaps I can begin to move my things in soon." Juan's eyes darted from one side of the barn to the other and then glanced at the house.

The corner of Alexander's lip curled up slightly. "You can start right away. Most of the house is cleared out. The barn is ready, except for our wagon and the oxen."

"I'll tell Wallace when I have vacated your other house."

"He thinks he may already have a buyer." Alexander chuckled. "Everything seems to be happening quickly. I suppose that happens when decisions are made and plans are executed."

Juan nodded. "I've wasted enough of your time."

Juan tipped his hat at Alexander and left.

Soon after, Juan rode up to Randall's place. He started for the porch when he heard the unmistakable sound of a six-shooter, cocked and ready to fire.

"I should shoot you for putting the idea of moving to California in my brother's head."

Juan turned around and laughed. Randall had a gun pointed at him. "Suspicious as ever. Old friend, how have you been?"

Randall chuckled and stowed his weapon. He walked up to Juan and shook his hand. "It's good to see you. I never thought you'd come back. Are you here to rob stagecoaches or banks or both?"

"I gave that up long ago. I have all the money I need. I made a fortune in California with gold."

Randall narrowed his eyes. "I heard you were in town looking for me."

"You still got someone there spying for you?"

"Of course."

"You ain't never going to change, are you?"

Randall shrugged. "I got better." Randall walked toward the porch. "Let's sit and talk for a bit. Start by telling me why you're back here."

Juan tied his horse to the hitching post and sat across from Randall. "California wasn't right for my family. We're here to stay."

"Did my little brother come back with you?"

"Nope." Juan half-smiled. "I already bought a place here."

Randall cocked his head, his eyes narrowed slightly. "How is Joseph doing?"

"He's well. He made a fortune, too, even more than I did. Joseph is a well-respected sheriff. Can you believe that? A sheriff."

"I got something for you." Juan went to his horse and returned with a small leather pouch. He handed it to Randall and sat down.

"What's this?" Randall opened the pouch.

"Your brother asked me to give you this for his son."

Juan withdrew a folded piece of paper from his pocket. He glanced at Randall, who was rummaging through the pouch. A wrinkle formed between Randall's brows, and his nose scrunched upwards like he'd encountered a particularly pungent odor.

Juan put the paper back in his pocket. He took a deep breath, let it out slowly, and said, "Why don't you move out there? You could make all the money that you could ever want."

Randall shook his head. "Nah. By now, they've pulled out all the gold from the ground. Besides, I like it here."

"I'm moving into the old Swanson house. You know which one. Right?" Juan's face brightened. "My wife and I can hardly wait to move in."

"What?" Randall asked, confused. "I thought Alexander lived in that house."

"They're moving to California. They're almost ready to leave."

Randall's face went pale. "I should pay him a visit."

"They'll be leaving in a few days. I spoke with him this morning, and he asked me to tell you they were moving away."

Juan gazed at the pouch in Randall's hand. "You gonna give that to Thomas?"

"No!" Randall tossed it back to Juan.

"I gotta go." Juan shook his head and went to his horse. He stowed the pouch and the note from his pocket into the bag hanging from his saddle. "We can catch up later."

"Sure thing." Randall waved goodbye as Juan left.

Randall ran to his desk and pulled a six-shooter from the top drawer. He smiled as he wrapped it in the oilcloth he used to clean it. Within a minute, he was on his way to Alexander's house.

Randall rode up to the Swansons' house. He'd never been this close to it before. A memory of Mrs. Swanson screaming at him and calling him a monster startled him. He shuddered and shook the vile thought away.

Alexander was on the front porch enjoying a cool lemonade. He jumped up to greet Randall.

"Howdy," said Randall.

"What a sight for sore eyes," said Alexander, smiling. "I thought you moved down south."

"I did, but I came up to check on my place. My friend Juan said you're moving away."

"Yeah. We're moving to California. I bought a ranch from him."

Randall smiled broadly. "Juan mentioned it. Congratulations!"

Randall walked to his horse and withdrew the six-shooter. "I got a present for you."

Alexander instantly recognized the six-shooter. It was his father's.

"My pa knew I liked it."

Randall handed it to Alexander. "I think you should have it. I've used it several times and always kept it oiled up."

A barely perceptible quiver ran across Alexander's lips. "Thank you." He examined the gun. The faded initials 'C.J.' were on the handle.

"Deep down, he cared for you as much as me. He's the only real friend I've ever had."

Alexander hugged Randall briefly and then returned to admiring the weapon. "You've always been great to me," Alexander said.

A warm smile crept onto Randall's face, revealing profound wrinkles on his sunburned, leathery face.

"I got an idea. Maybe you could come with us to California. We're leaving in a few days."

Randall's nose wrinkled. "I'll think about it."

"You going for the gold out there?"

Alexander chuckled. "I don't think so. Martha and I are adventurers, and we are excited to make a new start there. I already have a job at the Sacramento bank waiting for me."

"Juan said it was exhilarating to live out there."

"Pa!" yelled little Alex as he ran out the door.

Alexander rushed to his son. "This is my boy." Alexander picked up Alex. "My wife is napping inside."

A small smile tugged at the corner of little Alex's lips, his eyes wide with curiosity.

Randall blinked in surprise—the boy was a mirror image of Thomas at that age.

The memory slammed into Randall like a physical blow. He could almost feel the phantom grip of tiny hands clinging to his leg, hear the echo of a young voice pleading, "Don't leave. I love you."

Randall's eyes floated up to Alexander and then settled back on Alex.

He grinned as he crouched down and locked eyes with little Alex. "And who do we have here?"

"I'm Alex. Who are you?"

Randall laughed as a wave of warmth washed over him. It was a sensation he hadn't felt in years, uncomfortable but enjoyable nonetheless.

Randall patted Alex's arm. "I'm Uncle Randall."

Alex smiled at Randall and then turned to Alexander. "I like Uncle Randall."

Randall stepped back and tilted his head curiously. Little Alex stirred something in him that he had thought long dead.

Randall said, "I gotta go."

Alexander picked up Alex. "I hope you seriously consider joining us on our trip."

Randall hesitated and thought of Thomas and little Alex. "I promise I'll think about it."

Alexander and little Alex waved goodbye as Randall left.

Randall was mesmerized by an unfamiliar feeling of euphoria. He planned to get a solid night's rest before heading back south to the big ranch. Randall shook his head and smiled as he thought about little Alex and Thomas.

Randall grimaced. Frank's and Thomas's horses were out front when he rode up to the house.

"Frank!" yelled Randall as he dismounted.

Frank rushed out onto the porch.

"What are you doing here? I thought I told you boys to wait till I got back."

Frank grinned. "We thought you might be in trouble since you didn't get back this morning."

"Don't bullshit me."

"We just wanted to come back to check out the place. We didn't go into town, just here."

"We'll head back in the morning."

"Sure thing."

"Where's Thomas?"

"He's down by the creek."

"Did you know anything about Thomas having a bastard child?"

CHAPTER TWENTY-THREE

Westward Bound

As the sun rose on April 1, 1864, Alexander's family embarked on their cross-country adventure. Twenty-eight wagons – all full of families, provisions, hopes, and dreams lined up, waiting for the word to go.

Martha's eyes were filled with excitement. "Isn't this wonderful?"

She sat next to Alexander with little Alex on her lap. Gertrude was behind Martha.

Gertrude nodded. "We have a ways to go." She reached into her pocket and pulled out a small silver medallion. She held it in her hand and rubbed it between her thumb and her forefinger. It was older than she was, and most of its face had been worn smooth. Her father told her, "It belonged to your mother. It will bring you luck."

Alexander was grinning ear to ear. "This wagon is sturdy and will get us to California. It's a lot bigger than I expected. I'm amazed we could fit everything. It'll be comfortable."

Gertrude looked inside. The interior was orderly but very cramped. She held her lips tight to hide a smile. "I'm sad that Agnes isn't coming with us."

Alexander said, "They'll catch up to us once they get someone to drive them."

The wagons toward the front started to pull away.

"Let's get a move on," came the yells from the wagons ahead.

Alexander's wagon was fifth in the train, followed by the wagon holding the doctor's family.

"Let's go," Alexander yelled to the wagon behind.

It sounded like an echo as the command to go was repeated from wagon to wagon. And just like that, the journey west to California began.

The initial days were smooth. They would rise early each morning, travel for hours, stop, and go some more. Several uneventful weeks passed, and things went well, giving the travelers a false sense of ease. It was more challenging than the day-to-day life they'd been used to back home, but it wasn't as life-threatening as the guidebooks suggested.

Back at Randall's 'outlaw' ranch forty-five miles south of his house, Frank and Thomas were target practicing in the backyard.

Thomas aimed at a tin can some thirty feet away and pulled the trigger. "I'm tired of living here. I liked Randall's house better. This place is nothing but a hideout for outlaws." The can went flying. He lowered his gun as one of Randall's men sauntered by.

"Great shootin', boy!"

Thomas narrowed his eyes and wrinkled his face as the man walked past him. "That guy needs a bath. That long, greasy hair is disgusting."

Frank laughed. "That mostly described you a while back."

Thomas chuckled. "I look handsome now, don't I? I think it's time for me to settle down and get married."

"Married?" Frank guffawed. He aimed at the next can and was about to pull the trigger when Thomas said, "Maybe I'll start a family someday."

Frank shot at the can, and the bullet grazed its edge, barely moving it. He shook his head. It was a long, arduous journey weaning Thomas from his addiction. It took months to knock sense into him.

Frank scoffed. "A family? You already have a kid."

Frank gasped, instantly regretting his words.

Thomas's breathing slowed. "What?"

Frank put his gun down and stood frozen with guilt for having revealed a secret that wasn't his to tell. "I mean..."

Thomas lowered his gun and took a step toward Frank. "What are you keeping from me?"

"Randall told me not to tell you."

Thomas stepped closer. "Tell me."

Frank grunted. "I guess that woman you attacked had a boy after you..."

Thomas thought about Martha and the day he'd hurt her.

"Randall talked with Alexander the day we went to Randall's

house. Alexander's boy walked up. Randall says he was the spitting image of you as a kid. He said he could have been your twin."

The air rushed out of Thomas in a whoosh, leaving him gasping for breath. He shook his head, his voice a rasp. "A boy? Me?" His gaze darted to Frank, a mix of disbelief and anger twisting his features. "That's impossible!"

"You told me you didn't remember what happened after she shot you."

"I think I would remember that!"

Thomas put his gun into his holster and sprinted to the hitching post. "I hate it when you keep stuff from me."

"Where're you going?"

"To see for myself." Thomas jumped on his horse.

"You can't go there. It's likely to get you killed. That woman hates you for what you did to her. Leave her alone."

Thomas smiled at Frank. "I've made many mistakes, and thanks to you, I'm much better. I owe you my life. You know I have to see the boy. I'm not drunk or taking those pills anymore. I'm thinking clearly."

Frank glanced at the house and then back at Thomas. "Wait. I'll go with you if you promise we'll come back today."

Frank gritted his teeth and shook his head. "It's gonna take us three hours to get there. I'll get us something to munch on."

Thomas rolled his eyes.

"Okay. But hurry."

Frank rushed into the house and walked out two minutes later with a bag. "I got us some water, apples, and—"

Thomas half-smiled. "Took you long enough."

Frank jumped on his horse and muttered, "Randall ain't gonna like this."

Thomas grinned. "Let's go!" Thomas clicked to his horse and raced away. Frank chased after him.

They slowed after an hour as Thomas led Frank along a path that made him nervous.

"I sure hope you know where you're going. This is getting rough for our horses."

Thomas pointed to a trail that disappeared behind a hill. "It gets easier around that bend. Let's stop to give the horses a break. We've got another hour till we get there."

Frank narrowed his eyes, the right corner of his lip curled up. "That's a whole lot shorter than this trip is supposed to take. How do you know about this shortcut?"

"I went there several times after we moved to Randall's outlaw ranch." Thomas grimaced. "I couldn't bear seeing Martha with Alexander and stopped going."

Frank shook his head, gnashing his teeth.

Soon after, they rode up to the trail leading to Martha's house. Tens of workers were next to the barn, hammering away.

Thomas stopped. "Something isn't right."

He leaned forward and clicked. His horse obliged and raced toward the house.

Frank chased after him. Thomas stopped, jumped, and ran to the front door without tying his horse to the hitching post.

Thomas knocked.

Frank hitched his and Thomas's horses and rushed to the porch.

With a bewildered frown, Thomas raised his fist and pounded on the unyielding door.

Juan opened the door, annoyed at the two men for the intrusion. He threw them an irritated glance. "What do you want? You boys lookin' for work?"

"Mr. Cortez?" he choked out. He remembered Mr. Cortez, a friend of his father's.

Frank cocked his head back in surprise. Randall told him that Juan had organized the trip that had taken Thomas's father to California.

Juan squinted and leaned forward. "Is that you, Thomas?" he turned to Frank. "Frank? It can't be."

Thomas nodded.

Juan smiled and motioned to them. "Come inside. Welcome to my home."

Thomas tapped Frank's arm with his elbow and followed Juan inside. Thomas noticed that the furniture had been rearranged. He recognized where Martha had fallen, or rather where he'd knocked her down years before.

Juan led them to the study and motioned for them to sit. Thomas and Frank sat. The bookshelves were filled with books.

"The last time I saw you both, you were rascally boys with quite a lot of time on your hands." Juan smiled. "I see that you both are still inseparable."

"You took my father to California. I remember." Thomas leaned forward, his face wrinkled in anger.

Juan's smile disappeared, and his brows went up. "Yes. And you were supposed to come with us." Juan's smile returned. "Are you going to go to see him now? Is that why you're here?"

Thomas's shoulders slumped. "Randall told me that he was dead."

Frank shook his head ever so slightly.

Juan chuckled. "Dead? No, he's not dead." Juan shook his head. "That Randall, always spinning the truth to suit him."

Thomas narrowed his eyes at Frank and gritted his teeth.

Juan took a deep breath and let it out all at once. "Randall will always be Randall." Juan went to the desk and withdrew a folded paper from the center drawer. He handed it to Thomas. "Your father asked me to give this to you if I saw you. And here you are."

Thomas hesitated as he took it. He unfolded the paper and read it aloud, "Son, I miss you. I've written you many letters throughout the years and never received one back. I gave up writing a while ago. It occurred to me that Randall might have kept them from you. Juan suggested I write this letter to be certain that you receive it. Please come to California. You can live with me and my wife, Elizabeth. I'm a sheriff and have made a decent, honest living. I've sent you a small sample of the gold that made me rich. Please come, Your Pa."

"I never got any letters." Thomas narrowed his eyes at Frank again. "Did you know anything about those letters?"

"I didn't know. I wouldn't keep something that big from you."

"At least you got this letter." Juan pulled a small pouch from the desk. "You're important to your pa."

Thomas's gaze darted from Frank to Juan. "He wants me to go to California?"

Juan nodded and handed Thomas the small leather pouch

Joseph gave him.

Thomas fell back into his chair, speechless, as he examined the contents of the pouch.

Frank straightened up. "Juan, what happened to the woman who was living here? Her name is Martha."

Juan smiled. "They left for California about three days ago." He turned to Thomas. "It's too bad you didn't go with them."

Juan picked up a rolled-up paper from his desk. "This is a map of the way they went. Perhaps you could catch up to them. Your father is most anxious to see you. After your ma passed, it took him a long time to get his life straightened out. His new wife doesn't let him go near a drink. He's a respectable man."

Thomas was overwhelmed. His face relaxed as he put the items back into the leather pouch. He realized that Juan presented him with a way to travel to California, visit his father, and escape from Randall. He could see the little boy Frank told him about, too.

Thomas leaned forward. "I don't have the means to go to California."

Frank's right leg started to bob up and down, his heart racing.

"That's not a problem. I'd be happy to help you with that. Three wagons weren't ready to leave on time. They're looking for someone to help drive one of them. It's not too late to help them catch up to Alexander's wagon train."

Juan didn't notice Thomas wince when he mentioned Alexander.

Thomas hesitated. "But, I hadn't planned to—"

"The wagons must leave tomorrow. If they leave later, they won't be able to catch up to the rest of the wagon train. They could sure use your help." Juan leaned in toward Thomas. "Do you think you'll be ready to go tomorrow?"

"I don't have much of anything holding me here." Thomas felt a surge of excitement. He hesitated. His eyes shot to Frank and then fell on Juan. "Yes," he said.

"Excellent."

Frank stood. "I can't go. You can't either. You have to stay."

Thomas shook his head. "You're gonna tell Randall, aren't you?"

Frank gasped. "I—I—"

"Frank, I gotta do this. You know I do, for a lot of reasons."

Frank stared at Thomas, his mouth open.

Thomas narrowed his eyes at Frank. "I want you to promise me something."

Frank closed his mouth and blinked several times.

Thomas relaxed and nodded at Frank. "I know you'll tell Randall, but you've got to give me enough time to get away. I don't want him coming after me."

Frank, his lips tight, nodded.

Juan stayed quiet while Frank and Thomas talked. They reminded him of his friendship with Joseph, Thomas's father.

"You two are terrific friends," said Juan.

The three wagons took about a week to catch up to Alexander's wagon train. Thomas drove the lead wagon, which belonged to the old couple. The old man was fragile and slow-moving, but the old woman, Agnes, was full of spunk. The three wagons were at the tail end of the train, and Thomas was careful to avoid the other people. Agnes preferred they keep to themselves. It worked out well for Thomas. Thomas felt invigorated, almost like he'd been given a new life.

One day, the travelers were served a tiny dose of reality. The wagon ahead of Alexander's, fourth from the lead, seemed unsteady. The day before, it pitched to one side. Alexander told the owner that perhaps the weight needed to be redistributed inside the wagon. That wagon belonged to a wealthy couple. The husband was headstrong and not prone to listening to anyone. He was one of the bank's oldest customers. They were traveling with their two sons, who were about sixteen or seventeen years of age. Unlike the father, the sons were very polite and respectful to Alexander.

Alexander watched their wagon from his bench while Martha sat beside him. She had a book with her that she tried to read, but with all the shaking, it was impossible.

Alexander glanced at Martha. He pointed to the wagon in front of them. "I told them their wagon was leaning to one side."

Martha pointed at their right wheel. "Yesterday, the wagon was leaning the other way. Their wheel on this side seems unsteady."

A loud crash came at them from that wagon. Alexander's eyes widened. "No!" yelled Alexander.

The right wheel of the wagon in front of Alexander wobbled wildly and flew off its axle, careening toward Martha's side.

Martha yelled, "Oh my God. It's coming right at us."

Alexander pulled hard left on the reins. The wheel was heavy enough to hurt anyone or anything in its path. His wagon was about to plow into the back of the now-stalled three-wheeled wagon.

"Whoa!" screamed Alexander to the oxen. He pulled hard on the reins. Alexander was an expert with his horse, but not with these oxen. The escaping wheel crashed into Alexander's wagon.

Alexander's oxen stopped inches away from the hobbled wagon.

Gertrude peeked out from the back. "What's going on out here?"

Martha turned to Gertrude and pointed ahead. "They lost a wheel."

The errant wheel was leaning against Martha's side of the wagon.

Out the back, Gertrude could see the trailing wagons. "Everyone behind us is stopping."

As Alexander stood, a chorus of deep, guttural grunts erupted from the oxen.

He handed the reins to Martha.

The wealthy couple's wagon was stopped with a bowed, bare axle poking into the ground.

Alexander shook his head. "Perhaps they should have taken care of that wagon as I told them."

Martha exhaled in a huff. "Someone could have been hurt."

Alexander shook his head. "I suppose that we'll be staying here for the night."

He jumped down, inspected the wheel leaning against his wagon, and rolled it back to its owner.

Several men from the other wagons were walking toward the tilted wagon. The owner and his two boys inspected the damage as Alexander and the other men stepped up.

Alexander let the wheel lean against the man's wagon. "Your wheel is in excellent shape."

"The axle is okay, too," said the man. "But there's too much weight on it. We need to get that wheel back on it." He pointed to his boys. "Boys, help these men get that wheel back on its axle."

Alexander stepped forward, "Wait a minute. I told you yesterday your wagon was leaning to one side."

The man tipped his head back and narrowed his eyes at Alexander. "We did rearrange things in there. I did as you asked. It didn't help any. It appears it made matters worse."

"Then you've got too much weight in your wagon."

"We just brought some things that we'll be needing over there, a stove—"

A gasp ripped through Alexander's lips, shattering his silence as his eyes widened in astonishment. "What? A stove!"

He peeked into the wagon and saw the man's wife in the front, staring back at him, crying.

Alexander grimaced and turned back to the man. "You get rid of that stove."

"I'll do nothing of the sort. You told me to move that stuff around, and it's your fault that my wagon is in this state. Moving those things over this wheel caused it to fail."

Alexander marched close to the man. "You get rid of that stove. You don't need that for this trip."

The man pushed Alexander hard and yelled, "You're not in charge."

Alexander stepped closer and narrowed his eyes. "I told you to get that stove out of your wagon. I'm not asking again."

The wealthy man shoved Alexander again. Alexander stumbled backward and fell to the ground. Six of the men from the other wagons rushed up behind Alexander. Before Alexander could get up, the wealthy man had his gun pointed at him. The men became rowdy, and several began charging at the rich man.

A booming shot rang out.

Randall stepped up and helped Alexander to his feet.

"What seems to be the problem here?" Randall asked, his gun pointed at the rich man. "It looks like your little wagon lost one of its wheels." Randall holstered his weapon and stood inches from the wealthy man's face. "I suggest that you do whatever Alexander tells you to do. You don't have a choice."

The wealthy man, who had never been spoken to in this manner, stuttered. "O-, O-, Okay."

Shame washed over the faces of the two sons as they exchanged a silent glance. Their eyes, filled with regret, dropped to the ground.

The wealthy man told his boys, "Let's get that stove and the other heavy things out of the wagon."

He turned to the men who were standing nearby. "If I could oblige you to help us, I would be grateful."

Randall walked up to Alexander. "Can I have a word with you?"

Alexander nodded and led Randall away.

"I thought you weren't coming with us," said Alexander.

"You convinced me. I sold my interest in my ranch. I would have caught up to you sooner, but obtaining wagons and supplies took me a while."

Alexander squinted toward the end of the wagon train, expecting to see Randall's wagons. Confused, he turned back to Randall.

Randall locked eyes with Alexander. "My men are a day's ride behind you. I rode ahead to ensure you were okay with us joining you. We got three wagons back there. We'd be happy to help keep people in line if that's what you want. Although we aren't looking for trouble."

"Of course, that would be great if you joined us. I didn't expect that we'd need to keep the peace. We're not even one-quarter of the way there, and people are starting to get tired of this."

Randall half-smiled. "I can see that."

A loud thud came from the rich man's wagon. Alexander's jaw dropped when he saw the stove had left a crater where it had fallen.

Randall shook his head. "I bet there are other wagons that might be carrying stuff they shouldn't."

Several men lifted the rich man's wagon as another two pushed the wheel into place.

Alexander's brows went up, thankful that the wagon was whole again. "We'll have a meeting today about ensuring that all the wagons can make the trip safely." He nodded at Randall. "These are good people. This is new to all of us."

"Yeah, for me, too," said Randall. "I never thought I'd leave New York."

"Is everything okay?" yelled Martha from the wagon.

Randall's eyes darted to Alexander's wagon and saw Martha standing beside it, holding a little boy.

Alexander waved at Martha and turned back to Randall. "Come meet my wife."

Randall shook his head. "I really gotta go, or my men won't arrive here before dark."

Randall raised his hat at Martha, rushed to his horse, and rode away.

Alexander walked back to their wagon.

"Who was that?" asked Martha.

"That's Randall. He and his men are going to join us. I think they'll be helpful."

Martha nodded. "He looks familiar."

As the trek's initial excitement faded, the travelers' determination strengthened. They adjusted to the trip's demands and found a new normal. The camaraderie fueled their commitment to make the journey comfortable and safe. The trip was not taxing since they shared the work and helped one another. Randall and his men stayed to themselves almost a mile from the tail of the wagon train.

CHAPTER TWENTY-FOUR

Savages

The quasi-trail before them, traveled by many others over the last ten years, beckoned Alexander forward. Gripping the reins, he felt a surge of exhilaration, unlike anything he'd known. This wasn't just driving a wagon but navigating their destiny across a vast frontier. Martha, his loving companion, sat beside him, her eyes reflecting a mixture of apprehension and excitement. Inside, nestled amongst the sacks of provisions, Gertrude hummed a lullaby, the soft melody a counterpoint to the rhythmic creak of the wheels. Curled next to her, Alex slept soundly, oblivious to the grand adventure unfolding around him.

Martha glanced inside. "I'm glad that Alex likes to take frequent naps. That's why he's so healthy."

Gertrude smiled. "That lemonade every day helps, too. It keeps us all healthy." She urged everyone to drink her special lemonade, which consisted of citric acid, sugar, a few drops of lemon essence, and water.

Martha chuckled. "Yes, that too." She nudged Alexander. "This trip has been wondrous. The weather has been mostly comfortable, except at night. Sometimes it's a little chilly, but snuggling under a warm blanket is delicious."

Alexander turned to her, "It might get a little cooler as we get closer to California."

Martha's eyes went large, and her mouth fell open as she pointed ahead of the train. "What is that?" Martha's voice creaked with worry.

Martha grabbed Alexander's arm. A dozen thin towers of smoke rose from behind the hills in the direction they were headed. The smell of cooking meat permeated the air.

Alexander sat taller and squinted at the oncoming adventure. The four lead wagons slowed to a snail's pace and finally stopped. "It's smoke." He cocked his head back. "Yes. Riders are headed this way, too." He pulled hard on the reins, and his wagon halted.

The others behind them did the same.

Martha gasped. Several men on horseback were traveling fast toward them. They had darker skin than she was used to seeing. "Those are Natives. I read about them in the history books. Christopher Columbus encountered them when he first arrived. He thought he had landed in India and mistakenly called them Indians. That guidebook we got from Juan warned that we might encounter savages."

Little Alex woke from his nap and crawled out. "Ma!"

"Come here, darling." Martha scooped Alex up, her eyes sharp.

Alexander thought of a fly caught in a spider's web. "We have nowhere to go. We're trapped."

Gertrude squinted at the approaching strangers. "They don't look like savages to me."

She climbed down and started toward the riders, waving her arms up and down at them.

"Gertrude!" Alexander yelled. "Where are you going? Come back here."

A weak smile flickered on Gertrude's lips as she turned. Her voice, though strained, held a hint of defiance. "Don't worry," she said, "I'll be alright."

She reached the lead wagon and kept going, slowly waving her arms back and forth. She saw only ten Natives.

Martha's heart pounded as the scene unfolded, and fear coiled in her stomach. "Alexander, we have to do something," she cried, her voice barely a panicked whisper.

Alexander grabbed his rifle and jumped to the ground. "Gertrude!"

Gertrude spun around.

Alexander stood with his weapon pointed menacingly at the figures approaching Gertrude.

She held her hands on her hips as if scolding him and shook her head. "No."

Alexander, his face a mixture of frustration and worry, slowly lowered his rifle, the defiance draining from his posture.

As Gertrude trudged away from safety, her heart pounded in her chest. She gasped. Now, dozens of them were on horseback to her left, right, and as far as she could see. They were like statues, sitting on horses, staring at her. Her legs almost buckled as she realized she might have made a mistake. She froze.

Three Natives in the middle of the group closed in on her. Two stopped fifty feet from her while the man in the center continued toward her.

He narrowed his brows in surprise when he got close to her. Her face was painted with fright. He got down from his horse and strolled to Gertrude, holding something in his hand. He smiled and then bowed his head. He spoke words she couldn't understand.

Gertrude tilted her head and squinted at the man. Her fear transformed from worry to doubt and hopefulness. When he smiled at her, she settled on optimism. Not knowing what to do next, she curtsied and then bowed.

The man grinned, showing his chiseled chin, defined face, and beautiful white teeth.

Gertrude's face flushed a dark crimson. "You're so… tall."

His grin disappeared as he shook his head, confused.

She remembered something she had read in Alexander's guidebook. She raised her right hand, locked eyes with him, and said, "Hello."

He chuckled, and his head bobbed up and down excitedly. "Hello."

He opened his hand, revealing a necklace crafted from smooth, cool stones strung with thin leather strips. He offered it to her.

She took the gift and put it on. She smiled at him and pointed at the necklace. "Thank you. This is lovely."

She reached into her pocket and pulled out the small silver medallion that had once belonged to her mother.

She kissed the charm and brought it toward her heart. Then, she gave it to him.

He accepted her gift and touched it to his chest.

"Are you the Chief?"

He pointed to himself. "Chief."

Gertrude was pleased that they were communicating. "Chief."

He pointed to the wagon train and then pointed to a trail. "Home. Rest."

He winked at Gertrude, pointed to the trail again, and said, "Rest."

Gertrude's face lit up with understanding. "Are you inviting us to your home?" She surmised he'd learned a little English as travelers went through here.

He made a sweeping gesture as he pointed from the wagon train to the trail. "Home. Rest."

Gertrude breathed a sigh of relief. "Yes. Home. Rest."

The man returned to his horse. He rode to the trail from the main road and waited for the wagons.

Gertrude rushed back. She told each family in the four lead wagons, "Follow the Chief. He's offered us a place to rest. We'll be safe; he has my lucky charm."

Her fellow travelers were hesitant at first, but she convinced them. She had an endearing way of persuading people to her way of thinking. It helped that the rest of the Natives, except the Chief and two others, had left.

The Chief examined the silver medallion. It was smooth with faint lines where an impression used to be. It was worn down. He turned it over. The back was also smooth. He put it in his palm and bounced it, weighing it. It was heavy. He looked back at Gertrude. She was climbing into her wagon. A small smile wrinkled his cheeks. The wagons started to move. He stowed the silver piece away and led his guests to a scenic plain near hundreds of teepees.

The wagons took almost an hour to position along the trail's side. Some pulled up close to each other because they were still worried and preferred to bunch up together, just in case. "Safety in numbers," some of them said. It wasn't necessary because there was ample space.

Once they were settled, some ventured into the village. Soon after, their fear and apprehension disappeared.

Gertrude said to Martha and Alexander. "I think our new friends are in the middle of a grand celebration. They're quite lively."

Alexander marveled at the group of small fires situated away from the teepees. "They must be cooking a feast over there."

Martha said, "It reminds me of the picnic fairs we attended in the park. The fire pits were on one side, the performers were on the other, and people were eating all over. The guidebook suggested that not all Natives were savage; most were peaceful and enjoyed trading with passing travelers. 'Bring a trinket, get a trinket,' it said."

The practice of trading spread quickly throughout the caravan of wagons. None of the travelers considered anything they traded or received in return mere trinkets. Their hosts gave them clothing, blankets, fine jewelry, and more.

Martha and Gertrude stood together, watching little Alex play with the children.

"The children are beautiful," said Martha.

Gertrude said, "These are marvelous celebrations."

"This must be a festival for them."

"I'll say. They look like they're having a good time."

Martha patted Gertrude's arm. "I'll be right back. I'm going to get my shawl."

Gertrude nodded, and Martha rushed away.

A few seconds later, the Chief tapped Gertrude's shoulder.

Gertrude turned and smiled broadly. "Hello."

The Chief towered over her. The creases on his face softened. "Hello."

Gertrude said, "My name is Guuuurtrooood." She pointed to herself.

He repeated her name in the same exaggerated way, "Guuuurtrooood."

He pointed to himself. "Chief."

A woman with long braids and a gentle smile approached, balancing two steaming cups on a small wooden tray. The Chief spoke to her in a soft murmur. She nodded and offered one of the cups to Gertrude. The woman's dark eyes sparkled with kindness.

Gertrude graciously accepted the cup. The aroma wafting up was unlike anything she'd encountered—earthy, slightly sweet, and intensely inviting. Taking a tentative sip, she was surprised by the burst of flavor. It was better than any tea she'd ever tasted— complex, soothing, and strangely invigorating.

"This is delicious," she exclaimed. "I've never had a beverage quite like it."

The Chief, his weathered face creased with amusement, let out a hearty chuckle, the sound rumbling deep from his chest. Just then, Martha appeared by Gertrude's side, her brow furrowed with curiosity.

The Chief nodded to the woman. She offered Martha the remaining cup.

"Chief," he rumbled, pointing to himself with a twinkle in his eye.

Martha followed suit, pointing to herself. "Martha."

His smile widened as he repeated her name, his voice a low, musical rumble. "Martha."

Taking the cup, Martha expressed her gratitude. "Thank you." A cautious sip revealed a flavor explosion – earthy yet surprisingly refreshing.

Having finished her tea, Gertrude held it out expectantly. "More, please?" she inquired with hopeful eyes.

The Chief said something to the woman, his gaze flickering to Gertrude's empty cup. The woman nodded and gestured for her to follow.

"Bye," the Chief boomed with a grin, winking at Gertrude as he left.

Gertrude's eyebrows shot up in amusement, followed by a giggle.

Martha let out a hearty laugh. "Gertrude!"

"A girl can dream, can't she?" Gertrude countered with a playful glint in her eyes. She turned to follow the woman to discover the tea's secrets.

Martha rolled her eyes playfully. "Wait! Have you seen Alexander anywhere?"

Gertrude glanced back toward their wagon. "There he is," she replied, pointing. "Talking with Randall." Gertrude left with the woman.

Martha's brow furrowed as she spotted Randall by the wagon. His head shook in what appeared to be disapproval as he spoke with Alexander. The exchange seemed to end abruptly as Randall's gaze flickered toward her. Without a word, he turned and stormed off in the opposite direction.

She glanced over at Alex, who was sitting with the other

children. He was enthralled by the dancers in colorful clothing performing for the group. She kept an eye on him as she walked to Alexander. When she reached Alexander's side, she said, her voice laced with concern, "He doesn't seem too pleased."

Alexander took her hand reassuringly. "Randall doesn't feel comfortable with these people. He's taking his group ahead, and we likely won't see him for days."

"These people?" Martha's unease intensified as she watched Randall's retreating figure disappear into the horizon. "Something about him rubs me the wrong way," she confessed. "The way he always seems to vanish whenever I approach... it feels deliberate, almost like he's avoiding me."

Alexander shrugged. "He's certainly been a help getting us this far. Maybe he's the loner type." A flicker of doubt crossed his eyes despite his words, a silent acknowledgment of Martha's unease.

Gertrude made multiple trips to the wagon with the gifts from her new friends. Gertrude had chatted with many of the women in the camp. They couldn't understand her words, but Gertrude developed a knack for explaining with her hands. One family invited Gertrude to spend the night inside their teepee. She thought it was an exciting opportunity to become enlightened in their ways. Martha politely declined her invitation. She couldn't imagine spending the night away from her husband and child.

Their hosts were very generous. They shared food, supplies, clothing, and blankets for their journey.

The celebrations went late into the night.

The travelers found getting up early the following morning challenging. A cup of strong black coffee helped them prepare to continue their trip.

Gertrude returned to her wagon at sunrise. She regretted accepting their invitation to spend the night in a teepee, sleeping on a thin blanket on the hard ground. Her crowded, makeshift bed in the wagon was considerably more comfortable.

Alexander and Martha were beside the wagon when the Chief rode up and got down from his horse.

The Chief walked up to Alexander. "Guur..., Guurtrude...."

Alexander was confused at first, and then his face lit up.

"Gertrude! You're saying, Gertrude. I'll go get her." Alexander held his palm facing the Chief. "Wait."

Alexander rushed to the back of the wagon and peeked in. Gertrude was hard at work making room for all the "trinkets" and food they'd gotten from their new friends.

"Gertrude, the Chief is asking for you."

She stepped out of the front and jumped down.

Like a silent promise, the Chief, his eyes warmed with kindness, handed her a gift.

Gertrude gasped, her eyes glistening with surprise. Her good-luck charm was now part of an elaborate necklace. It was extraordinary. Her cherished medallion stood as its centerpiece. The work of art was designed to hang from her neck with a crafted string of polished beads, smooth brown woven leather, and silver at its heart.

Her eyes swelled with tears. "It's stunning!"

Martha's face filled with amazement. "It's spectacular."

Gertrude held it close to her heart and bowed repeatedly to the Chief.

He closed his eyes and bowed his head slightly.

Turning to Alexander and Martha, he pointed to the trail and said, "Go."

He rode to his awaiting men.

In no time, the Chief and his men led the wagon train out of the prairie on a path that would save them several days of travel. Once the travelers were safely beyond the unfriendly terrain, the Natives left.

Martha sat with Alexander, holding little Alex. "Those wonderful people. I fell in love with their beautiful children."

"Why can't we stay?" asked Alex. "I liked playing with my friends."

Alexander laughed. "You'll love our new home when we get there. I'm sure of it. And you'll meet more friends there."

Martha turned to Gertrude. "Weren't you scared marching up to those Natives on the trail alone?"

Gertrude leaned back in her makeshift seat next to the provisions. She clenched her teeth into a grin and nodded.

"I was terrified. I'll never have the courage to do that again."

CHAPTER TWENTY-FIVE

Chance Encounter

The wagon train forged ahead over the next few months. Ever since the day they met the Natives, their trip had been mostly uneventful but challenging nonetheless. The travelers grew tired of the monotony. They became skilled at working together to face the many adversities. However, none of them would consider making the trek again. "Never again" was a mantra often muttered. It didn't help that heavy rains forced them to stop for two days until the rain left and the roads dried. The mood transformed into hope when the sun peeked through the clouds. Then, the news spread like wildfire that they were about a week away from arriving at their new home. There was a renewed vigor. The mantra changed to: "That wasn't so bad."

Alexander and Martha saw the mirage not far from the road: a big, still water hole reflecting an orange-colored sunset at them. The rains gifted them this beautiful, crystal-clear pocket of water. The promise of a cool, refreshing bath was too much to resist. The driver of the lead wagon signaled for the rest to pull over. It was the perfect place for a weary train to gather around this unexpected oasis.

Alexander turned to Martha. "We're stopping."

Gertrude peeked out. "Today, I'm cooking. It's time for you to relax."

Martha smiled. "I'll take Alex for a walk and investigate that waterhole. It looks inviting."

Alexander kissed Martha. "Enjoy. I'll head over and find Randall."

Gertrude said, "Martha, just stay on the trail and be careful of snakes. It'll be at least an hour before dinner is ready."

"Come, Alex." Martha helped him down from the wagon. "Off we go."

As Martha passed the other wagons, the aroma of tasty food permeated the air. Women busily prepared their specialties. As she neared the last of the three wagons, Agnes, Gertrude's best friend, sat outside the first one. Her family preferred to stay to themselves and keep their distance from others. Even so, now and then, she would bring her family to the clearing where Gertrude, Martha, and Agnes would have a fine time chatting while little Alex played with Agnes's grandchildren.

As Martha drew near, Agnes jumped up, surprised. She turned to her wagon. "Thomas, stay inside!"

For the most part, Thomas kept to himself. He'd managed to stay hidden from Alexander and Randall, the two people who might do him harm, although he hadn't seen Randall in weeks. An image of him mauled by a wild animal flashed in his head.

A month after the trip began, Thomas told Agnes about some of his encounters with Martha. She was furious with him at first, but she became sympathetic when he recounted the whole story, thanks to her prodding. Thomas was unaware that Agnes was Gertrude's best friend and had known Martha since birth.

Thomas glimpsed a young boy with Alexander from afar once when he snuck up to the wagons closer to the front. But he'd never seen him up close and never talked to him. Weeks passed, and he never dared approach the child.

"I can't do it," he thought. "They'd shoot me dead as soon as they saw me."

Initially, he thought meeting the boy was a good idea, but now he felt asserting himself where he was not wanted might hurt the child or his family.

"What was I thinking?" he muttered. "When I get to California, I'll find my father and forget about Martha's family."

Thomas rode alone with the old couple in the first wagon. Agnes's husband often rested inside, and Agnes sat beside Thomas. He usually drove, although she would sometimes take the reins. Now and then, she would yell at him for no particular reason. He assumed that the trip was difficult for her at times. The other two wagons had two young, rambunctious children in each. Their oldest son, wife, and two children were in the next wagon. The third wagon had the youngest son, his wife, and two children. In the evening, after a long day of riding, they would gather and enjoy a nice meal prepared often by the grandmother (Agnes) and occasionally by her daughters-in-law.

The four children grew fond of Thomas, affectionately calling him Uncle. He appreciated them, although they were sometimes too "wild" for him. He preferred to retreat to the solitude of the wagon for an hour before supper to grab a nap. That's when they were at their wildest. They were all under ten years old. He felt a little awkward with them. He'd never been around youngsters.

He heard Agnes tell him to stay inside the wagon. He was leaning against a grain bag. A cool breeze blew, causing the fabric curtain at the back to flap loudly. Another curtain hung in the front, just behind where the driver sat. The rain had come and gone a few days before. He could hear the children playing outside, laughing and giggling. He tried to get comfortable, crossed his arms, and closed his eyes. Then, he heard Agnes talking loudly, followed by a familiar voice. His eyes shot open.

Agnes said, "Martha, didn't Gertrude tell you I didn't want to be disturbed here at my wagon?"

"She did. I'm sorry. Agnes, would you mind watching Alex?" asked Martha. "I've got to cool off in that water hole. I'm burning up."

Thomas pulled back the curtain that kept the light from coming inside. He peeked outside and saw Martha holding her young son's hand, talking to Agnes. The boy glanced in his direction. Thomas gasped, fumbled to shut the curtain, and muttered, "He doesn't look that much like me."

Alex noticed the curtain close suddenly. It piqued his curiosity. It reminded him of when his mother would pretend to hide behind the curtain and then peek out, laughing.

"Those women over there are making a spectacle of themselves," said Agnes. "Cackling like a bunch of geese."

"Hopefully, they won't be too much of a nuisance so that I can cool off there in peace," Martha said.

Agnes cocked her head back and squinted slightly at Martha. "You look flushed. There's no sense in overheating in this heat." Agnes motioned to one of her daughters-in-law. "We'll be happy to watch your boy. We love little Alex."

"Thank you. He enjoys playing with your grandchildren."

"Alex will have a fine time," Agnes said, taking a cookie from a box on a table next to the wagon. Her eyes darted to the curtain by the driver's bench. "I have some cookies left from the batch I baked yesterday."

Alex turned away from the curtain. "I like cookies."

Agnes gave the dessert to Alex.

Alex took the treat and ran to play with the other children.

Martha said, "I won't be long." And rushed away to cool off.

Thomas peeked out again and watched Alex for a few minutes. A wave of guilt suddenly consumed him. He leaned back, closed his eyes, and fell asleep.

What seemed like an instant later, he was jarred from sleep. A sharp prod against his arm jolted him awake. His eyes snapped open wide with terror, sure that his arm was shot. Panic surged through him. He jumped back, his eyes filled with fear as the scene came into focus.

Little Alex peered at him through the open curtain, using a stick to poke his arm.

"Hey, mister. Are you awake?" asked Alex.

Thomas pushed himself up and smiled at the little boy.

Alex dropped the stick.

"I'm waiting for my ma to come back from the water. She left a while ago."

Thomas gasped. "Where's your pa?"

"He went off to find Uncle Randall."

Thomas sat taller.

Alex leaned in and tilted his head. "Where's your pa?"

Thomas flinched. "Uhh. He's in California. I don't rightly know where."

Alex's face lit up brightly. "That's where we're going! When my pa gets back, maybe he can help you find your pa."

Thomas shrugged and tried to get comfortable. "How old are you?"

"I'm almost four." Alex held up his right hand, showing four fingers.

"You're smart." Thomas's face softened as his heart warmed.

"My ma taught me. She's real smart."

Thomas's heart skipped a beat. "I don't think she likes me much."

Alex chuckled and shook his head repeatedly. "Ma likes everyone. When she comes back—"

Thomas sat up. "No. Don't tell her about me. Do you know how to keep a secret?"

"Yeah," Alex said slowly, glancing down with a faint smile. "Well. Ma told me I could have one cookie, but I didn't tell her I took another one."

"I won't tell. I'll keep your secret if you keep mine." Thomas locked eyes with Alex. They were full of warmth and childhood innocence. Thomas took a shallow breath as his heart raced with guilt.

Alex giggled. "Okay. I'll keep your secret." Alex wrinkled his nose.

Thomas smiled. "Your ma is a good person—"

The wagon rocked. The curtain opened wide, and its collected dust swirled above little Alex.

"Alex. What are you doing up here? Disturbing this—"

Martha saw Thomas staring back at her.

Thomas leaned back, exposed. He held up his hands as if in a hold-up. "I'm sorry. He just walked in and surprised me." His gaze dropped to her midsection and then back to her face, her mouth open in shock.

The curtain fell back in place after Martha briskly picked Alex up and left.

Thomas sat there, prepared to atone for his sins. Soon, Alexander, or worse, Randall, would come for him. He waited and waited and waited.

"Dinner's ready, Thomas," yelled Agnes. "You've been sleeping long enough!"

CHAPTER TWENTY-SIX

Sick and Tired

Martha rushed back to their wagon, tugging at little Alex's hand along the way.

"Ma, why are you crying?" asked Alex, struggling to keep up. "That man said he was sorry."

Alex always told his mother that he was sorry after he'd done something he wasn't supposed to do. She would smile, hug him, and say, "Don't do that again. Okay?"

Martha pulled Alex closer to her as she walked faster.

"Ma, you're hurting my hand."

Martha stopped and knelt next to Alex.

"We need to get back right away."

She wiped her tears and forced a smile.

"You're such a beautiful boy." Martha picked him up. "Oh my, you're getting heavy. Before you know it, you'll be going off to school."

"What's that?"

Martha felt lightheaded as she battled to maintain her composure. "It's a place where you learn with other children your age."

Alex grinned. "Do big boys go there?"

"Yes, they do."

Martha was gasping as they arrived at their wagon.

Gertrude was putting vegetables into a pot and smiled at them. "Dinner will be ready soon."

Martha caught her breath and waited while Gertrude moved a large pot to the fire pit. "Could you look after Alex?"

"Of course. Are you okay? You look a bit pale, and your eyes are puffy."

Martha rolled her eyes and exhaled in a huff. "I'm fine." She put Alex down next to Gertrude.

Gertrude took Alex's hand and led him away from the cooking

area to where they usually sat to eat.

Martha rushed to the wagon and pulled the bag with her gun from below the driver's seat.

Gertrude looked up from the stew she was preparing. "Martha, where are you going?"

Martha walked past her as if she hadn't heard her.

Gertrude watched, confused, as Martha marched away.

When Martha reached the back of their wagon, she fell against the back wheel and held herself up. She was motionless for a few seconds.

Gertrude gasped. She turned to Alex. "Sit down here and don't move."

She ran to Martha.

Martha slumped to her knees, rubbing her forehead. Sobbing erupted from her like a dam bursting, raw and unrestrained.

Gertrude knelt next to Martha. "Martha, what's wrong?"

Martha shut her eyes and tried to breathe normally through her tears.

Gertrude waved for help to the women who were watching nearby.

Martha opened her eyes. Her face hardened as she wrangled her emotions. "I think I've been in the sun too long. I feel nauseated."

Several women gathered around them. One of them yelled as she ran away, "I'll go get Dr. Martin."

Martha choked out, "Give me a minute."

Gertrude's eyes flickered with alarm.

Martha doubled over, "I'm going to be sick." She let loose whatever was in her stomach. Afterward, she leaned back, closed her eyes, and sat motionless.

When the doctor walked up, Gertrude said, "Help me get her inside."

Martha grabbed her bag as they helped her inside.

Once in the wagon, he examined Martha while Gertrude watched from behind the driver's seat.

Martha looked up, surprised, as if she'd forgotten the doctor was there.

Dr. Martin smiled. "I'm almost finished, Martha. You need to relax. Your heart is racing."

Gertrude turned to leave. "I'll get her something to eat."

The doctor barked out, his irritation barely veiled. "Rest and calm; that's what she needs. Food can wait. I'll talk to you outside when I'm done."

Gertrude's jaw clenched, but she kept her voice even. "Okay." A grimace flickered across her face as she left, leaving the doctor alone with his patient.

"I feel better now," Martha chirped, but a tremor in her voice betrayed the lingering weakness.

The doctor gave her a curt nod. "Get some sleep. I'll be back to check on you."

Martha inhaled deeply, the air catching in her throat as she released it in a shaky exhale. "I will," she whispered.

He patted her hand, his expression softening, before crawling out of the cramped space. He rushed to Gertrude, concern creasing his brow. "Gertrude, Martha—"

He was cut off by a raspy voice peeking out from the wagon's opening. "Alex, come take a nap with me. You must be tired, little one."

Alex, ever obedient, hurried inside, disappearing behind the canvas flap.

Gertrude watched the curtain fall shut, listening to the hushed conversation within. A momentary frown creased her face. Whatever the doctor had to say, she'd listen.

Dr. Martin took a deep breath. "Carrying a child can be demanding. She requires plenty of rest for her and the baby's well-being."

"I understand. You're right." Gertrude gritted her teeth.

The doctor nodded slowly. He'd expected a confrontation of some sort. He hesitated briefly and then left.

Gertrude was lost in thought as she watched him march away. At the trip's beginning, the doctor had an excellent bedside manner. But now, he seemed worn and short-tempered. Perhaps, as the only doctor traveling with them, there was little time for himself or his family. He was pulled in all directions, day and night. She smiled and yelled to him, "Thank you, Dr. Martin. I do appreciate your help."

Already halfway to his wagon, Dr. Martin glanced back at Gertrude, nodded at her, and smiled.

Gertrude grinned and then went back to preparing supper. She didn't have much to work with: some dried meat, grain, and this and that. Their trip was nearing its end, and she was determined to create a meal to celebrate the conclusion of their long journey. Worried about Martha, it took her a little longer to prepare than usual.

She looked at the wagon's curtain gently swaying as the soft talking from inside the wagon ebbed away. A wave of relief washed over her. "The doctor's right," she muttered.

A half-hour later, Alexander walked up. "Where's Martha?"

"She's sleeping now. She had a rough day, and the doctor examined her."

Alexander's eyes grew with alarm. "Is she alright? I should go see."

"Dr. Martin says she needs rest. Alex is napping in there with her."

Alexander nodded with concern. He fixated on the wagon.

Gertrude continued preparing supper. "How's your best friend?"

Alexander exhaled, his face still tight with worry. "Randall? I wonder why he's not riding with us."

Gertrude snickered. "I'm sure he's hiding something he doesn't want us to know about."

"I don't understand why you don't trust him."

Gertrude shrugged. "He's—"

Harsh coughs erupted from the wagon, followed by a peaceful silence. Gertrude and Alexander both turned to the wagon.

Gertrude's face seemed to be a combination of hopefulness and optimism. "Why don't you go check on her?"

Alexander rushed to the wagon and pulled back the curtain. Martha was sleeping while Alex played quietly next to her.

Alexander whispered, "How are you doing, my little man?"

"Ma threw up in that bucket." Alex pointed to the bucket. "Then she fell asleep again. I'm waiting for her to wake up."

Alexander went to Martha's side and patted her arm.

"Martha. Wake up. It's time for supper."

Martha continued to breathe softly. Too softly.

He reached under her neck, raised her head, and lightly tapped Martha's cheek. "Martha!" His voice was laced with raw panic. "Can you hear me?" The silence that followed seemed to amplify his pounding heart. He glanced at Alex. His eyes were filled with worry.

The wagon shook, and then Gertrude peeked in. "What's wrong?" Her eyes grew wide with shock at the scene before Alexander could answer. She grabbed her bag and retrieved a small bottle. "Move over."

Alexander moved out of her way.

Gertrude acted fast. She waved the vial under Martha's nose.

Martha cocked her head back and pushed the vial away. "What?" she asked, sneezing and coughing.

Gertrude touched Martha's forehead. "She's burning up! Go get Dr. Martin. I'll stay here with her."

Alexander rushed out.

Worry was etched into Alex's tiny face.

Martha patted Alex's cheek. "Everything is going to be fine," she rasped.

Gertrude smiled at Alex. "Alex, peek out that curtain and let me know when you see your pa and Dr. Martin walking up."

Alex nodded and did as he was told.

It didn't take long. "They're coming. They're coming," yelled Alex.

Gertrude moved aside as Dr. Martin stepped in.

Dr. Martin had to kneel to get comfortable. "Alexander, could you take the boy outside? I need some room in here."

Gertrude started to leave.

The doctor cleared his throat. "Gertrude, please stay."

Alexander reached for Alex's hand. "Let's make room for the doctor."

Alex kept his eyes on his mother as he crawled over to Alexander.

Dr. Martin smiled at Alex. "Your ma is going to be just fine."

Martha fixated on Alexander and offered him a weak smile. "Alex needs to eat something." Her voice was raspy and hoarse.

"You should eat too, dear. I'll be alright."

"Okay," he whispered.

Alexander took Alex to a makeshift table next to the wagon and served him some stew.

"This is Gertrude's famous stew." Alexander tried his best to hide his unease.

He spooned some stew and beans on his plate and sat beside Alex.

Alex used his spoon to push it around in his bowl. "Is ma sick?" Alex's small voice trembled.

A smile tugged at Alexander's lips. "She's going to be fine." He took a bite of the stew, but his gaze flitted between Alex and the wagon, betraying a flicker of worry beneath the surface.

"But, Ma..."

Alexander moved closer to Alex and squeezed his hand. "Your ma needs rest, that's all. She's stronger than anyone I know. Before you know it, she'll be back riding her horse, shooting her gun, and making cookies."

Alexander tickled Alex. Alex laughed.

"Now finish up."

Alex ate a spoonful of the stew. "Mmm. This is delicious."

Alexander nodded.

The doctor stepped down from the wagon and walked up to Alexander, shaking his head. "Swimming in a stagnant water hole is never a good idea. It looks like she drank some of that water, and who knows what was in it."

A sharp and sudden gasp tore from Alexander's throat.

The doctor turned back to the wagon. "Gertrude is cleaning up in there. The best thing is to get rid of anything bad from her stomach. I gave her some medicine to help her with that. She told me she went into that water to cool off. Other women went, too. She likely already had a fever when she went there." He shook his head. "That cold rain followed by that hot sun. It isn't healthy for her, especially in her condition. She needs to be careful out here. We all do."

"Thank you, doctor," said Alexander, the worry still on his face.

"She'll be fine. She needs rest. And after her stomach settles, encourage her to eat." The doctor exhaled. "I better find those women and treat them, just in case."

"I appreciate your help."

The doctor nodded and left.

Alexander picked up Alex and climbed up on the wagon. He peeked in. Martha was lying down, her eyes closed, and Gertrude sat beside her.

He put Alex down next to Martha. "Why don't you keep your mother company?"

"Okay, Pa."

Gertrude helped Alex get comfortable.

Alex took Martha's hand, held it close, and closed his eyes. The edge of her lips curled upward as she dozed off.

As Gertrude was about to leave, Alex opened his eyes. "I'm not sleepy. I already took my nap."

Martha half-opened her eyes. "Go with Gertrude and get some supper."

"I already ate," said Alex.

Martha, her eyes drooping, smiled at Gertrude. "Maybe we can find a cookie."

Gertrude glanced at Martha on her way out with Alex. Martha's eyes were shut, and her breathing was normal.

Gertrude and Alexander kept their voices low so as not to wake Martha.

Alexander sat tapping his foot on the ground. "It's been an hour. I wonder if I should go check on her."

Alex glanced back at Alexander and returned to flinging little rocks into the wilderness.

Gertrude and Alexander exchanged worried glances.

Martha peeked out from the wagon. "It's so quiet out here."

Alexander jumped up. "Martha, how do you feel?"

"I feel much better."

Martha got down from the wagon.

Gertrude rushed to Martha. "The color in your cheeks is starting to show." Gertrude put the back of her hand on Martha's forehead. "You're not warm. That's a wonderful sign."

"Please stop fussing over me, Gertrude. I need fresh air. It's stuffy in there."

Alexander hugged Martha and led her to a chair.

Alex ran to Martha. "Ma, I love you."

Martha hugged Alex. "I love you very much, Alex. I would do anything to keep my family safe."

Alexander looked puzzled at her. "Are we not safe?"

Martha's gaze darted away and then back to Alexander. "Of course we are." She inhaled deeply and blew it out. "The cool air feels so good. I could use a little something to eat."

Gertrude smiled at Martha. "I'll get you some stew."

The following day, Martha peeked out of the wagon. Gertrude was sitting in the driver's seat right outside.

"I feel wonderful. Dr. Martin must put some potent medicinals in his tonics."

Gertrude rolled her eyes. "There's plenty of spirits in there and some other goodies, I'm sure." She patted Martha's shoulder. "You look well. I'll go inside and freshen it all up."

Martha nodded as she stepped down. "I'm going to get some coffee."

The sun was peeking over the horizon. She stopped and watched Alexander and Alex sitting a few feet away from the fire. They hadn't noticed her. Alexander was drinking from his favorite cup and chatting with his son. The coffee pot was perched precariously over the small fire nearby.

"How do you like this trip so far?" Alexander asked.

Alex chuckled. "It's fun."

Alexander laughed. "What have you liked the most?"

Alex thought for a second. "Our new friends."

"The Natives were incredible people."

"I like the toys they gave me."

"I'm glad you're having an exciting time on this trip. In a few days, we'll be at our new home."

"Yay! I want to sleep in my old bed."

Alexander stifled a chuckle. They hadn't brought any beds. Juan told him the house was fully furnished. Alexander smiled.

"Sleeping in a soft bed in our California home will be nice."

"Yes, Pa."

* * *

Out of sight of her family, Martha reached under the bench where she usually sat and withdrew the pouch with her gun. She had returned it there the day before when she had called for Alex to join her for a nap. She crept around the wagon's opposite side and walked away toward Agnes's. She was at ease as she passed her fellow travelers, nodding at anyone who saw her. She felt lightheaded, but nothing like before. "Pace yourself," she muttered.

She approached Agnes's wagon. A young man was perched above, sitting on the bench. She blinked in confusion.

"Hello, ma'am," said the man. "Ma is in the next wagon."

She recognized him. He was Agnes's older son.

"There was a man here yesterday. He was talking to my son."

"He was gone when we got up this morning. My ma is furious with him. He was supposed to drive them the rest of the way."

Martha was relieved. She imagined Thomas running away like a spineless coward. The gun was heavy in the sack hanging from her shoulder. She sighed.

"Well, I'm sure my husband can find someone to help y'all out." Martha was starting to feel a little better.

"No need. We're just a few days out, and Ma insists she can finish the trip. It won't be a problem."

Martha smiled and nodded. "Tell your ma I said hello. And if she needs anything, just let us know."

"Will do."

Martha strolled back to her wagon.

Halfway there, Gertrude stood with her arms on her hips. "Dear girl, what are you doing here? I thought you were going to get some coffee. You're supposed to be taking it easy."

Martha grinned. "It's such a beautiful morning. I thought I'd take advantage of the fresh, cool air, enjoy a little stroll, and savor the quiet, peacefulness."

Gertrude tilted her head forward and held a tight smile. She linked arms with Martha's. "Let's finish our walk, get that cup of coffee, and warm you up. And afterward, you've got to lie down."

Martha nodded.

As they neared their wagon, Alex ran to his mother.

223

"Ma! You're up."

"I love you. Let's sit down for a bit and relish this beautiful day." Martha brought Alex close and hugged him. She turned to Gertrude. "You've got a cookie for my little cowboy here, right?"

Alex's eyes lit up.

Gertrude's face brightened with a grin. "I suppose so." She reached into a small box and withdrew a cookie. "It might be a little crunchy since I baked it a few days ago."

Alexander said, "He doesn't care as long as it's sweet."

"I like 'em that way, too," Alex exclaimed, a wide grin splitting his face. He snapped the cookie in half, the loud crack echoing. He devoured each bite, crunching as he chewed, savoring the flavor.

Alexander giggled. "Slow down, Alex. You don't have to eat it all at once."

Alex held his bulging mouth and nodded.

Alexander poured Martha a cup of coffee, leading her to a comfortable spot near the fire. "You look well rested," he said.

Martha hugged Alexander tightly. "I hope everything is going to be okay. It's hard to believe that we're almost home."

Alexander nodded. "Just two or three days, and we'll be there."

Gertrude brought a light blanket for Martha and put it over her shoulders. "I thank God for keeping us safe."

Thomas peeked out from behind Agnes's son.

"I'm glad she's gone." Thomas tossed him a small gold nugget, smaller than the size of a pea.

Agnes's son examined the little treasure. "She seemed disappointed that you weren't here. I think she had a gun in that sack of hers. She must have a good reason to want to shoot you. What did you do?"

"I did her a wrong that I can't undo."

CHAPTER TWENTY-SEVEN

First Day Home

On October 1, 1864, the wagon train pulled into Sacramento's town center. After saying goodbye to the others, Alexander drove to their new home.

A choked sob escaped Martha's lips as she looked at the house. Her hand flew to her mouth, tears blurring her vision. "I never imagined it could be this beautiful."

Alexander's eyes darted from the house to the barn and into the seemingly endless fields. "All of this land! And the barn is gigantic."

Gertrude held Alex's hand while her eyes soaked it all in. "This house is enormous, and there's a lot of acreage here."

Alexander picked up Alex and hugged Martha. "We made it."

Martha pulled Gertrude in. "I'm so happy."

They walked into their new home.

Little Alex disappeared into the kitchen and then back to the front room. "The inside is bigger than the outside."

Gertrude chased after Alex. "I bet your room is huge."

Alex giggled. "Let's go hunting for it."

Alex ran down the hallway opposite the kitchen. He ran around the corner.

Gertrude bolted after him. "Let's look for my room too."

Alexander chuckled and then glanced out the window facing the barn. "I'm going to find the caretaker. Juan told me that he was staying in a house nearby."

Martha nodded at Alexander. "I'll go join those two and figure out who's getting what room. There are enough rooms for each of us to get two."

Alexander grinned. "Or room for more children." He winked at Martha and left.

Martha, Alex, and Gertrude continued to explore the house.

* * *

Alexander ran into the barn. His jaw dropped. "Incredible." The space was clean and orderly—one of the three horses whinnied. A wave of emotion washed over him. His lips curled upward as he marveled at its vastness.

The metallic sound of a cocked six-shooter wiped the smile from Alexander's face.

Alexander froze. "Is that you, Charlie?" Alexander turned around. "I'm Alexander Johnson."

Charlie clumsily withdrew his gun and holstered it.

Alexander smiled. "You never can be too careful."

"I—I'm sorry. I wasn't expecting you yet."

"Glad to meet you, Charlie."

Charlie nodded.

An amorous rooster chased a screaming hen into the barn.

Alexander jumped out of the way. "I didn't know there were chickens."

Charlie shooed the chickens out.

Alexander chuckled at the sight.

Charlie rushed back to Alexander. "Now and again, that darn rooster breaks out of his enclosure. You have cows and horses, too."

Alexander's jaw dropped as he took it all in, "I didn't realize —"

"You've got at least ten or fifteen acres here."

"Juan told me there were fifteen. It's going to take some getting used to."

"Mr. Holt asked me to ensure you had enough food to feed your family for a week or two. There's plenty. I just put an ice block in your kitchen box yesterday. It will last two or three more days."

"I sure do appreciate that."

"I'll give you some time to settle in before I move out."

"I thought that you'd be living here permanently. I'd pay you to take care of this place."

"I told Mr. Holt that this had to be temporary. He paid me well. You don't have to worry about it. You won't have trouble finding someone to work here if that's what you want."

"I understand."

Charlie blinked twice and shifted his weight from foot to foot. "I was getting ready to head out. All I have left is to inspect a fence post near the south entrance."

Alexander perked up. "Would you like some company? There's no time like the present to explore my property."

"I'm sorry, but I'm in a hurry. I have to meet somebody in a couple of hours."

"No problem. I should probably head into town and figure out where everything is."

Charlie half-smiled and nodded. Then, he went to his horse and rode off.

Alexander was leaving when he saw Dr. Martin riding up in a cart. "Dr. Martin!"

Dr. Martin pulled up. "I wanted to check up on Martha."

"I appreciate that. She's on the back porch, happy as ever."

The doctor nodded as he got down from his cart.

"Is your home to your liking?" asked Alexander.

"It's a grand house less than a mile from here."

"Martha and I are glad you live nearby."

"Dr. Martin!" said Gertrude as she walked up.

The doctor smiled broadly. "Gertrude!"

"I came by to see Martha. I brought her some more tonics."

Gertrude cocked her head with a suspicious smile.

Dr. Martin grinned. "I assure you that these are safe and effective. I take them myself."

Gertrude chuckled. "Maybe I should take some of those concoctions. I'll need more energy sprinting from room to room in this enormous house."

Dr. Martin's eyes sparkled with excitement. "My place is twice the size of the last one. My wife and I are beyond pleased with everything. I even have enough space for a proper examination room or two."

"If you'll excuse me," said Alexander. "I'm going into town to see where things are. I'll be back a little later."

With the innocence of a child exploring a wondrous new adventure, Alexander rushed to his horse and rode off.

Gertrude smiled as Alexander disappeared, leaving a plume of dust.

"Martha is doing so much better. I'm sure she'll be happy to see you."

Martha sat relaxing in a reclining wooden chair on the back porch. She was too excited to spend the day in bed. After what she endured getting here, she wanted to explore her home. She loved everything about it. It had ample space everywhere. There were enough bedrooms for more children. The kitchen was enormous and had a huge table. There was an icebox in the corner. A partially melted ice block was already inside the icebox when they arrived.

She spotted the cows grazing in the field. She couldn't wait for the promise of fresh milk. Toward the barn, she saw the chickens clucking away in their coop and thought of the eggs they would enjoy each morning. A vegetable garden on the sunny side of the barn was bright green with spots of red. It was undoubtedly full of vegetables of all kinds.

Gertrude stepped out to the sun porch, followed by the doctor. "Dr. Martin is here to see you."

Martha stood, smiling. "Dr. Martin, how lovely to see you. I'm in heaven."

Dr. Martin walked up to Martha. "We are delighted that we moved here."

Martha seemed to wobble on her feet. She closed her eyes, rubbed her temple, and shook her head.

Gertrude took Martha's arm. "Martha, why don't you sit down for a bit?"

Martha obliged. "I suppose I'm a little overwhelmed."

"You should be in bed. You're recovering nicely, but it'll take a few days to return to your old self. I promise."

Martha took a deep breath, exhaled slowly, and smiled.

Gertrude's face was creased with worry.

"Okay. I'll go lie down for a little while. I must be in bad shape for Gertrude to be worried about me."

Gertrude's head slowly bobbed up and down.

The doctor felt Martha's forehead and then examined her eyes. "Do you feel any pain?"

"Occasionally, my baby affectionately pokes and prods me at

night."

"I'm delighted that your fever is gone. I brought some tonics that will help you regain your strength. As I told Gertrude, my wife and I both take these, and they're safe. Rest in bed as much as possible."

The doctor handed Martha the bottles of brown liquid. "You should take them once a day in the morning. If you follow my instructions, you will have optimal health for the birth."

"I can't see myself relegated to a bed for long, but I'll try."

Dr. Martin picked up his bag and started for the door. "Come get me if needed."

Martha said, "Say hello to your wife."

Dr. Martin winked. "I know the way out."

Gertrude turned to address the doctor, but he had already left the room. She helped Martha down the hall to her bed and rushed out the front door. The doctor was stepping down from the porch.

"Doctor, I'm glad you stopped by. I'm worried about Martha. Sometimes, she is energetic and wants to conquer the world; other times, she's lethargic."

"Don't worry. Martha is sturdy. I'm convinced her resolve will enable her to have a healthy delivery. The illness she endured during the trip was quite taxing and left her in this precarious state. The baby growing inside of her is even more demanding of her body. If she wishes to save her baby, she must take every opportunity to regain her strength."

Gertrude sighed. "You're right. It's unlike me to worry like this. I guess I'm a little tired."

"I have a tonic for that."

Gertrude chuckled. "Take care."

The doctor nodded as if everything was going to be okay, and then he left.

Charlie rode along a narrow path to the south side of Alexander's property to a rarely used gate. Traveling on that winding and uneven trail was quite a trek. He preferred to take the road near the house and ride around the property to the south gate because it took only minutes to reach the secluded spot. But he didn't want to raise any suspicion with Alexander.

Several men pointed guns toward Charlie when he arrived at the 'hideout.'

Charlie pulled back on the reins. His horse neighed as he came to a stop. "It's just me, damnit!"

The men put their weapons down and shuffled away, shaking their heads. A shorter man marched up as Charlie got down from his horse.

"Why'd you come through this way, sneaking up on us?" asked John Walker, Charlie's brother-in-law.

"The owner of this property arrived early. We got to clear out of here. He's talking about riding around his property, exploring it."

John laughed. "Well, ain't this a damn coincidence. Come on over. I want you to meet someone."

Charlie followed John.

Two men stood just outside John's tent as they turned the corner.

John walked up next to a tall, mean-looking, rugged man. "Charlie, this is Randall."

Frank peeked from behind Randall and waved clumsily at Charlie. "I'm Frank."

Charlie ignored Frank and extended his hand to Randall. "Have we met before?"

Randall shook Charlie's hand. "Nope, I've never been to California."

Charlie stepped back and squinted his eyes at Randall for a second. "Do you know Sheriff Joseph Pruitt?"

Randall laughed. "I sure do. He's my brother. I knew that I'd find someone who came across him. I was talking to John about him."

John looked sideways at Charlie. "How do you know his brother?"

"Years ago, when I lived in Sacramento, I rode up to Auburn and did some work there. Mrs. Pruitt paid me well to fix the barn and other odd jobs. She was fair." He was about to say how much he hated her husband, and thought he better not.

Randall laughed. "Well, I'll be. Finding Joseph was a lot easier than I thought."

John approached Charlie. "I reckon so. Been talking with Randall, and he's proposed that we combine forces." He grinned at Randall. "Randall and his crew used to rob stagecoaches in New York. I think we're a good match."

Charlie chuckled. "I think it's a great idea."

"How about our men head to my brother's place? It isn't safe here. My friend who used to live here told me that my brother's ranch is much bigger."

"It sure is," said Charlie, his yellowed teeth showing through his snarly smile. "There are lots of hiding places on Joseph's property. It must be over a hundred acres."

Randall winked at Charlie. "Charlie, you're going to be my new best friend."

Charlie grinned. Charlie could see already that Randall was nothing like Joseph.

John said, "We'll leave tomorrow morning."

CHAPTER TWENTY-EIGHT
Sick Again

Alexander woke up early the next day and was excited to go into town to meet the bank owner, Douglas Holt.

Martha smiled as Alexander went to her bedside.

He sat on the edge and took her hand. "How are you, my darling?"

"I'm fine. There's no need for you to worry about me. Gertrude will take care of me while you're gone."

"I could go there tomorrow or the day after."

"I want you to visit Mr. Holt and tell me if he's as nice as his brother, Wallace. I'm going to sleep in. I'll be up and about by the time you return."

"Are you sure you're okay? You're a little warm."

"I'm positive. I know you're excited to go meet him."

Alexander nodded. He kissed her cheek and left.

Martha waited for the door to close behind Alexander. Her smile twisted into wrinkles of pain as she squeezed her eyes shut.

Alexander walked into the kitchen. Gertrude was reading the newspaper, and little Alex sat eating breakfast.

"Martha wants to sleep in. I'm going into town to see Douglas Holt. Would you look in on her after a while? Her forehead was a little warm."

Gertrude's face was tight with worry. "Of course. Rest is exactly what she needs."

"Son, you be good for Gertrude. I'll be back in a few hours."

Alex nodded several times.

Alexander patted Alex's shoulder and left for the barn. His horse was saddled and ready to ride. He smiled at Charlie's efficiency.

His eyes darted toward the house as he led his horse out of the barn. A flicker of worry tugged at his heart. Martha, held up in bed, had always been his anchor. He knew her strength, her unwavering spirit. He clung to the hope that this new town, a mixture of opportunity and uncertainty, would allow her to flourish. He swung onto his horse with a sliver of optimism and rode away.

He knew the way since he'd ridden into the city the day before to familiarize himself with the area. Minutes later, the valley came into view as he approached the bend about a mile from his home. He stopped to admire the countryside. It was luscious, with trees sprinkled throughout the flat lands and bounded by sloping hills. It was flatter than he had expected. In the far distance were majestic mountains. A gentle breeze blew the dust from the well-traveled road. When he lived in New York, he spent most of his time in the city and never ventured to the less inhabited surrounding areas. He was amazed at the difference between New York City and Sacramento.

New York was a bustling, ostentatious city where half a million people hustled and bustled about. A handful of people held onto their riches, and the rest struggled to make a living for their families. The influx of immigrants continued to flow in from all corners of the globe, adding a rich tapestry of diversity and ingenuity to the middle class.

Sacramento wasn't as large as New York City. It was a place where 10,000 people lived. Unlike in New York, the wealthy people had dirt in their fingernails. He'd seen some of them the day before. He surmised they had to work hard to get the earth to give up its bounty. The land was rich and greedy with its minerals, but not as much with its food and water. Off in the distance were the planted fields of crops. Waterways were plentiful throughout the region. The weather was cool and calm. It was slow, peaceful, and synchronized with the pace of nature. Alexander smiled and shook his head at the wonder.

The horse whinnied, snapping Alexander from his thoughts.

Half an hour after leaving home, Alexander arrived at the bank. The exterior seemed more weather-worn than the New York bank. As he got off his horse, a man sitting on a bench near the entrance yelled, "Howdy."

Alexander secured his horse and nodded to the man. "Hello."

The man wore a hat that partially covered his leathery face and had a trimmed beard. He was dressed in a loose-fitting suit.

His leather boots were shined and decorated with fancy inlaid patterns.

Alexander approached the man. "I've never seen a pair of boots like that."

The short man was awkwardly squinting at him. The man smiled as he stood and put forward his right foot. "I'm mighty proud of these boots. Getting them just how I like them cost me plenty. There ain't no one else here in town that has a pair like these."

Alexander raised his brows, not understanding why a pair of boots should be valued that way. "Very nice," he said.

"Excuse me, I have an appointment with someone inside."

The man chuckled and then extended his hand. "You must be Alexander."

Alexander blinked, confused.

"I'm Douglas; Douglas Holt."

Alexander laughed nervously. "I'm sorry. I had no idea."

"I'm not the picture of a wealthy bank owner. I like to ride my horse and be out in the country more, but I gotta keep this bank healthy and come into work now and then."

Alexander nodded. "I can understand that. This place is majestic and full of opportunity, more than I could have imagined."

"Yup. It needs someone to keep it that way," Douglas said. "Let's go have a chat."

The door creaked as Douglas opened it and stepped inside.

Alexander followed and was surprised by the decor. The floors and counters had quite a bit of wear on them. There were two counters where the tellers worked. The bottom was made of wood, just like the desks. But there were metal bars that stood between the tellers and the customers. The wooden floors were clean but marred by scratches and were heavily gouged. The bank was about the size that he expected.

They continued through a door that opened to the offices. This space was in better shape, but was far from as manicured as the New York bank. The floor plan was similar to Wallace's bank —a center area with four desks and three offices at the end.

Douglas stopped at his corner office door.

Alexander's eyes darted from side to side as he surveyed the room, distracted by the decor.

"It's not as fancy as my brother's bank. It's more chaotic out here. We have a lot of miners in this region who bring their riches into the bank in all sorts of hand carts. Last week, a customer brought a rickety cart full of his bounty. It fell over and caused quite a stir with the other customers."

Alexander's eyes went wild with excitement. "So it's true that this land is still giving up its riches." He walked past the desks and followed Douglas into his office.

"It is. We assist the miners in refining their gold and other precious metals. We don't turn any of the law-abiding folks away."

Douglas sat behind a massive oak desk, its surface polished to a gleam. Across from him, Alexander settled into a creaky wooden chair with well-worn arms.

"Your brother said you have a big problem with stagecoach robbers."

"Those vermin are coming from all over. They think that they can come into this town and get rich. That's why the miners bring their bounty here as soon as possible. They can't risk keeping it loose in the mines…" He shook his head. "…or in their homes."

"That's not good. I suppose the Law helps out with that?"

"Absolutely! I asked Sheriff August to stop by today. He's a respectable, law-abiding man. He's polite, too. But don't let that fool you. He'll put any man in his place and have him begging for mercy."

"I look forward to meeting him. I used to work closely with the Law back in New York. We had a great relationship."

"I have no doubt you'll like him. Wallace wrote me that you prefer to do bookkeeping, but I need you to help me eliminate those robberies."

"I understand. I would still like to do some bookkeeping."

"For now, I'll give you one account. It would be too much if I gave you more."

Alexander's face loosened, and the right side of his lips curled downward.

"Listen, these accounts here are nothing like those you're used to. Most of those New York accounts belong to people with a few dollars. And there are only a handful of accounts belonging to wealthy people." Douglas grinned. "It's the opposite here. This bank primarily handles people with newfound fortunes."

Alexander's face brightened. "I see."

"That's why I need your skills to protect the stagecoaches. It's a chronic problem, and I have some ideas about attacking it. After you reduce those robberies to a manageable level, you can do all the bookkeeping you want."

Alexander nodded.

"I have a spot for your wife, too, if she wants it. Wallace wrote me about how pleased he was with Martha's work."

"She would love that. However, we have a young son and another on the way."

There was a knock at the door.

Douglas saw Sheriff August through the glass in the door and yelled, "Come in."

Alexander stood and extended his hand to Sheriff August. "Sheriff, I'm Alexander Johnson. I look forward to working with you."

Sheriff August rushed up and shook Alexander's hand vigorously. "Douglas has told me all about you. I can't wait to work with you to get rid of those damn robbers."

Alexander smiled as his enthusiasm grew. "I'm confident that we'll get them under control."

They sat down.

Douglas continued, "Several stagecoaches travel between here and the surrounding cities. Most of them are sending their bounty to this bank. I have another smaller bank in Auburn. We move a lot of money between the two banks."

Alexander looked at Douglas. "How far is Auburn?"

Sheriff August straightened up. "It's about thirty miles, two or three hours by stagecoach. It's faster on horseback."

Douglas shot a mischievous grin at Sheriff August. "You have a friend out there, don't you?"

Sheriff August smiled. "Yup. I do. But she's married. I never go up there unless I have to." He wrung his hands as if he were caught talking about something forbidden.

Douglas turned to Alexander. "We'll have to travel to Auburn to familiarize you with that bank. I wired the manager there that you and I would visit soon."

Alexander turned to Sheriff August. "Do you know the sheriff in Auburn?"

Sheriff August grunted. "Yes. His name is Pruitt."

Douglas half-smiled. "He keeps his town safe. I'll introduce you to him when we go there."

Alexander, his brow furrowed, looked pensively at Douglas. Alexander had heard rumors long ago about Randall's brother Joseph Pruitt running off to California, but had never thought much about it. It was a coincidence, he thought.

Douglas continued, "I have some smaller banks in other towns. Those operate alongside a post office or a general store."

"I see."

Douglas nodded. "They hold the wages of most of the workers. And, they don't have much trouble with robbers."

Douglas handed a folder to Alexander. "Here is a compilation of the latest robberies. It used to be that no passengers got killed. Although they often wounded the driver."

The first sheet contained a columnar list written on a page from an accounting journal. Detailed, copious notes of the robberies, mainly between Auburn and Sacramento, with a smattering of robberies on routes leading to other towns, were included.

Alexander's eyes grew wild with enthusiasm as he shuffled through the papers. "This will be beneficial. They've been killing a lot these past few days."

"Yup," said Sheriff August. "They got no respect for life. In the last two days, we've had several robberies where they killed everyone on the stagecoach and made off with the strongboxes, along with anything of value from the passengers. It was less bloody before."

An unwelcome image flickered in Alexander's mind — the ransacked inside of the Swansons' stagecoach and their dead bodies lying outside. He winced, startled by the intrusion of the memory.

Douglas shook his head. "You've come just in time to help us. It's turning bad here. Now and then, we see an increase in stagecoach robberies. But now they're more bloody, and half a dozen or more robbers are working together to down a stagecoach — instead of just two or three."

The sheriff leaned forward. "In the past, we were able to catch them and get the bank's money back, but it's been getting harder. They pop up here and there and then disappear. Those robbers know the schedules, and they pick spots along the trails that are vulnerable and difficult to protect."

Douglas turned to Alexander. "I don't expect you to do this alone. I have skilled men who will report to you. And the sheriff also has men. My brother wrote me that you took care of his stagecoaches and assured me that you would not disappoint me. I believe him."

Alexander sat up taller. "I swear. We will resolve this problem."

Douglas jumped up from his chair. "It's almost noon. I'll introduce you to the men later. Let's go across the way to the restaurant. They serve the best steak and potatoes in the West."

"I'm afraid I can't stay. My wife has been ill, and I need to check on her."

Douglas looked disappointed. "Of course. When you're ready, just come on back. I wasn't expecting you for another week anyway. I still need to get that center office fixed up for you."

Alexander liked the center office. He said his goodbyes and left.

It was almost noon when Gertrude lightly tapped on Martha's bedroom door. There was no answer, so she peeked inside. Martha's arm was hanging from the side of the bed. Panic crawled up her spine as she rushed over. Martha was burning up, breathing hard, and she wouldn't wake up no matter how much she called to her. Gertrude couldn't find the smelling salts, so she ran to fetch the doctor. Ten minutes later, they walked in. Martha was drenched in sweat and crying. The bedsheets clung tightly around her, limp and heavy, like a sopping wet rag.

Martha held a pillow like a baby, rocking back and forth, sobbing. "I've lost my baby!"

A lump formed in Gertrude's throat as she rushed to Martha's side. "I'm sure the baby is fine. Dr. Martin is here."

The doctor, his face filled with panic, examined Martha. "Her fever is too high. It's dangerous for the baby. She needs a cool bath. Help me get her to the tub."

Gertrude and the doctor helped Martha into the tub. It was next to her bedroom and intended to be filled with warm water. Gertrude rushed back and forth and returned with buckets full of well water. Martha moaned as the water touched her skin through the thick robe she was wearing. Martha shivered as the water level rose around her. The doctor held on to her as she trembled.

The doctor told Martha, "This will help to break your fever once and for all."

Martha moaned and shivered as the fight left her. Her wails softened to a whimper, her voice trembling. "It's so cold."

The doctor's face was unemotional. "Just one more minute. You can do this. You must fight for your baby."

Martha closed her eyes and began breathing slowly and assuredly. After several breaths, she opened her eyes and nodded to the doctor. "I-I-I think I'm better."

"That's long enough. Help me get her up." He pointed to a wooden chair near the bed.

They helped Martha to the chair. Water dripped to the floor from her robe, which clung tightly to her body.

Gertrude smiled and pointed to the door. "Doctor? If you don't mind."

"I'll be in the hallway," said Dr. Martin as he left.

Gertrude assisted Martha into the warm, dry robe. Martha sighed with relief, her posture softening. Gertrude carefully wrapped a towel around Martha's damp hair.

Martha sat up tall.

Suddenly, she lurched forward, her eyes widening in alarm. Gertrude instinctively reached out to steady her. "Careful there," she cautioned.

Martha squeezed her eyes shut, a grimace twisting her features. "The room..." Her voice trailed off, a whisper barely audible. "Spinning."

The world tilted alarmingly for Martha, a swirling vortex replacing the familiar surroundings. She fought back a wave of nausea, clinging to Gertrude's arm for support.

After a moment, Martha let out a sigh. "I sat up too fast. I'm okay now." She leaned back and watched Gertrude silently.

Gertrude gathered the damp bed linens and tossed them out of the way. She pulled fresh linens from the closet and made the bed. She assisted Martha back into her freshened bed.

Gertrude yelled, "Doctor, she's ready for you."

The doctor rushed in. "I'm right here, Martha."

Martha struggled to smile at the doctor.

"Have you taken your tonic today?"

Martha glanced at the bedside table and nodded.

He examined the bottle from the table and went pale. It was almost empty.

"This elixir should have lasted at least another week."

Gertrude looked crooked at Martha.

Martha opened her eyes slowly and looked at the bottle, still in the doctor's hand. "I took a big dose this morning. I need to be well." She closed her eyes, inhaled deeply, and blew it out with a sigh.

"It causes hallucinations if taken in excess." The doctor shook his head and said, "Those effects will soon disappear. I'm pleased the fever has broken, and the baby is doing well."

Gertrude heard the front door slam shut. She rushed to the living room.

A wide-eyed Alexander asked, "Why is the doctor's cart here? Is Martha okay?"

"Martha's fever has broken. She's—"

Alexander ran to the bedroom, his heart aching with worry. When he walked up, his eyes were filled with panic. "Martha, how are you?"

Martha opened her eyes halfway and shook her head at Alexander. She started to cry.

Alexander stood shocked as Martha's wails grew louder. Gertrude walked up.

The doctor tapped Alexander's shoulder. "Sir, may we speak in private?"

Gertrude took Martha's hand. "You'll be okay." Gertrude turned to Alexander. "I'll be here. Go talk to the doctor."

Alexander led the doctor to the next room and closed the

door.

"Your wife had a high fever and left me concerned for the baby's life."

Alexander stood dumbfounded, terrified at what the doctor would say next.

The doctor met Alexander's gaze. "Gertrude couldn't awaken her earlier. We were able to reduce her fever quickly." He glanced at the bottle still in his hand. "She's hallucinating. She thinks that she's lost her baby. But her baby is alright, at least for now," said the doctor. "She—"

"Alexander! Alexander!" Martha yelled from her room.

Alexander and the doctor rushed into the bedroom. Little Alex, who'd been napping, had snuck in to see his mother after he awoke. He didn't understand what was happening and was scared for her. His eyes were tainted with fright.

Martha held her hand over her mouth. "Don't let him see me like this!"

Gertrude ushered Alex out of the room. "Everything is fine, Alex. Let's get a cookie."

Martha's gaze drifted out the window, trying to make sense of her distorted sense of reality. "My baby." Martha's voice was reduced to raspy whispers, and her eyes were filled with puddles of hopelessness. "How cruel!"

Martha always prided herself on being ready for anything life might throw at her. But this was more than she could bear. How could her God be so cruel to her, her child, and her family? How could he have taken her baby, she thought.

Her hallucinations faded into dreamy imagery as she drifted off to sleep.

"She needs to rest now." The doctor turned to Alexander and walked with him into the parlor. "She will be better in the morning."

Alexander shook his head. "Martha has been through so much for this child."

"She's resilient."

"I can't stand to see her suffer."

The doctor patted Alexander on the shoulder. "I doubt that she'll remember any of this. That baby is most certainly a fighter.

It's kicking up a storm, anxious to be born."

Alexander tried to smile. "She wants this child more than life itself."

"Her determination, I'm sure, keeps her going."

The doctor took another bottle from his bag and handed it to Alexander. "See that she takes only one teaspoon of this tonic each morning. It will restore her strength. The tonic she took earlier today was intended to be used sparingly. It was responsible for her hallucinations and likely why Gertrude had trouble waking her. The new one will help flush any lingering toxins from her body and invigorate her. I'll stop by tomorrow to check in on her. Please keep her calm and see that she drinks plenty of water and rests."

Alexander shook his head. "She was warm this morning when I left. I should have stayed and called you then."

"She'll be alright. Those toxins in her body caused her fever. Once they're flushed out, she'll be healthier than ever. The fact that her fever was so easily tamed this time tells me that she's at the end of her illness."

Alexander nodded.

The doctor turned to leave. "I promise you, the worst is over."

CHAPTER TWENTY-NINE

Recovery

Late the following morning, Gertrude walked into Martha's bedroom. "How are you feeling?"

Martha stretched out her arms, tilted her head from one side to the other, and loudly yawned. "Terrific!" Martha sat up, bewildered. "But I had some terrible dreams."

"You've been sleeping since yesterday afternoon." Gertrude touched Martha's forehead. "Your fever is all gone, and your color is back to normal." Martha tensed up and then relaxed. A slight pressure pushed at her from her swollen belly.

Martha's eyelids fluttered open and closed rapidly. She motioned to Gertrude. "The baby... he just kicked. He's kicking. Come quick."

Gertrude gently placed her hand on Martha's rounded stomach. A faint flutter pulsed beneath her touch.

"I felt it!" she exclaimed, her voice choked with emotion. Her glistening eyes met Martha's, mirroring their shared joy.

Martha laughed. "Today, for the first time in a long time, I'm hopeful and filled with optimism. A happily ever after, not just for me, but for all of us, is right around the corner."

Gertrude went to the curtains and opened them wide. "Your wellness, this incredible house, this fertile land, and this charming city are but a small sample of the happiness we deserve."

"I want to leave this bed and explore this new world. I don't even know what the town is like."

Gertrude glanced at Martha and opened the window. "You'll love it. I'm surprised you haven't mentioned work or target practicing yet."

"Before you walked in, I was thinking about that. I'm not sure I want to do bookkeeping anymore. It doesn't seem that important to me, and it's not exciting, either. Alexander told me that Douglas from the bank had a position there for me. But, now, with Alex and a new baby on the way, I don't know if I should."

"You know you could count on me to care for the children if you decide to work there."

"I'm tempted to help Alexander protect those stagecoaches instead. I know my way around a six-shooter, a rifle, and a shotgun."

Gertrude gasped. "You—I mean—You want to protect the stagecoaches?" She rushed to Martha and lightly touched her forehead again. "I thought those hallucinations were over."

Martha laughed. "I'm fine. The thought of protecting innocent travelers fills me with a sense of purpose. I know I can handle its challenges. It sounds thrilling, and I have the skills and courage to excel at it."

"It's dangerous."

"A few bumps and bruises won't stop me. It's the kind of adventure I crave."

Gertrude shrugged. "Perhaps this is something that you might want to discuss with Alexander. I don't think he'd be too excited about you doing that."

Martha winked at Gertrude, her eyes twinkling with mischief. "I'll talk to him."

Gertrude's smile softened. "I'll be honest with you. I can't imagine you working on those stagecoaches. But I will support you and help you attain whatever you're passionate about. But I ask you to please think hard about this. You have a family now."

"I know. As soon as the doctor says, I'll be outside shooting up those cans." Martha glanced at the door. "When is he supposed to be here?"

"I'm expecting him any minute now."

Martha took a deep breath and let it out smoothly. "What happened yesterday? It's all hazy. It seemed like a bad dream." Martha rubbed her arms. "I remember shivering, and I couldn't get warm."

"You fainted. You had a high fever; the bedsheets soaked up some of it. We had to put you in an icy cold bath to break its hold on you."

Martha grinned. "Wow. That's a lot of drama. I'm glad it slipped my mind."

"Oh, yes. One more thing. You had way too much of the

doctor's tonic."

Martha glanced at the side table with a mischievous grin. "After Alexander left, I figured I needed to speed up my recovery, so I took an extra dose." Martha shook her head slowly. "I won't do that again."

Gertrude laughed. "You said the room was spinning, and you were imagining crazy things."

"Today, I'm fine—better than fine." Martha sat up and was about to get out of bed.

Gertrude reached for Martha. "Oh, no, you don't. The doctor said you need to get plenty of rest, drink lots of water, and eat well. He wants you resting in bed as much as possible until you have your baby."

"I can't stay in bed. I have lots to do, cans to shoot."

"Martha, I insist that you follow the doctor's orders. Before you know it, your baby will be here."

With a playful scoff, Martha bumped Gertrude's arm. "Okay, I surrender. But I'm hungry. I feel like I haven't eaten in days. My stomach is growling like crazy."

"I'll be right back." Gertrude pointed her finger at Martha. "Don't get out of bed."

Gertrude rushed away and returned a few minutes later with a plate of food on a wooden tray. It had legs on either side so Martha could eat in bed. "I've brought you some tea to settle your stomach, a little lunch, and a small dessert. It's called a Queen Cake. I got it from a lady that I met in town. They're delicious."

Gertrude placed the tray in front of Martha. "I added honey to your tea."

Martha sat up taller a little too quickly. She closed her eyes briefly, opened them again, and said, "I guess I'm a little lightheaded."

"Maybe you should lie down."

"I need some food in me. Until then, I'll move more slowly."

Martha sipped the tea. "This reminds me of the one my mother used to make for me when I was not feeling well."

"Your mother showed me how to make the perfect brew."

"She taught me too. But this is much better than the one I make."

Martha poked the little cake with her fork and glanced at Gertrude. "So you've already made another friend."

"Yes. I'm glad to have a friend here."

"What about Agnes?"

"Agnes is clear on the other side of town. And you know how she and her family like keeping to themselves. I guess Agnes is overwhelmed with the move from New York to here. I think she needs some time to acclimate to her place here. I'm sure we'll continue with our weekly outings soon."

Remembering her encounter with Thomas inside Agnes's wagon, she set her teacup down a little too hard. Agnes, it seemed, intentionally hid Thomas from her. "Is it because of Thomas?"

Gertrude raised her eyebrows. "Agnes should have told me she was hiding him. She's never kept anything from me."

Martha rolled her eyes. "I wanted to kill him. I had my gun with me, ready to shoot him. But…" Martha brushed the thought away and reached for the cake.

Gertrude shrugged. "At least he's gone."

"Yes." She took a bite. "My goodness, this dessert is delightful. It has a slight floral scent to it."

"Those cakes are heavenly."

Martha nudged Gertrude playfully, a teasing smile gracing her lips. "Tell me about your new friend."

"Well, Helen's family lived back east. Her younger brother passed away a long while back. He had one child, Elizabeth. She's a woman now. Elizabeth is fifteen years older than you. Helen and Elizabeth moved here after Helen's brother passed. I think Elizabeth had a husband who died shortly after they arrived here."

Martha liked it when Gertrude talked about people and jumped from person to person, just like in the old days. It took effort to keep track of everyone Gertrude spoke about. Martha loved that everything was settling back to normal.

Gertrude continued, "Helen said that Elizabeth's second husband is a womanizing man." Gertrude laughed. "Helen doesn't like him at all. He's thirteen years older than her and a sheriff in a small town nearby. I think the place is called Auburn. She said that Elizabeth should have instead married Sheriff August, the sheriff here in Sacramento. Helen asked me to come by her home this afternoon to meet Elizabeth for some tea and cakes."

"You learned all that this morning?"

Gertrude's eyes lit up. "I haven't told you the half of it. Turns out that Elizabeth's husband had a boy back in—"

Alexander walked in with Dr. Martin. "Look who I found outside. He's here to make sure that you're okay." Alexander rushed over to Martha and kissed her on the cheek. "Darling, you look beautiful. How are you doing?"

"Wonderful!" Martha glanced at Gertrude to finish the rest of the story. Gertrude seemed frozen mid-sentence, her mouth seemingly unable to utter any more words. Martha smiled at her and then looked at Dr. Martin. "I don't know what I had, but I'm glad it's over."

The doctor stepped up to Martha. "I'm thrilled to see you bright and cheerful. Your eyes are sparkling, and your color is back." He looked at her tray. "And it looks like your appetite is back, too. Excellent!"

He used his stethoscope to examine Martha.

"Doctor, please tell me what I must do to return to my normal routine. I'm dying to get out of bed and see my new home, the barn, the fields, the animals, and everything."

Martha winked at Alexander, who was standing quietly, smiling at her.

Dr. Martin chuckled. "Your heart sounds much stronger than in the last few days. I want you to go slow and pay attention to your body. I want you to rest when you feel tired. And don't overexert yourself."

Gertrude cleared her throat. "And take your tonic, too."

A playful eye-roll escaped Martha. "Okay, I got it: Rest and Tonic."

The doctor chuckled. "Yes. One spoonful each day, no more. That other tonic and your high fever were likely responsible for your hallucinations."

Martha grinned. "Thank God. I remember having trouble keeping track of what was real and imagined. It's a mostly forgotten bad dream now."

The doctor smiled. "Tomorrow, if you're up to it, you should take short walks. The exercise will do you good."

Martha's face lit up with a broad smile.

Alexander's brows rose, and his eyes twinkled with delight. "Just let me know, and I'll accompany you. It would be the highlight of my day."

Martha blew Alexander a kiss. He pretended to capture it and then brought it to his heart.

The doctor stowed his stethoscope away. "I'll let myself out. Please don't hesitate to call on me. You are well on your way to a quick recovery."

Martha's eyes sparkled with excitement. Soon, she would be taking walks outside. "Thank you, doctor."

Dr. Martin picked up his bag and left.

Gertrude tapped Alexander's shoulder. "Little Alex and I are headed into town to visit my friend Helen."

A teasing smile graced Alexander's lips. "You have a new friend already?"

Gertrude held her lips closed tight to stifle a chuckle. "I do."

A mischievous glint twinkled in Martha's eyes as she wrinkled her nose in a playful tease. "Before you know it, she'll have friends everywhere."

"Alex is out in the barn exploring," he said.

Alexander sat on the side of the bed, picked up Martha's hand, and kissed it gently. "I'm sorry, you'll have to spend your day alone with me."

Martha winked at Gertrude. "Gertrude, take your time. I'm ecstatic to spend some alone time with my husband." She gazed at Alexander. "The only man I have ever loved and will ever love."

"You two love birds are perfect for each other," Gertrude said as she left the room.

Martha smiled at the memory of when Gertrude called them lovebirds back at the park in New York.

CHAPTER THIRTY

Family Reunion

In Auburn, Sheriff Joseph Pruitt read the newspaper at the kitchen table, and his wife, Elizabeth, poured Joseph a cup of freshly brewed coffee.

Swirling patterns of steam floated away from the top as she placed it before him. "I've got to get to town to catch the morning stagecoach headed to Sacramento."

"Is your aunt okay?" he asked out of habit. He didn't care at all for her. He secretly hoped that she would join her husband in heaven or hell. It didn't matter to him which one.

A playful smirk danced on her face. "Yes, she's fine. I wrote last week that I'd visit her for a few days."

Elizabeth rushed to the bedroom and returned with her bag.

He put the newspaper down. "I can't bear the thought you'll be away from me."

"Oh yeah, I won't be with my protector." She chuckled as she stowed the small leather pouch into her bag. "Can't travel without my gun."

"Slow down. You'll get there soon enough. That coach ain't leaving without you."

"I know. I don't like to keep people waiting on me."

"That's what I love about you. Always thinking about others."

"I love you, too. Please keep the house in order. I'll be back in two days."

"I'll count the hours, the minutes, and the seconds until you return, dear."

Elizabeth giggled. "Ever the romantic. I'll leave my horse at the hotel stables if you don't mind picking her up when you can."

"You sure you don't want me to take you in the wagon?"

"Nope. I'll be fine." She kissed Joseph and rushed out the door.

Joseph smiled as she rode away. The sound of her horse's

hoofs hitting the hard clay soil faded quickly into the distance.

He took a sip of his coffee. And spread the newspaper onto the table. He usually read the paper front to back as soon as he got it. He especially enjoyed reading about New York City. He was hoping to find news about his old home. He thought he might see something about his son, Thomas. Some reports named people he knew, like the bank owner, Wallace. Wallace was mentioned several times in association with stagecoach robbers. He grimaced as he thought about his brother Randall.

He heard the sound of horse hooves riding up. He smiled as he jumped up from his chair. He rushed to the door, still smiling.

"Did you forget something?" yelled Joseph as he opened the door.

His smile faded. He gasped in disbelief.

"Hello, little brother," said Randall.

Joseph's eyes filled with fire. "Randall? What in the hell are you doing here?"

"Is that how you greet family?"

Joseph went out onto the porch and slammed the door shut behind him. "You ain't my family." Joseph put his hand on his six-shooter, ready to draw. He squinted toward the road near the front gate. Someone was there, but he couldn't see who. "Is Thomas with you?"

Randall smirked. "No. That boy has been nothing but trouble since you left. I should have let you take him with you."

A flicker of surprise crossed Joseph's face before his expression hardened. He narrowed his eyes at Randall, suspicion creeping into his voice. "Why are you here? You aren't welcome."

"Frank and I need someplace to stay for a spell."

A rumbling sound grew louder from the main road near the entrance of his ranch. Joseph squinted toward the chaos. A massive plume of dust hung like a fog over the road. Dozens of men on horseback were headed their way.

Joseph's eyes widened with astonishment. "What the hell?"

"Oh yeah. My friends need a place, too. It seems you have plenty of room for my men to camp."

"No! I'm the sheriff here. I can't have outlaws on my property."

Randall wrinkled his face. "You ain't got a choice, brother. We found a secluded piece of land here; no one has to know we're there. It's next to an abandoned mine near the creek."

Several men carrying rifles walked up.

Randall glanced back at the men and then smiled at Joseph.

Joseph took a deep breath and blew it out as he locked eyes with Randall.

Randall stepped closer to Joseph as if he were about to tell him a secret. "Would be a shame if your new wife discovered you killed your first wife."

Joseph narrowed his eyes. "We've been married for a long time now, and we ain't got no secrets." Joseph repeatedly blinked in shame as he realized that he had only told her that Rose died in an accident, but not that he shot her.

Randall saw a glint of shame in Joseph's eyes. "It seems like we have an understanding. The rest of my men have already set up camp there. We'll come and go through the south side. No one will even know we're there."

Joseph reached for his gun. The six men pointed their rifles at Joseph. He pulled his hand away from his weapon.

Randall half-smiled. "As I said, you won't even know we're there. I got something for you."

Randall walked to his horse.

Joseph squinted hard to see who was hiding by the fence. He finally recognized Frank. Odd, he thought. Frank and Thomas had always been inseparable. However, when Randall and Frank chased him out of town, Thomas was nowhere around.

Randall took something from his saddlebag and sauntered back, grinning ear to ear. He winked at Joseph, put the sack on the chair, and left.

One by one, the men pointing their rifles at Joseph got on their horses and rode away after Randall. Joseph fixated on Randall and Frank as they led the squatters away past the guest house and across the creek. Randall was right. No one ever went to that part of his property. It was secluded and the perfect spot for outlaws to hide.

Joseph watched for a long time as the men disappeared down the trail. He shook his head and then noticed the sack that

Randall had left on the chair. He took a step toward it. It wasn't moving. He thought it might have contained a poisonous snake, which might deliver him a deadly bite. Randall would never shoot him dead with a bullet. He had a warped sense when it came to family. "Family takes care of family," Randall told him many times. Perhaps, Joseph thought, that's why Randall couldn't kill him back in New York.

Randall poked the bag with the barrel of his gun. There was a loud clink. He used the barrel to open the bag and peeked inside. Joseph stepped back in shock as he realized what the gift was. It was a bottle of whiskey.

Elizabeth peeked out the window of the stagecoach as it pulled up to the hotel across from the bank. She saw Aunt Helen waiting in a cart. In the back were two crates filled with colorful fabrics. Elizabeth stepped down, and the driver pulled her bag and handed it to her.

"Thank you, Robert." Elizabeth visited this town often and knew most drivers who rode between Auburn and Sacramento.

The driver smiled. "Have a pleasant visit."

Elizabeth nodded and went across the road.

Helen sat on the passenger side of the cart and waved at Elizabeth. "You're right on time."

Elizabeth rushed up to Helen and hugged her. "It's wonderful to see you. It only took two and a half hours."

Elizabeth put her bag into the cart beside the crates.

"It looks like you're getting ready to sew up a storm?"

Helen nodded. "I sure am. I came early and did some shopping."

Elizabeth climbed and picked up the reins. "You haven't moved, have you?"

Helen let out a loud belly laugh. "I'll never move out of that house."

"Just checking." Elizabeth shook the reins, and the horses took off.

Helen held on to the seat. Elizabeth usually drove the wagon a little faster than she did. "By the way, I made those desserts you love so much."

Elizabeth's eyes twinkled with surprise. "I was hoping you'd bake those fabulous Queen Cakes."

"Of course." Helen could barely hold back her enthusiasm. "I met a friend. She's coming over this afternoon."

"Friend? That's wonderful. I sometimes worry that you spend too much time alone."

Helen shrugged.

Elizabeth smiled fondly. "Who is your new friend?"

Helen chuckled. "Her name is Gertrude. She's a lovely woman, close to my age. She just moved here from New York with her niece and family. And she can talk up a storm."

"Nowhere near as you, I'm sure."

Helen burst out laughing. "That was my first thought when I met her, but no. She's a delightful person. Gertrude's niece is Martha, and Martha's husband is Alexander. They have a young boy of three or four—I don't remember—the boy's name is Alex."

"Is Martha coming with Gertrude?"

"No. Gertrude is bringing Alex. She said Martha was resting and recovering from her trip, and Martha is expecting another child."

"Oh, dear. I look forward to meeting Martha and her new baby."

Helen nodded. "I asked Gertrude to meet us at the house. I hope that we get there before she does."

Elizabeth glanced at Helen, her eye twinkling with mischief. With a flick of her wrist, she flung the horse's leather reins. The horse sped up. Helen laughed with glee and held on tight to her seat.

Helen and Elizabeth arrived at the house. A buggy was parked out front, and a woman sat on the porch with a young boy.

"Gertrude!" yelled Helen as Elizabeth stopped the wagon next to Gertrude's. "I was hoping to get here ahead of you. This is my niece, Elizabeth."

Gertrude stood.

Elizabeth stepped down from the cart and walked over to Gertrude. "It's my fault we're late. My coach just arrived from Auburn."

Gertrude said, "We left early in case I had trouble finding your house."

Helen walked up, out of breath, carrying one of the smaller crates. She turned to Elizabeth. "Would you be a dear and get the other crate?"

Elizabeth nodded.

Gertrude turned to Alex, sitting on the bench, and whispered something. Alex nodded as he snuck several brief peeks at Elizabeth and Helen. Gertrude went to Helen's cart, pulled down the other crate, and brought it to the porch.

Helen opened the door. "Thank you, Gertrude. Please go inside and set that crate anywhere."

Alex was quietly swinging his legs back and forth while he waited. Helen walked up to him. "Alex, it's a pleasure to meet you. I've heard a lot about you. Come inside. I have some tasty desserts."

Alex smiled and jumped down. "Thank you. My favorite dessert is cookies."

"I have something else that you might like even more. But if you don't, I have cookies too."

Alex nodded and then followed Helen inside.

Elizabeth went to the kitchen to make tea. She lit the stove and put a pot of water to boil on top. She set four plates and cups on the square table on the other side of the enormous kitchen.

In no time, Elizabeth served tea and Queen Cakes. She poured lemonade into Alex's cup.

"Come sit," said Elizabeth, pulling out a chair. "Alex, this is your seat."

Alex climbed in. His eyes grew wide when he saw the cake. It was as large as three stacked cookies. Gertrude sat on his right and grinned at Alex.

Helen sat to Alex's left and tapped his arm. He was halfway done with his cake. "Would you like the cookies instead?"

Alex's eyes filled with glee, and his mouth was still chewing. "No, thank you. I like these better."

Helen's brows rose with amusement.

Gertrude sipped her tea and then tasted the cake. "These are delightful, and the tea is delicious."

Elizabeth sat; Helen was on her right, and Gertrude to her left. "Aunt Helen's Queen Cakes are from a family recipe handed down for generations. I'm sure she'll share it with you. It took me a while to master them. Aunt Helen's are much better than mine."

Helen chuckled. "Thank you, darling. You're too modest. Yours always turn out better." She held out her hands. "These old hands don't work as well as they used to. These days, it's hit or miss if the cakes turn out well."

Elizabeth patted Helen's hand.

Gertrude took another sip. "I'd love to know how you make this tea. It's delicious."

Helen pulled her chair closer to the table. "The secret to the tea is how you prepare it. I'll show you. But I'm sure that yours is just as good."

Gertrude nodded with delight. "Thank you. Mine is good, too, but I'm always looking for ways to improve it. Oh! Before I forget. This morning, I gave Martha the cake you sent for her. She loved it."

Helen glanced at the cupboard. "I'll give you some to take home with you."

Alex's eyes followed Helen's and then fixated on the cupboard.

Elizabeth chuckled. "I can see that little Alex loves those cakes, too."

Alex turned to Elizabeth and bobbed his head up and down quickly.

Elizabeth winked at Alex and turned to Gertrude. "I'm looking forward to meeting Martha."

Gertrude's eyes brightened, and her face lit up. "Soon, she'll return to her normal, healthy self."

Elizabeth sipped her tea. "That's good to hear. Helen said that she'll be giving birth soon."

"Yes. I'm guessing she'll have her baby in another two months. Although she had Alex about a month early." She glanced at Alex. He was munching on his cake. "He turned out pretty good."

Alex grinned and pretended he hadn't heard Gertrude.

The three women chuckled.

Elizabeth's gaze lingered a few seconds on Alex.

"Have you any children?" asked Gertrude.

Elizabeth's face softened and turned to Gertrude. A hint of moisture caught the light in her eyes. "No. We've tried, but..."

Helen grimaced. "It's her husband's fault. All that drinking he did early on messed him up." She turned to Elizabeth. "It's not too late for you. You still got time."

Alex's brows furrowed slightly as he fixated on Helen.

Elizabeth held her lips tight. "Aunt Helen! That's got nothing to do with it." She glanced at Alex and then looked at Gertrude. "We're still hoping."

Elizabeth wiped her eyes and smiled.

"Are you okay?" Gertrude asked.

Elizabeth rolled her eyes, her shoulders dropping slightly. She held a large grin and shook her head at Helen. She tapped Gertrude's hand. "Of course I am. Let's get back to the party." She looked across to Alex. "Have you tried the lemonade, Alex? It's also from an old family recipe."

Alex put his cake down and tasted the drink. "It's delicious, but I don't usually have lemonade with my dessert."

Elizabeth held her lips tight as her brows went up. "Oh dear. What was I thinking?" She jumped from her seat and brought a glass of water for Alex.

Alex drank nearly half of it.

Elizabeth turned to Gertrude. "What brought you to California?"

Gertrude chuckled. "I just came along for the ride. It was Alexander and Martha's decision. Alexander came home from work one day with a little booklet about traveling to California. Juan Cortez, who used to live here, gave it to him."

Helen leaned in, her voice tinged with excitement. "I know Juan. Mrs. Cortez didn't like it here. The lifestyle was much too crude for her. She and I chatted all the time." She sighed. "I still miss her."

Gertrude continued, "Alexander bought his ranch. It's lovely."

Helen sat up taller. "Oh, my. That's nearby."

"Yes. Dr. Martin moved into the place down the road from us."

Helen clasped her hands together. "That'll be convenient to have a doctor close by. My doctor is as ancient as the hills and quite far away."

Gertrude smiled. "Dr. Martin is an excellent doctor. I help him now and again, especially when treating women."

Elizabeth nodded. "I know what you mean. Those doctors could learn a bit from us in that regard."

Gertrude and Helen both laughed and said in unison, "Yes!"

Gertrude asked Elizabeth, "Helen told me your husband is a sheriff."

"Yes, he's the sheriff over in Auburn. We came on the same wagon train from New York about fifteen years ago. That's when Aunt Helen bought this house. We stayed here, and he moved to Auburn."

Helen sighed. "That's when Elizabeth's first husband passed, right after that trip." Helen patted Elizabeth's hand.

Gertrude furrowed her brows. "Oh dear, I'm sorry."

Elizabeth's face softened. Her eyes were bright and cheerful as she remembered her first husband. "I'm okay. I've made peace with it a long time ago. I loved him, and he's in a better place now."

Gertrude nodded. "I understand. My husband passed away years ago. I still love him to this day. I honored his memory by letting him go. He's in heaven now."

"My husband's first wife died in some accident before leaving New York. Joseph was devastated and never said much about it."

Helen stood. "Enough talk about death." She served Gertrude, Elizabeth, and Alex another cake. "Gertrude, you told me that Martha is a bookkeeper. Is she going back to work at the bank? It's quite rare to find a woman doing that work."

"She might work there someday, but for now, she wants to focus on that baby growing inside her. I think you both would love her. She's a firecracker. She's an expert with numbers and is as good a shooter as any man."

Elizabeth's face brightened, and she excitedly pointed to her leather pouch on a small table by the front door. "I'm good at shooting, too. I can hardly wait to meet Martha and maybe do some target practice together."

Alex looked up from his cake. "Ma can shoot better than Pa."

Gertrude stifled a chuckle. "She sure can!"

Elizabeth, still glowing, said, "She sounds like a wonderful woman. I have an idea. My best friend Rebecca lives nearby and is visiting me in Auburn next Tuesday. Gertrude, why don't you take Martha and Alex up there?" Elizabeth turned to Helen. "And you can come with Rebecca. It will be so much fun."

Gertrude nodded. "That's eight days away. Martha will no doubt be healthy and want to go. We'll have to check with the doctor to ensure it's okay. But knowing Martha, she'll think it's a fabulous idea. She's looking for an adventure."

Alex's head was bobbing up and down excitedly at Gertrude.

Gertrude, her face filled with excitement, winked at Alex.

Elizabeth smiled. "Rebecca has a cute little coach."

"I'm not riding to Auburn in that rickety cart of hers. It's uncomfortable for me and won't be for Martha. I'll charter a stagecoach for us. Martha needs a smooth ride," said Helen. "If Martha's husband comes with us, six will be inside the cabin. I'll reserve it for Tuesday morning at eight."

Gertrude said, "Tuesday is perfect. Although I don't think Alexander would go. But if he did, he'd ride up top with his rifle, ensuring we're safe."

Elizabeth cocked her head curiously at Gertrude. "He's a lawman?"

"No. He works for the bank protecting stagecoaches. He's skilled at that. And he does bookkeeping for them, too."

Elizabeth rubbed her hands together excitedly as if warming them. "I can't wait to meet them."

Gertrude leaned in toward Elizabeth. "Elizabeth, Helen said your husband has a son in New York. That's sad that they're apart."

A wave of sadness washed over Elizabeth's face. "That's true. He was supposed to move here with us. I don't know why he didn't come. We've written letters inviting him, but he's never answered them. My husband has never given up hope. It tears him up that his son isn't here with him."

Gertrude said, "I'm sorry. I hope he never gives up. You never know."

Elizabeth exhaled loudly. "We'll never stop hoping his son finds his way to us."

"What's his name?"

"Thomas Pruitt."

Alex looked curiously at Elizabeth.

Gertrude blinked repeatedly as her smile melted away. She choked out, "Your husband is Joseph Pruitt?"

"Yes," said Elizabeth. She stood, worried, and took a step toward Gertrude. "Are you okay?"

"I'm fine. I need to get home. You know, with Martha being ill and all."

"Of course," said Elizabeth.

When Gertrude returned from Helen's house, she found Martha sitting in bed, humming a melody and reading the newspaper. Martha smiled as Gertrude and Alex walked in. Alex rushed to his mother.

"Ma! I missed you."

"I missed you, too." Martha kissed Alex and then glanced at Gertrude. "How was your visit?"

"It was lovely, and Elizabeth and Helen are looking forward to meeting you."

Gertrude hesitated as she decided whether or not to tell Martha about Thomas and Joseph.

Alex looked from Gertrude to Martha. "We found that man's pa."

Gertrude's eyes filled with shock.

Martha smiled at Alex. "Which man?"

"Thomas."

CHAPTER THIRTY-ONE

Conflict Resolution

On the other side of town, three days later, Agnes hobbled over to the chair next to Thomas and sat down. Although some women her age were content to sit quietly in a rocking chair as they aged, Agnes was quite active. Her face was tanned and leathery. It belonged to a woman who worked hard much of her life. She cooked, cleaned, and sewed when she needed to. She never learned how to read and thought reading was for affluent folks. She preferred being alone except when her friend Gertrude visited. When they lived in New York, Gertrude would visit with her almost every Sunday. Agnes met Gertrude sometime after Gertrude left the orphanage, long before Martha was born.

"My boy told me you wanted to talk to me. I got my chores to get to. What do you want?"

Thomas moved uncomfortably in his seat and leaned forward. During the trip from New York, Agnes was strict and stone-faced serious with him. Whenever she talked to him, she spoke monotonically and condescendingly. He'd never seen her smile except when she was with her grandchildren. When she smiled, her face would crack into a million wrinkles.

"I want to thank you for everything. I still don't understand why you've helped me all these months."

"Son..."

Thomas gasped. She sounded exactly like his mother for an instant.

Agnes pursed her lips, her wrinkles accentuating her mouth. "Everyone deserves a second chance if willing to try."

Thomas slumped in his seat. "Thank you."

Agnes narrowed her eyes, looking off in the distance. "That day on the trip, when I saw Martha marching our way, I knew that trouble was coming. She was carrying that leather bag of hers. That's where she carries her six-shooter."

Thomas leaned back, and his eyes grew large with shame.

260

"I told my boy to get to the wagon and hide you. Martha was red-faced and angry."

Thomas relaxed his face. "She had a good reason to shoot me."

Agnes's voice trembled slightly. "I know all about you and a little something about your family. And I know what you did to Martha."

Thomas fell back to his seat, shocked. "But—"

"Don't interrupt me." She sighed and then continued, "There's redemption in you. You're not like the rest of your family. You have your own life. You need to make restitution to those you've harmed and let go of those who have hurt you. Do you understand?"

Thomas blinked, confused. "I think so." He had expected to thank her and move on. He had managed to stay hidden from Randall and hadn't decided if he could muster the courage to meet with his father.

Agnes shook her head. "This is the part where you tell me you know what you must do."

She turned her head slightly, expecting Thomas to say something.

Thomas nodded. "You knew all these things about me and still took me in."

"We needed a driver. My husband is old and wouldn't have been able to get us here."

Thomas took a deep breath and let it out. "I'm grateful to you. You've helped me more than I ever deserved. I think I understand. I'm sorry about what I did to Martha. I know now that I should have gone with my pa all those years ago."

"Son, there ain't nothing for you to be sorry for with me. You gotta tell her directly. Tell her yourself." Agnes locked eyes with Thomas. "You can deal with your pa later. But now it's time that you made peace with that woman."

"But, she'll shoot me dead."

"We all gotta die sometime. And it'd be better to go with a clear conscience. Don't you think?"

Thomas nodded, and then his gaze fell to the floor.

"Now you go get the buggy ready. They live on the other side of town. And even though I don't care much about riding on that hard, worn-out bench all day, I'll go with you. Maybe she won't kill you if I'm there. I need you to be able to bring me back home."

"Yes, ma'am."

Agnes cocked her head back. "Damnit! Call me Agnes."

Thomas jumped back. "Agnes, I'll be right back."

A faint hint of a smile revealed a small fissure of a crack at the edge of her lips. "I'll be out here waiting."

Ten minutes later, Thomas rode up with the buggy. He had put a pillow on the bench for Agnes. He wanted to assist her in climbing up, but he knew she would scold him if he tried. "When I want help, I'll ask for it," she would likely say.

Agnes stepped in and smiled when she saw the pillow.

Soon afterward, Gertrude and Martha sat on the porch chatting. They talked about Helen and Elizabeth and traveling to Auburn to visit them.

Martha shook her head. "It'll be exciting."

A plume of dust kicked up from the main road as a buggy approached. As it turned toward the house, Thomas and Agnes came into view.

Martha jumped up and ran inside the house.

The buggy stopped next to the porch, and Gertrude walked up close to the edge.

Agnes got down. "Gertrude, we're here to talk."

Martha burst out of the house, pointing a six-shooter at Thomas.

"I knew you were helping him. I knew it," Martha said to Agnes, tears of rage simmering. "I can finally be rid of him."

Martha's razor-sharp eyes locked on Thomas as her hand trembled.

Gertrude's gaze darted from Thomas to Martha in total shock. She rushed to Martha's side, her voice tight with urgency. "Martha, Alex is just inside the door. Please!"

Agnes hobbled over much quicker than expected and stood before the gun. "Now you put that damn thing down. He ain't got a weapon. I saw to that."

Martha's chest rose and fell with ragged breaths. A tremor ran through Martha's hand, gripping the gun.

Agnes leaned in defiantly toward Martha. The glint of steel pressed against Agnes's flowery blouse. "Look at me, Martha."

Martha's gaze flickered to Agnes for a fleeting moment. With a forced effort, Martha inhaled deeply, then exhaled slowly. Finally, she took a hesitant step back and lowered her gun.

Agnes seized the opportunity. "You and Thomas will talk while Gertrude and I chat inside. It's been too long since she and I talked, and we have plenty to catch up on."

Martha blinked once, twice, then raised an eyebrow as if to say, 'Are you serious?'

Agnes whispered so only Martha could hear, "I know exactly what he did. You don't have to forgive him. You've got to talk it out with him." She glanced sideways at Thomas. "I've got his gun, and I'll shoot him myself if he tries anything. You understand?"

Martha grimaced. She narrowed her eyes at Thomas. "I'll be okay. You two have some of that tea and keep Alex inside."

Gertrude hesitated.

Her face filled with resolve, Agnes held the door open and pointed for Gertrude to enter. Gertrude's eyes flitted to Thomas, and then she marched in. Agnes's eyes darted from the gun to Martha. "This ain't about giving him another chance. This is about talking and listening. Get whatever you got off your chest. You don't want this hanging over you for the rest of your life."

Little Alex came flying out onto the porch. "Grandma!" He hugged her. He'd started calling her Grandma after spending so much time around her grandchildren on the trip from New York.

Alex hadn't noticed Thomas. Agnes smiled broadly at Alex. "Let's have some of those cookies you like so much."

Alex ran in, followed by Agnes.

Gertrude peeked out the door, narrowed her eyes at Thomas, then said to Martha, "Call out if you need me." Gertrude sent one more suspicious glance at Thomas and then went inside.

Thomas stopped breathing for an instant. He hadn't been alone with Martha since that crazed day at her house.

Martha stood, and Thomas sat on the buggy.

Thomas stood up. "Can I sit down on the porch? It's hot up

here."

Martha raised her gun. "You'll be dead before you take a step onto this porch."

"Okay. I got it. I'll stay right here." Thomas threw his hands up in surrender and collapsed back to his seat. His body was twisted at an awkward angle to face Martha.

Martha lowered her gun but held it at the ready.

Thomas glanced at the door. "That boy is my son. Isn't he?"

Martha's face contorted into a caricature of disgust. "No. He's not."

Disbelief crashed over his face, pulling his breath away in a startled blink. "But he looks like me."

Martha pulled her gun up again. This time, her arm trembled. "He's not your son. I don't want any more trouble from you. My family is happy. You have no rightful place in my family."

"I—I know. You're right." His eyes, filled with shock, focused on the gun that was pointing at him. As his gaze swept up to her face, he noticed she was pregnant. "I'm not here to ask for your forgiveness, although I'm sorry for what I did to you. I was a monster."

"You still are, following me here. Why didn't you stay in New York? I came here to get away from the likes of you."

Thomas shook his head. "I told Agnes I didn't want to see you because I knew you would shoot me dead. I spent the past few months with her and her family, keeping my distance."

"Hiding the whole time." She kept the gun pointed at him, shifting her weight from foot to foot.

"Yup. I was hiding. But not just from you. I was running away from my past, fearing it would find me."

Martha gasped. She felt like she had also run from her past, from New York and its painful memories.

"You killed my parents," yelled Martha.

"No. I didn't. I've never killed anyone. I'd never do that. My pa taught me to be better than that. My uncle shot them right in front of me." Thomas shuddered, trying to wrangle his guilt and sadness away.

"Why should I believe you?"

"He told me that he wasn't going to hurt anyone. It was a lie.

I'm surprised that your husband and he are so close."

Martha blinked several times. She lowered her gun and stepped closer. "What do you mean—close?"

"My uncle, Randall, has always been looking out for Alexander."

A sudden gasp tore from Martha's lips, her eyes widening in disbelief. Her voice rasped. "Randall Pruitt?"

Thomas nodded slowly.

Martha yelled, "Gertrude, come out here."

Gertrude rushed out. She had been in the front room next to the door, listening while Agnes was in the kitchen with Alex. "I heard everything." She turned to Thomas. "We know your pa is Joseph Pruitt."

Thomas nodded hesitantly. "Yes. My pa left New York years ago and is somewhere out here. Juan Cortez told me you bought his house. He gave me a letter from my pa asking me to come here. Juan gave me money and asked me to help Agnes and her family travel here."

Martha's breathing slowed. "Some of this sounds made up."

"Yeah. I suppose it does. But it's the truth. I swear. I'm a better person thanks to Agnes. I got a lot more to learn, I know." He glanced down at the gun resting at Martha's side. "Assuming I have enough time to."

Martha rolled her eyes and said. "Okay. I'm listening. I'll never forgive you for what you did to me, but I won't kill you. At least not yet."

"Can I get down from here and sit on the porch? It's really hot."

"No! Tell me about the stagecoach robbery. Tell me exactly what happened."

Gertrude placed her hand on Martha's arm and said, "Martha, we should let him tell Alexander."

Martha locked eyes with Thomas. "No. I want to know everything. Don't leave anything out."

Thomas spent the next twenty minutes telling her in minute detail about Randall, Frank, and the stagecoach robbery. A couple of times, he stopped as Martha wiped her tears away, about to cry.

"Shall I stop?"

"No! Keep going. Tell me why Randall shot my father."

"I didn't have my gun out, and your father was about to shoot me. Frank wounded him, and then he fell to the ground. But then Randall, with his crazed eyes, shot him dead. I didn't know he was going to do that. I'm sorry," he said as his eyes teared up.

"And my mother?"

"I should have known better. I found her hiding inside the stagecoach. She was scared. I took her around to the front. She ran to your father, and then Randall just shot her. I didn't...."

Martha sat down, crying from the excruciating pain of closure. "I'm gonna shoot him." Her voice trembled with rage. "I'm gonna kill him for what he did to my parents."

Martha felt the tremendous weight begin to lift away from her.

Thomas watched in horror at what he and his family had done to Martha. He was just as guilty as Randall for the disgusting mess he'd burdened Martha with. He wanted to apologize, but understood why his words would have meant nothing.

Martha took a deep breath, wiped away her tears, and then turned to Gertrude. "I'm okay now."

Gertrude grimaced at Thomas. "Come on down and sit across from us."

Thomas got down and shuffled to the bench at the end of the porch, keeping his eyes on Martha's gun. A cool cross-breeze relaxed him a bit. "Thank you," he said.

A wave of sympathy washed over Gertrude. She brushed it away and stared stone-faced at Thomas. "You have a lot to answer for. But now tell us exactly what's going on with your uncle. And tell us why your father is living in Auburn as its sheriff. And what happened to your ma?"

Martha nodded approvingly at Gertrude. Despite her tears, she appreciated that Gertrude was good at learning every detail of the people she met.

Thomas blinked, a prickle of unease creeping up his spine. "How do you know so much about my family?"

Gertrude answered without hesitation. "I met Elizabeth and her aunt three days ago. Elizabeth said your pa is all torn up about you not moving here with them."

Thomas went breathless. He rubbed his neck, breathing

slowly, and then inhaled deeply. He let it out with a sigh.

"It's Randall's fault that my mother is dead. He shoved her into my pa's gun. I'm certain that he pushed her on purpose. Anyhow, that's when the gun went off."

Martha gasped.

Thomas continued, "I was supposed to go with my pa to California the next day, but Randall persuaded me to stay. He's good at persuading people to do what he wants." He took a breath. "I don't know anything about Elizabeth."

Gertrude's eyes darted to Martha. "Alexander needs to hear his story." She turned to Thomas. "Are you staying at Agnes's place?"

"Yes," said Thomas.

Agnes walked out onto the porch. She looked over at Thomas. "You don't have any holes in you that don't belong there, do you?"

Thomas glanced nervously at Martha and then stood slowly. "Nope."

"I gotta get home. I got chores to do."

Thomas, his face void of emotion, nodded at Martha and Gertrude and then rushed to the buggy. He waited for Agnes and then helped her up to her seat.

"Don't tell anyone you helped me get up here. Got it?"

"Yes—I mean—no—I won't tell a soul."

He hurried to his seat and briefly glanced at Martha and Gertrude. He wanted to say goodbye, but didn't. He shook the reins to go.

CHAPTER THIRTY-TWO

Truths and Wounds

Alexander sat at his oil-finished desk, its surface marred by a chaotic canvas of half-hidden scratches. He thought it must have once been a beautiful specimen.

Douglas walked in. "It's almost lunchtime. How do you like your office?"

"It's nice. It's quite functional. It's exactly what I like."

"Good. I was afraid that the hifalutin lifestyle of New York would have tainted you into expecting a fancy, ornate desk."

"Nope. I never really liked that. Your brother told me he thought the customers expected the bank to have an air of upper-class splendor. He said that when they enter, they should feel like the bank symbolizes wealth and prosperity."

Douglas laughed. "If I made this place in that image, every law-breaking thief would want to rob it blind. I have more than enough money to do that, but we're practical here. I bet we have more money flowing through this building than Wallace has in all his banks out there."

Alexander smiled and nodded, pleased that Douglas shared similar tastes in practicality over aesthetics.

"How's your wife doing?" asked Douglas.

"Doctor says she's healthy now. Before I left, she was up humming and cooking an incredible breakfast. She's back to her old self." Alexander rubbed his neck. "I'm still worried about her, though."

"I don't want to see you working here in the afternoons for the rest of the week. You have a wife to care for and need to settle into your new place."

Alexander relaxed his shoulders. He wanted to stay home with Martha, but Martha had prodded him to go to work. "Thank you."

Douglas looked expectantly at Alexander. "It's about that time, ain't it?"

A flicker of confusion crossed Alexander's face as he looked at

Douglas.

Douglas grinned. "Let's have some steak and potatoes at the restaurant across the way. They have the best food anywhere around."

"Oh, lunch, yes."

Douglas said, "That restaurant has excellent service, delicious food, and a sensibly priced steak."

"You're so different from your brother."

Douglas nodded. "Why in the hell do you think that we're on opposite sides of this great continent? I love my brother, but I have my limits."

Alexander laughed as he patted Douglas on the shoulder. "Let's go have some of those sensibly priced steaks," he said.

"I'll be out on the porch waiting for Sheriff August."

"I'm right behind you."

Alexander quickly pulled his six-shooter from the drawer and holstered it. He reached for his rifle out of habit, then decided against taking it. He grabbed his hat and rushed out the door.

When Alexander came out, Douglas and Sheriff August were chatting and sitting on the bench.

Sheriff August jumped to his feet. "Alexander, it's good to see you again. I hope you're hungry. They have the best steak and potatoes."

"So I've heard." Alexander winked at Douglas.

Sheriff August bobbed his head repeatedly. "We've got a lot to talk about. Mostly about those stagecoach robbers."

The three of them walked across the street to the restaurant. They looked like long-lost friends talking with each other nonstop.

As they stepped onto the restaurant porch, Randall and Frank walked out. Randall's face was sour as he passed. Frank winced and glared at Alexander.

"I'll join you in a minute," Alexander said to Douglas.

Douglas nodded, and he and the sheriff went inside.

Alexander rushed after Randall. "Randall!"

Randall's face exploded into a million fissures of wrinkles as he grinned. "Alexander!"

Alexander firmly shook Randall's hand. "I've been meaning to see how you're getting along."

Randall nodded to Frank to go ahead and turned back to Alexander. "I just had lunch, and I'm headed out of town after I get some supplies. You were right about moving here. This part of the country is much grander than I had expected."

"I love it here, too. It's quite a bit more peaceful than New York. I'll be home in a couple of hours if you want to stop by before you head out," said Alexander.

Randall pulled out his pocket watch. "Tell you what. I'll be there at four o'clock. I got a lot to do before I head out."

Alexander extended his hand. "Four o'clock is perfect."

Randall gripped Alexander's hand, grinning, and brought him in for a hug.

Frank was by their horses and stood glaring at Alexander.

Alexander said, "To get to my house, you—"

"I know where your place is." Randall patted Alexander's shoulder.

Alexander's smile faded.

"You're at Juan's old ranch, aren't you? It's on the map that he gave me."

"Yes." Alexander relaxed. Juan had written the location on his maps for each traveler.

Randall winked at Alexander and went to his horse.

Frank stood next to his horse with his eyes narrowed at Alexander.

Alexander locked eyes with Frank.

"Frank!" yelled Randall. "Let's go."

Frank snapped out of his mean-spirited gaze and got on his horse.

Alexander grimaced as they rode away. Shaking his head, he stepped into the restaurant. Toward the back, just beyond several booths, Sheriff August and Douglas sat at a secluded table.

"It's about time you get in here, Alexander," said Douglas. "We've been making all sorts of plans for you."

Alexander chuckled as he sat. Douglas was to his right, and the sheriff was to his left. With a view of the whole place, Alexander counted at least twenty folks sitting at the other tables.

"Mighty fine place here," said Alexander. He liked that it was clean and orderly. It was much louder than the bank but wasn't loud enough to interfere with their talking.

Douglas said, "We ordered the steak and potatoes. We didn't know what you drank, so we got you their famous lemonade. You can order something else if you want."

"Sounds perfect to me. So, what have you men been planning?" asked Alexander.

The sheriff straightened up. "I'm glad you asked. You can talk to Douglas later about your banking duties. But, I wanted to bring you up to speed on the stagecoach problems."

Alexander nodded.

The sheriff was very animated, using his hands as he talked. "Lately, we've had a rise in stagecoach robberies. They seem to be hitting the routes west of here, especially between here and San Francisco. But the latest one was early this morning, Northeast of here. The coach was headed this way, and the driver said men were wearing covers over their faces."

Douglas sat up. "No one got killed, but the two protectors, the driver, and one of the passengers were injured. They took the strongboxes." Douglas shook his head. "They were moving a lot of money on that coach."

The sheriff nodded. "Usually, there are only two or three robbers. And it's relatively easy for the lawmen riding with the coach to chase them off. But this time, there were at least a dozen robbers."

Alexander tilted his head as if he had partially solved a complicated problem. "That's unusual. A group that size makes me think they're organized like soldiers on the battlefield. I'm betting there are more than a dozen of them in all. We should start now."

Douglas shook his head no. "You need to settle in and look after your wife. August can take care of this for now. I'm hiring more men. They'll report to you once August has trained them. They'll work with him until then."

"I like that idea. How many deputies do you have?" asked Alexander.

The sheriff said, "I have two right now, but I'll deputize several more. We ain't going to mess around. We'll get this under control."

"I hope so. I'll pay them a decent wage, August." He turned to Alexander. "And I'll do the same for your men, too."

Alexander blinked in surprise. "It looks like we've got a plan."

Douglas's eyebrows lifted as he leaned in toward Alexander. "When Martha is better, please have her stop by the bank. We certainly could use her expertise. Wallace wrote me that she was responsible for straightening out his bank's records."

Alexander's head bobbed as a faint smile played on his lips. "She is gifted in that regard. I'll pass the invitation on to her. Although—"

A woman placed a plate filled with food in front of each man. "I'll be right back," she said.

Alexander's eyes widened at the size of the thick, juicy steak. The steam, filled with a tasty aroma, wafted up and made his mouth water.

Douglas smiled at Alexander's reaction. "Eat up. It's the best."

They spoke very little for the rest of the lunch, except for Alexander, who said occasionally, "This is marvelous. I've never tasted steak this juicy. I've got to bring Martha here."

It was almost two o'clock when Alexander rode up to his house. Martha and Gertrude were sitting on the porch. Little Alex was playing in the far corner.

Alexander ran up to Martha and kissed her gently on the cheek. He sat next to her. "Boy, do I have a lot to tell you? But first, Douglas told me you could work at the bank whenever you like. He said that his brother had written him all about you. Over dinner, I thought we'd discuss what I'd be working on with Douglas and Sheriff August."

Martha tried to smile. "That's wonderful, dear."

"Oh, I saw Randall in town, and he's off to who knows where."

Martha winced and turned to Gertrude. "Would you mind taking Alex inside? Maybe give him a cookie or two. And then come back. We need to tell Alexander about our visitor."

Alexander looked with concern at Martha.

"I'll be right back." Gertrude walked over to Alex. "Alex, let's go get some cookies."

Alex dropped the little twigs he was playing with and ran to the door. "Yes. Cookies. I want two."

A minute later, Gertrude stood in the doorway. "I'll keep an eye on Alex from here."

Martha half-smiled.

"What's going on?" Alexander asked, confused.

"Agnes came over this morning. It turns out that she had hired a man to drive her wagon from New York."

Alexander furrowed his eyebrows. "I was wondering how that old couple managed to handle that wagon alone."

"It was Thomas who drove the wagon for Agnes. And he was the man who brought me those personal items from my parents' stagecoach. He was here with Agnes."

Alexander straightened up. "Did he hurt you?"

"No. But I wanted to kill him until he told me all about my parents' stagecoach robbery. Things were clear for the first time after talking to him."

"What did he say?"

"You should go talk to him. He's at Agnes's house."

"I'll head to her place after you tell me a little more."

"Okay. He told me how my father and mother died. He never mentioned anything about anyone else on the coach. I thought a protector or a deputy always rode up top with the driver or inside with the passengers."

Alexander gasped.

Martha continued. "Why wasn't someone there with a shotgun or rifle or something?"

"I was there, but I arrived too late."

"I know that. But, I had assumed that someone else was protecting that coach."

Alexander took a deep breath and let it out slowly. "I was supposed to go with them, but I was working on your father's account. I would have been riding in that coach if I had left right away. I might have been able to save them."

Martha went silent and glanced away. "So you're saying that my parents' life was worth less to you than correcting a bookkeeping error?"

Gertrude gasped. "There's no way to know what would have happened. If it's God's will to go, it's God's will to go."

Martha looked at Alexander and let out a huff. "How could you lie to me all these years? You could have told me."

"I didn't lie to you. I've never lied to you."

Martha turned up one corner of her mouth and shook her head. "You should have told me."

"I'm sorry." Alexander took her hand and kissed it gently. "I made a mistake that cost you dearly."

Martha exhaled loudly. "Today has been a day of clarity. Is there anything else you should have told me, Alexander?"

Alexander furrowed his eyebrows. "No."

"We can't afford to keep these sorts of things from each other." Martha sat back down. "I know it's not your fault that my parents are dead. However, I will not rest until their killer is brought to justice."

Alexander half-smiled and nodded his head.

"You should go visit Thomas before it gets too late." Martha chuckled. "And don't shoot him until he tells you everything. We can talk when you return. We can see if he told us the same thing."

Alexander kissed Martha and rushed off to his horse.

As Alexander left, Gertrude leaned over to Martha. "Why didn't you tell Alexander about Randall?"

"Because I'm going to go kill him myself. And I don't want Alexander trying to stop me."

CHAPTER THIRTY-THREE

Confrontation

Alexander rode through the city, amazed at the many houses. They seemed closer together than where he lived. It reminded him of the houses by the bank in New York. He loved the wide-open countryside much better. He pulled up to a watering hole and examined the map while his horse sipped water. A minute later, he knew exactly where to go.

After five minutes of navigating the dirt paths, he arrived at the road to Agnes's house. Turning the corner, a modest house came into view. Agnes and Thomas sat on the porch, watching him approach.

Agnes jumped up when Alexander stopped in front of the house. "I don't want any trouble. Got that?"

"Yes, Agnes, I understand. Can I talk to Thomas — alone?"

"Nope. I'm gonna stay right here. If you cause any ruckus, my son is in the barn." She glanced at Thomas and turned back to Alexander. "Sit down." She pointed to a bench across from them.

Alexander grimaced. For a long time, he had wanted to shoot Thomas dead for what he did to Martha. He sat, his eyes narrowed and fixed on Thomas.

"Tell me everything about the Swansons' stagecoach robbery."

Thomas blinked. Alexander's eyes bore into him mercilessly. "I already told Martha what I knew."

Alexander leaned back. "We didn't have a chance to talk about the details. Did you kill her parents?"

"No! I've never killed anyone. I promise," said Thomas as if pleading for his life.

Alexander snarled at Thomas. "Sometimes hurtin' someone is the same as killing 'em."

Thomas's shoulders slumped, and his brows furrowed. "I know. But I'm not like that anymore. I'd never do anything to hurt... Alex's mother."

Alexander bristled.

Thomas squirmed in his seat and then settled down.

"I don't understand why you're here. Why did you follow us?" asked Alexander. "Did you come to harm Martha again?"

"No! My uncle said that Martha had a boy who looked exactly like me. I didn't believe him at first, so I went to see for myself, but you all had already left. Juan Cortez was at your house and gave me a letter from my pa, asking me to come to California."

Agnes cleared her throat. "That's when he came over, needing a way to get to California. Thomas was a God-send."

"I never saw Thomas once during that trip," said Alexander to Agnes.

Agnes continued. "We stayed at the end of the train, far away from your wagon. Everything was fine until your boy climbed into my wagon and found Thomas inside."

Alexander winced. Martha hadn't told him that. He sat taller and glared at Thomas, "You lured him into the wagon?"

"No. I was sleeping. He came in and woke me up, poking me with a stick. I was stunned. And then he just started talking to me, asking me stuff. He was chatting away like a grown person. He asked me where my pa was. I said he was in California, and he said that's where he was going and that his pa would help me find him."

Alexander wanted to smile because Alex was just as Thomas described, but his rage wouldn't let him. "What else?"

Thomas glanced away. "Nothing more. That's when Martha came in and told me to stay away. After she left, I was up all night expecting her to come to shoot me. And, I would have let her."

Alexander went silent. His eyes bore into Thomas, and then he turned to Agnes.

"Agnes, why do you trust him?"

Agnes's lips curled up as the rest of her face went small. "Oh, I don't trust anyone. Not even you."

Thomas stifled a grin and turned away to hide his face.

"Why haven't you gone looking for your father?" asked Alexander.

"I can't. Not yet." He glanced at Agnes. "I don't know why. I want to, but—"

Agnes narrowed her eyes at Alexander. "He'll visit him when

he's ready."

Alexander grimaced and then pulled out his watch. "Damn, it's three-thirty. I have to get going soon. Now tell me, who killed Mr. and Mrs. Swanson?"

"My uncle did. He shot them both. I didn't want to go with him that day. He assured me we wouldn't hurt anyone."

Alexander shook his head as he stared at Thomas. "I wish I had known this back in New York."

Thomas tilted his head and narrowed his brows at Alexander. "He's not in New York. He's here."

Alexander cocked his head back as if he'd been punched. "He's here? Where?"

Thomas shrugged. "I don't know. I thought you did. The last I saw him was a week or two before we arrived."

"How would I know?"

"You know him. He's your friend, Randall," said Thomas. "He's my uncle."

"What!" Alexander jumped to his feet. "You're lying."

"No, I'm not. He's my uncle. He came out here chasing after me. He didn't want me to go looking for my father." Thomas gritted his teeth. "He's to blame for my mother's death."

"You're a Pruitt?"

"Yes. And my father is Joseph Pruitt."

The color drained from Alexander's face. "I invited Randall to join our wagon train. Earlier today, I told him to stop by my house before he left town. It's my fault." Alexander's eyes filled with dread. "He said he'd be there at four o'clock."

Thomas jumped up, startling Agnes. "Martha knows all about Randall. She won't have a chance against him if she raises a gun at him," said Thomas. "And I know she will."

Alexander stood up, realizing he had foolishly trusted Randall, and looked incredulously at Thomas.

Agnes jumped up. "She said if she ever got the chance, she would kill him."

"I gotta get home." Alexander sprinted to his horse. "Thomas, get Sheriff August and bring him to my place."

"Sure thing," said Thomas without hesitation.

Alexander raced away.

Agnes handed Thomas his gun. "My boy is in the barn. Send him after Sheriff August. You go help Alexander."

Thomas rushed to his horse.

Thomas tore out of the barn in no time and raced after Alexander.

Then, her son rode out and yelled, "I'll be right back, Ma."

Agnes nodded. "Hurry!"

Agnes went back to the porch bench, shaking her head. "I was right about Thomas. He has a good heart."

John, Randall, and Frank led the gang out of the south entrance of Alexander's property and headed north to Joseph's ranch.

"It was fine of your brother to let us stay on his land up in Auburn. Charlotte told me that it's secluded up there," said John. "She's got it all set up and ready for the rest of us. Sorry to be leaving this place."

"The owner would have discovered us here sooner or later," said Randall.

John nodded. "Yeah. There wouldn't have been much trouble if it were just my handful of people hiding. But now, with your men and mine, there's no way we could hide everyone, including those covered wagons you brought with you."

"Yup. I almost got rid of those wagons after we arrived here. They sure make it easy to transport our captured bounty without raising any suspicion."

"We made a lot of money working together on those jobs."

Randall grinned. "We gotta make this a regular thing."

"That last stagecoach was an easy target," said John. "Some of the others were a bit harder."

"It's easy when a dozen of us work to bring a coach down." Randall glanced at Frank behind him. "If it weren't for Frank wounding the driver, we wouldn't have been able to stop that coach. No one could have made that shot but him."

Frank smiled.

Randall's gaze surveyed the wagons and everyone following them. "Combined, we got at least twenty, maybe thirty men."

John's head bobbed up and down wildly. "I think we got more. And don't forget my wife, Charlotte."

Randall wrinkled his face, his lips curled down. "She doesn't count."

John chuckled. "She counts. She'd say she's a better shot than your Frank."

Frank snarled at him, but John didn't notice.

Randall rode up closer to John. "You guys go on up ahead. I'll wait here for the rest of my men to catch up."

"Sure thing," said John. "I'm anxious to join Charlotte and the rest of my group there."

Randall motioned for Frank to move to the side of the road. Randall turned back to John. "Keep your men hidden from Joseph. I told him it was just a few of us staying there."

John chuckled. "He doesn't have much choice in the matter."

Randall grunted, then rode up to Frank.

Randall said in a lowered voice, "The rest of my men should be coming soon. I'll be back in ten minutes."

Frank's brow furrowed in confusion. "Where are you going?"

"I've got to stop by Alexander's place and tell him goodbye. Stay here and wait for the men."

Frank looked incredulously at Randall.

Randall pulled out his pocket watch, ignoring Frank. "It's almost four."

John rolled his eyes and exhaled in a huff. He turned back to his men, whistled, and waved for them to go. After he snapped the reins, his horse broke into a gallop. Most of the men on horseback followed closely behind John. A handful of them rode with the slower-moving wagons.

The sound of the galloping horses and wagons was deafening.

Randall and Frank waited for the wagons to pass by at the end of the procession.

Martha and Gertrude sat on the porch chatting while Alex napped inside.

Martha giggled. "I hope that Alexander didn't shoot Thomas."

"If he had shot him, Alexander would have been here already, sitting here with us. He would have ridden up there, had a little gunfight that might have lasted two minutes, and ended with Thomas sprawled in the dirt."

Martha chuckled. "Oh, but Agnes wouldn't let Alexander go without scolding him."

"That's true. She thinks Thomas is worth saving."

Martha smirked. "I'm not entirely sure why, but I don't want him dead anymore."

"That's good to hear."

A slow-rising rumble came from the road that cut across the east side of their property.

"What's that?" asked Martha.

"Sounds like a stampede."

They ran to the edge of the porch where they could get a better look.

Several men were riding on horseback, followed by wagons stirring up plumes of dust.

"Looks like they're headed north," said Martha.

Gertrude scrunched her forehead. "They're mighty loud. I wonder where they're coming from."

"I don't know, but they sure did kick up a lot of dust. I hope all that racket didn't wake Alex."

"I'll check on him." Gertrude hurried inside.

Martha watched the road as the noise faded into the distance. A slight breeze blew the dust cloud toward the house. She pulled her scarf and covered her mouth. She heard a lone horse riding her way.

"Thank goodness." She expected to see Alexander coming down the trail. She squinted, trying to see through the fading haze. Her eyes felt gritty, and her vision was blurry. A silhouette of a man approached. She leaned forward and squinted again. An instant later, her eyes filled with shock. Randall was riding tentatively toward her. A chilling dread hit her. She ran into the house. Randall was getting down from his horse when she returned to the porch. He was less than twenty feet away from her.

"What are you doing here?" asked Martha.

"Alexander told me to come by at four o'clock before I head out of town." Randall pulled out his pocket watch, opened it, and showed her the face. "It's four."

Martha gasped at the sight of the timepiece.

"Where did you get that watch?" Martha asked accusingly. The chain was silver and didn't belong to the gold watch.

"It's nice, ain't it?"

Martha didn't say a word. Her breathing was forced, her chest heavy as she fixated on the timepiece.

When Randall snapped it shut, Martha shuddered.

He narrowed his eyes at her and stared at her for a second. "Why don't you use those pretty little legs of yours and go get Alexander? I ain't got all day."

Martha squinted at him. "Wait here," she said in a slow, deliberate tone.

Randall snickered. "Good girl."

Martha turned as if she were going inside. Instead, she pulled her six-shooter and pointed it squarely at Randall.

Randall laughed. "Is this a joke?"

Martha glared at him. "That woman on the front of that watch —that's a picture of my mother. She had that watch made special for my father. Those tiny, little stones all around the edge—no one else had anything like that. He loved that watch because my mother gave it to him. He was never without it."

"You're mistaken. I bought this watch in New York." He looked down at her belly, past the gun. "You're expecting. That must be why you might be imagining things."

Martha glared! She felt exposed. She pointed her gun squarely at Randall. "You killed my parents!"

Randall stepped back, grinning, and winked at Martha.

"Ain't that gun a little heavy for your dainty little hand?"

"Don't you take another step. I know all about you," said Martha. "Thomas told me everything."

Randall's grinning face froze as his jaw clenched hard. He narrowed his eyes like a panther about to pounce on its prey.

Martha fired a shot at his feet.

Randall laughed. "So you're the mother of Thomas's boy? Where is he?" Randall tried to peek behind Martha. "You know, he's the spitting image of Thomas when he was that age."

Randall took a step closer to Martha.

Martha fired a second shot an inch from Randall's right foot. Bits of rock and dirt flew up at Randall. Randall shielded his eyes, pulled his gun, and shot at Martha. Martha fell, her arm bleeding from the bullet.

Randall wiped his face and pointed his gun at Martha.

Gertrude rushed out the front door, pointing a six-shooter squarely at Randall. A loud boom of a shot echoed, nicking Randall's arm.

Frank was startled by the commotion and grabbed his rifle as he jumped from his horse. There was an older woman on the porch aiming a gun at Randall. He aimed at her. Behind him, Thomas barreled toward him as he jumped from his horse. The rifle went off as Thomas fell hard on Frank. He wrestled the weapon away from Frank. "You're not a killer." Thomas held Frank pinned tightly, face down.

Gertrude yelped as a bullet whirred past her and landed in the wall behind her.

Randall twisted around, and his eyes grew large. Thomas was attacking Frank. Randall aimed his gun at Thomas, and before he could pull the trigger, Alexander plowed his horse into Randall. Randall slid against the unforgiving, rocky dirt between the house and the barn. His arm cracked loudly when he crashed into a huge rock jutting from the ground. He moaned as he tried to stand but couldn't.

Martha jumped to her feet, gun in hand, and towered over Randall. "You're going to pay for what you did to my parents."

Randall, seething in pain, couldn't manage a laugh. "The only reason I didn't shoot you dead is because you're Alexander's wife."

Martha's hand trembled.

Sheriff August and two deputies hurried to Martha. "You don't want to do that. The laws out here aren't as forgiving as they are back in New York."

Martha, still breathless, fixed Randall with a sharp glare. A glint flickered from his pocket—a pocket watch catching the light in a brief, telling flash. Without hesitation, she reached down, her grip firm around her gun, and snatched the watch.

"This isn't yours."

The flimsy chain snapped as she tore it free, the fabric of Randall's pocket giving way under the force. She gathered the broken links and the watch into her palm, holding them close to her heart. Without another glance, she turned and strode back to the porch—to Gertrude.

Alexander rushed to Martha. "You're arm is bleeding."

"It's just a scratch." She pointed to Thomas. "He's not going to hold that man down forever. You better go help him."

"I got him," said one of the two deputies. He ran over to Frank and Thomas. Thomas stood and helped Frank stand.

"Give me that gun," said the deputy to Thomas.

"What?"

The deputy said forcefully, "The gun, hand it over."

Thomas blinked repeatedly, confused, and handed the gun to the deputy.

"You two sit down. We're going to be a while."

The other deputy was guarding Randall.

Sheriff August walked up to Alexander and pointed to the cart beside the large boulder Randall had crashed into. "We'll need your cart to get them to the jail."

Thomas called out to the sheriff. "Can't we let Frank go? He didn't kill anyone."

Frank looked astonished at Thomas.

Sheriff August was flabbergasted and yelled, "He would've if we hadn't arrived in time. He's going to jail. And so are you."

CHAPTER THIRTY-FOUR

Shootout

Gertrude ran inside. "I'll keep Alex company inside."

Martha nodded as her eyes surveyed the front yard.

Alexander stood beside Randall while Thomas and Frank sat further away next to the cart, guarded by a deputy. Sheriff August and the other deputy were inspecting the cart.

Alexander turned to Martha. "You okay?"

"Yes, I'm fine." She narrowed her eyes at Randall. "That scoundrel needs help standing. He looks like a turtle on his back."

Alexander tried lifting Randall.

Randall roared like a wounded animal. "Damnit! That arm's messed up." He struggled to stand on his own but couldn't.

Alexander went to his other side and helped Randall to his feet.

Randall leaned up against the four-foot-tall boulder that had broken his fall. The giant rock was halfway between the barn and the house. He was breathing heavily. "Son, I watched out for you. And this is how you repay me?"

"You've made a fool of me. I thought you cared about me."

Randall's chest rose and fell. "Your father was my best friend. I promised him I'd take care of you." He shook his head. "And I kept my promise."

Alexander glared at him. "You're as crooked as he was." Alexander turned to walk away.

"I know who murdered your pa."

Alexander stopped. "You're lying! You said he ran away."

Randall nodded. "It was Frank's father, Sam Williams. He hated your pa. The coward shot him in the back."

Alexander couldn't recollect that name, but it sounded familiar.

Frank pointed at Alexander. "His pa was weak. Pa told me he deserved what he got."

Randall cocked his head in surprise and eyed Frank. "He told you?"

"Of course he did. He never kept secrets from me."

Randall hissed at Frank, "What else did he tell you?"

Frank grinned with a sinister, sideways glance at Alexander.

Randall leaned forward and glared at Frank. "You keep your damn mouth shut."

Alexander said, "I think you're lying to me. I think you both are."

Randall said, "You've met Sam before. I'm sure you have. You were a young boy when Juan, Sam, and I came to your house. We'd all play poker—your ma, too."

A shiver passed through Alexander as a vague memory surfaced. He pointed at Frank. "I remember a man who resembles him. My parents didn't like him. I think they got into a fight or something."

"Yup, that was Sam. After that, he never came over again. After your pa disappeared, I searched for him for days. It didn't make sense that he'd up and leave without telling me. I didn't know what happened to him until the day Frank's pa died."

Randall winked at Frank. Randall's eyes found Alexander again. "Sam was recovering from the bullet wound you gave him. That's when he confessed to killing your pa. When I defended your Pa, Sam went wild-eyed. He was going to come after you. Then he attacked me." Randall took a breath. "I shot him in self-defense."

Frank gasped as the air fled from his lungs. He stood motionless at the revelation.

Randall's gaze darted from Thomas to Martha and then to Alexander. "Let me tell you about them. Thomas was soft on her way before you ever knew her."

Thomas growled, "You shut your crooked mouth."

A gravelly chuckle escaped Randall's lips. "He met her at the school. That's no place for a woman unless she's there to clean or service the men."

"That's enough," said Alexander.

Martha moved to the edge of the porch like a viper preparing to pounce.

Randall smiled at her and kept on. "Thomas went to her house and asked her why she abruptly left. She broke his heart."

"You're lying," Martha snapped at him.

Alexander stepped threateningly close to Randall. "I know you killed Mr. and Mrs. Swanson back in New York. I know the whole story. You, Thomas, and I suppose the third was Frank over there."

Randall grimaced, and then a smile snuck back onto his face.

"That boy of yours looks exactly like Thomas."

Alexander's face exploded into a patchwork of crimson, and his eyes grew large with contempt.

Alexander pulled his gun and pointed it at Randall. "I ought to kill you right here."

A loud rumble came from the road. Randall chuckled and edged himself behind the giant rock while Alexander was distracted. A cacophony of thunderous shots followed. With their guns drawn, riders shot as they rode toward the house.

Martha and Gertrude ran inside.

The deputy next to Alexander managed to shoot two outlaws before he was shot. He fell, still breathing.

Alexander and the sheriff dragged the wounded deputy to the side of the house.

Randall hid behind the boulder and held his bloody arm.

The other deputy, Thomas, and Frank had retreated to the backside of the barn nearest the southern trail. From there, the deputy fired at the outlaws.

Randall yelled out, "We have you surrounded. Let us go; no one has to die today."

The deputy peeked out from behind the barn and shot down two men. The deputy was too distracted by the outlaws coming from the road to pay any mind to Thomas and Frank, who were a few feet away from him. He continued to shoot.

Thomas pleaded with Frank. "You can stay and settle down here. Randall killed your pa, just like he did my ma. Don't trust him. He doesn't trust you."

Frank tilted his head. "The sheriff said I'm going to jail. You too. Ain't nothing you can do about it."

"No. We haven't killed anyone. We're going to be okay."

Frank glanced at the deputy, crouched down, reloading his weapon.

Frank punched Thomas. "Sorry." Thomas stumbled and fell. Frank lunged at the deputy. Frank wrestled the gun away from him and shot him dead.

Thomas fell back in horror as he watched Frank's crazed look and shouted, "Nooooo!"

Frank narrowed his eyes at Thomas and pointed the gun at him. "Now, I killed someone. You can't keep me from my destiny. Randall's men won't stop until everyone here dies. You should come back with us. We're your family."

"No. That's not true. You're my friend."

Frank cocked his head back. "You don't understand. Randall is all I got. Now go inside and bring me a damn horse before I decide to shoot you."

Thomas froze. "I won't give up on you. Just don't kill anyone else. I'll tell them that one of Randall's men shot that deputy."

Frank glared at Thomas. "Get me that horse!"

Alexander continued to fire. He and the sheriff had shot three outlaws. He counted another three outlaws still firing their guns. The deputy was lying motionless where Thomas and Frank once stood.

Alexander rose taller. Frank crawled out from behind the barn, ready to fire his gun at him. Alexander dropped down as a bullet splintered the wood above him.

Martha was enraged when Frank almost shot Alexander. She fired several shots from the window facing the barn.

Frank temporarily retreated.

"You okay, Alexander?" Martha yelled from the house.

"Yes."

Alexander turned to Sheriff August. "Go to the back of the house."

Seconds later, he and the sheriff landed safely behind the house. From that spot, he peeked around the corner. Randall was by the boulder, and the side of the barn was just beyond him.

Martha reloaded her rifle. "Gertrude, take Alex to the back room.

Alexander will keep the back of the house safe."

Gertrude crouched down as she led Alex to safety. Concern painted Alex's face. He flinched every time a shot was fired. He never uttered a word, though.

Martha pointed her weapon out the front window. She imagined the cans standing precariously on the table in the backyard. Three of the men were close to the road. One was climbing up the big oak tree she admired, another was near the ground, hiding by the shrubs, and the third was high in the tree.

It was suddenly quiet. She calculated the optimal order to dispatch her targets. She preferred to think of them as targets rather than to humanize them. Her family's life was more important than thinking of them as sentient and rational people. They were there to kill her family.

She put a bullet in the first one, who was crouched down. Then she hit the next one, climbing the tree. She shot the third man before he could seek the cover of another branch.

Randall's eyes darted to the barn when Frank peeked out from around the back. Frank motioned to him. Randall hesitated when Frank raised his gun in his direction and then fired. A surge of fear shot through Randall as the bullet buzzed past his ear. He stopped breathing until he realized he hadn't been shot.

Frank became more animated, waving his arm frantically for Randall to come to him. Frank fired at the house where Alexander and the sheriff hid. Randall took the opportunity and sprinted toward Frank. Frank fired several more shots. Randall flinched as more bullets streaked past him. He reached Frank, his eyes filled with fire.

Half out of breath, Randall growled at Frank, "What the hell were you thinking shooting at me?"

Frank choked out incredulity. "What are you talking about? I was keeping you from getting shot! I just saved you!"

Thomas held the reins of a horse. Randall grabbed them from him.

Frank glared at Thomas. "What about a horse for me?"

Thomas pointed to the doorway. "He's right there."

Randall struggled to climb onto the horse. His grip failed when he tried, and he tumbled down and landed with a thud. Frank helped him up. It was almost comical. Randall snapped the reins and took off down the southern trail.

Frank jumped on his horse, dug in his heels, and took off after Randall.

Martha peered out the window, searching for any movement from the trail to the main road. The sound of horses' hoofs racing away echoed into the house. Martha figured it was Randall getting away. No matter, she thought, she'd track him down and kill him soon enough. She continued to survey the front of the property. There was a deputy down, moving his arms slowly. Further away, a gun-toting man was sneaking up on the deputy. The brush and trees mostly obscured the figure. She wasn't sure if it was one of the outlaws or Thomas. She pulled the trigger anyway, and he fell. Another man came around from the back of the barn, walking toward the house. He staggered, his head turning from side to side, his arms half-raised. It was Thomas. She pointed the gun at him. Her finger twitched at the trigger, and then the side of her mouth curled up. She surveyed the area for more threats. When she was satisfied, she lowered her gun.

"Is it safe?" yelled Gertrude from the back room.

"Yes," said Martha, turning to Gertrude.

Alex gripped Gertrude's hand tightly and tried to look brave. A slight furrow in his brow betrayed his worry.

Martha ran to Alex and hugged him.

"Martha!" yelled Alexander as he ran in from the back door.

"Is everyone okay?" asked Alexander.

Martha hugged him. "We did it."

She glanced out the window. "Looks like a deputy out there needs some help."

Alexander pulled the bullet-riddled curtain aside and looked out. "Sheriff and Thomas are getting him into the cart. I'll go help them."

He leaned over and hugged Alex. "You were a brave boy today."

Alex nodded as if the shootout hadn't bothered him. "I know. You and Ma took care of those bad men. And I took care of

Gertrude."

Gertrude and Martha smiled.

Alexander nodded. "You sure did."

"Alexander," came a yell from outside.

Alexander kissed Martha and then rushed outside.

Thomas was propping up the wounded deputy against the cart.

The deputy was holding his bloody arm and breathing hard as Alexander walked up. "Thomas said Randall and Frank went down the trail in the back of the barn. We have to go after them. They killed my brother over there."

Alexander gasped as he glanced at the body of the other deputy. "I'm sorry. I promise we'll get them. How bad are you hurt?"

"I think I got shot twice in my arm. But we gotta go after them," said the deputy.

"You're bleeding badly," said Sheriff August to the deputy. "We'll take care of your brother."

Thomas's eyes were filled with shock. "You have to see a doctor right away. I got shot like that before. You're losing a lot of blood. You're likely to pass out soon."

Alexander led one of the horses to them and secured it to the cart. Sheriff August climbed up to the seat, and Alexander handed the reins to the sheriff.

The sheriff's gaze surveyed the carnage. "I'll send someone to collect the dead."

Thomas climbed up next to the sheriff. "Am I going to jail?"

The sheriff half-smiled. "Maybe someday, but not today." The sheriff pulled on the reins, and the horses took off slowly at first.

As they drove away, Alexander overheard the sheriff say, "I'm looking to hire deputies. Are you any good with a gun?"

Thomas said, "I'm a better shot than Frank. And he's the best shooter I know."

Alexander grimaced at the absurdity. He squinted at Thomas, a flicker of suspicion dancing in his eyes. He shook his head and walked down the trail toward the road. He found several horses tied to a post that marked the edge of his property. He exhaled sharply. He returned to count the outlaws on the ground to ensure that none would surprise him later. He collected their guns. He marched to the porch and put the weapons on the bench.

Martha walked out. "I'll take care of these."

"These men have been hiding in plain sight all this time. They were right there in front of me," he muttered.

Martha smiled affectionately. "We got them, Alexander."

Alexander shrugged and then returned to the yard. He counted five more bodies and took their weapons, placing them with the others on the porch.

Martha had placed the bullets into a small box and had lined up the pistols neatly.

He smiled at her and then walked around to the back of the barn. There, the grass was flattened along a path leading southward. He walked down a ways, where the trail went straight for several hundred feet, then made a sharp bend into a grove of trees. It was the perfect place to ambush him if he were to head that way. He decided to go back to be with his family.

He hadn't solved the Swansons' murder. All of the facts were right there in front of him. He'd been blinded by people he trusted. The murder of Martha's parents had been solved despite him.

Alexander jumped when a shot came from the road. He ran to the fence line of his property. The sheriff was standing by the cart. Further away, Thomas was chasing a man. Seconds later, Thomas tackled the man and walked him back. The sheriff waved to Alexander, saying that everything was okay.

Alexander exhaled loudly. "This whole thing is all my fault."

CHAPTER THIRTY-FIVE
Joseph's Refuge

Randall and Frank rode to the camp at Joseph's place.

The intense throbbing in Randall's shoulder kept breaking his concentration. "Damn it," he muttered.

His horse glanced back, uncertain if a command had been directed toward him. He returned to looking forward, and his pace settled into a steady rhythm.

Randall's mind wandered chaotically as images of his dead men flashed at him. Too many of his men had been killed in that encounter with Alexander. "I should have stayed in New York." His horse lurched to one side when he stepped into a rut in the road. Randall almost lost his balance, and his left arm banged into his chest.

"Dangit," he screamed. "Damn you, Alexander. You ingrate!"

Randall closed his eyes for a few seconds and inhaled deeply. When he opened his eyes, he let out a loud sigh. His self-pitying thoughts continued. Alexander had turned on him after all these years of caring for him.

Randall glared back at Frank. He's been keeping things from me all this time. Randall kicked at his horse, and his horse took off in a gallop. Randall moaned and inadvertently tugged at the reins when he tried to right himself. The horse immediately slowed.

Frank rushed to catch up and almost ran into Randall.

"You okay?" asked Frank.

Randall ignored him and snapped the reins.

Frank shook his head as Randall raced away.

Frank grimaced as a flood of memories accosted him of the day his father died.

Over breakfast, Frank's father, Sam, confessed to Frank that he'd killed Alexander's father. When Sam confessed, it reminded Frank of when his mother forced him to admit his sins to the parish priest as a child. "You never know when you might die," she told him.

Frank's pa must have thought for sure he was dying. Why else would he need to confess his sins, he thought. His father was very talkative that morning.

"Son, don't tell Randall. The doctor says I'm lucky to be still breathing. But, that bullet is still stuck in my chest and...."

His pa grabbed his chest as he coughed. "Feels like I got a hot poker jabbing at me." He held his breath as he sat up in bed, his face wrinkled with pain. He checked the blood-stained bandages covering his wound. "I wonder if this is how your ma felt before she passed."

Frank shrugged. "I was way young. You told me she died of consumption, not a gunshot."

"I just meant she was coughing up blood and babbling about her chest burning. She wasn't shot."

"I don't remember much about her except her telling me I was going to end up in hell."

Sam chuckled and then immediately winced. "She loved that bible of hers. I'll probably see her there."

"You ain't going nowhere for a while as long as you stay put."

Sam's lips curled up slightly.

"Alexander is a good shot."

"Pa, you're going to be fine. You've been shot before. Right?"

Sam forced a smile. "You've been a good son to me. I'm proud of you."

Frank shook his head.

"After I'm gone, promise me you'll kill Alexander for taking me from you."

"You're going to be okay, Pa," Frank said.

His father glanced out the window, scrunched his face, and his gaze landed on the shed. "You ever wonder why Randall is so protective of Alexander?"

"It's because—"

"Damnit!" yelled Randall as his horse recovered from an unexpected crevice in the road. Randall slammed his eyes shut, cursing in agony. He stuffed his left hand into his shirt to keep his arm from hanging loose. Then, he leaned forward and shook the reins hard. "Get going!" His horse obliged. Randall shuddered as the pain shot up his arm.

Frank glowered at Randall and chased after him.

As the south gate of Joseph's property came into view, Randall rode a ways past it and turned right after a large grove of trees.

Frank stopped and wondered why Randall hadn't used the ranch entrance. A trail continued from the main road. Further down the trail, far into the property, was a lone shack dwarfed by a large barn. To the right stood a house.

Seconds later, there was a loud commotion. Randall was shouting, and his horse was shrieking unnaturally.

Frank rushed to the trail by the trees and found Randall shaking the reins while his horse stood defiantly at the creek's edge, refusing to move.

"Go, you damn horse. What the hell is wrong with you?" Randall yelled.

Frank calmly rode into the ankle-deep water and gently tugged at Randall's horse's bridle, saying, "Come on. Let's go."

Randall's horse, his nose flared, and his ears pinned back, whinnied and then glanced back at Randall.

"Look at me," said Frank to the horse. "It's okay."

The horse shook his head and stepped into the water. His ears began darting about, listening for threats, as he took more steps and splashed the water.

Frank let go when Randall's horse started to follow him across the creek.

Ten minutes later, they approached a dense grove of trees hugging the road. Men's laughter filled the air. Randall raced ahead of Frank and turned onto the trail. Two of his men stood guard just outside the entrance. Charlie and John were inside the camp.

Randall grunted at the sentries and stopped next to them. "I could hear all of you from a mile away. Anyone could have snuck up on you." He stared at them for a second, waiting for a response. They said nothing.

Randall groaned. "Help me get down from this damn horse."

Charlie pushed past the two men and helped Randall.

Frank glared at Charlie.

Randall stormed over to John.

"Most of my men are dead because of you. You couldn't have missed the gunfire," yelled Randall. "Why didn't you come to help us?"

John leaned in. "I heard shots from behind us. And then there were riders raising dust coming our way. We were lucky to get everyone hidden in the trees, including your wagons. I figured you could handle whatever you got yourself into. Once they were out of sight, we got the wagons back on the road and tore out of there. I'm surprised the wagons didn't come apart. It could have been bad if the law had gotten what's in them."

"The sheriff and two of his deputies were in that group of riders. You could have shot them."

John narrowed his eyes at Randall. "We weren't ready for a fight."

Frank cleared his throat. "Alexander was with them. We should have shot him dead." Frank grinned. "I killed one of the deputies."

John shook his head at Randall. "Alexander? I heard what you told Frank before we left. Sound carries far out on the open road. It don't matter if you talk soft or loud." He glanced at Frank and then took a step toward Randall. "That man is working with the law, and you seem to protect him."

"I'll handle Alexander myself." Randall shot a sideways glance at Frank.

John scoffed, shaking his head. "You stopped to visit his place, led your men straight into that gunfight—and now they're dead. That's on you."

Randall merely shrugged. "Not all of them," he said, gesturing toward the men standing off to the side. "I still have some men here."

John stepped up. "Most of these men are mine, not yours. You and Frank and the few men you have left can stay with us, but don't you forget I'm in charge."

"Joseph is my brother. He won't hesitate to toss everyone out of here without me."

John choked out a laugh. "Charlotte knows Joseph. He's a friend of hers. She can sweet-talk him if she needs to."

Randall glared at John, ready to lunge at him. "Your wife?"

Charlie rushed up between them and grabbed at Randall's arm.

Randall yelped like a wounded dog.

Charlie stepped back. "What's wrong with your arm?"

Randall was breathing hard, his eyes fixed on John as he struggled with the pain.

Charlie's brow furrowed as he reached for Randall. "Let me take a look at it. I know a thing or two about mending people. I promise I'll take care of you."

Randall nodded. He tried to raise his injured arm and then screeched. "I can't move my arm. And my shoulder hurts like the devil."

Charlie patted Randall's other arm and asked, "Did you get shot?"

Randall whimpered like a child crying about an injury to his father. "A bullet grazed me. Not bad." Randall turned so that Charlie could see his arm. "Alexander slammed me into a damn rock."

John chuckled.

"What's so funny?" said Randall, his face crumpled with pain.

Charlie grimaced at John and reached over to Randall's left side. "It's stuck in your shoulder. I can fix that." Charlie grabbed Randall's left wrist and yanked down hard in one powerful, swift motion.

Randall let out a guttural scream.

Frank pulled his gun on Charlie.

Charlie stepped back, his hands up. "Your arm was jammed into your shoulder. Ain't no other way to fix it."

Randall wiggled his fingers in his left arm, lifting it slightly and moving it from front to back. "It doesn't hurt as much. You fixed it!"

Frank lowered his weapon and narrowed his eyes at Charlie.

Charlie said, "It'll take a few days to mend itself the rest of the way. You need a sling."

Randall patted Charlie's shoulder. "You're a good man."

Charlie winked at John and said, "That stagecoach we robbed this morning was some of the best we've ever done. You can't deny that."

Randall was rubbing his arm, shaking his head in amazement. "It sure was!"

"We're down some men, but if we pull together, we can make this work. You and Randall worked great on that job. You two should be partners in this. What do you say, John?" Charlie asked.

"He's right, John," said Randall.

John stood stone-faced. He gritted his teeth and blew a puff of air through his nose.

"Well?" asked Charlie.

Randall raised his brows expectantly at John.

John nodded as adrenaline slowly seeped into his veins, and a slight grin formed. "Let's plan the biggest robbery ever. We've got to do it soon because it won't be long before that Sacramento sheriff comes here and gets into our business."

Randall extended his right hand to John. "Bygones?"

John let the rest of his grin turn into an unflattering smile. "Sure. I'm all about business."

Charlie yelled, "Let's drink to that. Where's Howard? He's always got whiskey."

John grimaced. "He's not here. He got off the wagon when we stopped. We couldn't wait for him. I already sent someone to collect him."

Charlie took a menacing step toward John. "You left him behind?"

"John!" said Charlotte as she pushed Charlie aside. If it weren't for her blond hair, pigtails, fancy necklace, and bracelet, she might have been mistaken for one of the men— a petite one.

Charlie narrowed his eyes, annoyed, at his sister. An instant later, his jaw fell open, and his breath stuck in his throat. Joseph, carrying a small bag, walked up next to Charlotte. He stood like a giant beside her.

"Look who I found skulking up the trail a ways from here," said Charlotte. "And he's got a little present for us."

Joseph grinned at Randall and said, "Well, well. You got a great crowd here."

Randall stepped back, shocked. Not a trace of the smile he'd worn earlier remained.

Joseph chuckled. "Aren't you happy to see me, Randall? You

traveled all this way to visit me. You look ragged, and you're all banged up. The men out here are rougher than you're used to."

John walked up between Randall and Joseph. "You must be Sheriff Joseph Pruitt. Charlotte told me plenty about you, including that she trusts you."

John glanced at Charlotte with a mischievous smile and said, "She says she likes you."

Joseph extended his hand to John. "And, you must be John. She seems to like you, too."

Charlotte giggled.

John curled up the corner of his mouth like a dog bearing its teeth in a growl. "So what are you doing here? This is supposed to be our secret hideout."

Randall narrowed his eyes, his face growing a crimson red. "Yeah, what are you doing here?" he snarled.

Joseph snickered at Randall and turned back to John. "I brought you a little gift," Joseph said, handing John the bag he carried. "Just a little peace offering."

John peeked in the bag and smiled at Joseph. He pulled out a bottle of whiskey. "Well, look what our new friend got us."

Fire filled Randall's eyes. The whiskey was the same one that he'd given Joseph.

Joseph glanced at Randall and winked at him. Then, he leaned toward John and whispered, "You and I need to talk—privately."

Randall stepped menacingly close to Joseph, "He and I are partners here."

Half-smiling, Joseph locked eyes with John. "I was about to offer you and your men a deal. But not to Randall."

John tipped his head at Charlie. "Charlie, why don't you help Randall get his arm into that sling? Nobody is better at making one than you."

Joseph grinned at Charlie, "Hey, Charles. I didn't see you standing there."

"It's Charlie. You know that." Charlie turned to Randall. "Let's take care of your arm. You'll be in a world of pain later if it doesn't heal right."

Randall glared at Joseph and then followed Charlie away.

Frank stood momentarily, glanced at John and Joseph, and

followed Randall.

John waited until they were out of sight and smiled at Joseph. "What's the deal between you and your brother?"

Joseph grimaced. "He threatened to kill my wife when he got here. It's his fault that my first wife, back in New York, is dead, and he separated me from my boy."

"Damn! That's a...." John shook his head. "Okay. I'm listening,"

"You can't stay here forever. Sooner or later, the Law from the other towns will come up here and find you."

John laid his hand on his gun. "You gonna turn us in?"

Joseph's face wrinkled like he'd seen something ugly. "Of course not. I'd go down with you."

"What do you want then?"

"You gonna be here long?" asked Joseph.

"We'll be gone soon enough. Most of my men have a wife, and some have kids. They need whatever we can make to live."

"I know this life ain't easy for you and your men. Give me a chance to do something for them. In exchange, I want your word that you won't harm my wife. She doesn't know anything about you or your men," said Joseph. "Hell, I don't think she knows about this place."

John stepped back and eyed Joseph suspiciously. "I never thought I'd be making a deal with a sheriff. It doesn't make sense."

"I just want to keep my wife safe and maybe help your men out, too. There's nothing complicated about that, is there?" asked Joseph.

John half-smiled. "I can't promise anything about Randall or the handful of men he has left. His little side-kick, Frank, just killed a damn deputy back in Sacramento. My men don't kill people unless we have to."

Joseph shook his head. "Randall's not to be trusted. Eventually, he'll try killing me or my wife. He'll probably turn on you, too. But in the meantime...."

"Okay. Let Charlotte know what you want. She takes care of our money."

Joseph nodded and grinned as he pointed toward the trail,

asking permission to leave.

John smiled at Charlotte. "Charlotte, why don't you escort our guest back the way he came? Make sure he gets there without someone shooting him."

Randall, wearing a sling, rushed up next to Joseph. "I'd watch myself, brother. I'm looking forward to meeting your new wife."

Joseph brushed up against Randall's injured arm. Randall winced and then reached for his gun.

John jumped between Randall and Joseph. "Settle down, Randall!"

Randall glared at John, spat beside Joseph's feet, and stormed off.

Joseph locked eyes with John. "Like I said, don't trust Randall. He'll turn on you."

Charlotte said insistently to Joseph, "Let's go. I haven't got all day."

John stood, shaking his head. Charlie and Randall marched down the trail to the clearing where the tents were. In the opposite direction, Charlotte and Joseph sauntered off to the path that led to Joseph's house.

Charlotte turned to John and yelled, "I'll be right back, darling."

John smiled back at her. She's the only thing that ever made any sense to him.

Charlotte and Joseph reached the creek's edge, where Joseph's horse was tied to a tree.

"I like your horse. He's mighty handsome," said Charlotte as she patted and gently rubbed the horse's face. He moved closer to her and tilted his head down. She switched to his other side.

He let out a soft whinny.

Joseph smiled. "I'd say he likes you, too. He doesn't let just anyone near him like that."

"I can tell he's close to you by how he keeps glancing at you, making sure you're okay with me rubbing his face."

"He loves getting his face rubbed," said Joseph.

"I know you don't know much about me, but I'm grateful you helped get me out of that pickle back at the saloon last year.

Those men didn't have any right to be treating me that way."

"You didn't deserve that. No one does."

"I'm smarter now. I can take care of myself, and John watches out for me. He doesn't let anybody mess with me."

"That's good," said Joseph. "Charles should have been there for you back then."

Charlotte giggled. "My brother hates it when you call him Charles."

"That's his name. Ain't it?" said Joseph with a mischievous grin.

"I wish my nickname was Charlie. It somehow fits me better than Charlotte," she said. "That name, Charlie, is more masculine. People don't think twice about someone named Charlie wielding a gun. They don't like a woman who knows her way around shooting."

"My wife, Elizabeth, is an excellent shooter, probably even better than me. Maybe someday you'll meet her," said Joseph. "I think you two could become friends."

Charlotte chuckled. "I doubt that. I'm not the fancy, refined type."

Joseph glanced away and then smiled at Charlotte. "I need a favor. Do you know the names of all the men here? Both John's and Randall's men?"

"I suppose so," she said suspiciously. "Why?"

"I asked your husband if I could help some of his men. He said a few of them have families."

"Some of John's men do. Randall's men aren't as civilized. They're mean and bloodthirsty," said Charlotte. "I don't think they care much for families."

Joseph nodded. "Would you be willing to write their names down for me?"

"I guess so."

Randall went to his horse, took a piece of paper and a pencil from his saddle bag, and handed them to Charlotte.

"Wow. You came prepared," said Charlotte.

She took the paper and quickly wrote the names: "That's all of them, including Randall's men." She started to hand him the list and then quickly took it back. "Oh, I forgot one."

She wrote another name at the bottom. With a mischievous smile, she handed the paper to him.

He read the names and smiled when he reached "John and Charlie." He chuckled when he read the last entry.

"Can I have the pencil?" asked Charlotte. "It's hard to keep records for John without a pencil."

"Sure thing."

"I gotta go," said Charlotte. She patted the horse and then rushed away.

Joseph stood there for almost a minute as Charlotte disappeared down the trail. He watched for a few more minutes until he was sure no one else was there. He got another pencil; it was broken. He pulled a small knife from the pouch and sharpened it until it was ready for writing. He scribbled something on the paper, folded it in half, and put it away. He smiled, hopeful about his plan to peel John and his men away from Randall's. If the plan worked, John's men would enjoy a nice chunk of money and perhaps become more sympathetic toward law and order. He might even employ some to protect his town and the stagecoach routes. Most importantly, he would be able to keep his wife safe.

He got on his horse and rode home.

CHAPTER THIRTY-SIX

Plans

Alexander and Martha dumped the lifeless bodies of the outlaws in the back of an old, dilapidated cart. Gertrude stood on the porch watching them, occasionally pacing back and forth as if standing guard. Alex was napping inside.

"That's it," said Alexander. "That's all ten of them."

"Nope. There were eleven. There's one more over by that tree," said Martha. "He thought he could hide from me up in the branches. I saw him fall to the ground after I shot him."

Alexander followed Martha, and sure enough, another one was sitting at the base of the tree, his face forever contorted in pain and his eyes partially open.

Alexander stepped closer. He stared wide-eyed at the man, shaking his head.

"What's wrong?" Martha asked.

"I know that man. He was a deputy in New York. We worked together on the stagecoaches for Wallace's bank."

Martha gasped. "Randall's corruption and influence, no doubt."

"I thought he was a friend. Instead, he was working with Randall. I should have known."

She pointed to the body. "And there he is dead. He paid the ultimate price for his betrayal."

"He knew which stagecoaches were worth robbing."

Alexander cocked his head back and threw a sideways glance at Martha.

Martha stepped back and glanced at the man. "He was the deputy assigned to my parents' stagecoach. Wasn't he?"

Alexander, his face wrinkled with regret, nodded hesitantly. "This is all my fault. If I hadn't invited Randall, he wouldn't have brought these killers from New York."

Martha smiled at Alexander. "It's not your fault."

Alexander tried to smile at Martha. "I—"

"She's wrong," said the outlaw deputy, pointing a gun at them. "We couldn't have done any of this without you."

Alexander and Martha turned, shocked, to the man they thought was dead.

The outlaw deputy's hand trembled as he held his gun.

Alexander reached for his gun.

"Don't." The outlaw deputy aimed his gun at Martha.

Alexander stopped and put his hands up. "I thought you were my friend."

"Randall made me a deal I couldn't pass up. He was real good to me." The outlaw deputy coughed and spat up blood. He kept his gun on Martha. "Randall told me to keep you off that stagecoach."

Alexander winced.

Martha's face wrinkled at him. "It's your fault my parents are dead, yours and Randall's."

The outlaw deputy curled his lips and said, "I suppose so. It was easy to convince the driver to head out early."

Alexander narrowed his brows. "You're lying. He told me Mr. Swanson gave him twenty-five dollars to leave without me."

Martha gasped. "My father would never do that. Especially not while traveling with my mother."

Alexander's mouth fell open.

The outlaw deputy chuckled. "Swanson said he wanted to wait until you got there. And that you were better at protecting stagecoaches than his money." The outlaw deputy coughed again. "I assured Swanson that I'd be riding my horse behind them. He didn't like the idea much, but I convinced him that you said it'd be safe. I gave the driver some money and told him it came from Swanson."

Alexander shook his head. "You lied to me."

The outlaw deputy laughed and then reached for his side in pain. "Swanson did say that you could go to hell."

Alexander tried stepping in front of Martha.

"Don't," said the outlaw deputy as he straightened up. He stood, keeping his weapon pointed at Martha. The right side of his chest was bright red with fresh blood.

Alexander raised his arms as if surrendering. "You're not getting out of this alive."

The outlaw deputy grinned through his blood-stained teeth. "At least one of you ain't either." His finger twitched on the trigger.

A sharp snap of twigs distracted the outlaw deputy. His eyes shot toward the sound. Alexander pushed Martha to the ground and rolled over her to keep her safe. A loud blast exploded after Martha grabbed Alexander's gun from his holster, about to fire at the outlaw. She pulled the trigger. Her bullet caught the tree dead center.

"He ain't gonna shoot anybody," said Gertrude, smoke oozing from her shotgun. Her arms trembled as she lowered the heavy weapon.

Alexander and Martha quickly stood, both dumbfounded and relieved.

Martha rushed to hug Gertrude. "You saved us."

Gertrude stared at the mutilated mess of the outlaw. "I did what needed to be done." Gertrude's nerves were rattled.

Alexander's eyebrows shot up in surprise. "Thank you, Gertrude."

Gertrude, her heart racing, exhaled in a huff and nodded. "You two make a good team. You might want to think about working together on this sort of thing. I don't see what you two like about it."

A surprised smile tugged at Martha's lips. "That's a marvelous idea. Imagine us, a team against outlaws. Now, that would be exciting."

Dread washed over Alexander's face. He shook his head vehemently.

Gertrude winked at Martha and said, "I'll check on Alex. It wouldn't surprise me if this blast woke him. After you're done and cleaned up, I'll get us some lemonade, and we can relax on the porch."

In no time, Martha, Alexander, and Gertrude sat relaxing on the porch. Alex was still sleeping.

Martha sipped her lemonade. "Wouldn't it be great if we knew someone in Randall's group?"

Alexander fixated on the bodies lying in the cart. "Maybe we could reason with Randall."

Martha looked incredulously at Alexander. "No."

Gertrude shook her head. "He's beyond redemption."

The sound of thundering hooves from the road grew louder.

Alexander rushed to the corner of the porch to see who it was. "It's Sheriff August."

Martha and Alexander walked hand-in-hand to the sheriff as he rode up.

"We loaded those outlaws onto that cart. They're ready to go," said Alexander.

The sheriff glanced at the bodies as he got down from his horse and grinned. "You've arranged them neatly, except for that one."

Martha half-smiled. "One lived a short while longer than he should have."

The sheriff raised his brows. "After what they've done to your family, I'm surprised you didn't just pile them up like the garbage they are."

"I like things to be neat," said Alexander, then winked at Martha.

Martha chuckled.

The sheriff said, "Anyhow, earlier, as we were leaving, we came across a drunkard staggering along the side of the road. He bolted into the fields toward the trees when he saw us."

Alexander shrugged. "What was he doing there?"

"He had an empty six-shooter on him. He said he was shooting at crows because they were out to get him."

Alexander scrunched his face, confused.

"After a while, he wouldn't shut up. He said he got left behind. He told me he knows Randall."

Alexander's mouth fell open.

Martha smiled as her eyes filled with enthusiasm. "Someone on the inside," she muttered.

"It turns out there were a lot more outlaws than those that attacked us," he pointed to the pile of dead men. "He didn't know where they were headed. His name is Howard, and he's plenty drunk. We brought him back with us. Do you want to talk to him?"

Martha leaned forward. "Of course we do."

"He's not making much sense now." The sheriff shook his head and then chuckled. "He says a lawman is letting him and his friends stay on his property. I asked him which one, and he just shrugged. There ain't no sheriff around here that would work with the likes of those outlaws."

Alexander glanced at the back of the cart at the crumpled body of his deputy friend from New York.

The sheriff led Alexander and Martha to the road where a man, his eyes closed, sat on a rock stroking his long beard like a wise man deep in thought.

The deputy chuckled as he got off his horse and approached Howard. "He fell off when he was getting down from his horse."

The sheriff shook his head. "Go get the cart ready."

"Sure thing," said the deputy, leading the horses away.

Alexander cautiously approached the man. He was hunched over, his short legs awkwardly splayed before him, almost like a turtle if they could sit. "Howard?"

Howard jumped to his feet and nearly stumbled. He squinted at Alexander and then at Martha. He shook his head. "I don't know you."

"I'm Alexander, and this is Martha."

Martha smiled and took a step toward him. "Hello."

Howard's gaze dropped to his feet, and he nodded. He tried straightening his hair and brushing the dirt from his clothes. "Hello, ma'am."

Alexander stifled a smile. "How do you know Randall?"

Howard's eyes shot up and narrowed at Alexander. His face stiffened as if he'd smelled something disgusting. "He's been nothing but trouble to my friends since he joined our group. He's all about shooting and hurting people. I don't shoot people like he does. The only thing I shoot is crows. I hate them."

Alexander's eyes twitched.

Howard glanced at the house and then back at Alexander. "You wouldn't happen to have some whiskey. I'm mighty thirsty."

Alexander said, "We might. But first, tell me, what are you

doing here?"

"We've been living here for a few months. We set up camp over there on the south side of this property." Howard pointed toward the barn. "We had to move 'cause the new owners moved in. It was nice and comfortable. I was sorry that we had to leave."

Alexander stepped back in shock. He shook his head and glanced at Martha, apologizing again.

"I was riding in one of the wagons, and when we stopped, I got down to...." He shot a sideways glance at Martha and then said, "...to have a visit with nature. Then, I saw some crows, and I guess I got distracted. Those crows are nasty. Anyhow, when I went back, my friends were all gone. Then I heard all these shots, so I took off running." Howard straightened up, held his hand, his thumb touching his forefinger, and said to Martha, "I'm so thirsty. Maybe I could have a tiny bit of whiskey?"

Martha smiled at Alexander and said to Howard, "It's quite a coincidence. We were talking about someone just like you. Why don't you come with me, and you can sit on the porch. I'll get you some tea or lemonade." Martha winked at Alexander and started for the house. "I might even put a spot of whiskey in it."

Howard lit up bright, followed Martha, and sat on the bench by the front door. She hurried inside. Gertrude had the whiskey hidden in the far back of the kitchen cupboard. Now and then, Gertrude enjoyed a drink. "It keeps me young," Gertrude would say.

Alexander watched Howard sitting obediently, smiling like little Alex did while waiting for a cookie.

Alexander turned to the sheriff. "Martha suggested that we need someone to infiltrate their group."

The sheriff smiled. "We've been secretly planning a huge payroll shipment on the ten o'clock stagecoach on Wednesday morning. The bank's nervous about it. We could schedule another stagecoach run for the same time on Tuesday. We can have that Tuesday stagecoach with enough deputies and firepower, instead of money, to eliminate those robbers. We could tell Howard that Tuesday's stagecoach will have a bounty worth robbing and then let him go."

Alexander said, "I'll ride with them to ensure nothing goes wrong."

The sheriff nodded and smiled broadly. "Let's go have a chat with Howard."

Alexander and the sheriff sat up against the rail across from Howard. Martha was sitting to their left on the porch swing.

Howard took a sip of his lemonade laced with whiskey. "This is the smoothest whiskey I've ever had."

Martha grinned.

The sheriff asked Martha, "May I have a drink?"

Martha poured the sheriff a whiskey.

The sheriff took a small sip. "Thank you. I enjoy a smooth one now and then."

She handed Alexander a lemonade.

Alexander smiled at her. He rarely drank whiskey, and Martha never did.

Alexander said, "Martha, on Tuesday, I'll be riding up top on the payroll stagecoach headed to Auburn."

Howard perked up, his gaze darting from left to right, and sipped his drink.

Martha's brows raised slightly.

The sheriff glanced at Howard. "We shouldn't be chatting about our business in front of a robber," said the sheriff.

Howard moved uncomfortably. "I ain't no robber... Well... I won't tell no one."

"Hmm," said Alexander. "Do we have your word? That shipment is worth more—"

"Alexander, I was going to let him go, but now that he knows.... That shipment is too valuable. We either got to kill him or keep him until—"

Martha brought her hand to her mouth and stifled a chuckle.

"No, don't kill me. I've never killed anyone. I know I shouldn't be with those people, but some of them are my friends. I ain't got no one else. Please—"

"Sheriff, let him go. I think we can trust him." Alexander turned to Howard. "Will you promise to keep our secret?"

Howard nodded awkwardly. It was more like how a pigeon shook its head than a nod.

The sheriff finished his drink and stood abruptly. "Okay.

You're free to go."

Howard grinned, showing his yellow-stained teeth. He jumped up, extended his hand to shake Alexander's, and fell back onto the bench. He leaned back and then closed his eyes. "I just need to rest for a minute. I stood too fast."

Alexander glanced at the sheriff and shook his head.

The sheriff half-smiled. "I'll take him into town and let him sleep it off in jail."

Howard choked out, "No! I don't want to go to jail. Leave me at the saloon. My friends will come to get me. They always do."

The sheriff held his lips tight. He wanted to laugh at the absurdity. "Let's go. You can ride in the cart with your dead friends over there."

Howard staggered to the cart. His face tightened, and his nose scrunched at the sight of the bodies lying in the back. A shudder shot through him. "Those aren't my friends." He made a sour face and walked to the front, weaving left and right as he went. "Those are Randall's men. I don't like any of them one bit. None of us do."

Alexander watched Howard make several attempts to climb up to the bench seat.

The deputy rushed over and helped Howard up.

The sheriff chuckled at the sight. He tossed some coin at the deputy and said, "Leave him at the saloon."

Once the deputy was seated, he waved to the sheriff and snapped the reins, and they took off.

"He seems harmless enough," said Alexander. "Shouldn't we follow him and his friends when they pick him up?"

The sheriff shook his head. "I think our surprise ambush on Tuesday will take care of all of them instead of the one or two that come for Howard."

Alexander nodded. "I wish he'd told us more."

"He's told us a lot. We have the advantage now. There are two groups: his group and Randall's group. And it sounds like none of them like Randall and his men. They're divided. And another thing, if those dead outlaws were Randall's men, I'd bet he's running out of men. I wonder how many they brought with them."

Martha said, "At least two or three wagons full."

The sheriff shook his head. "Those wagons can hold enough supplies for a lot of men."

Alexander exhaled loudly. "Howard is going to tell them everything we told him. I hope we told him enough."

Sheriff August's face lit up bright. "He'll tell them plenty after his friends pick him up at the saloon."

Alexander laughed. "They'll find him there for sure. Sounds like he's been left behind before."

The sheriff said, "Now we gotta ensure Tuesday's 10:00 a.m. stagecoach is heavily fortified."

Soon after, Howard sat at the bar and smiled broadly when the bartender poured him a whiskey. Howard was about to take a sip when a man walked up next to him and whispered, "It's time to go."

Howard turned annoyed and then grinned when he recognized him. He quickly drank it and said, "Why don't you join me for a drink?"

The man's eyes darted from side to side nervously. "Let's go."

Howard grimaced as he slammed his glass down on the counter.

"Everyone is always in such a hurry!"

Howard clumsily got down from the stool and nearly stumbled. The man helped Howard out of the saloon to a waiting horse.

Soon after, they rode into the camp. Howard struggled to get down from his horse.

Charlie ran to Howard and helped him down. "Howard, what happened?"

Howard stood wobbling back and forth, his arms moving slowly to steady himself.

"Everything is spinning. I've been riding too long. I need a drink to calm me. That Alexander gave me a drink. He's a good man, and his wife is too. He's going to protect that stagecoach. It's gonna have a lot of money to pay people. That's what they said."

Charlie leaned in. "What coach?"

Howard took unsteady steps toward his tent. "Tuesday at ten.

It's got lots of money. I like Alexander. He's gonna keep it safe."

Charlie propped Howard up as they walked to his tent. "Let me help you. Tell me more."

"I'm not supposed to say anything. Don't tell anyone. It's a secret. But, they got a lot of money on that stagecoach headed here."

"Today?"

"No! Tuesday. Ten o'clock. I need a drink," said Howard as he pointed at his tent and straightened up, determined to get to his bottle of whiskey.

Charlie smiled and then rushed off to find Randall.

Charlie spotted Randall arguing with John outside John's tent. Frank was standing a few feet from Randall. Charlie shoved Frank out of his way and stood across from John and Randall.

"You two are fighting too much. Now, shut up! Both of you!" said Charlie.

John and Randall, their mouths open, turned to Charlie.

John, his face sour, said, "What the hell?"

"I got great news. It turns out that Howard found out about a stagecoach that's traveling from Sacramento to Auburn with a payroll shipment. It's supposed to be heavily loaded."

Randall stepped closer to Charlie. "When?"

"It's this coming Tuesday at 10 a.m. Your friend Alexander is going to be on that stagecoach," Charlie said.

Randall's annoyance melted away into a grin. "Well, what do you know? Our luck is changing."

John smirked. "It'll be the perfect time for you to get rid of Alexander."

Randall narrowed his eyes at John and leaned menacingly close to him.

Charlie stepped between them. "Dangit, you two. We've finally got a chance to strike it rich. There's no telling how much gold dust or script that coach will be carrying. I have a plan."

Randall's eyes fluttered as he stepped back. "You're right." He nodded at John.

John let out a huff and turned to Charlie, "Okay. Let's hear it."

Charlie continued, "We have to execute this carefully. We'll have to ambush them and wallop them hard. Half the men will hide ten miles outside Sacramento, and the other half will hit them from this side."

"I like that. Once they try racing away from the men on the Sacramento side, they'll run smack into the men on the Auburn side," said Randall. "They won't be expecting to be surrounded."

"They won't have a chance. They'll surrender for sure before things get out of hand. And with that much cargo, they won't have room for passengers," said John. He winked at Charlie. "I knew there was a reason I kept you around."

Charlie grimaced.

Randall nodded approvingly at Charlie. "It's an excellent plan. My men and I will camp outside Sacramento, and your men can head out from this side. My men will have downed the coach outside Sacramento by the time your men get there."

John gritted his teeth. "Don't get overzealous. They won't give up without a fight. It'd be better if we hit them together."

"You're right," said Randall with a smirk. "I'll go talk to my men."

John shook his head as Randall rushed away.

Frank smiled and ran after Randall. With barely a gasp of air, he said, "I heard you talking."

Still grinning, Randall stopped walking. "We're gonna rob the Tuesday 10 a.m. stagecoach from Sacramento. It'll be fantastic!"

"You can trust me, Randall. I promise I'll work harder than I ever have before."

Randall's face soured. "Son, you ain't got what it takes to be anything more than you are." A faint hint of a smile formed on Randall's lips. "We're cut from the same cloth, you and I. But what would make you think I would ever trust you? I never have trusted you. I don't want you on this job. You'd be likely to shoot me, just like you tried at Alexander's. You'll be staying behind."

Randall snickered and then walked away, shaking his head.

Humiliated, Frank stood there for a whole minute and remembered what Thomas told him. "He doesn't trust you."

CHAPTER THIRTY-SEVEN

Frank Gives It Up

Agnes walked out to the porch, where Thomas sat looking off into the distance. She shook her head and sat next to him. "Ever since you got back from that shootout at Gertrude's place, you've been trudging through your chores, not saying much. It don't make one bit of sense when people get stuck in their heads that things are hopeless. People should spit out what's on their minds and work on it. And move on to the next thing that pops up and deal with that. There's always something new to worry about." She took a breath and asked, "Well? Why are you moping around here?"

Thomas straightened up. "I always mope around here."

Agnes half-smiled and nodded. "Yeah, but this time it's different. Something heavy is weighing on you. You got to let it out sooner or later."

Thomas shrugged. "It's about my father."

"Your father? It's about time you go see him."

"I'm not ready."

Agnes guffawed. "Yes, you are. If you wait any longer, it might be too late. If your ma were here, she'd tell you to get your rear in that buggy and visit with him." She smiled and scooted closer to him. "Your mother was a friend of mine."

Thomas turned, astonished at Agnes.

Agnes continued. "The clothes I made for her were spectacular. While Rose was at my house getting fitted, she told me how much she loved her little boy. She never brought you into the house. You'd be waiting for her out on the cart."

A nostalgic smile played on Thomas's lips. "She did love to dress up in colorful dresses." Thomas glanced away. "I loved riding into town with my mother. We talked quite a bit on those rides." He looked up at Agnes. "Do you think she loved my father?"

"There's no question about that. She must have seen plenty of good in him to love him that much." She shifted in her seat. "She told me that your pa loved you too. That's why you two should work things out. You didn't come to California to just brood around here."

"In the letter my pa sent with Juan, he wrote that I should move here."

"Let go of the past and everything that happened all those years ago. Think about the last few months and how you've helped people. Your ma and pa would be proud."

Thomas laughed. "Things get clearer for me when we talk."

Agnes smiled. "Does that mean you'll go see your pa?"

"Yes. I'll head out after I finish my chores and get cleaned up." Thomas took Agnes's hand and kissed it. "Thank you."

"You can take the buggy after lunch," Agnes said with a playful grin. "Just bring it back in one piece."

After enjoying lunch with Agnes's family, Thomas left for Auburn to meet his father.

When he arrived in Auburn, he felt queasy. A drink might settle his stomach. The hotel clerk smiled as Thomas pulled up in front of the hotel.

"Are you Thomas Pruitt?" asked the clerk.

Thomas looked at him, confused, and said, "Yes."

"We received a telegram from Mrs. Agnes Jenkins. Your room is on the first floor," said the clerk. "We'll take care of your bag."

Thomas smiled. "Thank you." He stepped down from the buggy and looked up and down the road.

"I'll take care of your horse. The saloon is across the way if you like." The clerk stood waiting beside the buggy.

"Thanks. I think I'll get a drink." Thomas tossed a coin to the clerk.

The clerk caught it and excitedly led the horse and buggy to the back.

Thomas walked inside and was about to order a drink. He cocked his head in surprise. Frank was sitting at the far corner table with a glass in his hand. A tall bottle of whiskey and an empty glass were on the table next to a lamp.

Thomas took tentative steps to Frank's table. His friend's hair was messy, and his face was outlined with dark stubble. Frank's clothes were wrinkled and dirty. This wasn't the Frank he knew.

The acrid tang of sweat stung Thomas's nostrils as he approached. He scrunched his nose in distaste and then called, "Frank!"

A pale face etched with despair peered up from his misery. It brightened for an instant before he scrambled to his feet. "Thomas!" His voice was raspy, devoid of its usual boisterousness.

"How are you, my friend?" Thomas asked, concern lacing his tone.

Frank grinned, revealing a perfect set of pearly whites. "Join me for a drink." He pointed to the empty glass on the table, his hand trembling. "So that's why they brought me a second glass."

Thomas sat on the rickety chair opposite him, the creak echoing the unease in his gut. He poured himself some whiskey. "You don't look like yourself."

Frank sipped his drink, "Randall is being an ass, as usual."

"Yeah. What else is new?"

"Aren't you mad at me?" asked Frank, slurring his words.

"Nope. You're my best friend."

Frank cocked his head back, confused. "Then why didn't you come with us?"

Thomas shook his head. "I'm never going back. Things are clearer now. Randall is rotten. Everything he touches goes to hell."

Frank narrowed his eyes.

Thomas leaned forward. "Don't trust him. Randall only cares about himself. And don't forget that he killed your pa."

"My pa was dying already. That bullet that Alexander put in him was lodged in his chest. The doctor couldn't get at it. It was just a matter of days before my pa died a horrific, painful death. He was scared. Randall did him a favor by putting him out of his misery."

Thomas choked on his breath. "I'm sorry. Why didn't you tell me?"

Frank's eyes caught the light of the lamp. They were swimming in pain. He guzzled down the rest of his drink and poured himself more.

"I admire Randall." Frank gazed down and shook his head.

316

"But he doesn't trust me anymore. He said he never did."

Thomas said, "Alexander is the only person Randall ever trusted."

Frank stared at Thomas for several seconds as if he were about to say something.

Thomas shrugged and waved his hands. "What?"

"Nothing." Frank sat up and took a drink. "You still live in Sacramento?"

"Yeah, with the old couple from New York. I'm grateful to them. Agnes Jenkins, the old lady, helped me a lot. Her place is on the north side by the river at the end of 45th Street. You'd love it."

"They won't appreciate a person like me. I'm a wanted killer, you know," Frank bellowed.

"Hey! Don't say that so loud." Thomas looked around. "I told the sheriff that you didn't kill anyone."

Frank's right cheek twitched, and then he leaned in, the light in his eyes fading. "Why did you come up here to Auburn?"

Thomas winced. "To meet my pa. He's the sheriff of this town."

"Sheriff Joseph Pruitt."

Thomas straightened up. "You've seen him?"

Frank hesitated. "Yeah. Are you sure you want to see him?"

Thomas slumped back into his seat. "Well. I started having second thoughts as soon as I got here."

Frank sat up taller in his seat. Randall's and John's men were on Joseph's property, a secret Thomas shouldn't know. Randall would likely kill him for working with the Law. "Better for you to go back home."

Thomas looked cock-eyed at Frank.

Frank glanced down at Thomas's glass. "Why haven't you touched your whiskey?"

Thomas's face soured. "I don't care for it much anymore."

Frank chuckled. "Me neither, but it sure does make things easier to deal with."

Thomas watched the reflection of the flame from the lamp dance along the surface of his brown concoction.

Frank cleared his throat.

Thomas scrunched his nose, grabbed the glass, and gulped it down. His face wrinkled in disgust as he slammed the glass on the table.

Frank grinned and poured more into Thomas's glass. "Drink up."

A mischievous glint danced in Thomas's eyes. "You've got to be kidding me." He took the glass and drank it down. His face contorted, his tongue extended as if trying to cough up a hairball. "It's still awful." He poured himself a little and pushed the glass away.

Frank slapped the table with his hand. "Think of it as a tonic prescribed by your doctor."

"Yeah. Right." He remembered how they laughed and had fun back in New York. "Why are you here in this corner all by yourself? Something lousy must have happened. You're always boisterous. I'm surprised you don't have a woman sitting with you now."

Frank shook his head. He glanced from side to side, leaned forward, and whispered, "Randall and the men are planning to rob the 10 a.m. stagecoach tomorrow coming from Sacramento, and Randall doesn't want me with them."

Emotion drained away from Thomas's face. "That doesn't make any sense. You're his right-hand man. He doesn't go anywhere without you."

"Randall thinks I was shooting at him at Alexander's place. He says he doesn't trust me." Frank took another drink and slammed his empty glass down on the table.

Thomas inhaled and let it out in a huff. "You kept him from getting shot. Everyone was distracted while Randall ran to you. Otherwise, anyone would have had a clear shot of him."

Frank held out his hand, mimicking a gun. He squinted through one eye as he focused past his thumb, aiming at an imaginary target. "If I hadn't protected Randall, Alexander would have gotten one of my bullets. I almost got him." Frank smiled.

"I guess you have a good reason to want Alexander dead after all."

"You got a reason, too." Frank narrowed his eyes at Thomas. "You still like Alexander's wife, don't you? If Alexander were gone, she'd be all yours."

318

"No! I wronged Martha. I made a mistake." Thomas shook his head. "I'm not going to hurt her anymore."

"Because she's your boy's ma? Was that boy the mistake?"

Thomas, his face riddled with pain and confusion, crumpled back into his chair as if Frank had struck him.

Frank leaned in toward Thomas. "I'm sorry."

Thomas took a deep breath and let it out all at once. "Don't worry about it. We each have our demons to face."

Thomas sat up taller. "Come back to Sacramento with me. You'll like it there. We can hang out like we used to."

Frank grimaced and glanced down. "That kind of life isn't for me. Excitement is." His face brightened up. "Wish I could go with them tomorrow. They've got a good plan. Half a dozen men will camp just outside Sacramento, near the stagecoach run. They'll wait for the coach to travel a few miles and then pounce on it from the rear. The other men will ride out from here tomorrow morning and catch them from the front while they try to escape the first bunch. Damn!"

Frank sat back with a cynical grin and said, "Alexander's supposed to be riding on that stagecoach tomorrow. He'll be dead soon."

Thomas gasped. "They won't have a chance."

A sinister smile crept onto his face as he nodded. "That's the whole point." Frank jumped up and then stumbled to the floor.

Thomas sprang from his chair in time to catch Frank.

"Come on. Let's go. You can sleep this off in my room at the hotel."

"I know a secret," Frank mumbled and struggled to stand.

Thomas helped Frank to the hotel room. When Frank saw the bed, he sat, took off his boots, and lay down. His eyes shut the instant his head hit the pillow.

Thomas shook his head. He walked to the basin and wiped his face with a rag dipped in the cool water.

"I know Randall's secret," Frank mumbled.

Thomas tossed the rag next to the basin and turned back. Frank was lying in bed, his eyes closed.

"What secret is that?"

"My pa told me that Alexander is Randall's son. His mother

ended her life after Randall told her husband the truth. Randall's never forgiven himself. Why couldn't he have been my father instead?" Frank said, his voice filled with sadness.

Thomas gasped. The air fled from his lungs. He walked up to Frank. "What?"

Frank's breathing slowed into a smooth pattern, and then he shrieked out a loud snore.

Thomas jumped.

Frank fell into a rhythmical, annoying snore.

Thomas shook his head. His mind raced as he made sense of it all. His head ached as he thought about Alexander and Randall. Randall had been protecting his son all along. That's why Martha's boy looked like a Pruitt.

Thomas plopped into the cushioned chair next to the door, got comfortable as best he could, and fell asleep.

When Thomas woke up the following day, his back was sore, and his head was pounding. It took him a moment to orient himself. The bed was empty.

"Frank?" he whispered to an empty room.

He checked the time. It was almost 6 a.m. He bolted for the door and left town to warn Alexander.

CHAPTER THIRTY-EIGHT
Ladies Day

Martha woke up early before the sun brightened her day. The glow from the full moon shone through the window. The cool morning breeze from the open windows smelled delicious. Alexander shifted in the bed as she sat up. She tiptoed to the door lest she wake her husband and took a candle from its holder. The aroma of baked bread and mouth-watering smells welcomed her when she opened the door. From the hallway, a flickering light came from the kitchen. She put the unlit candle on the shelf next to the door and continued to the kitchen.

"Gertrude!"

Gertrude jumped. "Goodness, you startled me!"

The table was loaded with chicken, vegetables, crackers, and more.

"I was going to fix something tasty for our outing. But...." Martha chuckled. "This looks like the feasts you prepared for those picnics we'd go on back in New York."

Gertrude rushed to the stove. "You could have slept another hour." She opened the firebox and used the poker to redistribute the fuel. Bright glowing red-orange embers shot out in all directions as the fire flared. She dodged them as they fell, their glow fading to ash on the floor. "Most everything is ready. The bread needs five more minutes. We can have breakfast when the boys wake up."

Martha took a cracker from the table. "That's wonderful. How can I help?"

"After it's all cooked, you can stow it in the picnic basket."

"Sure."

"How are you feeling?" asked Gertrude. "You've had a rough recovery."

Martha grinned. "I feel great. That illness lingered much too long. I never want to go through that again."

"Dr. Martin thinks going to that water hole was more than

your body could handle. Sad about the woman there with you."

Martha shook her head. "She coughed up a lot of water after she fell in. When she left, she seemed fine."

Gertrude patted Martha's arm. "May she rest in peace."

Martha nodded. "About those tonics the doctor prescribed...."

Gertrude's brows went up. "Dr. Martin claims they had some nasty side effects. But he assured me they were otherwise safe."

"Let's hope so." Martha's face brightened with a smile. "I'm excited about going to Auburn to meet Elizabeth."

"She's a lovely woman," said Gertrude.

"Did you tell Agnes we're going to Auburn?"

"No. I haven't gotten to chat with her since before Randall and his thugs attacked us."

Martha shook her head. "It's incredible that he brought all those outlaws from New York. It's clear now why he didn't join our wagon train."

Gertrude nodded. "He must have had at least three wagons."

"Yup. Alexander blames himself for inviting Randall to California."

Gertrude poured scrambled eggs into the hot skillet. "It wasn't Alexander's fault."

"Nope. Randall won't bother us anymore. He knows better than to show his face around here."

Alexander walked out of the hallway. "Who knows better?"

"Good morning, dear," said Martha, almost dancing as she went to hug him. "Randall. He wouldn't dare come back here."

Alexander rubbed the sleep from his eyes. "He's like a wounded animal. Once he recovers, he'll attack us again. Why don't you postpone your trip until after he's apprehended?"

Martha chuckled. "We scheduled this before you and the sheriff planned your ambush. And besides, if those outlaws dare look at our coach, they'll regret it. I'm taking my guns. They'll be under the rear bench. Gertrude and I have discussed what to do if anything unusual happens. We'll use those weapons while Alex is safe in the compartment below the front seat."

Gertrude pulled the bread from the oven. "Too bad the rest of the coach, where the passengers are, isn't as well fortified as the strongbox compartment."

Alexander grimaced. "The stagecoach would be much too heavy." He tilted his head at Martha. "Will the traveling be too taxing for you?"

Martha rolled her eyes. "Now you're just looking for excuses for me to stay. You don't have anything to worry about. I feel wonderful. I haven't felt this well in a long time. Terrible as that shootout was, it left me invigorated and hopeful." She glanced at Gertrude. "I think Gertrude was right. We should work together more often."

Alexander half-smiled. "We're going to get a deputy to sit up top and another inside."

"There isn't any room inside. There are five of us already," said Martha. "And besides, we'll have our bags inside with us."

Alexander smirked, "Well, one deputy can ride on the rooftop and the other with the driver."

Martha rolled her eyes. "Anyone seeing two lawmen on our coach will make it a target." Martha raised her brows as her lips curled upward. "Instead of babysitting the 10 a.m. 'payroll' stagecoach to Auburn, why don't you join us on the 8 a.m. stagecoach? You can sit next to me. Let the deputy go on the other one. That way, we arrive together in Auburn."

"I have a duty to Douglas. It's my job."

Little Alex walked out of the hallway, rubbing his eyes as the light from the morning sun seeped into the house. "Are we leaving yet?" He was looking forward to this trip.

Martha rushed to Alex and knelt beside him. "Yes, after breakfast. But first, let's get you dressed."

At six-thirty, Alexander, Martha, Alex, and Gertrude arrived at the hotel in the buggy, where the stagecoach awaited. Helen stood on the porch next to a tall woman with wavy dark hair pinned tight to her head. The deputy was across from them by the stagecoach.

Alexander tipped his hat at the women and turned to Martha. "Go ahead, darling. The deputy and I will load your things."

Martha, Gertrude, and Alex stepped down from the buggy and approached the two women.

Rebecca extended her hand to Martha. "Martha, I'm Rebecca, and this is Helen."

Helen smiled and said, "Welcome. I'm so glad you made it."

"It's lovely to meet you both," said Martha. Rebecca was an inch or two taller than her and had gorgeous, greenish-blue eyes. Martha shook Rebecca's hand and then pointed to Gertrude and Alex. "This is my aunt, Gertrude."

Rebecca smiled at Gertrude. "I've heard wonderful things about you."

Gertrude winked at Helen and then turned to Rebecca, "That was kind of Helen to paint me in that light. Once you get to know me, you might change your mind."

"I love you already," said Rebecca.

Rebecca glanced at Martha's stomach. "Martha! You're not even showing."

"Thank you. These pants hide a lot. Thankfully, they're comfortable. They're the only loose-fitting pants that fit me right now."

Alex was watching his father load the stagecoach. Martha tugged at his hand. "This is my son Alex."

Tilting his head up, Alex gazed at Rebecca.

"What a handsome boy you are," said Rebecca.

Alex giggled.

Helen hugged Gertrude. "Great to see you again, Gertrude." She tapped Martha's arm. "Martha, it's a pleasure to meet you." She leaned over and handed Alex a small bag. "I got you a present."

Alex nodded as he took the sack. "It smells like something I like a lot."

Martha leaned in and smiled at Helen. She understood why Gertrude had described Helen with such delicate, loving words.

Alexander rushed over and removed his hat. "Everything is all loaded, Martha."

"This is my husband, Alexander. He'll be joining us in Auburn, but he's leaving on the 10 a.m. coach, unless…." Martha winked at Alexander.

A smiling Alexander shook his head slowly at Martha, and his eyebrows bounced up.

"A pleasure to meet you," he said to Rebecca.

Rebecca tapped Martha's arm. "You've snagged a mighty

attractive husband."

Helen gasped. "Rebecca!"

Martha and Gertrude chuckled, and Alexander blushed.

Alexander cleared his throat. "I'll check in with Douglas now. Good to meet you both."

He rushed across the road to the bank.

"Did I say something wrong?" asked Rebecca, giggling.

Helen shook her head, amused. "Rebecca makes a sport of embarrassing men."

Rebecca said, "It's a pastime of mine."

Laughter from the women filled the air with delight.

Martha patted Rebecca's arm. "We're going to have so much fun."

There were more giggles all the way around.

Martha glanced down. Alex wasn't there anymore. Her smile faded. "Alex!"

The other women's eyes darted to Martha, alarmed.

"Yes, Ma," said Alex from a few feet behind her.

Little Alex sat in a chair eating his Queen Cake, crumbs on his shirt and pants.

Martha shook her head, rushed to Alex's side, and hugged him. "You were supposed to save that for later," she said.

Alex nodded. "I ate half and saved the rest."

Helen pulled out a pocket watch that used to belong to her husband. "Everybody's ready to go," she said.

Martha looked down the road toward the bank. "But we're not supposed to leave until eight. Can't we wait another hour?"

Helen started to the stagecoach. "We've been here since six. We'd have been halfway there if we had left then."

Gertrude stepped up to Martha. "Waiting any longer won't make any difference."

"I suppose you're right." Martha got the driver's attention. "Let's go. We're all here."

The driver signaled to the deputy.

"Give me a minute while I have the clerk send a telegram to Auburn that we're headed out," the deputy said and rushed off.

The women and little Alex boarded the stagecoach, and after a few minutes of shuffling bags and deciding where to sit, they found their spots.

The deputy returned, sat beside the driver, and said, "I don't know why they needed me on this trip. It's just a bunch of women passengers. Who'd want to rob them?"

The driver nodded. "I know, but Sheriff August wanted us to have a deputy riding up top with me. He said that we had 'delicate' cargo."

The deputy chuckled. "Oh yeah. He used to have us accompany Elizabeth to Auburn when she lived here."

He shot a sideways glance at the deputy. "I think he had feelings for her." He shook the reins, and the stagecoach lurched forward on its way to Auburn. Once they left the city, the terrain changed from streets and buildings to patches of trees, followed by long stretches of barren vegetation. "I've made this trip many times and never encountered any trouble I couldn't handle." He glanced over at the deputy, fidgeting in his seat.

Soon after, the deputy checked his watch. "We've been traveling for almost twenty minutes, and they've been too quiet. Something's wrong."

The driver chuckled. "Give them a little more time. I'm guessing they start on some snacks, and once they're done, the conversation begins. Soon after, the laughter and chatter will continue for the rest of the trip."

The deputy shook his head and surveyed the road ahead. He looked from side to side and then behind. The horses and the coach wheels kicked up a dust storm, following them, making it hard to see the trail behind.

"Everything's okay. How about I close my eyes for a bit?" asked the deputy.

"I'll wake you if—"

A raucous cacophony of laughter came from inside the coach. The deputy grabbed his rifle and sat taller, adrenaline rushing through him.

Inside, Gertrude wiped the tears from her cheeks as she tried to contain her laughter.

Rebecca continued, "I told that man in the saloon that I could out-drink him or his friends any day or night of the week. He laughed at me. Back then, I drank quite a bit, and I could hold my liquor better than anyone except maybe my older brother. I challenged the man, and he accepted. We each ordered a round of shots, and we began drinking. I took my shots down like tea, and he started looking pale. It went on for a while, and finally, he gave up. He couldn't believe that a woman could out-drink him. I don't like drinking much anymore, but at the time, I was proud of myself! For proving that I was just as tough as any man, or maybe just as stupid."

Martha burst out laughing. "Stupid? I don't think so. You proved that you could outsmart a man. They have strange ideas of what a woman is."

Rebecca shrugged. "They don't know any better. That's their weakness. They want people to think they're smarter than anyone, even other men. It's all in their imagination."

As Helen listened to Rebecca's story, she remembered that she was very much like Rebecca at that age. Rebecca was strong, independent, and unafraid to stand up for herself.

Gertrude held up her hands, palms up. "So what happened after that?"

Rebecca's face relaxed into a delicate smile. "Well, after he gave up, he bought me a coffee. We ended up talking for a while, and we became friends. He's a righteous man, and I'm glad I met him. Oh, it turns out that he was the new minister at the church Helen and I go to."

"What?" Martha said. "That must have been awkward!"

Rebecca nodded. "It was for him. For me, it was a night that I'll never forget."

Helen chuckled. She was proud of her friend.

Martha smiled at Rebecca. "I can see you and I becoming marvelous friends."

Rebecca nodded. "Yes. I would love that I—"

The wheels skidded and slammed into the well-worn grooves in the road as the horses surged forward. The stagecoach lurched and swayed as it tried to outrun the hail of gunfire coming at them.

CHAPTER THIRTY-NINE

Ladies vs. Idiots

A plume of dust billowed from the side road ahead, moving quickly toward the main road. At its center were eight riders. Their fierce expressions and frantic pounding of hooves left no doubt about their hostile intentions. Their guns drawn, they fired mercilessly at the stagecoach.

The deputy, perched atop, shot at the gunmen. The deputy grinned as one of his bullets found its target. One outlaw tumbled to the ground, and only seven were left.

"You gotta go faster. We won't have a chance unless we get ahead of them — before they reach the main roadway."

The driver's face was etched with panic. He cracked the whip in a relentless rhythm, urging the horses to a desperate gallop. "Faster!" the driver screamed, his voice laced with urgency.

The horseshoes pounded the hard clay, and the low rumble echoed louder to the driver. The stagecoach shuddered violently as it rattled forward at a breakneck speed.

The deputy snickered and squeezed off several shots at the approaching riders as the coach hurtled past the side road. The pursuers scrambled to avoid the deputy's bullets.

The driver, his eyes filled with terror, said, "We can't keep going this fast."

"You gotta. They're behind us now."

The shudders turned increasingly violent and chaotic as the stagecoach fled from its pursuers.

Inside, Helen wailed when her shoulder crashed into the wall. Alex tumbled down. Martha jumped up and nodded to Gertrude. Gertrude knew precisely what to do and rushed to Alex.

Martha yelled over the chaos, "Everyone, get down close to the floor."

The sound was deafening: the horses, the road, the shots, and the two men above yelling at each other.

Gertrude opened the compartment under the front seat.

"Alex, I want you to lie down here. You'll be safe in there," she said, her voice intense and her tone wrought with equal parts of worry and courage. Alex, his eyes wide, crawled in.

Martha withdrew two rifles from the rear bench. One was for her, and the other for Gertrude.

Helen sat frozen and cried, "No. Please, no."

Rebecca helped Helen down next to Alex. "Helen, everything is going to be all right. Take care of little Alex. He needs you."

Helen forced a smile. Alex's face had cake crumbs around his mouth.

A bullet whizzed into the cabin on Gertrude's side; splintered wood flew in all directions.

Helen moved closer to Alex and gripped his hand, her touch steady and strong.

"We're going to be fine, Alex," said Helen, her voice frightened with panic. "We'll take good care of each other. Okay?"

"My ma's going to protect us both. Don't worry," said Alex, his voice soft but sure.

The corner of Helen's trembling lips curled up slightly.

Gertrude peeked out the window as another bullet cracked a hole in the wood a few inches above her.

"There's a bunch of them. They're riding over to your side," Gertrude yelled to Martha.

Martha stuck her rifle out her window and waited for the riders.

Gertrude hesitated before reaching for the rifle.

Rebecca grabbed it instead. "Gertrude, I got this," she said, pointed the weapon out the window, and glanced back at Gertrude. "Take care of Helen and Alex. Martha and I can handle those idiots."

"You don't have to tell me twice." Gertrude quickly crouched down next to Helen.

Martha grinned at Rebecca. "Let's keep them guessing where our bullets are coming from. There's more ammunition and another two rifles down there," said Martha.

They took turns shooting at the outlaws until they forced them into a narrow corridor behind them. The deputy up top fired at the outlaws, causing them to disperse.

Martha pounded her fist on the roof. "That deputy is gonna get us all killed. We had them where we wanted them."

The deputy fired again and downed another one of them. The robbers returned fire with a vengeance.

"Uggh," came from up top, followed by a loud thump.

"The deputy's shot!" shouted the driver through the chaos.

Martha yelled out the window to the driver, "Veer right and stop the coach on the road when you hear me shoot. And then get down low and don't let them see you."

"Okay," he screeched. "Whatever you say. We ain't got a chance."

Martha shook her head. She narrowed her eyes and counted the men. "Rebecca, you got that side?"

Rebecca nodded. "Yup."

"Gertrude, grab the other rifle and take the front window on the same side as Rebecca."

"Yes, ma'am," said Gertrude.

"As soon as the coach stops, fire at anything that moves. There is no place for them to hide. It'll be as easy as shooting tin cans on a fence."

Rebecca chuckled. "They aren't too bright."

"Nope. The deputy shot two of them. So that leaves six," said Martha.

Martha leaned out her window, pulled the trigger, and shot one of the men. He fell to the ground. "Five more to go!"

The stagecoach suddenly slowed, veered to the right, and abruptly stopped. Rebecca and Gertrude had clear shots of the approaching riders. They each shot one man.

Martha burst out of the door, ran to the side, and looked around the corner at the outlaws. She shot the first man when he came into view. The last two men were about to take shots at the stagecoach but hesitated. Gertrude and Rebecca had them in their sights. Martha aimed at them from the other side. She pulled the trigger, and the first man fell dead. Before the last one knew where the bullet came from, Martha shot him, too.

Martha was breathing hard, her adrenaline pumping with

excitement. She gripped her weapon tightly, ready to shoot as she walked toward each of the bodies. She counted six of them. She yelled back to the coach, "We got six here, plus the two the deputy shot, accounts for all of them."

Rebecca and Gertrude were yelling, "Get down!" They were waving frantically at her.

Time seemed to stop as she thought someone inside the coach might have been shot.

Two shots came simultaneously: one from the stagecoach and another from behind her. Martha fell.

Gertrude ran to Martha, who was lying motionless.

"Martha!" exclaimed Gertrude.

Martha grunted and then got up. She brushed the dust away from her clothes. "I didn't know what was happening, so I dropped."

"One of those men from the side road wasn't quite dead yet. He was running at you fast. Rebecca took care of him. Come. Let's get back to the stagecoach and get ready in case more of them come."

Martha followed Gertrude. "I'll talk to the driver and figure out what to do."

They reached the stagecoach as Helen was tending to the deputy's wounds. The driver was checking the wheels. Martha squinted in the direction of the road leading to Auburn. A plume of dust from a fast-approaching buggy was headed their way.

Gertrude cocked her head back, surprised, as she pointed to the buggy. "Is that Agnes?"

"No. It's a man. Everyone, get inside," said Martha.

Martha hid behind the stagecoach with her rifle aimed at the looming threat.

An instant later, she let out a huff as the buggy neared. It was Thomas.

Thomas slowed his buggy. The stagecoach seemed lifeless and was crooked on the road. He was confused and grew alarmed as he got closer. Just beyond the coach were two dead men. There was no driver. The horses were motionless, staring straight in front of them. He got down. He was vulnerable where he was. He surveyed the area to see if there were any threats. He crept toward the coach. Perhaps there might be an injured survivor, he thought. Another dead man came into view.

A shot came at him. He flinched and crouched over.

"I'm here to help!" he yelled.

There was a long silence, and then Martha walked out, her rifle ready.

He relaxed when he saw it was her.

Another shot came near his foot. He stopped breathing for an instant.

"Are you with us or with them?" asked Martha as she glanced sideways at the dead outlaws.

Thomas looked incredulously at her. "I'm with you!"

Martha kept her rifle on him. "Why are you here?"

"I came as fast as I could to warn Sheriff August. Randall and his men are planning to ambush the ten o'clock stagecoach headed out of Sacramento to Auburn. He has men waiting just north of Sacramento to intercept it," said Thomas, barely breathing between words. He pointed at the bodies. "These must be the men that planned to cut off their escape."

"How do you know that?" asked Martha.

Thomas's breath got choked in his throat. "It's a long story. Agnes loaned me her buggy so I could visit my pa yesterday. I couldn't do it. Then, I came across an old friend who told me about Randall's plans."

Martha scoffed. "Alexander won't have any trouble handling those outlaws. That coach is loaded with plenty of firepower. Whatever's left of Randall's men won't have a chance."

"There are probably two dozen men about to descend on them. They're going to kill Alexander. None of them, not even Alexander, will survive."

"I have to get there to warn them," said Thomas.

Martha walked closer, her rifle still pointing at Thomas. She thought of Agnes and gritted her teeth hard. "Bring your buggy on the other side of the stagecoach."

"Yes, ma'am."

As he passed the stagecoach, the deputy was sitting on the ground, wounded. The driver was standing next to him with a six-shooter.

Thomas glanced at the coach. Cries came from inside. Gertrude's muffled voice said, "Everything is going to be alright. I promise."

Thomas led his horse to a large bucket of water. Immediately, his horse gulped it down.

Martha locked eyes with Thomas. "You help the driver get the coach over into those trees. Understand? I want you to protect them."

Thomas nodded.

Martha patted Thomas's horse. She took his weapons from the buggy and handed them to him. She put her rifle and the heavy pouch full of ammunition on the seat. "Give me a hand getting up."

"Do you know how to drive a buggy? It's not that easy."

Martha rolled her eyes. "I don't have time for this." She climbed up and took the reins. "You make sure that you take good care of them. If they die, then you die." She snapped the reins. The buggy shot forward, leaving a swirling dust cloud behind.

Thomas shook his head and watched Martha race away. He walked to the coach's entrance and peeked inside.

"Is everything alright in here?" asked Thomas. He gasped when he looked up at Rebecca.

Rebecca smiled and asked, "And who might you be?"

Thomas took a step back.

She chuckled. "Don't be rude. What's your name?"

"I'm Thomas—Thomas Pruitt."

"What a tasty treat you are," said Rebecca.

Thomas blushed and started to smile.

Gertrude looked out the window. Martha was riding away. Gertrude turned back and glared at Thomas. "Where's Martha going?"

"She went after Alexander."

"Why'd she do that?"

Thomas cowered and told Gertrude about Randall's plan. "Martha threatened to kill me if I don't keep you all safe."

Gertrude narrowed her eyes. "You get on one of those horses and go after her. Make sure Martha's okay. You owe it to her."

CHAPTER FORTY
Coach Ambush

Martha rode for half an hour. It was a challenging ride. She thought she could handle the buggy, but it was more complicated than the one she was used to driving. As she went, cramps accosted her now and then. Most of the way, the well-traveled road was smooth. Even so, the occasional rut in the road caused the buggy to shudder. It wouldn't have been that uncomfortable if the buggy had been going at a proper speed.

She worried that she had rushed into this rescue to save her husband at the expense of risking her baby's wellbeing. As she drove, she thought about when she was younger. She would leap into any endeavor without regard to consequences. Now that she had a family, her carefree attitude felt out of place. Others depended on her now.

Gunshots echoed from the distance.

She gasped, pushed past her discomfort, and snapped the reins, sending the horse racing toward the gunfire. She approached cautiously. She rode inconspicuously up a side trail barely wide enough for the buggy. She rode another hundred feet and stopped at a slightly elevated spot with a perfect view of Alexander's stagecoach. Her body was aching as she got down. The gunshots continued as she grabbed for her rifle and ammunition.

Thomas's horse was unnervingly frightened by the constant gunfire. "Everything is going to be fine," she said to the horse as she rubbed his head. She tied the horse to the tree and rushed to where she could see Alexander's stagecoach.

She took a second to recover from a cramp by leaning against the tree. She looked at the scene below.

Alexander's stagecoach was pinned down near a tall canyon wall, which on one side provided shelter from the outlaws' barrage of bullets.

She counted five to ten seconds between gunshots fired from the stagecoach. The outlaws were shooting much more frequently.

"The good guys must be conserving their ammunition," she muttered. "They've probably been under siege for a while."

The horse whinnied and stared at her curiously.

She nodded at the horse, then at the shootout below. "Okay. Let's make my bullets count." She counted the outlaws she could see and estimated a few more from the shots behind the trees.

She aimed and waited for anyone to approach the stagecoach. A moment later, two men snuck up to the coach from the right, and she shot them both. As soon as they fell, the gunshots stopped.

She glanced at the horse. "Two down, at least eighteen to go."

The horse stared at her curiously.

There was no sign of Alexander, only rifle and shotgun barrels protruding from the back of the stagecoach.

Martha winced at a slight pain and gasped. Four outlaws were crawling toward the coach's left.

"This is too easy."

She quickly dispatched the four men.

"Fourteen more to go."

It got silent again. Martha squinted as she strained to see anyone from the stagecoach. She smiled as she caught a fleeting glimpse of Alexander. A feeling of warmth washed over her, soothing her aches and pains.

Down below at the stagecoach, Alexander and four deputies were pinned down. It kept them safe from the outlaw's bullets. However, they couldn't take a shot without peeking out from behind the safety of the stagecoach.

Alexander squinted up at the ridge. "Someone's up there helping us. Whoever it is must have come from Auburn."

One of the deputies looked up there. "I think you're right. Our friend up there could pick them off if we could draw them out to the open."

Alexander's voice carried a note of urgency. "Yes! Let's all aim toward the road leading to Sacramento. That's where most of the outlaws are."

Four shots rang out from the stagecoach. Silence. The outlaws stopped shooting. Alexander peeked out in the direction of the sniper who was helping them.

Up above, Martha was lying quietly and uncomfortably on the ground. She tried lying on her stomach but quickly found that very uncomfortable. She ended up in an awkward position on her side with her rifle balanced on a tree stump in front of her.

She grimaced. Five outlaws were crouched down and stealthily running toward the stagecoach. Three of them ran from the left, and two of them from the middle. She fired, reloaded, and fired again. She'd only shot four of them. Another two shots came from the stagecoach, and the fifth outlaw buckled backward when one of their bullets hit him.

Martha winced. "That leaves us with nine. Now, Alexander, that should be a manageable number."

Martha drew a deep breath, her eyes squeezing shut from the sharp pain of a sudden leg cramp.

The sound of a heavy footstep crushing, snapping twigs sounded behind her. She opened her eyes, ignoring the pain.

A burly, menacing outlaw with eyes blazing with fury grabbed her weapon away from her and tossed it aside. He pointed his rifle at her. "You didn't count on me finding you, did you?"

Martha gasped as she sat up and put her hands on her knees.

He wrinkled his nose. "You ain't got a right to shoot people like fish in a barrel. It ain't right."

Martha chuckled. "All of you are outlaws. Your gun-toting friends down there are trying to kill those people in the stagecoach! Isn't that right?"

"Yup, that's right." His stubble-filled face was severely scarred. "I'm gonna kill you for killing my friends down there. You shouldn't have done that."

Martha slowly reached down to her ankle. "They deserved what they got."

The outlaw's face went red with rage, his eyes bulging. "Any last words?"

In one swift move, she pulled out her gun. A loud blast exploded in front of her.

Her arm was extended with a pistol pointing to where the outlaw once stood.

Thomas lowered his shotgun and ran next to her. "Are you okay?"

As she stowed her pistol, she looked incredulously at Thomas.

"What the heck are you doing here? Why aren't you guarding that coach like I asked?"

"Gertrude told me to go after you."

Martha half-smiled. "I was getting ready to put a bullet in that half-wit's head. You know that, right?"

Thomas nodded. "Let's take care of the rest of those outlaws."

"That shotgun won't do you much good. They're too far." Martha shook her head and turned back to shooting at the outlaws.

Thomas grimaced, then rushed to the horse and returned with his rifle. He crouched several feet from Martha and pointed his rifle at the battle below. He glanced at Martha as she fired her rifle with deadly precision. He followed her sight line, and her targets fell to the ground after each of her shots.

"Are you going to join in, or are you just watching?" asked Martha.

He nodded and quickly shot two outlaws. From the right-hand side of the bloody battle below, his uncle, Randall, stepped out from the brush.

"Dog gone it," Thomas whispered. "I should have known you'd show up."

Martha glared at him with a sour look, shook her head, and returned to her targets.

Thomas aimed at Randall. His finger twitched as he tried to pull the trigger. He had a clear shot, and his rifle was pointed at Randall's middle. Thomas gritted his teeth, lowered his gun slightly, and then fired at Randall's leg to wound him. Randall fell hard, face-first to the ground. Then he rolled to his back and grabbed at his leg. Thomas gasped, and then a hint of a smile caught his lips as Randall screamed.

Martha glanced at Thomas. He was fixated on something below. She followed his gaze. There was a man on the ground holding his leg. It was Randall. Another man helped him up, and they shuffled away. She half-smiled.

She squinted. "Who is that man with Randall? He looks familiar."

Thomas leaned in as if it would make it easier to see. A man was helping Randall, and several others were hurriedly following behind. At first, he thought Frank had joined them, but it wasn't him. "I don't know. They're all running away. The cowards."

"Why didn't you kill him? You didn't seem to have trouble killing those others down there."

"He's my uncle. I couldn't do it."

"You know he'll come after us again, right?"

Thomas nodded.

Martha half-smiled. "If he dares mess with us again, it'll be his last."

"I should have shot him, huh? I never shot anybody before today."

Martha took a deep breath and let it out slowly. "No sane person deserves to die. But sometimes, they become corrupted. They become dangerous when enraged. They focus their hate on killing. When they have the means and the intent to kill you, you have to defend yourself, your family, and your friends. All those outlaws down there, including your uncle, would kill to steal something of yours. They're not just thieves; they're killers." Martha grimaced. "We aren't killers. Our rifles are loaded for justice."

Thomas glanced down at the stagecoach and then back at Martha and nodded. "I guess we delivered justice."

Martha half-smiled and slowly bobbed her head up and down. "Let's go."

Martha climbed into the buggy. "You can drive."

Thomas tied the horse he'd ridden there to the back of the buggy, hopped up next to Martha, and grabbed the reins.

Down below, Alexander surveyed the area, looking for any movement.

Alexander hesitated. Headed straight for him was an approaching horse and buggy pulling a lone horse. He recognized Martha sitting side-by-side with a man in the buggy.

Without hesitation, he ran toward her. Thomas sat snugly next to Martha.

Martha smiled at Alexander when the buggy reached him. "Help me down."

Alexander narrowed his eyes at Thomas and then helped Martha down. "What are you doing here? You're supposed to be safe in Auburn."

Martha collected her rifle and bag from the buggy and winked at Alexander. "I was saving my husband. There's no way I would let those scoundrels hurt you. That's what I'm doing here."

He hugged her.

Alexander's eyes fixated on Thomas as he got down. "Why's he here?"

"I helped a little," said Thomas. "Now, if you don't mind, I'll head home."

Alexander cocked his head in confusion and put his hand on his gun, ready to use it.

Martha exhaled loudly. "I borrowed his buggy earlier. It's a long story." She turned to Thomas. "Do me a favor. Tell Alexander what happened before you go. Thanks for your help. I'm going to go lie down."

Alexander bristled. "He was probably helping them."

"No. He wasn't. I need to rest for a little bit. Talk with Thomas. He saved my life." Martha had over-exerted herself and worried she may have endangered her baby. She kissed Alexander and walked away with her rifle.

Alexander waited for Martha to go into the stagecoach. He pulled his gun on Thomas.

Thomas cocked his head back in surprise. "I'll tell you everything if you put that damn gun down. I came to help."

Alexander glanced at the coach and then holstered his gun. "I promise I'll shoot you if you pull something."

Thomas grimaced and told Alexander about Randall's plan. "I rushed back here to warn you and the sheriff about it. But on my way here, I came upon Martha's stagecoach. Some half a dozen or more men attacked them. All of the outlaws were dead when I got there."

Alexander asked, "What about the passengers?"

"They're all okay. Gertrude sent me after Martha."

"How'd you save her?" asked Alexander in a condescending, mocking voice.

"Martha was on the ground, a gorilla of a man towering over her with a gun, about to pull the trigger. But I was faster." He glanced at the stagecoach. He wanted to chuckle but didn't. "After the man fell out of the way, I saw that she had a gun in her hand, ready to fire."

Alexander's right lip twitched upward. "How do I know you weren't in on this?"

"I wasn't." Thomas's lips tightened around his clenched jaws, his patience waning. "I'll head back to Sacramento and tell Sheriff August what happened here."

Thomas turned to leave.

"Wait!" Alexander's eyebrows went up. "What were you doing in Auburn?"

Thomas grimaced. "I was going to meet someone there, but changed my mind. I ran into an old friend who told me about this robbery."

"Coincidence. Huh?"

Thomas nodded half-heartedly. "I guess so."

Alexander glanced back at the stagecoach and then at Thomas. "I think it's best to keep your distance from Martha from now on."

"I just saved her life. That man was going to kill her." Thomas shook his head.

Alexander leaned in. "The way I see it, this is your fault. You've been trying to weasel your way into her life, and you've done nothing but hurt her."

Thomas tilted his head forward, his eyes narrowed and locked with Alexander's, and stepped toward him. "You're the one who invited Randall here. Your fa—friend." Thomas took a deep breath. "It sounds like all this is your fault. I'd have protected her from all this if she were my wife."

Alexander's eyes grew sharp as daggers and were filled with fire. He pulled his gun and used it to point from Thomas to the buggy.

"You can leave now. I'd think twice about going near my wife again. I'm likely to kill you."

Thomas shook his head and then glanced at the stagecoach. He snickered and then walked to the horse at the back of the buggy. He untied the horse and tossed the reins at Alexander's feet. "This horse belongs to the other stagecoach."

Thomas winked at Alexander and then left in the buggy.

Alexander kept his gun on Thomas as he drove away.

He stowed his gun, turned to the stagecoach, and muttered, "I'll always protect you, Martha."

CHAPTER FORTY-ONE

Regroup

Elizabeth paced back and forth on the porch of the Auburn Hotel. Occasionally, she looked down the road for the coach. According to the telegram from Sacramento, it should have arrived already. Nervous and anxious, she sprinted to the sheriff's office. When she walked in, Joseph was at his desk, reading the newspaper.

"Elizabeth!" Joseph put the paper down and stood to greet her.

"The coach is late. Something terrible must have happened."

Joseph checked the time. "It's an hour late." He grimaced at his deputy. "Let's check up on that coach."

"I'm sure they're fine," Joseph reassured Elizabeth, gently kissing her cheek. He turned to his deputy, his concern evident in his eyes. "Let's go."

Elizabeth, her steps quick and restless, returned to the hotel porch. She continued to pace back and forth in a desperate attempt to distract herself from her mounting anxiety. Dread pounded on her chest as her mind filled with unpleasant thoughts.

A half-hour later, the stagecoach, riddled with bullets, arrived. Elizabeth went to the coach as it stopped a few feet from her.

Rebecca stepped out, her hair disheveled, her dress torn. "I'm glad that's over!"

Elizabeth gasped. Her face was pale, her heart racing as she hurried to the coach to help Rebecca. "Oh my!"

Rebecca winked at Elizabeth. "We're a little banged up, but we're fine!" She turned to Helen, who was slowly exiting. "Come on, Helen. You'll feel better once you are out of that stuffy coach and get some fresh air."

Helen looked like a frail old woman with shaky legs, barely able to walk.

Elizabeth choked on her breath. "Aunt Helen, are you okay?"

Helen didn't say a word. She patted Elizabeth's arm as she shuffled, stone-faced, past her and sat on the bench outside the hotel. Helen closed her eyes, put her head down, and rested it on one hand while gripping her purse tightly.

Elizabeth's forehead creased, her eyes filled with worry as she looked at Helen.

Rebecca glanced at Elizabeth. "Stop worrying, Elizabeth. She'll be fine. She needs to rest for a bit."

Gertrude and Alex walked over to Elizabeth. She turned to Gertrude, still worried about Helen.

Gertrude stood grinning as if nothing were wrong. "Hello, Elizabeth."

Elizabeth's face softened. "It's lovely to see you again." She smiled when she saw Alex. "Hello, Alex."

Gertrude knelt beside Alex. "Sit quietly with Helen while we wait for your mother."

"Okay." He ran to the bench and sat.

Rebecca touched Elizabeth's arm. "I'll get a couple of hotel rooms. I'll be right back after I get Helen settled."

Elizabeth said, "Tell the clerk to bill my husband's account."

Rebecca nodded and went to get Helen.

Helen stood and turned to Alex. "Thank you for protecting me. You made me feel safe."

Alex took a deep breath and let it out with a smile. "I like you."

A smile almost escaped Helen's lips. She patted Alex's arm and left with Rebecca.

Alex's smile faded as he sat alone, worried about his mother. He glanced at Gertrude and then returned to staring at the road, hoping she would arrive safely.

"Where's Martha?" Elizabeth's eyes darted to the coach and then back at Gertrude. "Why isn't she with you?"

Gertrude's eyes momentarily darted to Alex, saw he was okay, and then said softly so Alex couldn't hear, "Our stagecoach got attacked by outlaws. We took care of all eight of them. After that, Martha left on a buggy after discovering more of them planned to attack her husband's stagecoach. Your sheriff showed up about ten minutes after she left."

"She went alone?"

"Yes, but I sent someone after her. Martha shouldn't have been driving in her condition, especially not to a gunfight. I don't know what she was thinking."

Elizabeth shuddered. "I knew something wasn't right."

"Martha and Rebecca put bullets into most of those attackers. I might have shot one, too."

Elizabeth looked down the road. "Why didn't my husband come back with you?"

"The sheriff?" Gertrude asked tentatively. Elizabeth had told her that Joseph was the town sheriff when she met her at Helen's the week before. When she saw Joseph for the first time, he looked so much different than the photograph she'd seen of him back at Wallace's office. Of course, he was twenty years younger in that picture and looked more like Thomas.

"Yes."

"He's still out there. He and the deputy were trying to figure out what to do with those dead men. He got one of their horses and hitched it to the stagecoach, and then we left. That horse didn't like being hitched like that."

Rebecca stepped out of the hotel and sat with Alex. She yelled to Elizabeth, "Helen is resting in bed."

Elizabeth nodded at Rebecca and then turned back to Gertrude. "Let's go join them. I have some desserts."

Elizabeth and Gertrude walked over to where Rebecca and Alex were talking.

Rebecca talked to little Alex, and he politely smiled and nodded in return. Now and then, his smile would change into a frown as his gaze drifted toward the road.

"Alex, look who is joining us," said Rebecca.

Elizabeth took the Queen Cakes from her picnic basket and offered one to Alex.

Alex sat up tall, his frown transformed into a smile. He looked at Gertrude.

Gertrude nodded at Alex, saying that it was okay for him to eat one.

"I want one," said Rebecca.

Elizabeth handed her a cake. "I have plenty." She held one for

Gertrude. "Would you like one, too?"

Gertrude's mouth was crooked, and her eyes glistened with worry. She glanced at Alex and then shook her head. "Maybe after Martha arrives."

Rebecca walked close to Gertrude and spoke so Alex couldn't hear. "Come sit. I'm sure that Martha is fine. Thomas will help her. You're making Alex and me nervous."

Gertrude forced a smile. "I suppose you're right."

Rebecca and Gertrude walked up to Elizabeth and Alex.

Elizabeth smiled at Gertrude. "I wanted to talk to you about Thomas. You were tight-lipped the other day when I mentioned that my husband and I have hoped for a long time that he would come here."

A streak of guilt flashed across Gertrude's face. "I'm sorry. I should have told you about Thomas. It turns out that he followed us here to California."

Elizabeth's eyes filled with hope. "He's here? Oh my goodness! I can't believe it."

"Yes. He's living in Auburn with my friend Agnes. He's the one I sent after Martha today. I'll leave it to Martha to tell you the rest."

"I understand. I'm flabbergasted."

Gertrude took a deep breath and let it out slowly. "I can't think about him now. I'm worried about Martha."

Elizabeth nodded.

Gertrude tried to relax, but her heart raced instead. Her eyes darted often toward the road, hoping for Martha to arrive.

Alex jumped up and pointed at a fast-approaching stagecoach. "It's Ma!"

Seconds later, a bullet-riddled stagecoach pulled up in front of the hotel.

Alexander stepped out and extended his hand to Martha. Gertrude and Alex rushed over.

"Ma!" Alex's face was painted with excitement as he ran to his mother.

Martha pulled Alex into a tight embrace.

"How's my little cowboy?" asked Martha. "You've got crumbs all over your face."

He pointed to Elizabeth. "That lady over there brought cakes. Gertrude said it was okay for me to eat one while we waited for you."

Martha looked at the woman and smiled at her.

Alexander kissed Martha's cheek. "I'll be back after we take this coach to the bank." He leaned over and hugged Alex. "You take care of your ma."

Alex giggled. "I will."

Alexander climbed up next to the driver.

Martha blew him a kiss.

Alex waved goodbye to his pa.

Gertrude patted Martha's arm. "Are you okay?"

Martha chuckled. "I'm fine. I'm just tired and sore. My hair is a dreadful mess, and my clothes are ruined. Earlier, I had cramps. Thank goodness they're gone."

"You gave us quite a scare," said Gertrude, grinning.

Elizabeth walked up to Martha. "Martha?"

Martha's eyes lit up bright, and her smile filled her face. "Elizabeth! You're exactly as I pictured."

Elizabeth hugged Martha and said, "Gertrude told me lovely things about you. It's such a pleasure to meet a like-minded soul."

A wave of warmth washed over Martha, and her breath stuck in her throat. The last time she'd felt this was when her mother hugged her.

Rebecca walked up. "Martha is beautiful, both inside and out. She can handle any gun, rifle, or situation better than anyone I know."

Martha took Rebecca's hand. "How kind of you to say. I think we made a good team back there. I'd say we're evenly matched when it comes to shooting, but you're the true beauty here."

Rebecca blushed. "Thank you!" She glanced away for an instant as if embarrassed. "Where is that Thomas fellow? Is he okay? Gertrude sent him after you."

Martha smiled. "He's fine. He went back to Sacramento." She shook her head. "He more or less saved me."

Gertrude chuckled. "I'm sure Martha had everything under control." Her gaze swung from Elizabeth to Martha. "I told Elizabeth a little about Thomas. She's excited to meet him."

Martha looked surprised at Gertrude. She wondered for a second if Gertrude had shared every single detail about Thomas with her. Hopefully, she hadn't mentioned anything about that terrible assault.

Gertrude's mouth fell open, and her eyes opened wide as if Martha had accused her of betraying a confidence. "I wasn't being my usual gossipy self."

Martha patted Gertrude's arm and shrugged. "Sorry." She turned to Elizabeth.

Elizabeth's eyes moistened. "Joseph has missed him ever since the day he left New York. When I get home, I'll tell him that Thomas is in Sacramento. I'm sure Joseph will want to see him right away. It's a miracle. After all these years, they'll be reunited."

Gertrude patted Elizabeth's arm. "I told her he's living at Agnes's. I'll tell Agnes to expect him."

"Thank you." Elizabeth took a handkerchief from her bag and wiped her eyes. "I want to talk to Thomas first and ensure he feels welcome here." She turned to Rebecca. "I'll return to Sacramento with you. We can meet Thomas together."

Rebecca's cheeks went rosy bright with delight. "Oh yes. That would be fabulous."

Elizabeth put her handkerchief away. "Martha, Rebecca got two hotel rooms. One is for you, your husband, and Alex. The second room is for Helen, Gertrude, and Rebecca. Helen is already napping in her room."

Martha shook her head. "Poor woman. I hope she's okay. She had a hard time earlier."

Rebecca affectionately patted Martha's arm. "She's fine. She was quite shaken, but she's been through worse. She insists we take the 6:00 a.m. stagecoach back tomorrow."

Martha chuckled. "I don't blame her. I'm anxious to get home, too. This trip was more taxing than I expected. On the way here, Alexander and I had agreed to leave first thing in the morning. We'll join you on the 6:00 a.m. coach."

Rebecca shrugged. "Sounds good to me. The sooner we get there, the sooner I see Thomas."

Gertrude chuckled.

Martha said, "I'd like to nap in a soft bed before lunch. I'm still achy. Would it be possible to have a late lunch?"

Rebecca nodded. "Yes! Helen said to wake her for lunch today. She said she didn't travel all this way to starve. How about two o'clock?"

"That's marvelous," said Gertrude. "Helen and I have plenty to talk about while we eat. We have a lot in common."

Rebecca leaned over to Gertrude. "You did a wonderful job easing her nerves on the way here. You've got a gift."

Gertrude put her hand on her cheek and turned her head in a glamorous pose. "Don't forget, you promised to give me some beauty tips."

Martha laughed. "I need some hints, too."

Rebecca rolled her eyes. "Oh, please! You two are beautiful women. Later, I'd love to share some of my beauty products. I always travel with them."

Martha planted one hand on her hip and wiggled her shoulders. "Maybe I'll wear a nice dress to lunch."

Gertrude asked Elizabeth, "Will the sheriff join us for lunch?"

"I doubt it. With those robbers, I'm sure it will be a long day for him. We're not used to seeing this level of aggression from robbers around here. My husband takes pride in keeping this town safe."

At the site where the women's stagecoach had been attacked, Sheriff Joseph Pruitt watched as the deputies loaded each of the dead men onto a wagon. He gasped when he recognized one of them. The man had been standing near John at the outlaw camp when Joseph delivered the whiskey to John.

He shook his head. In no time, the outlaws would be traced back to him. He'd be accused of aiding them. He'd spent years earning the townspeople's trust and keeping the town safe. Sometimes, he resorted to paying off outlaws to leave and do their dirty deeds elsewhere. Other times, he used brutal force on those who refused to act peacefully in his town. It appeared that John was someone he could deal with rationally—his men, although outlaws, might be inclined to become peaceful for the right price. But Randall was a problem that wouldn't be so easily resolved. Randall, a bloodthirsty killer, would never stop being a threat to

Elizabeth and his town. Randall wouldn't hesitate to kill his wife. Protecting her would be justification enough for killing Randall, he thought.

The ground shook at the hideout on Joseph's property as horses' hooves pounded the hard clay dirt outside. Men were yelling, while others were grunting. Frank rushed out of his tent to investigate the commotion.

The men from the robbery had returned and were in sad shape. Some were wounded and moaning as they got down from their horses.

Frank spotted Charlie and another man helping Randall get down from his horse.

Frank rushed to Randall. "Your leg is bleeding!"

Randall grinned, happy to see Frank. Randall showed Frank his bloody leg. "Someone shot me good. The bullet tore into my leg. It hurts like hell," he whined. "It stopped bleeding after Charlie wrapped it up."

Frank asked, "What happened to your eye?"

"I went face-first into the ground when I got shot. It feels like I have something in it."

"Shoot!" said Frank.

Randall shook his head. "They were shooting down on us—picking us off, one by one."

Charlie said, "Could it have been Alexander? I saw him peek out from behind the stagecoach, aiming his gun at us."

Frank went red-faced. "We've gotta get rid of that man. He's a menace."

Randall winced as he tried to put weight on his bloody leg. "It wasn't him. The shot came from up the hillside. I sent one of my men up there to handle the threat. I thought it was dealt with, so I walked out, and someone shot me in the leg. It doesn't make sense. It was like they knew we were there."

Frank went pale.

"What's wrong?" Randall barked. "Was that you shooting down at us? Did you follow us?"

Frank cocked his head back like he'd seen something revolting. "No! I was here. Ask anyone." Frank gasped and then

349

glanced away as if remembering something.

Randall stared at him, his anger simmering. "Don't look away. You know something. Don't you?"

Frank shook his head with a tremor. "I told Thomas. But he wouldn't have shot at you. He wouldn't have."

Charlie stepped back, surprised.

John rode up and jumped down from his horse. He sprinted to Randall and shoved him to the ground. "We're done. Your stupid, 'brilliant plan' didn't work. Thanks to you and Charlie, eight of my men are dead. You both botched that robbery. I've had it with you."

Charlie stood, shocked that all of them had died. He was supposed to go with them, but decided, at the last minute, to join Randall's men instead.

Randall moaned in pain as he struggled to get to his feet. "It ain't my fault. You agreed to this. Some of my men got killed, too."

Frank started to pull his gun on John, but Charlie pulled him aside and whispered, "Let them finish their fight. You and I can help Randall after they're done fighting."

John closed in on Randall. "I don't think you care about any of your men. You keep getting them killed." John kicked at the dirt. "To be clear, I'm in charge now, not you, not Charlie."

Randall shoved John, "Get out of my face."

John lunged at Randall.

Randall fell to the ground and squirmed, his eyes bulging with hate and contempt. "I—"

"Shut the hell up!" yelled John. He eyed Charlie and then turned to the group. "Everybody, get ready. We'll stay here as long as we can. We might have to run if the law comes looking for us. In the meantime, we'll be lying low. I don't know if it will be days or weeks—no way to tell." He narrowed his eyes at Randall. "If you and your men come with us, you'll do as you're told. Got it?"

Randall, his upper lip twitching, glared at John.

John didn't wait for Randall to answer. He stormed away and signaled his men to follow him.

Frank stood frozen in shock as the men, including some of Randall's, followed John. No one had ever treated Randall like the wounded dog that he was.

"John is a dead man," Randall muttered. "He's soft. He's weak."

Frank rushed to Randall. "Everything will be okay, Uncle Randall." Frank was surprised by what had come out of his mouth. He wanted to call Randall his pa.

Randall looked astonished at Frank. Frank had never called him uncle before.

"Shall we head to the doctor?" asked Frank.

Charlie said, "Let me take a look at his wounds."

Frank hesitated. "And his eye, too."

Frank and Charlie led Randall toward the tents. Frank looked around and quietly said to Randall, "Charlie and I are both on your side."

CHAPTER FORTY-TWO

The Sting of Justice

Rebecca sat across from Helen and Gertrude in the restaurant. "You two are yakking away like children. I feel left out."

Helen shook her head, grinning.

Gertrude chuckled. "All she wants to talk about is Thomas."

Rebecca glanced at Helen. "What's wrong with that?" She turned to Gertrude. "Please, tell me more about him."

Gertrude hesitated for several seconds. "Thomas seems like he's changed from when I first met him. You should slow down and get to know him a little. Let him tell you about himself."

Rebecca rolled her eyes and dropped her shoulders. "You're right. I'll ask him myself when I see him."

Helen sipped her drink. "You'll meet him soon enough. Be patient."

When Martha, Alexander, and Alex entered the restaurant, Alex raced off to a giant stuffed bear near the entrance. Alexander chased after him, and Martha walked to the table where the other ladies were.

Gertrude leaned in toward Rebecca. "Please don't mention Thomas to Martha."

"Okay." Rebecca stood to greet Martha. "Oh, my goodness. That's a gorgeous dress."

Martha turned from side to side so that Rebecca could get a better look. "Isn't it? I love it. It used to be my mother's."

Rebecca was astonished. "You sew too?"

Martha leaned in with a smirk. "A little, but nowhere near as good as Gertrude. She altered it for me."

Helen said, "It's stunning."

Martha's head bobbed up and down, and then she patted her belly. "Gertrude had to let out the waist because of the baby." She took a deep breath and exhaled quickly. "It's so lovely to see you all. It was quite a journey we had today."

Martha sat down and glanced toward the front of the restaurant. Alexander and Alex were inspecting the giant stuffed bear.

Helen nodded. "Thank you for keeping us safe earlier."

Martha's eyes lit up. "You're welcome. Those criminals won't be bothering us anymore."

Alex ran up to Martha. Alexander scooped him up and put him in the chair next to her.

Alexander kissed Martha's cheek and smiled at the other women. "I'm sorry I can't stay. I have work to do at the bank."

Rebecca leaned forward and winked at Alexander.

Martha laughed. "Alexander, you better get going before Rebecca climbs across the table to try to hug you or something."

Rebecca let out a chortle.

"Goodbye, ladies." Alexander grinned and hurried away.

Five minutes later, Elizabeth arrived. She rushed to the group and said, "What have I missed?" She quickly sat.

Rebecca said, "Martha—"

Gertrude cleared her throat.

Rebecca smiled at Gertrude. "I wasn't going to bring up Thomas."

Gertrude rolled her eyes and laughed.

Martha chuckled. "I figured that Thomas would come up in conversation."

Elizabeth leaned forward. "I want to tell my husband everything I can about him."

Rebecca giggled like a schoolgirl.

Martha moved to get more comfortable. "I'll tell you what I know."

Gertrude's face was painted with caution. "Martha, are you sure?"

Martha glanced at Alex; he was staring intently at her.

Alex tapped Martha's arm. "Ma, why is he scared of you?"

Martha smiled at Alex. "He's not scared of me. He's developed a sort of respect for me."

Gertrude stood. "Alex, let's visit with that seven-foot-tall creature up front."

Alex jumped down from his chair and sprinted to the bear.

"Yay! It's giant and scary."

Gertrude chased after Alex. "Wait for me! Only I can protect you from that old bear!"

Martha laughed at the spectacle. "Alex is growing up so fast."

Gertrude caught up to Alex, and they stood small next to the enormous animal frozen in his most vicious pose.

A pang of regret tugged at Elizabeth's heart as she watched little Alex. She hoped she and Joseph would have a child—maybe a boy—someday. "Alex is a wonderful boy," she said.

Rebecca cleared her throat. "You were saying about Thomas…"

Martha looked sideways at Rebecca as a smile grew. "Is there some sort of spark between you and Thomas?"

Rebecca flashed a sly smile. "He's handsome."

Martha locked eyes with Rebecca and let out a sigh. "Don't rush in. Take your time and get to know him." Martha hesitated. "I think he's changed for the better. But, for a time, he was awful."

Rebecca blinked several times. "You make him sound like he used to be a monster."

"For a while, he was." Martha's mood turned icy. She tried to get comfortable in her seat and let out a sigh. "I might as well tell you. He and I had a very unpleasant encounter a few years ago when he forced himself on me. He left me bruised, physically and emotionally. I wanted to kill him. It took me a long time to overcome, but I have—mostly."

Rebecca gasped.

Elizabeth rested her hand on Martha's and patted it softly.

"I'm sorry, Rebecca. That was a bit crude." Martha's face softened. "He used to be an outlaw who appears to have taken a turn toward redemption."

A mischievous glint danced in Helen's eyes. "He sounds like his father."

Elizabeth half-smiled at her aunt, "Then he must not be all that bad, huh?"

Helen sat back in her seat. "Sorry, dear. I couldn't resist."

Rebecca squirmed impatiently in her chair.

Martha's brow furrowed as she leaned closer to Rebecca. "Are you alright?"

Rebecca wiggled once more in her chair. "This dress I decided to wear bunched up on me. It's ridiculous."

"That's why I prefer wearing pants," said Martha.

Rebecca adjusted her dress and got comfortable. "Please tell us some nice things about Thomas instead of...."

Martha grinned. "You should think about wearing pants more."

Rebecca looked astonished at Martha. "But men won't look at me."

Elizabeth chuckled and rolled her eyes.

Martha held her lips tight and stifled her urge to laugh. She took a breath and went back to her story. "I first met him when I was going to school—"

Rebecca gasped. "You went to school? How wonderful. You're so talented."

"I met him at the university. He—"

Rebecca's gleeful eyes were filled with surprise. "Wait. He went to the university, too?"

"No. He said he went there to meet me."

Rebecca let out a sigh. "How romantic."

"Ewww! He had long, oily hair and the beginnings of a beard, and he smelled of whiskey and sweat. It wasn't romantic at all. He was disgusting."

Rebecca sat up and turned up her nose slightly. "He cleaned up well."

Elizabeth leaned forward. "Maybe it's his path toward redemption. Some people have to hit rock bottom before they start doing good." She glanced at Helen.

Helen smiled softly and nodded.

A woman rushed up to their table with several plates of food.

Gertrude and Alex walked up. "Yay! The food has saved us from that bear."

The women spent the afternoon enjoying each other's company and chatting away.

"Heavens, where has the time gone?" said Elizabeth. "I've got to get supper ready." She turned to Martha. "Thank you for your lovely stories. I'll be sure to let Joseph know about Thomas. He'll be delighted."

Helen said, "I'm going back to the hotel to rest. I'm taking some bread with me."

Helen and Elizabeth said their goodbyes and left.

Gertrude, Rebecca, Martha, and Alex strolled in the park and chatted for half an hour.

Martha pointed to the bench next to the pond. "Let's sit over there."

They talked for another twenty minutes about Martha's baby while Alex sat on the grass.

Rebecca took Martha's hand. "Thank you for telling me about Thomas. I know it was selfish of me to want to know, and I know he did you wrong. I'm so sorry."

Martha patted Rebecca's hand. "You and I are going to be great friends."

Randall's wagon pulled into the road leading to Agnes's house the following day and stopped just outside the gate to her property. The house seemed modest, reminding Randall of his friend Sam's house. The barn was relatively small. He'd expected to find Thomas sitting on the porch drinking whiskey or working in the barn, but it was quiet there.

He grunted when he tried to move his injured leg. He stepped down from the wagon and almost fell. He grimaced and started limping to the house.

Thomas burst out of the house, aiming his six-shooter at Randall.

Inside, Agnes yelled, "Thomas, what's going on?"

Thomas tilted his head back and said, "Stay inside. I'll take care of this."

Randall stopped at the bottom of the stairs. "I'm alone. I came to talk."

Thomas narrowed his eyes at Randall. "I've got nothing to say to you. You turn around and get out of here. I'll shoot you if I have to."

Randall cocked his head. "You're the one who shot me yesterday. Aren't you? I know Frank told you about our plans."

A tremor ran through Thomas's voice. "I could have killed you if I wanted. I got you in the leg instead. The same as you did to me back in New York when I tried to escape you."

Randall chuckled. "I suppose I should be grateful that you spared my life, like I spared yours?"

Randall glanced back. "Frank, come on out."

Thomas's pupils went pinpoint sharp as Frank, his gun pointed at Thomas, strode to where Randall stood.

Frank's voice seemed strained as he said, "You better put your gun down, Thomas."

Thomas shook his head incredulously at Frank.

Thomas aimed his gun higher at Randall's chest. Randall's bloodshot right eye distracted him. "You're not my family anymore. I don't care what happens to you. You best go back to New York."

"It's your fault I'm losing half my sight," said Randall. "It got hurt when you shot me."

Thomas felt a pang of guilt and lowered his gun slightly.

Randall pulled his gun and had it squarely pointed at Thomas's middle.

"I'd holster those guns," said Agnes's eldest as he snuck up from the side of the house. "I'd do as he says," said her other son, walking out from the other side.

The barrel of a shotgun poked out from the porch window.

"You two had better turn around and leave," yelled Agnes from inside.

Randall grinned as he held his gun sideways. "I guess I ain't got family here."

Thomas's brows went upward as he glanced at Frank. "You too, Frank. Holster your gun, and let me see your hands. Looks like you made your choice between me and Randall."

Frank stowed his gun, shook his head slightly, and let his gaze fall to the ground.

Thomas took a step forward. "Randall, put that gun away and leave before I shoot you."

Randall's eyes bulged from their sockets as his rage consumed him. He brought the gun to his holster and then, in an instant, sharply swung it up and pointed it at Thomas.

Thomas pulled the trigger. Randall's gun, covered in blood, crashed to the ground.

Frank stood frozen, horrified that Thomas had shot Randall. Thomas would never shoot at his uncle.

Randall screamed, "My hand! You put a bullet through my hand." His eyes darted to Thomas, disbelieving at what he had done.

"I'm not that little kid who used to look up to you. I don't feel anything for you." He glanced at Frank. "You should take care of his hand. He won't be able to use it for much anymore."

Thomas grinned at Randall. "I know you're lousy at shooting with your left hand."

Randall bristled. He leaned over and reached for his gun.

Thomas fired, and the bullet landed an inch away from the fallen weapon. "Leave it. No sense in messing up your other hand, too."

Randall growled. He spat at Thomas and turned to leave. Frank ran over to help Randall.

"One more thing. I saw that boy of Alexander's," said Thomas, his weapon still trained on Randall.

Randall and Frank both spun back, startled.

"I'd say he's your spitting image, his grandpa."

Randall's jaw dropped, his head shook, and he trembled. He looked up at Thomas with broken eyes. Randall's mouth moved, but no words escaped his shock.

"You're responsible for killing my ma, Martha's ma, and — Alexander's ma."

Randall fell to his knees, clutching his hand. His face was etched with creases as his deepest, darkest secret was laid out for all to hear. His jaw hung loosely as his eyes darted from Thomas to Frank, to Agnes's boys, and back to Thomas. For the first time in forever, Randall's eyes glistened in shame. His gaze fell to the ground.

Frank's eyes grew wide with shock. Never before had Randall seemed so small, broken.

Frank looked disdainfully at Thomas and told Randall, "Let's go."

Thomas's face flushed with satisfaction. For the first time, he felt powerfully in control of his destiny. "Next time I see you, Uncle, I might just put a bullet in that cold heart of yours. Your stagecoach-robbing days are over."

Randall, breathing hard, stood and turned away.

"And stay away from my pa!" Thomas yelled.

Randall hesitated for an instant.

Frank helped Randall as he limped away. Randall struggled to get into the cart.

Frank shook his head as he shot a menacing glance at Thomas. Frank's eyes were swimming in tears.

Thomas felt nothing for Randall, but his heart felt hollow as he fixated on Frank's eyes. Frank ran to the other side, climbed up, and then the wagon raced away.

Agnes stepped out onto the porch, and one of the boys went to retrieve Randall's six-shooter.

Her face held a soft, supportive smile. "I'm proud of you, Thomas."

Frank flung the reins, and the horses flew into a gallop. Frank glanced at Randall.

Randall wrapped his hand with a filthy rag he'd found on the bench. Blood turned the once-white cloth into a soggy, red mess.

"We're almost at the doctor's place," said Frank.

Frank's heart raced as he snapped at the reins again. How could Thomas shoot Randall like that?

Randall was breathing hard. For the first time in his life, he was scared.

"I can't stop the bleeding. Blood's gushing from my wrist," screamed Randall.

Frank's eyes widened with shock when he realized it was much worse than he thought.

"Press harder." His eyes darted back and forth from the road to Randall.

Randall's face was turning pale as the blood pooled up in the foot well. Randall leaned back in the seat and closed his eyes.

"Randall, there's the office."

Dr. Martin was sitting on the porch, reading the newspaper. He stood up when Frank pulled up.

He looked at Frank. "I remember you. What's happened?"

"His hand is bleeding. It's not stopping."

The doctor climbed up to the wagon and examined Randall's hand.

Randall opened his eyes and looked menacingly at Dr. Martin.

"Come into the office before you pass out. We've got to patch that wound up quickly. You're bleeding from your wrist. That's a lousy place to bleed from."

Frank helped Randall down.

Between the doctor and Frank, they led Randall to a large room to the left of the entrance. Frank glanced to the other side of the entrance and saw an identical room with another bed.

Frank helped Randall into the bed while the doctor closed the door to the other room. He rushed back and administered a dose of ether, giving him extra because he looked like he could be troublesome.

Frank, his crazed eyes wide with worry, said, "Can you help him?"

Dr. Martin put a tourniquet on his upper arm. Then, he removed the makeshift bandage and worked quickly. Soon after, he cleaned the wound and sutured it shut.

"I'm not even going to ask what happened," said Dr. Martin.

"You've gotta fix him up. He's all I got."

Dr. Martin grimaced and stared at Frank for a few seconds. He was trying to remember if that was the same thing Frank had said when he brought his other friend to him.

"Did he try to kill himself? That's one of the ways people try it."

Frank cocked his head back like he'd been insulted. "No!"

Randall was unconscious. His breathing was noisy. It sounded raspy when he inhaled and like a whistle when he exhaled.

"Why was he limping?"

"He got shot in the leg this morning."

The doctor recoiled when he examined it. "This wound is dirty. It has caked blood. Did a doctor take care of this?"

Frank shook his head. Only Charlie had looked at it, and Randall said he could fix it himself. "No. He said it was a flesh wound."

The doctor rolled his eyes. "That isn't a flesh wound."

The doctor worked on Randall's leg. A minute later, he pulled out a bullet fragment. He cleaned the wound and said, "He's damn lucky. The bone isn't broken all the way through. He'll need to stay off it for a while." He bandaged Randall's leg.

Frank said, "His eye is messed up, too."

Dr. Martin examined Randall's left eye. The doctor wrinkled his nose as if he'd seen something disagreeable and went to the basin and drew a glass of water. He washed away the grotesque parts that didn't belong there. Once satisfied, he took a clean cloth, folded it into a small square, and placed it over his eye. The doctor used a piece of twine to keep it affixed.

He walked up to Frank. "Is there anything else that's wrong with him?"

Frank shook his head quickly. "Is he going to be okay?"

"His leg and eye will heal, but I'm certain the bones in his hand and wrist are shattered. I found fragments—bits and pieces of bone. That hand won't be much use to him anymore."

CHAPTER FORTY-THREE

Peace at Last

The following morning in Auburn, Elizabeth left with the group on the 6:00 a.m. stagecoach to Sacramento. Helen, Gertrude, and Rebecca spent much of the trip gossiping. Elizabeth, Martha, and Alex sat opposite them and mostly napped. Alexander rode up top with three deputies. The deputy who had defended the ladies' coach the day before had his arm in a sling. He sat next to the driver. The other two sat with Alexander up top and stood ready to shoot anything that moved.

The women, filled with anticipation and excitement, had decided to have afternoon tea at Martha's house. Elizabeth had stayed up the night before to bake a fresh batch of Queen Cakes for their party, her mind buzzing with the joy of their gathering. They eagerly planned to meet at Martha's at three, their hearts filled with the promise of a delightful afternoon.

The stagecoach pulled up to the Sacramento main hotel at 8:45 a.m. Martha stepped out with Alex. Across the road was Agnes's buggy. She smiled that Thomas might be there. Instead, Agnes's eldest climbed into the driver's seat and drove it away. Ten minutes earlier, Thomas had gone to the blacksmith's to settle the payment.

Helen, Rebecca, and Gertrude exited and stood next to Martha.

Alexander jumped down from the coach. He turned to the driver. "Wait here. I'll be right back with the carriage." He rushed away.

Rebecca tapped Martha's arm. "The hotel clerk is bringing my carriage. It was lovely to get to know you. Helen and I will see you later today at your house."

Martha hugged Rebecca and then Helen, her embraces filled with warmth and genuine affection. "It was a pleasure to meet you both. I can hardly wait until this afternoon," she said, her voice filled with anticipation and a hint of excitement. Rebecca and

Helen returned her embrace.

Alexander brought his carriage and parked behind Rebecca's, where the hotel clerks were loading her things.

Alexander loaded his and Martha's weapons and the luggage into his carriage.

Helen, Gertrude, Rebecca, and Elizabeth spent fifteen minutes saying goodbye while Alex waited with Alexander in the carriage.

Soon after arriving home, Gertrude wasted no time and rushed to Agnes's house. She turned in from the road and headed down the trail to Agnes's place. She pulled back on the reins and stopped in front of the house. Agnes was out front, relaxing on the porch.

Gertrude climbed down from the cart.

Agnes looked suspiciously at Gertrude. "What are you doing here, Gertrude? It ain't Sunday." Gertrude and Agnes usually went for a ride on Sundays.

Gertrude went up the stairs and stood facing Agnes. "I'm here to tell you about meeting some new friends today."

"I ain't going nowhere. I'm staying right here."

Gertrude grimaced and narrowed her eyes at Agnes. When Agnes said nothing, Gertrude crossed her arms and stared at her.

Agnes let her shoulders drop. "Okay. Where are we meeting these friends of yours?"

Gertrude laughed and sat next to Agnes. "We're having tea at three this afternoon at Martha's."

"Are we going to have those Queen Cakes you've been boasting about?"

"Yes. But first, is Thomas around?"

"No. I sent him and my son into town to get the buggy fixed up. It didn't look right after he brought it back yesterday. They should be back soon."

Agnes grinned, and her eyes lit up bright. "I got something juicy to tell you."

Gertrude's brows raised, and her jaw dropped.

Agnes held her hands before her, tapping her fingers together, about to gossip. "About seven this morning, a man came looking for Thomas. He was limping something awful. Anyhow, it turns out it was his uncle."

Gertrude gasped. "Randall?"

Agnes grew animated as she pointed here and there. "Yeah. Thomas came out of the house with his gun, yelling at him to leave and never come back. That uncle of his was stubborn. It didn't matter, though. My sons had their rifles, and I had my shotgun pointed at him. Another young man came over, pointing his gun at Thomas. Frank, I think he called him. Thomas wasn't afraid. He stood his ground."

"Did they leave?" asked Gertrude.

"Oh yeah, they did alright, but not at first. He told his uncle he'd shoot a hole right through his heart the next time he saw him, and he'd do it, too."

Gertrude let out a puff of air. "That man is as dark as they come."

"Thomas shot his uncle's shooting hand and kept his six-shooter. I'd swear that man cried when he got into his wagon when he and the young man rode away. He was moaning like he was in a lot of pain. He left here a broken man. He was limping and holding his bloody hand. And he was having trouble with one of his eyes, too."

Gertrude cocked her head to the side in surprise. "He's not worth talking about anymore."

Agnes shrugged. "I suppose not." A hint of a smirk crossed Agnes's face as she shot a sideways glance at Gertrude. "But I haven't told you the best part."

Gertrude rolled her eyes. "What?"

"Thomas blamed his uncle for the deaths of his, Martha's, and Alexander's mothers."

Gertrude's nose wrinkled. "Alexander's ma? Thomas told us about the other two."

"There's something big there, and I won't ask Thomas about it."

"That's not like you," said Gertrude. "You're not one to let a mystery sit unsolved."

"This is different. You should have seen Randall's face after Thomas accused him of that. That man's face went pale, his jaw dropped, and he looked like he had no breath left. Randall was keeping a secret as plain as day. If it got out, it would likely hurt Alexander, Martha, and who knows who."

Gertrude sat back and let out a sigh. "I suppose you're right."

Agnes nodded. "Let's keep this between us for now. Okay?"

"I will."

"But, I have to say I've never been prouder of Thomas. I wish you could have seen him."

Gertrude looked toward the road. "Thomas's father will likely come here tomorrow to see him."

Agnes sat up taller. Straightening up that way was unusual because of a slight hunch in her back. "Really? The saints are looking out for that boy. I tried to get him to visit his pa. And he went the other day. But something happened, and he didn't see his pa. He's been moping around again since he came back—much worse than after that shootout at your place."

"So that's why he was out in Auburn yesterday. I admit I don't care for him, but he helped us. We got attacked by outlaws while we were on the early morning stagecoach to Auburn."

Panic filled Agnes's face. "He didn't tell me about that. Is everyone okay?"

"Yes. The deputy who was 'protecting' our coach was wounded, but he's fine. It turns out Thomas kept Martha from getting shot."

Agnes slapped her knee. "I knew he'd do well if he had some proper loving and discipline. He owes his life to that woman. No one would blame her if she killed him for doing what he did to her."

Gertrude grimaced. "I don't know how, but she seems to be moving on."

Agnes shrugged. "When's that boy's father coming?"

"First thing tomorrow. His wife, Elizabeth, told us he'd ride out of Auburn at first light. Later, he'll head back to Auburn with Elizabeth."

"Great! I'll make sure Thomas stays around the house. I'll tell him his father will be here early. I know he wants to see him."

"Elizabeth asked me if you would invite Thomas over today at about 3:00 p.m. She wants to introduce her friend Rebecca to Thomas formally." Gertrude rolled her eyes. "For some reason,

Rebecca is dying to get to know Thomas better."

Agnes chuckled. "At breakfast, Thomas asked me how to spell Rebecca. He said he was writing a letter to her. I had no idea, but my eldest son's wife helped him."

"I guess those two match up pretty well," said Gertrude.

Agnes tilted her head and looked at Gertrude. "Wait. Is Alexander going to be there?"

"No." Gertrude grinned and shook her head slowly. "Alexander and Martha had words this morning. It wasn't a fight. But after saving Martha, Alexander told Thomas he'd kill him if he ever got near Martha again."

"I can believe it. That must be why Thomas was moping yesterday when he got home."

Gertrude rolled her eyes. "Something tells me those two will have a rough time seeing eye to eye. It's like they're siblings."

Agnes's heart skipped a beat as she glanced at Gertrude sideways. "I'll have Thomas take me over there for the tea party," said Agnes, checking her pocket watch. "I don't have much time to get all prettied up."

The two women giggled like gossiping children.

Rebecca, Elizabeth, and Helen were the first to arrive at Martha's house.

"Is Thomas here already?" asked Rebecca as Martha greeted them at the door.

Martha smiled, "No. Not yet. They should be here soon. It's not even three o'clock."

Elizabeth stepped in, arm-in-arm with her Aunt Helen.

"It's wonderful of you to welcome us into your home," said Helen.

Elizabeth hugged Martha. "Yes! Thank you."

Martha led them to the chairs in the front room. "Please come sit."

Rebecca stayed watching out the window that faced the road.

Helen sat down. "Oh, my! These cushions are marvelous. They're much more comfortable than those stagecoach seats and those on Rebecca's carriage."

Elizabeth smiled and turned to Martha. "This morning, you

mentioned Agnes Jenkins on the trip here, and I think I've met her before."

Gertrude stepped up, "You might have. She and I like to shop in that dress shop by the hotel, and we often stop at the general store. They have a post office there, and she receives a letter from one of her friends back in New York now and then. Sometimes I do, too."

"I guess we'll see when she arrives," said Elizabeth.

Martha said, "We have those delightful cakes you brought and Gertrude's famous lemonade and tea."

The desserts, drinks, cups, and plates were tastefully placed on the table.

Elizabeth admired Martha's efficiency. "It's perfect. I hope you didn't have to go through too much trouble."

Martha shook her head. "No trouble at all."

"Is your husband here?" Elizabeth sensed that there might be some friction between Alexander and Thomas because of what Martha had disclosed about Thomas.

Martha glanced at the door. "No. He's working at the bank today. Either he's out protecting stagecoaches or at his desk adding and subtracting numbers." Martha had asked him to stay at work until the party was over. She told him Thomas was going to meet Rebecca there. Alexander objected. They enjoyed a heated discussion, and after a short while, Alexander relented.

Gertrude said, "Martha does both things just as well as Alexander."

Elizabeth smiled at Martha and said, "That's impressive, Martha. Rebecca's excellent at shooting, too. When we get together, she and I like to go target practicing."

Rebecca turned back to the other women. "Elizabeth is starting to shoot better than me." She returned to looking out the window.

Elizabeth rolled her eyes, pointed to Rebecca, and whispered, "That girl! She hasn't stopped talking about Thomas. I'm anxious to meet him, too."

Rebecca chuckled without turning away from the window and said, "I've got a feeling about him. I want to get to know him to see if I like him."

Gertrude shrugged and shook her head at Martha.

A glint of mischief flashed in Martha's eyes. "I think it's lovely for you two to meet. If he ever gets out of line with you, I'm sure your gun-slinging talent will come in handy."

Rebecca squinted at Martha curiously but got distracted by the sound of an approaching horse. Rebecca looked out the window and saw a well-groomed man courteously helping an older woman down from a buggy.

Rebecca jumped away and ran to the door. "He's here! I'm going outside," she said, rushing out the door.

Agnes stepped in, grinning ear to ear. "Oh dear! That woman is a firecracker. I told them to sit on the porch and get to know each other."

Agnes closed the door behind her and walked up to Gertrude. "Let's get this party started. My lips are parched. I need some tea."

Elizabeth laughed. "You are delightful. Didn't we meet before, maybe at the dress shop?"

Agnes tilted her head in thought, and her face lit up. "I think I've seen you shopping there. That's probably where you saw me. You have excellent taste, and those fabrics you buy are costly."

Elizabeth shrugged. "I love to sew, and I can't resist some of those fancy patterns now and then."

"I do, too, but—" Agnes held her right hand so Elizabeth could see it. It was full of calluses, and one of her fingers was slightly bent. "But I have a little trouble these days with this hand. I spend more time gardening, preparing meals, and doing chores around the house. That doesn't leave me much time for sewing. I still sew, but I've been doing more mending lately."

Elizabeth smiled softly at Agnes. "That's a beautiful dress you have on, Agnes."

Gertrude stepped up. "She sewed that herself just last month. She picked out the fabric and put it all together."

Agnes moved closer to Elizabeth. "As long as I got the right measurements, it ain't hard to get a perfect fit. It just takes longer to make than before."

Elizabeth looked crooked at Agnes. "Are you sure we didn't meet back in New York? Now that I've seen you up close, I think we did. It was about fifteen years ago. You were a seamstress there, weren't you? I came in desperate one day needing some work done."

Agnes squinted at Elizabeth and burst out laughing. "I remember you now. You were a mess. You had two or three dresses in bad shape and told me you were leaving for California in a few weeks."

Elizabeth jumped up. "Yes! I moved with my first husband to New York just about a month before we left for California. I didn't have enough clothes to make the trip."

Agnes said, "I guess you and I are old friends."

Gertrude brought a tray of tea and cake to the group. "Your first husband?"

Elizabeth sat down and took a cup. "He passed shortly after arriving here. It took a while, but eventually, I fell in love with Joseph. He was kind and helped my Aunt Helen and me."

Helen wrinkled her nose. "Hmmm."

Elizabeth smiled. "She doesn't care much for Joseph."

Helen tilted her head back. "I adored your first husband."

"Of course, I did too. Joseph is a loving husband."

Helen grimaced. "He's a big flirt! He has a son out there on the front porch."

"Oh, dear!" Elizabeth rolled her eyes and shook her head. "When Joseph comes tomorrow, he plans to head straight to Agnes's house and meet Thomas." She turned to Agnes. "I hope that's okay with you."

Agnes bobbed her head several times. "Yes! Gertrude told me earlier, and Thomas already knows. He knows you're here to chat with him, too."

Elizabeth exhaled loudly as if a huge weight had been lifted from her shoulders. "Thank you, Agnes."

Agnes glanced at the front door. "I think Rebecca and Thomas out there have been mighty quiet. Elizabeth, why don't you go out there and chat with Thomas? There's no time like the present. We gotta get all this serious stuff out of the way. It's about time we have some fun."

Elizabeth nodded and walked hesitantly to the door. She wasn't sure what to say to Thomas. Her first thought was about how Thomas had been separated from his father for fifteen years.

She put her hand on the doorknob and glanced back at the other women. They all smiled at her with encouragement. None of them could imagine what they would say to a son estranged from his father.

Elizabeth stepped out onto the porch and closed the door behind her. Her jaw dropped at the sight of Rebecca and Thomas in a passionate embrace. She cleared her throat loudly.

Rebecca jumped up, and Thomas fell unceremoniously to the floor. Rebecca was clearly the aggressor.

Elizabeth covered her mouth to stifle a chuckle.

Thomas leaped to his feet and straightened himself.

Elizabeth regained her composure. "Agnes suggested I come out here and chat with you, Thomas. Is that okay?"

"Of course," said Thomas.

Rebecca winked at Thomas as she fixed her hair. "I'll be back in a few minutes. Perhaps you could take me for a stroll while the women have their tea party."

Thomas's brows bobbed up as he nodded.

She kissed his cheek and then hurried inside.

Thomas tilted his head slightly down. "You must be Elizabeth, my father's wife."

"Yes. I'm happy to meet you. We have much to talk about."

Thomas raised his head. "I'm nervous about meeting my father."

"I'm betting he's even more so than you are. He's talked lovingly about you almost daily since he left New York."

Thomas's face seemed to narrow as he tilted his head. "Really?"

"Yes. Believe me. Your father and I are close, and he and I keep nothing from each other."

Thomas's brows rose. "I've spent a long time wondering about him." He shook his head. "My uncle, Randall, hates him."

"I'm sorry about your uncle. I've never met him. I can assure you that your father loves you. I'm hoping you and I can become close, too."

Thomas nodded. "Did you and Pa have any children?"

Elizabeth blinked and took a small breath. "No." She smiled

at Thomas. "I haven't given up hope."

Thomas moved uncomfortably when he realized he had broached a sensitive topic. "Forgive me."

"That's okay. Ask me anything you like."

"Is my father here in town?"

"He's coming to pick me up tomorrow. He hopes you'll be amenable to meeting him then."

His eyes sparkled as his face grew bright red. "That would be perfect. Agnes mentioned it earlier. I told her that one more day would make me feel more comfortable. She said I've had fifteen years to get comfortable."

Rebecca peeked out the door. "Are you two done yet?"

Elizabeth rolled her eyes at Rebecca and grinned. She turned back to Thomas and took his hand. "I'm happy we talked. You are quite the gentleman," she said.

Thomas stood. "Me, too. You're a kind person. I'm thrilled I met you. You remind me of my mother."

Elizabeth smiled as her eyes moistened.

Rebecca marched over to Thomas. "I'm ready for that stroll."

Thomas's face grew bright red.

Elizabeth chuckled. "Thomas, please take her on that stroll before she makes a scene."

Rebecca leaned toward Elizabeth and whispered, "I'm almost certain I love him."

Elizabeth's eyes glistened in the light as her lips held tight in a smile.

Rebecca grabbed Thomas's hand and led him down the stairs. Rebecca glanced back at Elizabeth and winked at her. "We'll be at the park and return in an hour."

Elizabeth sat on the bench, watching the two walk away hand-in-hand.

"They're an attractive couple. It's time Joseph gets his son back, and Rebecca finds true happiness," she muttered.

Joseph traveled from Auburn to Sacramento early the following day and arrived at Agnes's house. When he got there, all was peaceful. The leaves in the giant tree in the front gently swayed to and fro as the cool breeze swept through it. Joseph had ridden straight from Auburn, taking a few brief stops to rest his horse. The cool air helped him calm his nerves. Agnes's house was well-kept and painted with a muted green color. The trim was a faded, light tan, almost white. He stepped onto the porch and noticed the path from the stairs to the doorway was well-worn. He knocked on the door, expecting the man of the house to answer. Instead, a small, thin woman answered the door.

Agnes studied his face. "You must be Sheriff Joseph Pruitt."

Joseph's head tilted, his face wrinkled with confusion. Her face hinted at familiarity. "Yes."

"He looks just like you. He's in the barn tending to the horses. Go ahead—"

"Pa?" Thomas walked out of the barn.

Joseph turned and saw his son standing several feet from the house. Joseph's face grew bright with a smile as he stepped down from the porch. He stopped the instant his foot touched the ground, almost as if asking for permission to return to his life.

"Thomas!" Joseph's voice cracked as tears moistened his eyes.

Thomas and Joseph stood motionless, staring at each other.

Agnes yelled, "Are you two going to stand there like statues all day? Go ahead and hug it out."

Joseph rushed to Thomas and hugged him. Thomas was speechless as he tried to hold back his tears. "I missed you, Pa."

CHAPTER FORTY-FOUR

Loaded for Revenge

At the outlaw camp on Joseph's property, Randall limped to his makeshift tent a hundred feet from the rest of the group, isolated from the others. He crawled inside and sat. Outside, far from his tent, he heard the men chatting as if nothing was wrong.

Randall inhaled uneasily and raised his right hand to his face. He used this hand for shooting, writing, eating, and even pulling himself up to the saddle. He gasped when he tried twisting it. The pain was excruciating. He closed his eyes, trying to ride out the torture. No luck.

How could this now useless hand become his weakness? His downfall?

With his left hand, the one that trembled now and then, he reached into his pocket and withdrew a little envelope with pills that the doctor assured him would alleviate his pain. The doctor had given him seven but warned him to use them only if the pain was unbearable. He looked inside. There were seven round white pills.

He poured one pill into his hand, swallowed it, and then put the envelope away. He shook his head and thought about how he had gotten here. A memory that he had long suppressed crept into his awareness.

A hint of a smile cracked from his mouth as he thought about a woman he once knew. He was almost a decent man back then. He was cocky and self-absorbed. He enjoyed spending time with his friends, especially his best friend CJ. One day, CJ introduced Randall to a woman. Soon after, Randall became obsessed with her. She wasn't like any of the women that he had ever known. He was persistent with her, always buying her gifts. She seemed unattainable, which encouraged him to pursue her even harder. Eventually, the woman relented. She had told him she had always loved him, but knew he would never be the man she truly desired. Soon after, he lost interest in her. The situation reversed itself.

Now, she was desperate to be with him, marry him, and spend the rest of her life with him. Randall was cruel in his rejection of her. After several months, she found love with another man, CJ. They married quickly.

Randall was upset with the union. He accused his best friend, CJ, of stealing his woman. It didn't take long for Randall to seduce the woman. In a moment of weakness, she was unfaithful to her husband. Once she told Randall that she was going to have his baby, he again said he wanted nothing to do with her. Nine months later, Alexander Johnson was born.

Eventually, Randall and CJ repaired their relationship, much to the chagrin of CJ's wife. She lived in constant fear that CJ would find out the truth. Randall was often at the house. As little Alexander grew, he became accustomed to calling Randall his uncle. Randall seemed to spend more time with little Alexander than CJ did. CJ was none the wiser. As Alexander's twelfth birthday neared, Randall told CJ's wife that it was time to tell CJ who little Alexander's father was.

"No," she said, crying. "You'll destroy our lives: Alexander's, CJ's, and mine. You can keep being his uncle, please."

CJ walked in.

He stared at Randall for several seconds.

CJ's eyes darted from Randall to his wife and then back to Randall. CJ's mouth fell open, and he started to shake his head.

Randall tilted his head and then cocked it back. "No. That's not it."

CJ looked confused.

Randall took a step toward CJ. "I think you should know the truth. I'm Alexander's father."

Silence filled the air as CJ stared blankly at his wife. Her mouth moved, but no words came out.

She ran out the door and soon after took her life.

Back in the present, Frank yelled from outside the tent, "Are you okay, Randall?"

Randall wiped his tears away. "Yeah."

At Alexander and Martha's house, all was peaceful. Martha

hummed a melodic tune as she cleaned the kitchen. Alex sat quietly at the table, scribbling on a piece of paper with a pencil his father had left for him earlier.

Martha glanced at Alex. "You be sure and put the pencil away when you're done."

Alex continued to draw. "I will. I'm almost finished."

Martha smiled. "Your pa will be home soon."

Gertrude brought the dirty breakfast dishes to the basin. "You prepared quite the feast this morning. It was delicious."

Martha's face lit up bright. "Thank you. It's been ages since I cooked breakfast. You work so hard around here, I thought I'd surprise you for once."

"At least let me wash these plates."

Gertrude reached for the soap, but Martha got to it first.

Martha chuckled. "I got this. I'd love it if you took Alex outside." Martha continued to scrub away.

Alex jumped up and put the pencil away with the other pencils.

"I guess I wouldn't mind doing a little gardening." She looked crooked at Martha. "You sure do have a lot of energy."

"I feel better than I ever have. I think I'll fix lunch, too." She glanced out the window overlooking the garden. "Would you mind picking some vegetables?"

Gertrude nodded. "I like this new Martha." Gertrude smiled at Alex. "Let's work in the garden while your ma finishes here."

Alex jumped up and ran out the door. He loved playing outside.

Martha grinned as Gertrude followed Alex outside.

"I'll be there shortly," said Martha.

In no time, Martha peeked out the back door. Gertrude was stooped over in the garden. Alex seemed busy with something on the ground a few feet away.

"Can I help?" Martha yelled to Gertrude.

Gertrude looked up, surprised. "You can bring me the basket from the porch."

Martha stowed her apron and walked out the door, picking up the basket.

She smiled at the scene as she strolled over: Gertrude kneeling in the garden and Alex sitting, playing with sticks and stones.

Gertrude stood and brushed her hands briskly across each other. Clumps of damp, fertile soil fell to the ground. She sprinted to Martha, took the basket from her, and returned to the garden. "I haven't seen the caretaker since we got here. Someone's got to pull these weeds before they take over."

Martha walked to the bench next to the garden and sat. "Alexander said Charlie moved on."

Alex jumped up and dropped a handful of rocks and twigs. Then he ran to his mother and hugged her. "I love you, Ma."

"You are the light of my life, my boy."

Martha's face softened, and her eyes grew bright as they glistened in the sun.

She glanced at Gertrude. "Today is a beautiful, rejuvenating day. Isn't it wonderful?"

Gertrude put the vegetables she had collected into the basket. "We'll always have plenty. We've got carrots, radishes, potatoes, onions, and more."

Martha smiled at the variety. "Those look tasty. That'll do nicely for lunch."

"They taste good, too," said Alex. "Gertrude gave me a baby carrot."

Martha laughed. "I love carrots. The young, tender ones are my favorites." She tickled Alex.

Alex giggled as he jumped down and ran back to the far corner of the garden. There was a large pile of moist soil with several earthworms attempting to retreat into the mound. Alex used a stick to pick them up and examine them as they wiggled and squirmed.

Gertrude grinned and shook her head. "Alex, I brought those here for the garden. Stop teasing them. They like to stay in the moist earth."

Alex returned the earthworm to the soil. "I wonder what they taste like?"

Martha gasped and recoiled in disgust.

Gertrude locked eyes with Alex. "I suppose they taste a lot like dirt. I wouldn't try tasting one if I were you. I doubt you'd like them anyway, especially with them squirming around in your mouth and then in your tummy."

Alex's face wrinkled tight around his nose. "Yuck. I'd rather have a cookie or one of those cakes from that nice lady."

A warm chuckle escaped Martha's lips. "Elizabeth truly is lovely. That was kind of her to give you one of her delicious cakes."

Martha went to the well and pulled a bucket of water. She took a cloth from her pocket and wet it. "Alex, come get cleaned up."

Alex ran to his mother. She usually said this before offering him a snack.

Martha smiled as she wiped his hands. "I left a little surprise for you just inside the door." Martha pointed to the door and then went back to the bench.

Alex giggled as he rushed to discover his prize. He returned with a cookie and plopped his bottom on the porch's edge, his little legs dangling over the side.

Gertrude stood, brought the heavy basket next to Martha, and sat.

"Wait right here," said Martha as she strode past Alex and entered the house. A minute later, she walked out with three glasses of lemonade. She handed one to Alex. "In case you get thirsty."

Alex took the glass. "Thanks, Ma."

Martha took another to Gertrude and handed it to her.

Martha grinned as Gertrude guzzled down nearly half of her drink.

Gertrude put her drink down and took a deep breath. "I needed that." She glanced at Alex and then at Martha. "I sure am glad that balance has been restored to our family."

A hint of a smile formed on Martha's lips. "I don't think we'll have any trouble from those outlaws, at least not for a while."

Gertrude shrugged, and then a flash of excitement sparkled in her eyes. "I wish I could have seen Thomas shoot that gun out of Randall's hand. Agnes said there was a lot of blood. He won't be using that hand to shoot anymore."

Martha nodded. "Randall is resourceful. He'll find a way to cause trouble. It doesn't matter, though—he won't have a chance if he tries something. Too bad he didn't stay in New York and be someone else's problem."

Gertrude's brows raised as she bobbed her head in agreement. She took a sip of her drink. "Something doesn't make sense about Randall and Alexander being close like they were."

"Alexander said Randall promised his father he'd look out for him," Martha said. "But now that Randall's betrayed him, Alexander won't speak about him."

Gertrude smirked. "I bet Randall doesn't care much for Alexander now."

"For Randall and Alexander to have cared about each other for all these years, I doubt their 'relationship' would be so easily undone. I'm sure there's something more to it."

"Hmm. I didn't think of that."

Martha tilted her head. "Something else is bothering me. Now, why didn't Thomas's father ever talk to us? He was at the stagecoach the day we left Auburn. He rode away when Alexander walked up."

"He probably doesn't like that his brother Randall is involved in this whole mess. It must be an embarrassment for him. That family, including Thomas, has some huge issues."

Martha's head bobbed up and down slowly. "Although it looks like Thomas might be breaking out of his family's drama."

"Or maybe re-integrating into it. Agnes told me Thomas and his father were thrilled to see each other. She says Thomas is going to stay living with her for now. And Thomas does more to help her on her property than her two sons do. She's going to miss him when he gets married."

"Married? To Rebecca? They just met!"

Gertrude giggled, about to reveal a juicy bit of gossip that Agnes had told her. "Rebecca and Helen went to Agnes's house the day after Thomas met with his father. And Rebecca proposed to Thomas. Agnes had never heard of such a thing. Imagine that!"

"I'm thrilled for them. I suppose we won't be invited to the wedding since Alexander threatened to kill Thomas." Martha shook her head. "Alexander shouldn't have done that."

Gertrude shrugged. "Those two will never see eye-to-eye. I'm sure Rebecca will invite us."

"I've decided I want to focus on the here and now for our family. We've traveled a great distance from New York, and this is our home now. This morning, Dr. Martin stopped by to drop off a tonic and check on me. He was pleased that I was doing well. Another few weeks and—"

Alexander walked over, carrying Alex. "Another few weeks?"

"We will welcome our new baby. The doctor is pleased with my health. Gertrude thinks we're having a boy."

Gertrude said, "What's his name going to be?"

Alexander chuckled. "Martha and I have agreed that if it's a boy, we'll call him Marcus. If it's a girl, then Marissa."

Martha smiled as her head slowly bobbed up and down.

Gertrude grinned. "Marcus is a beautiful name."

Three weeks later, a healthy cry pierced the bedroom's silence. Wrapped in a blue blanket, Marcus, a picture of perfect health, announced his arrival. The doctor busied himself on the side, a hint of relief etched on his face. Martha, pale but triumphant, cradled her newborn son close. Beside the bed, Gertrude beamed, her gaze fixed on the tiny miracle.

"It all went so smoothly this time," Gertrude said, her voice hushed with reverence.

Martha winced as another cramp rippled through her body and managed a weak smile. "Smoothly?" she rasped, her voice thick with exhaustion. "Giving birth is never smooth, Gertrude."

Gertrude's smile faltered. Shame flushed her cheeks. "Forgive me, dear," she murmured, reaching for Martha's hand. "I meant— Well—. The truth is, I was worried. When Alex arrived, you struggled, and you fainted. I was scared that you wouldn't survive. This time, you were strong and vibrant. There was a fire in your eyes. I no longer felt worried. I was relieved that your incredible strength prevailed. I'm in awe of you."

Sensing a shift in the room, the doctor gathered his things. He glanced at Martha. "Well, congratulations," he said kindly. "I'll let myself out. Get some rest, Martha." With a nod, he slipped out of the room.

Martha watched him leave and then turned back to her son, a surge of fierce love warming her chest. She squeezed Gertrude's hand, the silent gesture conveying many emotions—forgiveness, understanding, and a newfound sense of solidarity.

Martha kissed Gertrude's hand, then reached over and pulled back the baby's blanket. "Seeing his face makes me feel so grateful."

"Gertrude, could you ask Alexander to bring Alex? It's about time he met his little brother."

Gertrude nodded excitedly and then rushed out the door.

Martha picked up her baby, blankets and all, and held him in her arms.

Barely a minute later, little Alex walked in, holding Alexander's hand while Gertrude stood by the doorway. Alex was curious about what was going on there. He had not been allowed into the room earlier when the doctor was there. For much of the day, he sat alone on the back porch, playing with some wooden toys his father had made for him.

Alex tiptoed to the bed. His mother held what looked like a bundle of blankets. Alex's eyes widened as the bundle moved in his mother's arms, and then a wail louder than anything he'd ever heard startled him.

"Mommy's here. Everything is okay." Cradling her baby close, a radiant smile lit up her face. She waved for Alex to come over. "Come, Alex, meet your baby brother."

Alexander prodded Alex. Alex let go of his father's hand and stepped slowly to the edge of the bed. He crawled up and peered at the bundled blankets. He gazed in awe for several seconds before he asked, "Can we keep him?"

Martha giggled. "Yes, we can keep him. He's your baby brother. It will be your responsibility to look out for him. Your father and I will take care of you both. We love you very much."

Alex pretended to be calm but could barely contain his excitement. "What's his name?"

"Marcus," said Martha, smiling proudly.

"I like that name. I like it a lot." Alex carefully pointed his finger at the infant. Marcus quickly grabbed it. Alex smiled and said to Marcus, "I'll protect you from those outlaws."

Alexander noticed Martha's soft smile grow. "Are you okay?"

"Everything is wonderful." Her brows raised as she patted

Alex's back. "Our eldest son is going to take after you."

Alex glanced at his mother and nodded. He went back to Marcus.

Alexander grinned. "He'll be an excellent bookkeeper."

Martha chuckled. "If those outlaws return, they'll be sorry for messing with us."

"We'll be ready for them."

She winked at Alexander.

Martha felt a surge of energy. "You're darn right. We'll be ready. You and I, together." Everything that mattered to her was right before her. Her smile grew wider as she realized that everything in her life had led her to this wondrous and magical moment. Her eyes darted from Marcus to Alex to Gertrude and then back to Alexander. Her life was better now than she could have ever imagined. Her dreams of attending college, working, exploring the world, marrying, and having children had come true.

The time had come to till another garden of dreams and sow it with new seeds, including her loved ones' dreams. Nothing would keep them from the happiness they deserve.

Alexander took a breath and said, "Together, we can—"

Martha interrupted, "Together, we can face adversity with unity and keep our lovely family safe."

A surprised smile filled Alexander's face. "That's exactly what I was about to say."

Martha took Alexander's hand. "I know. I've always remembered it. You said that to me on our wedding day."

At the outlaw camp on Joseph's property, John gathered his men. Randall, his right hand bandaged, stood several feet away with Charlie and Frank at his side.

"Make sure you got everything. We're heading out in two days," said John.

"Everyone?" asked Charlie.

John snarled at Randall and then looked at Charlie.

"Yup. Everyone," said John.

Randall narrowed his eyes at John and said nothing.

Soon, the fractured outlaw group would begrudgingly move from

Joseph's property, seemingly restoring peace to Joseph's family in Auburn and Alexander's family in Sacramento. Next on the horizon, however, was Thomas Pruitt's wedding to Rebecca Buchanan, a joyous occasion overshadowed by the dark cloud of Randall's simmering resentment. Perhaps a vengeful reckoning awaited....

THE END

The **Dark Sheriff** series continues in
Loaded for Revenge

About the Author

Roger Mendoza lives in San Antonio, Texas, the seventh-largest city in the United States. In 2014, he moved back to his birth town of San Antonio from Parker, Colorado, where he had lived for fifteen years. Living on the outskirts of San Antonio, he still enjoys the taste of the rural life that he loves so much and the big city's conveniences.

He worked most of his life as a software engineer in the defense industry, where he cultivated his passion for computer programming, but he is now retired. Along with writing novels, Roger is also a professional photographer and can often be seen toting his camera, looking for photo opportunities in and around town. He loves to capture nature photography and beautiful scenery.

Family has always been a cornerstone of Roger's life. Born eighth in a family of ten children, he has a deep-rooted fascination with his family history. Over the years, he has painstakingly gathered his parents' family photographs and documents, cataloging and digitizing them all. He takes pride in keeping the family tree database updated with new family members, cherishing the thousands of family photographs and documents that tell the stories of his relatives.

Roger's inquisitive nature has always led him to ponder the philosophy of life, the intricacies of human behavior, and our place in the grand scheme of things. Despite life's occasional challenges, he remains a firm believer in 'happily ever after endings', a testament to his optimistic worldview that can resonate with many.

He's always been fascinated with unusual phenomena, the

most common of which is the drama of life itself. It still amazes him why so much drama fills the lives of his friends and family. Perhaps it is observing that drama that sparks his imagination and gives his characters life.